SUBVERSIVE ADDICTION

BEN PORTER SERIES – BOOK THREE

CHRISTOPHER **ROSOW**

SUBVERSIVE ADDICTION
Ben Porter Series – Book Three

For information about this title, contact the publisher:
Quadrant Publishing, LLC
354 Pequot Avenue, Southport CT 06890
QuadrantPublishing@gmail.com

Library of Congress Control Number: 2021902643

ISBN: 978-1-7347147-4-6 (print)
978-1-7347147-5-3 (eBook)

AUTHOR'S NOTE

WHILE THIS STORY IS is constructed in the real world, including but not limited to referencing actual companies, places, news outlets and articles, events, and things, it is a novel, and it is a work of fiction.

However, it's not entirely far-fetched.

PROLOGUE

NOVEMBER 6, 2019 – HYDE STREET, SAN FRANCISCO, CALIFORNIA

AN EYE-LIKE PAIR OF bright, round, automobile headlights pierced the ghost-like tendrils of a dissipating San Francisco fog that drifted down the steep slope of Hyde Street toward the bay at the foot of Russian Hill. Within the car, a dinner-plate-sized speedometer ticked up past fifty miles per hour—a reckless speed given the decline ahead but not nearly fast enough, considering the angry intensity of a second set of squinting, narrowly-horizontal headlights closing in from behind.

With a gut-flopping lurch, the silver Mini Cooper S convertible bottomed out on its suspension as the car sped unchecked through the briefly flat roadway of an intersecting street. Reaching the far end of the intersection in the blink of an eye, the little car's front wheels lifted clear off the pavement as the road crested and dropped again to follow the contour of the hill. Chirping as they reconnected with the asphalt, the front-wheel-drive tires regained traction, and the Mini careened down Russian Hill with silvery trolley tracks, flush to the pavement and moistened with fog, glistening in the glare of the convertible's headlights.

The descent would be over in a matter of two blocks. The penulti-mate intersection at Bay Street lay ahead, traffic light glowing red. The driver of the Mini tapped the brakes and, with a quick glance left and then right, a black ponytail flipping from side to side, she gunned the motor; the absence of oncoming traffic a blessing but also not unexpected given the hour.

Another traffic light, this one changing from a cautionary yellow to a demanding red. Beach Street. *Brake? Left? Right?* The driver's thoughts jumbled as she calculated the turn. *Too fast! I'll never make it.* Panicking at the speed, she closed her eyes for an instant, and the Mini shot through the intersection.

In the rearview mirror, the intense, squinting, horizontal headlights had crept closer. The pursuing black sedan had gained ground, perhaps due to more confident driving, or perhaps because of the Mini driver's brief hesitations at the intersections.

At the bottom of the hill, at the end of Hyde Street, the woman driving the Mini would have no reason to pause. She knew that continu-ing straight to the pedestrian-only area of Fisherman's Wharf would be a no-go. A left would lead to a dead-end on Jefferson Street. She downshifted the Mini into third gear and applied the brake.

Tires squealing, the Mini lost valuable time and distance as it skid-ded through a sloppy right turn. Its little four-cylinder engine whined almost to redline, turbocharger whistling under strain, no match for the dual electric motors of the trailing sedan as it carved an easy right.

Ahead on Jefferson Street, the snout of a white box truck poked out from the right as it began to amble through an intersection. Almost too late, the Mini driver tried to swing around it, but she oversteered and slewed left onto Leavenworth Street.

A dead end.

Boxed in by a warehouse to the right and, to the left, a chain-link fence that shined dully in the harsh glare of overnight security light-ing, the Mini screeched to a stop just shy of a red-painted curb atop a railroad-tie bulwark. Ahead, through the remaining vestiges of fog, the cold, black waters of San Francisco Bay glinted ominously.

There was no escape.

The black Tesla sedan rolled to a silent stop behind the Mini, a cheery red glow still shining through the Union Jack etched in the Mini's plastic brake light lenses. The front doors of the Tesla swung open, and two burly men dressed in black coats advanced to either side of the little convertible.

Reaching the left side of the open-top Mini and addressing the perfectly still figure sitting in the driver's seat, her Asian complexion placid, one of the men spoke quietly, a hint of a European accent of some kind clouding his words, "Miss Zhao, I'll remind you. We are always watching."

The woman's hands remained immobile, tightly clutching the steering wheel. As the Mini's motor ticked softly, the driver sighed, buying time to allow her heart rate to slow, breathing deliberately through her nose. With a haughty turn of her head to the left, she accosted her pursuer in a clear, lilting tone, "I'm clearing my head with an early morning drive. What in the world is the problem with that, you fool?"

The man's head moved back slightly, signaling his surprise at being addressed so directly. Recovering quickly, he placed his right hand on the protruding driver's-side door handle. "Be careful how you address me, Miss Zhao. I am—"

"I'll address you however I want." She cut him off brusquely, her voice strong and deliberate. "Remove your hand. And remember that I am well acquainted with your superior. I will—"

"On the contrary, Miss Zhao. For all your bluster, I'm quite certain that you won't want me reporting this outing to *our* superior."

"I doubt that he would care." Her voice had lost a bit of bravado.

Taking advantage of the woman's hesitancy, the man at the car door changed the subject. "You're in quite a hurry for your early morning drive."

The woman snorted. She leaned back in the seat and pulled her hands from the steering wheel, resting them folded on her lap. "Had I known it was your type, following me so closely, I would have stopped. But I did not know it was you. And thus, I meant to elude you."

"Miss Zhao. You are very valuable, as you must know. Perhaps we can avoid this kind of awkward encounter in the future if you would simply remember that we are always watching you. For your safety, of course."

"Is that what we're calling it?"

"Of course." The man pulled his hand from the door handle. "We will be happy to escort you back home."

"Don't go to the trouble."

The man leaned his face close to the woman's head, his hot breath uncomfortably close as he whispered, "Don't make it be trouble. Are we clear?"

Staring straight ahead through the windshield at the black water, the woman pushed the clutch pedal with her left foot and, with her right hand, shifted the Mini into reverse gear, its backup lights now clearly illuminating the front of the Tesla. Speaking loudly, she announced, "I'm ready to leave. *Now.* If you will."

Slowly, the men withdrew back to their black Tesla. Doors slammed shut, and the sedan reversed clear of the Mini. The small car executed a neat, two-point turn thanks to its tiny size, and the two vehicles convoyed away from the waterfront, back into the hilly heart of San Francisco.

With her left hand lightly gripping the steering wheel, and her right hand caressing the stick shift, the woman piloted the Mini up the incline of Russian Hill, opposing the careening descent she had made just moments ago. Examining the horizontal headlights of the Tesla in the mirrors, she exhaled through pursed lips with dismay, realizing she would be under physical and electronic surveillance for the remainder of the night.

She would have to find another opportunity, one when they would not be watching, so that she would have the freedom to speak. To make a phone call, to explain what was happening to the one ally that she had.

The one ally who still remained . . .

Otherwise, soon she would be in too deep, she would risk being alone, and in that case, there might be no escape.

Only more dead ends.

NOVEMBER

CHAPTER
1

TUESDAY, NOVEMBER 19, 2019 – BRISTOL, RHODE ISLAND

MY NAME IS BEN PORTER. I'm twenty-nine years old.

I'm a disgraced former Special Agent of the Federal Bureau of Investigation.

Now, I work at Dunkin'.

You know Dunkin', the place that used to be called Dunkin' Donuts. They took the "donuts" part off the name. I'm not sure I completely understand why, but that kind of decision is way above my pay grade as a "crew member." I pour coffee, put donuts in boxes and munchkins in bags, and occasionally microwave an egg sandwich or some other delectable treat. It's not glamorous, but when I was fired by the FBI for insubordination, they didn't exactly give me a glowing letter of recommendation. That kinda limited my job options.

Makes sense, right? Do you buy it?

I hope the Russians do. I hope my cover story, my "legend" as we say, holds up to the scrutiny of Unit 29155. After all, I now know that they know I was involved. And because that's the case, there's no doubt in my mind that they're looking for me.

And that's why I'm going into deep cover—not only to protect myself, but also because I'm going to be looking for them.

The incongruity of it all still astounds me. Just over two years ago, in July 2017, I was a faceless cube dweller doing data entry work in the FBI

Boston Field Office as an information management specialist. Now, on a Tuesday afternoon, November 19, 2019, I'm sitting shoulder-to-shoulder with a Deputy Assistant Director of the FBI, on a bench in a Bristol, Rhode Island, park overlooking Narragansett Bay, as we outline how I'm going to run a top-secret mission for the United States government.

It was a clear, balmy—for fall in New England, that is—afternoon, forty-seven degrees Fahrenheit, with a gentle west-northwest breeze blowing off the Bay, and we had the Walley Park waterfront to ourselves. It was a good setting for a clandestine meeting, and I had no concerns about being watched or overheard as I began to update my boss. "My new gig is in place. Very compartmentalized. Only one other person in the Bureau knows about it, at the moment. Two, if I now include you."

Deputy Assistant Director Bradford Macallister merely grunted, "Yeah?"

To those who didn't know him, Macallister came across, at first glance, as polished. His fair-skinned, five-eleven gym-toned physique was almost always nattily attired, currently with a navy-blue suit cloaked with a gray overcoat. However, observing his sometimes-bumbling mannerisms and listening to his limited vocabulary, a new acquaintance might assume that Macallister was merely a well-dressed but slow-minded and inept bureaucrat.

I knew better. This man had been my direct boss in 2017 as Supervisory Special Agent, and then Macallister did a stint as an Acting Special Agent in Charge. He had the credentials and the experience, and I knew not to underestimate him. I took his one-word response not as confusion, as I might have at one time, but as an invitation to proceed. "We're going to need to expand the circle, but only slightly. One or two people to help run the cover inside the Bureau. And there are two people on the outside."

"Dat's a big circle. You're up to potentially six people. I can count, you know. Dat's not compartmentalized."

"You're correct, of course. Let me run it down for you." There was a defensive tone to my voice. If I couldn't get this part of the op right, I had no chance against the Russians. And I knew I had kept the need-to-know group as small as possible.

"Convince me." Macallister's tone indicated that he was anything but convinced.

"Okay. I applied online for a job at Dunkin'."

"You gonna be drinking more of that coffee you love? I hope you like Dunkin' coffee."

"Yeah, of course," I replied. "I live in New England. A Dunkin' on every corner. Hell, you can give directions just using Dunkin' stores as landmarks."

"I know. There's one almost across the street from the Boston Field Office."

That was true. About six hundred feet away from the FBI Boston Field Office, over on Everett Avenue in Chelsea, there's a Dunkin' store. This is where you say, wait: Macallister said "Boston." And you'd be correct. However, because of the way the government works, the FBI Boston Field Office is not actually located in Boston, but instead in Chelsea, Massachusetts, on Maple Street. I continued, "Selecting *that* particular Dunkin' location, a stone's throw away from the Field Office, seemed a little too obvious. However, that outlet is owned by a franchiser who also operates seventeen other Dunkin' locations spread out in six towns surrounding Boston."

"Okay. So what? What does that get you?"

"Opacity." I wasn't sure if Macallister would know that word, so I clarified. "This is how it's gonna work. The franchiser put my name in the payroll system and then put me on the schedule. Per that schedule, I'm working part-time, between fifteen and twenty-five hours per week, moving locations within the franchiser's network of stores to fill in for other employees who were absent or missed their shifts. Across the seventeen stores, there are so many shifts and so many employees that one more isn't going to be noticed."

"Who helped set this up?"

"That's the one other person in the Bureau that I mentioned. Appleton."

"Appleton did it? Personally?"

"Yessir."

"Good," Macallister nodded. I could tell he was pleased. As he should be. Jennifer Appleton was the highly regarded Special Agent in Charge (SAC) of the Boston Field Office. "There's no one better than her. But you said two, um, outside?"

"Yes. The president of the franchise company, and her controller."

"Who are they?"

"You don't need to know their names."

Macallister laughed. "Nice, Porter. Good compartmentalization. Good tradecraft. You're learning. I presume they are known only to the SAC?"

"Yep. Appleton vetted them herself. She manages the relationship."

"Anyone else?"

"Like I said, one or two Special Agents. Appleton will select them. I don't know who, yet. But she will need someone to help her on the inside, and someone to make it look like my apartment in Chelsea is lived in. Make the lights go on and off, and make the television flicker occasionally, just in case the Russians are watching. One of those agents will monitor my personal email account. In case the Russians try to contact me directly, I suppose, but I think that's unlikely."

"Okay," Macallister murmured, repeating, "It's okay. It's a decent cover. Unfortunately, it's a lot of potential for exposure, but it's loose enough that the only way you'll get busted is if a Dunkin' employee realizes you never make your shift. It will check out electronically. It won't check out in person. It's a risk."

"Yeah," I agreed. "That's been nagging me. But I think it works. I'm a disgruntled ex-agent who works a part-time job with no benefits, pouring to-go coffees, and barely hanging on. I'm gonna be a ghost, barely on the grid and basically invisible in person."

Staring out at the water, Macallister chuckled cheerlessly. "Sounds like a ghost is gonna be chasing a ghost."

"Exactly," I agreed. "Let's talk about our target."

CHAPTER

2

"BEFORE WE TALK ABOUT the target of this mission, Porter, we gotta take care of some paperwork," Deputy Assistant Director Macallister intoned. The statement was completely out of place with the setting. I mean, who does paperwork while sitting on a park bench at the water's edge?

"Paperwork?" I asked. "Top secret mission, and there's paperwork?"

He grimaced and said nothing as he leaned to his side to extract a buff-colored manilla folder from his briefcase, which, as best I could tell, was genuine brown leather and looked very expensive. He handed the cheap, government-issue folder to me.

The flimsy folder contained a single sheet of white paper, emblazoned with the FBI logo at the top, and I read the laser-printed words:

```
On October 23, 2019, Special Agent
Porter was verbally warned for an act
of insubordination by Acting Special
Agent in Charge Bradford Macallister,
and on the following day, Special Agent
Porter was relieved of his badge and
weapon and placed on administrative
leave for a period of time while his
actions were investigated. Subsequent
to that internal investigation, as of
```

October 31, 2019, with an effective date
of October 23, 2019, Special Agent Porter
was terminated for cause by the Federal
Bureau of Investigation.

Macallister handed me a fancy, blue-and-gold pen and said, "Sign it. This closes the loop in our systems. As of that signature, you're officially fired from the Bureau for insubordination. Congratulations," he added, with a sarcastic but amused tone.

I had, in fact, been insubordinate, purposely contradicting Macallister's orders just last month. But, in doing so, I successfully stopped an unprecedented act of terror against the United States of America that had been orchestrated by an obese, Russian-born immigrant, Russian mafia-connected oligarch named Anatoly Petrikov, who had colluded with a shady Russian organization called Unit 29155, identified as a nefarious sub rosa cybercrime and spy group that operated on the behest of the Kremlin.

At the moment when we had resolved that case, Macallister, who was on the cusp of a promotion to his new role as Deputy Assistant Director, recognized an opportunity. A two-fer, if you will. He could shield me from Unit 29155 by creating the ruse that I was a disgraced agent, no longer a threat. And, at the same time, he could dispatch me under that cover, potentially working outside the homeland-constricted jurisdiction of the FBI, to track down Anatoly Petrikov, who remained at large.

I waved away Macallister's offered fancy pen, and I reached into my backpack and pulled out a black Sharpie marker. I signed my name with the Sharpie, just to ensure that the signature was legible after the document was scanned into the Bureau's permanent records. I'd never see it again. I'd never see my badge or my Bureau-issued Glock pistol again, either.

Macallister was shaking his head as he accepted the signed document from me. "Do you always have to be difficult, Porter? I mean, it's just a pen. And you pick a marker." He examined the back side of the paper, where the ink had bled through, and huffed, "Are you done with the theatrics, Porter?"

"Sure, boss. I'm done. Can we talk about the target? Can we talk about the plan?"

Macallister carefully slid the folder back inside his briefcase. Rearranging himself on the park bench, he crossed one leg over the other, flicking a piece of dried dirt off the toe of a polished brown wingtip shoe with obvious annoyance. "We need to talk about one other item first."

"What's that?"

"As you might recall, I have a partner in mind for you. In fact, it's non-negotiable. You will be working with Anastasia Volkov."

"Great," I replied flatly. "Volkov."

"What's the problem? You were the one who trusted her. You were the one who countermanded my direct orders and teamed up with her."

"That was then, and that was for good reason. I realized that she had been truthful and, well, that I was wrong. *We* were wrong. At the same time, I kept her at arm's length, and I'd prefer to keep it that way. You know. Because she tried to kill me, once."

"It's non-negotiable," Macallister repeated.

"Why? Some sort of *Art of War* thing? Keep your friends close and your enemies closer?"

"I thought that was from *The Godfather*," the Deputy Assistant Director replied. "Whatever. You're working with Volkov. Because there's more."

CHAPTER

3

I REMEMBER WHEN I FIRST met Anastasia Volkov in person. It was July 2017. Macallister, then my Supervisory Special Agent, assigned her to work with me. Because, back then, Volkov was an Intelligence Analyst working in the FBI Boston Field Office.

Volkov had joined the Bureau after graduating from the Massachusetts Institute of Technology, majoring in computer science. Her hint of an accent, with her olive skin and caramel-blonde, long straight hair, made her somewhat exotic, but it was her extremely agile and intelligent mind that made her notable.

And it was her collusion with Petrikov—who, the FBI discovered, to our collective shock, was her father—that made her a traitor.

Volkov, however, had surrendered herself to the FBI after realizing that her father's criminal tendencies went far beyond a line that she was willing to cross. In exchange for her cooperation, Volkov was granted temporary immunity against the laundry list of charges that were brought against her, provided, however, she continued to assist the Bureau in finding her father, Petrikov, to bring him to justice. With her inside information and her incredible computer skills, she would be a unique asset.

And, apparently, despite the fact that one of the charges against her was attempted murder—of me—Macallister was insisting that Volkov would be my partner. I turned to Macallister on the park bench beside me and asked, "Where is she?"

"As you might recall, we arranged for a death certificate to be issued in her name. On paper, she is dead. In person, currently, she's being held under an assumed identity at a Federal prison in rural Connecticut."

"Oh," I said without enthusiasm. Macallister was correct, earlier, when he reminded me that it was I who teamed up with Volkov. That, however, was in the so-called heat of battle. With time gone by since, my reservations about Volkov had resurfaced. I mean, if you get bit by a dog once, you're gonna be pretty hesitant to pet that very same dog later on. And in my case, Volkov didn't just bite me. She tried to kill me.

"Cheer up, Porter. I've spent some time working with her recently. She's a key player in this operation."

"Oh? What's the op? What's the plan?"

"Well," Macallister stalled, "That's up to you."

"Huh?" I queried, adding in a sarcastic tone, "The Deputy Assistant Director hasn't come up with a plan yet?"

"Watch it, Porter," Macallister grunted, obviously annoyed.

"What? You gonna fire me?"

Macallister laughed but then added in a more serious, even tone, "Don't let it go to your head, Porter. We've been down that road before."

Chagrined, I only managed a muffled, "Mmmmm …"

He's right, I thought. *I've let my ego get in front of me in the past. Tone it down, Ben.*

Collecting my thoughts, I asked, "Okay, boss, lemme get this straight. Other than assigning me to work with Volkov, you're asking *me* to come up with a plan? You're not dictating a plan from above?"

"Correct. Spot on," he answered. "Listen, here's what I think. I know that you're creative. You seem to work best when you get a little runway. Some freedom to think. Last we talked, you said you were going to hang out here in Bristol for Thanksgiving with your sister. Stay here until you build your own team and work up an Ops Order, or something that resembles one."

I started to smile, but the grin faded quickly as I realized what he was offering. A dream come true, perhaps, but also a shit-ton of responsibility.

I better not screw this up, I thought, as I asked an innocent question, "Do I have a budget? And can I use Bureau resources for a team?"

"No budget. And yes. Well, sort of. One, two people tops."

Inadvertently, my eyebrows shot up. "Did I hear that correctly, sir? No budget?"

"Not really," he replied, cryptically adding, "I've arranged a black book funding resource."

"Black book, huh?"

"Yeah. One of the many reasons Volkov must be on your team. It's part of our deal. She will tap her father's accounts. That's your funding resource."

Now *that* made sense to me. And I appreciated the symbolism; I'd be using Petrikov's vast stores of ill-gotten money to track down Petrikov. I thought that over and then asked, "When do I start?"

"Now. Anything else?"

I laughed. "Anything else? Really? How about *everything* else?"

"You'll figure it out, Porter. You've got your cover legend in place. The cover gives you some time. Lay low and take that time to work it out. Oh, and by the way, you gotta return your car. That's a Bureau vehicle. You can't be driving a company car around. Find new wheels. I'll coordinate with Appleton, and in a couple of days, we'll send a driver to pick up the car. I'll send you a new phone with the driver. Give him your current phone. Turn off the password. Don't mess with it otherwise, because we can take it over and use it to enhance your cover. Create activity, that sorta thing. I hope you got nothing incriminating on it," he warned.

"No, sir, I don't."

Damn, I thought, *I don't care about the phone, but I like that car.* It was a sweet, tricked-out black Dodge Charger. But, as I thought it through, two of Macallister's words came back to me: "no budget."

This could be fun.

"Yessir," I repeated. "Got it."

There was silence on the bench for a beat until Macallister said quietly, "Porter, we could have done most of this on the phone. I came to Bristol to meet you in person to make sure you understand what you're about to do. Once you start this, you're not coming out of cover 'til you finish it. You're going into deep cover. Off the grid. No contact with friends or family. You understand that, right?"

I smiled grimly and looked Macallister in the eye. "Yessir. And I don't take it lightly. I've been chasing Petrikov for over two years. His time is up."

Macallister rose from the bench and instructed, "All communication from here on out through me, and me only." He handed me a blank business card, on which was hand printed ten numbers. He explained, "Like I said, I'm gonna send you a new phone. Call me from only that phone, using this number. Eventually we can set up email or whatever. In the meantime, come up with a plan, let me know when you're ready for Volkov, and go get Petrikov."

"Yessir," I replied. As Macallister walked back to a black Bureau Chevrolet Suburban and climbed into the rear of the SUV, I looked out onto the cold November water, wavelets sparkling like millions of tiny diamonds. It was the water that told me what to do.

I have no idea where to find Anatoly Petrikov. But I know how I'm going to start looking.

CHAPTER

4

AVENIDA DE LAS LOMAS, CARACAS, VENEZUELA

ANATOLY PETRIKOV WAS uncomfortably hot.

The stretched skin over the broken capillaries on his ruddy-red face glistened with sweat. With his liver-spotted, plump hands, he tugged at the fabric of his shirt, moist and clammy and sticking to his flab.

They told him that the peak of humidity and precipitation in the capital city of Venezuela was in late July or early August, and the months of November through March would bring a welcome respite from the dampness.

They lied, Petrikov thought. *Again.*

His ire simmered like the heat. He recognized that his temper would boil over, as it had done when, in a fit of hot, blood-red anger, he murdered his wife and drowned her dogs. That uncontrollable rage had also alienated his daughter. She bolted, abandoning him. She turned against him.

Petrikov made a concerted effort to force himself to relax. He'd cool himself off, mentally, by doing so physically, and he retreated to the air-conditioned building hidden within the concrete-and-steel-fenced compound on Avenida de Las Lomas.

Returning to his private room, he mopped his face with a towel and extracted a chilled bottle of vodka from a small freezer, pouring himself a refreshing shot. The familiar liquid had a restorative effect, and it allowed Petrikov to regain his focus as he settled into the comfortable, upholstered, red velvet armchair in his quarters.

The bulk of his waking hours in the walled compound had been spent in that armchair, his time consumed with the game of chess. He would escape into the big-screen Samsung smartphone they had permitted him to use upon his arrival in Caracas. The phone had been stripped of all applications but one, a newish social network called <u>Trampoline</u> <u>.Live</u>, which included online games such as chess. Petrikov could compete against a computerized opponent or, better, match wits and skills with any number of players on the platform, presumably from around the globe—some amateurish, some devious, and some masterful.

His fury subsiding and his calculating mind clearing, Petrikov realized that the games on the smartphone had become a distraction. A time waster. He decided, at that moment, that it was time to play the *real* match—one that would have much higher stakes than the online contests.

They lied, he repeated to himself. They had promised him asylum in Moscow, far from the reach of the American Federal Bureau of Investigation. But since that promise was made, he had been virtually imprisoned, first in Canada, then offshore, and now in this South American city. His handlers took away the false Canadian passport that was used to get him out of the Northern Hemisphere; they said it was "не хорошо." "Ne khorosho." *No good.*

They will continue to lie, until I am no longer of use to them. Waiting it out is not an option, he thought. *I must find an opportunity. I must take control of the game.*

He began to plot out his moves. When the opportunity arose, at the opening, he'd access his vast stores of money. Then in the middlegame, he'd go on attack, bribing his way onto a private plane ride from Caracas to the United States border. He'd sneak into the country by stealing a boat. And finally, once in the States, he'd execute the endgame: he would find the man who had twice stymied his plans and his ambitions. He would find Ben Porter.

Nyet, the oligarch corrected himself. *I will kill Ben Porter.*

CHAPTER
5

THURSDAY, NOVEMBER 21, 2019 – BRISTOL, RHODE ISLAND

AS MACALLISTER HAD PROMISED, within two days, the Bureau sent an agent to Bristol to pick up my car. My sweet, murdered-out Dodge Charger. Gone.

On the bright side, if there was one, that agent was my former colleague, Special Agent Don Jordon. With his close-cropped blond hair, wire-framed eyeglasses, pale skin, and impossibly thin and tall body, the geeky-looking Midwesterner did not fit the image of an agent from central casting. I knew otherwise, and his taciturn composure together with a sharp mind made Jordon an exceptional agent.

As usual, Jordon picked up on my mood right away, reaching his hand out to accept the Charger's key fob. "Sorry 'bout the car, Porter." Closing his fingers around the fob, he added dryly, "You need to give me your personal phone, too. And I have more good news for you. This stunner is your new phone."

As I handed him my personal iPhone, now unlocked and unprotected without a password as instructed, Jordon handed me a charcoal-gray, plastic flip phone, devoid of markings. I inspected it carefully, saying, "Thanks. What does it do?"

"It's a phone. It makes calls."

"Yeah, of course," I said dismissively, going on with more enthusiasm, "But what else? Does it shoot poison-tipped barbs? Or is it a homing device that I can use if I get in trouble? Or maybe it can, like, explode, 'cuz there's C-4 packed inside." I was getting excited as I rolled the device over in my hands, careful not to open it until Jordon gave me the tutorial.

My giddiness for a cool secret agent toy faded as Jordon remained mute, apprising me with what might have been scorn. Finally, he repeated flatly, "It's a phone. It makes calls."

"That's it? All the tech at the FBI and they're giving me a plain vanilla flip phone?"

"Yes."

I rolled my eyes. "Great. I'm supposed to track down America's most wanted fugitive with this?"

"Yes."

Jordon scratched his neck, and for once, I remained quiet. I was rewarded when he added, "I know enough about your task, but I am not read in specifically on it. I'm not at liberty to talk about it. However, I can tell you Appleton assigned me to run your cover back in Chelsea. I will be responsible for your personal phone, your residence, and your cover life, so to speak, in general. I will take charge of the Charger. And, finally, I report only to SAC Appleton. Outside of that, you're on your own."

"Take charge of the Charger?" I smirked. "That was kind of funny, for you."

Jordon's left cheek may have crinkled with a hint of a smile, but the tell disappeared just as quickly as he asked, "Any questions?"

"No, because you're gonna say that you're not at liberty to answer any," I pouted. Jordon inclined his head once in a nod, and without so much as another word, he turned to the Charger.

As the black car pulled away, I tugged on a warm coat to ward off the chill and the brisk late fall breeze, and I went for a walk. I enjoyed wandering around my temporary home in Bristol, a charming small town on the banks of Narragansett Bay. My sister's place was maybe a quarter-mile, three-block stroll to the water's edge.

Reaching the waterfront and ambling along the seawall at Walley Park where I had met with Macallister two days ago, it was time to put my plan in motion. I pulled the gray flip phone from my pocket. I knew who I would call, where I would go, and how I would set off on my mission.

DECEMBER

CHAPTER

6

TUESDAY, DECEMBER 3, 2019 – DANBURY, CONNECTICUT

IT HAD BEEN A SUBDUED Thanksgiving with my extended family. Naturally, I couldn't tell them what I was really up to. For all my parents, my sister Grace, and my brother Joe knew, I was returning to Boston to work at a coffee chain while figuring out what to do next, after being fired by the FBI. They were supportive, of course, but it was a difficult topic to dance around.

The most awkward part of the annual traditional family meal had been toward the end when someone said, "Does anyone want coffee?" Of course, they all looked at me. Nice.

I had grabbed another beer and waited it out.

Come Monday after the holiday, I was more than ready to put my plan into action. I had needed one last favor from my sister, and I pleaded, "Any chance you can rent a car for me? I'll pay you back."

Grace had grimaced ever so slightly but replied, "Sure, Benbro. But why? I can give you a ride back to Boston."

"Well, I have a few stops to make on the way. Want to check in with a couple of friends."

"Oh," had been Grace's unenthusiastic reply. But she did it anyway, and she put a one-way rental with drop-off at Logan Airport in Boston on her credit card.

Though I felt bad deceiving my sister, I figured she'd forgive me. Eventually. For I had no intention of going to Logan.

✳ ✳ ✳

Located near the southern tip of the eight-square-mile, manmade Candlewood Lake, the Federal Correctional Institution (FCI) in Danbury, Connecticut, is what's known as a "low-security" prison. The facility houses approximately 1,000 prisoners, including several hundred female inmates at the FSL (Federal Satellite Low Security) prison camp.

Low security connotes an image of "Club Fed," perhaps a country-club-like lush green lawn with unguarded prisoners wandering pebbled paths, fed three squares a day as they did their penance for some white-collar crime in relative comfort. This, however, was not that kind of prison. Despite being characterized as a minimum-security facility, FCI Danbury remained a prison, with barren concrete and steel walls perhaps best-known for being fictionalized in the Netflix series *Orange is the New Black*, which was based on a memoir of an FCI Danbury inmate. Or at least that's what I'm told. I've never seen it. The show, that is. And, come to think of it, nor have I seen the inside of a prison.

When I arrived at FCI Danbury, driving a Kia sedan rented in my sister's name, the irony of using another name that didn't rightfully belong to the person I sought was not lost on me when I checked in at the main visitor's entrance, greeted gruffly by a Corrections Officer who queried, simply, "Inmate's name?"

"Ann Karin."

The CO shuffled pages on a clipboard, and while flipping sheets, asked, "You are?"

I gulped. I'm supposed to be undercover. But I don't have any identity other than my own. *I need to fix that, soon*, I thought, before stammering, "Porter. Ben Porter."

"License or photo ID."

I slid my laminated Massachusetts driver's license to the CO. He examined it briefly and passed it back. I allowed myself a sigh of relief; he did not take down the information or copy the card, and I realized that Macallister had greased this arrangement as the CO picked up a single sheet of paper from the desk surface. Tracing the few words that were handprinted on the sheet with a forefinger, the Corrections Officer explained, "This is unusual, Mister Porter, but it checks out." He looked up at me, finally making eye contact as he commanded, "Wait outside."

As I retraced my steps to the exterior, I caught a glimpse of the CO bringing a black telephone handset to his ear as he crumpled the single sheet of paper into a ball with his free hand, tossing the ball into a wire-mesh trash can.

✳ ✳ ✳

My wait outside the doors of FCI Danbury, in the freezing, windy, early December air, was long. Twenty-five, thirty minutes. I debated returning inside versus retreating to the rental car. Instead, I chose neither option and sucked it up, shivering.

Finally, the double doors swung out, and three shapes emerged, a tall male guard in uniform and a stocky female guard in uniform, both flanking a casually dressed, stunning woman with olive skin and caramel-blonde, long, straight hair. The guards stopped at the maximum swing extension of the doors, and the woman continued walking toward me, composed, with her shoulders back and her chin high. She did not acknowledge the guards, nor did they acknowledge her as they slinked back inside the building. The doors pivoted closed and latched with an audible click.

"Can I help with your luggage?" I asked, completely unnecessarily and sarcastically; her hands were empty.

"Thanks, but no. I travel light. You look good, Ben. You look like you've lost weight," Anastasia Volkov lilted.

"Maybe a little. Always a challenge. Care to go for a long drive?" I offered.

"You know, I was expecting Macallister."

"Disappointed?"

"Not at all. Where are we going?"

Such a simple question, I thought. But I wasn't ready to answer it.

I had to call the shots. I got to choose what to say and when to say it. I would need that upper hand, that control. This was the woman who had once attempted to kill me, and who had once been my adversary. And now, this woman has been assigned to be my ally.

Or so I hoped, wondering with a tinge of nervousness, *can I truly trust Anastasia Volkov?*

It was time to find out.

CHAPTER
7

AS ANASTASIA VOLKOV AND I walked side-by-side toward the parking lot of FCI Danbury, our shadows long on the ground in a weak afternoon sun, I asked, "So. How was your stay at, um, in Uncle Sam's digs?"

"Not altogether pleasant, but manageable. I am relieved to be done. I am done, right?"

She stopped in her tracks, turning to face me, looking me in the eye with a plaintive expression. I considered her carefully, knowing full well how manipulative and deceitful she could be. I chose my words just as cautiously, wanting to draw her out. "As far as I know. But in that particular case, I'd be willing to bet that you know more than I. What does *done* look like from your perspective?"

Volkov sniffed and began walking again. "Macallister made me a deal. I'll be absolved of my sins if I continue to aid and abet the FBI and the U.S. government in general, for now, and in perpetuity. There's been a bunch of lawyers here. Lots of documents. Signatures. That's why I figured it would be Macallister who would come for my release."

I chuckled mirthlessly, "To crow about his tactics and legal fortitude?"

"That, and to take credit," Volkov snorted. "To remind me it was his doing. That I was and will be beholden to him."

We reached the rented Kia, and I made for the driver's side door. Volkov halted, examining the sedan, finally blurting in an accusatory tone, "What happened to my car?"

"*Your* car?"

"My Charger. The one that I, um…" Her voice trailed off.

"The car that you chased me down with, and then tried to kill me?"

There it was. I said it. I addressed the elephant in the room, or at least in the parking lot of FCI Danbury. Volkov *had* tried to kill me, running me down in the black Dodge Charger that was eventually, and somewhat ironically, reassigned to my use, after Volkov was exposed as a mole within the FBI.

She faced me, hands spread and palms up. With the pleading face that she had employed just moments ago, she said, "Um, yeah. Something like that. Listen, I thought that was behind us. I thought that I had earned my way out of that mess. Which, I admit, I created for myself. But also, for which I have apologized. Made amends for. Made the deal with Macallister. Isn't that why we are here?"

I respected her for tackling the uncomfortable topic head-on. I nodded, trying to diffuse the bit of tension, as I agreed gently, "True. Hey, it's freezing out here, and we've got a long drive. How 'bout we hop in and get going?"

We made eye contact—and held it for a beat longer than necessary. It made me uncomfortable. I blinked rapidly to break the stare and slipped into the driver's seat of the Kia. She followed suit on the passenger side, closing her door gently and overly carefully.

As Volkov snapped the seat belt into place, she purred, "We good now?"

"Yeah. I guess."

She flashed me a smile and said nicely, "Great. Thank you. Now where? Where's our long drive going to take us together?" She coquettishly raised one eyebrow slightly and added, sweetly this time, "And again, where's my car?"

I swallowed and started the car, buying time to let my brain consider her tone on the "together." Maybe I was being paranoid, but her voice sounded, well, flirtatious. Manipulative. I didn't like it. I answered in a businesslike tone, "Well, *your* car was an FBI car. They reassigned it to me. But—"

"It actually was *my* car," she interrupted. "I bought it with my money. Then I put it on the FBI's vehicle manifest so that it wouldn't call attention to me, as if it was just assigned to me randomly. I guess that kinda backfired on me . . ." Her voice trailed off.

I resumed the even, professional tone that I had used before she had cut me off. "That's all ancient history. Let's focus on the present day. Your Ann Karin identity is all that links you to this world. Your Anastasia Volkov identity disappeared with a death certificate. Since Ann Karin doesn't exist except for a record as an ex-con with a minor rap sheet, you're invisible. And I'm supposed to be invisible, too. Therefore, the Bureau took my car, or your car, or whatever."

"Oh." Her voice was flat. "And the Bureau gave you this thing?"

"No. I rented it. Actually, that brings me to something else. Macallister explained that part of the deal that you and he agreed to was access to, um, well, your—"

"Money." She finished my stuttering, awkward sentence for me and started to laugh, "Well, Ben Porter, so nice of you to come spring me from jail and then try to get into my . . . wallet."

Her tinkling laugh annoyed me. Her phrasing was most definitely flirty. I didn't respond.

Her laugh trailed off, but her face still registered a kind and deep smile. With the corners of her lips curling up, she whispered, "Just trying to have some fun. It's been lonely in that prison. Is that okay, Ben?"

I have to work with her. Don't be an ass, Ben, I thought, and I agreed pleasantly, "Sure. Sorry to be so humorless. Let's get out of here." I pulled my seatbelt across my chest and clicked the buckle into place.

"Not sure what you've got planned for me, but we're only about an hour from New York City. Let's go there."

Whoa, I thought. *I'm the one calling the shots. Not her.* "Sorry," I said, "But New York is not on the itinerary."

Volkov inclined her head and offered, "But, in order to satisfy the conditions of my deal and get access to my money—or, rather to my father's money—we'll have to make a stop in New York."

I considered that for a moment.

Only a stop. I'm still in charge. And access to the money is a critical part of the mission.

"New York it is," I confirmed brightly, trying to keep the mood light and to cover my hesitation. "The big apple."

"How prescient of you, Ben. As usual, you're spot on. Apple."

I had no idea what she meant. But I didn't have the opportunity to think it over, because when I shifted the car into gear to drive to New York City, she draped her left hand on top of my right hand, on the gearshift, with a soft caress.

Her touch was cold. And unwelcome.

I didn't like it one bit that she was dictating the route but having thought of no other options at the moment, I decided to go with it. I promised myself that I would remain on high alert, and as the Kia rolled past the cold, leafless trees, crunching on the cold, lifeless gravel road, I shivered, side-eying Volkov.

Her gaze was straight ahead; her face was placid.

Was she relaxed? Or was she preparing to strike?

CHAPTER

8

NEW YORK CITY, NEW YORK

THERE'S NOTHING QUITE LIKE driving into New York City at nightfall, heading south on the Henry Hudson Parkway, passing under the brightly lit George Washington bridge, as cars and trucks and yellow cabs weave through the traffic while, to the right, you see the glistening waters of the Hudson River and, to the left, the glittering lights of the apartment buildings and billboards and skyscrapers of Manhattan.

Volkov had said very little during the hour-and-a-half journey. She had pulled her hand off mine as we exited the FCI Danbury grounds, and she'd spent most of the drive with her head leaning against the window glass. I focused on the road and on the in-dash navigation display. Without any direction or comment from Volkov, and without a clue as to where she specifically wanted to go in New York City, I had set the destination as Times Square.

As we passed the signs for the 79th Street Boat Basin, Volkov straightened, stretched her arms, then reached over and, touching the dash display, canceled the route guidance. She turned to me and finally spoke, "West Fifty-Sixth Street. It's the first traffic light. It's nice to be out of that prison."

I swiveled my eyes from the fast-moving congestion to look at her for a second. She grinned, "I know. Directions and inner thoughts, all at once."

Laughing, I confirmed, "Let freedom ring, right? I can only imagine what it was like, you know, in jail."

"I had time to think. But the time went quickly. Macallister was on it. He was really good about setting up our deal."

"What is it, exactly?"

"Pretty simple, really. If I cooperate wholly and in good faith with the FBI, in perpetuity, I am absolved of my crimes. Want the list as a refresher?"

I chuckled, but I was curious, thinking, *Let's see if she ticks them all off. Let's see if she's truly honest.* I said, "Sure."

"Item one, one count of murder. Item two, which you are intimately familiar with, attempted murder, two counts. Item three, terrorism as an enemy combatant, two counts. And a bunch of minor charges just for good measure. Racketeering, collusion, fraud, money laundering, aiding and abetting criminal activities, that sort of thing."

Her list was complete, but I couldn't help chiding, "Aiding and abetting criminal activities? Those count as minor, huh?"

"Compared to murder, yes," she replied indignantly. She turned her head to face me directly. "That is my single, biggest regret. My cross to bear, if you will. It was inexcusable. It will be with me forever, and there is absolutely nothing that I can do to truly absolve myself of that."

A yellow cab cut me off, and I slammed on the brakes of the Kia, the sudden loss of forward movement pressing us both into our seatbelts. Horns blared. Volkov continued speaking in an even tone as if nothing had happened. "If I survive your driving, I'll still have the guilt. And if I decide to turn against the FBI, or you, or Macallister, the deal is off, and my convictions are back on, to which I've pled guilty to on the record. There's no going back."

"Unless, of course, you decide to disappear again. You're pretty good at that."

"I am. But as you'll soon find out, the novelty and thrill of living invisibly, off the grid, wears thin quickly. Your turn is coming up. West Fifty-Sixth. Left lane."

I merged the Kia into the traffic that was haltingly headed into the heart of the city, looking over at my passenger for my next direction or for her next confession. *She seems sincere. But she has blood on her hands. And she's manipulative. Sincerity can be faked,* I thought with trepidation.

After we'd traveled four blocks, she began scanning the sides of the narrow, one-way street. Our progress east was stop-and-go until she barked, "Here. Left. Into that garage."

Exiting the car, I exchanged the key fob for a proffered claim ticket from the parking attendant, who asked, "How long?"

I shrugged, but Volkov quickly responded, "Overnight." My eyebrows shot up. This was an unexpected twist. The hairs on the back of my neck prickled.

Volkov looked at me, and she hooked her left arm into the crook of my elbow, leading me to the sidewalk.

As soon as we were out of the sightline of the parking attendant, I stopped, pulling my arm away from hers, stooping to fake-tie my shoelace. "Sorry," I muttered, adding, "Lead the way. Where are we going?"

"East. To Fifth Avenue." She didn't make another attempt to touch me. We walked in uncomfortable silence. Not gonna lie. I was not enjoying it.

We turned left on Fifth Avenue at the barricaded, police-line protected Trump Tower. The sidewalks were jammed; the locals walking with purpose and without regard to the tourists who gaped at the towering buildings of New York City. Horns honked as cars and trucks and buses whooshed by on the Avenue, the smell of their exhausts intermingling with the odors of street cart food. The lack of personal space combined with sensory overload was almost overpowering.

Volkov paid none of it any attention as we worked our way north on Fifth Avenue, passing one swank store after another. Gucci. Louis Vuitton. Bergdorf.

The city skyline opened as we crossed Fifty-Eighth Street. To our left, a park. To our right, a plaza peppered with glowing discs of light set in the paving and a giant, contemporary, glass cube looming above. The Fifth Avenue Apple Store. Duh. *That's* what she meant when she said "apple," earlier.

Entering the glass cube, we descended the stainless-steel, reflecting spiral staircase into the giant, subterranean store, its ceiling dotted with the disc-shaped skylights to the plaza above, and its floor lined with row after row of maple tables displaying Apple products in various colors and sizes. Volkov made her way to a business service desk tucked deep within the vast, crowded store. Addressing the suited clerk, she purred, "Good evening. I'm sure you can help me. My bag was stolen, along with, of course, the contents. My phone. And my wallet."

"I'm sorry, ma'am. I'm not sure there's much I can do to help," was the discouraging, flat response.

"Oh, I'm sure that's not the case. Kindly let me access a device. I'll input my profile into a new iPhone. I'll link the device to my Apple card. It will be quite easy for you to confirm my identity and to make the sale."

The suit's eyebrows raised, "You will recite your card number? And all of the verifying details? And all of your passwords and such?"

Volkov smiled, "Yes. Of course."

I hung back. I'd heard of the Apple card, which was released to the public in August, earlier this year. It is basically a branded MasterCard credit card, but with typical Apple marketing flair, the card itself is heavy, thick metal, not plastic, and it does not show any embossed numbers. Against a white background and an outlined Apple logo, the face of the card is marred with only a printed name and a gold chip.

The clerk disappeared for a moment, returning bearing a plain, white rectangular box. "Will the color do?"

"I'm sure it will."

✳ ✳ ✳

Ninety minutes later, the suited clerk and Volkov were best friends as they parted with a friendly handshake. Volkov handed me one of the two bags; mine held two white boxes containing MacBook Air computers, and hers was packed with two iPhone boxes, fast chargers, two iPads with matching keyboard covers, and two pairs of AirPods. We climbed the stainless-steel staircase bearing our loot, conspicuous because of the two white bags, flexing our tech prowess and our economic stature for the tourists, presumably.

I was impressed. Working solely from memory, Volkov had input all of her details, email accounts, and credit card information. I caught a glimpse of her work as she typed in her name for what had to be the tenth time: "Ann Karin." Clever. She had prepared for this, creating an identity in her assumed name.

"Does Macallister know?" I asked as we reached the open air of the Apple store plaza adjacent to Fifth Avenue.

"Know what?"

"That you'd set all that up? With your Ann Karin identity."

"Does he know? Yes, of course. Know *how?* Of course not. He set up computer time for me, even though Internet access is strictly prohibited for prisoners. Obviously, he pulled some strings, but it was subtle. Only took a few hours over two days. But he knew that if the FBI set you up with an identity, there might be a trail. We decided that you'd start with nothing."

"And with this, I will have, what? Something?"

Volkov laughed. "That's why there's two of everything, Ben. One for me, one for you. We'll set your new identity up tonight. Let's go find a place to stay. And something to eat. I'm starving."

"I presume you've already thought ahead," I stated petulantly. It wasn't a question. As usual, she was ahead of me. *This is my operation,* I thought, reminding myself, *Ben, you're in charge. Stay in charge.*

She halted on the sidewalk as people flowed around us, two invisible people in the throng of a New York night. "Of course. But it's your turn. Before we go further, what's the plan? What are we doing?"

Dammit. She's ahead of me, again.

"I have a plan, and I'll let you in on the details once we are done with this so-called detour to New York. Will that be soon?" I hated the way that sounded. Whiny. Sophomoric. But I had to take charge.

Volkov called me out, "No need to be so catty, Ben. We're in this together. I'm sorry if I've come across as calling the shots. But you have to admit, for this part, I'm more qualified than you."

I had to dial it back because she was correct. I replied, "You're right. Listen, I'll explain the details when we are not standing on a New York

City sidewalk. But you know exactly what we're doing. I'm guessing you want to hear me say it. We're gonna go find Anatoly Petrikov. We're gonna find your father and bring him to justice."

"Where do you plan to start? I mean, I have some ideas, but I want to hear yours. I have a tremendous amount of respect for you. You know that, right, Ben?" With her bag-free hand, she clasped my bag-free hand.

I shifted my bag from one hand to the other so that I could pull free of her controlling grasp, and I said, "I think so. And I do have a plan once we finish up with this detour to New York. We get set up, and then we backtrack Petrikov through Unit 29155. Who, we assume, is looking for me. But we have the upper hand."

Volkov's eyes narrowed. "How do you figure that?"

I replied confidently, "Because, if you'll recall, you died. And because of that, I'm quite certain they're not looking for you. For Anastasia Volkov."

That was my second mistake of the day.

CHAPTER
9

AVENIDA DE LAS LOMAS, CARACAS, VENEZUELA

"I MADE THE MISTAKE OF trusting you," Anatoly Petrikov spat, his flabby jowls red in anger, as he leaned back in the brown, leather boardroom chair. *Defiance,* he thought, folding his arms across his massive chest. *No more obsequiousness.*

"No, you made the mistake of making assumptions," countered the medium-height, dark-haired, dark-eyed man sitting across the table. Grasping a white porcelain coffee mug with both hands, the man leaned toward the table, signaling that he would not back down from the argument.

The two men sat in silence. Petrikov considered his options.

The first to speak in a stand-off loses. Signals weakness. Capitulation. However . . . the first to speak sets the tone. Makes the opening offer.

Deciding on the latter move, he growled, "Perhaps we meet in the middle. Perhaps you explain what assumptions I made, and then you explain why I should trust you on this."

"It is quite simple. You assumed a timeline. When I told you that you would be brought to Moscow, you assumed the schedule. I did not set a schedule. A deadline. It will happen. But it is not the time."

Petrikov snorted, "Why? Why is *this* not the time?"

"New information has come to light."

"Such as?"

The man raised the coffee mug to his lips and slurped, then set the mug delicately on the table. Standing, he paced the length of the long table, a heavy, ornate mahogany affair which fit perfectly in the opulent surroundings of the boardroom in the Russian Embassy to Venezuela. From the exterior, the structure was bland and mostly invisible behind a tall concrete wall capped with steel fencing. On the inside, however, no expense was spared in furnishing or décor.

Reaching the end of the table, the man turned, prompting, "Let us play a little game. Humor me, if you will. What do you know of me?"

Petrikov snorted again but acquiesced. "Not much, I'm afraid. I know what you claim to be your name. Vitaly Nikolaevich Rodionov. What you claim to be your occupation: the senior-most information technology officer of Unit 29155. And that you claim that you report only to President Vladimir Putin."

"Precisely," Rodionov confirmed. "Your memory is excellent. And, therefore, you'll recall that I've done exactly what I've said I will do. Except, of course, for not meeting *your* expectation as to the timeline for your trip to the motherland."

"Mmmph."

Rodionov shrugged. "I don't expect you to admit that I'm correct. However, I do expect you to also recall that my job is *information*. And, therefore, I believe you'll find the new information that I've obtained to be quite interesting."

"Perhaps," Petrikov parried, "but perhaps in addition to sharing information, you'll share good faith."

Rodionov sat, and parroting Petrikov's earlier query, asked, "Such as?"

"I am here in the Russian Embassy not as your guest, but as your prisoner."

"That is not true," objected Rodionov. "You are permitted to come and go from the grounds as you please. The perimeter guards are all trained to recognize you on sight."

"Be that as it may, but I am still a prisoner. You dole out limited spending money, you set my daily schedule, and you limit my travel. You know that I cannot leave the city, much less the country."

"You may. I don't know where you'll go that will offer you this level of hospitality, but you may do what you want." Rodionov reached into his jacket pocket and withdrew a small, dark blue folio, embossed in gold on its cover. He slid the item across the table to Petrikov.

"My worthless and wholly false Canadian passport. By what stroke of fortune did you happen to have that in your pocket today?"

Rodionov laughed genuinely. "Good question. I wanted to tempt you with it. To show it to you. But you've been convincing as usual, and I truly don't think you're going anywhere. Not when I tell you what I can tell you. Or do you still not trust me?"

"This," Petrikov said, waving the passport in the air, "is a start. A gesture, which I appreciate. Please, proceed."

Rodionov leaned forward, planting his elbows on the table and lacing his fingers together. Earnestly, he revealed, "We have good information that Anastasia Volkov's death certificate was false."

Petrikov sat up straight. "My daughter is alive?"

"Perhaps. As you might recall, a death certificate for her accomplice was issued on the same day. Same time of death, same place of death. But there is an inconsistency in the state file number on only one of the certificates issued."

"On my daughter's?"

"Yes."

"And might this just be that? An inconsistency? A problem with the bureaucracy?"

"Yes. But one would think, in such a matter of such interest to the American Federal Bureau of Investigation, such inconsistencies would be quickly resolved and corrected. Or, to your point, it may be a simple clerical error."

Petrikov grunted, "And what do you propose?"

"We will do our job. Unit 29155 is uniquely and expertly qualified for this type of electronic investigatory work. We first complete our research on this certificate. If it turns out to be questionable, we make the assumption that your daughter is alive, and we look for her. Perhaps we find her. Perhaps we don't."

Nodding, Petrikov laboriously brought himself to his feet, making a show of pocketing the passport. He crossed to a small table, where he extracted a clear bottle from a bucket of ice. Selecting two cut-crystal glasses, he poured a clear liquid from the bottle as he asked, "And what of Ben Porter?"

Standing, Rodionov laughed, "As you are pouring vodka, former Special Agent Ben Porter is toiling behind the counter at a fast-food chain, pouring coffee. Quite a fall to a somewhat demeaning position for a man who was specially trained as, what do they call them? A G-man."

Petrikov, however, remained grim, not joining Rodionov's mirth and instead flatly stating, as he handed the other man one of the two glasses, "Now I believe it is you making assumptions. While I shall wait for more of your news on my daughter, I'll remind you that Porter seems to be persistently difficult. And, therefore, I would offer that you might also utilize your unique and expert qualifications, as you say, to ensure that Porter is no longer a threat."

Accepting the offered glass and touching it to Petrikov's glass with a high-pitched ding, Rodionov agreed. "I'll drink to that thoughtful counsel. And I'll disclose something else to you. Just as we've been investigating the potentially fraudulent death certificate for your daughter, we've remained quite interested in Ben Porter."

CHAPTER
10

WEDNESDAY, DECEMBER 4, 2019 – 6:10 AM – BOSTON, MASSACHUSETTS

"CAN I TAKE your order?"

The voice was disembodied. Female, it sounded. Tinny, through the rusted, black, rain-streaked speaker grill, built into a garishly colored, back-lit menu board. The driver of a bland, silvery-gray Ford Fiesta mumbled, "Ah, okay, ah, a large coffee."

"How would you like it?"

"Ah, black. Just black."

"Okay. Two twenty-two. Pull to the window."

The Fiesta rolled forward over shiny, wet pavement to the partial shelter afforded by a stub of roof that protected the drive-up window. A pale woman's face peered from within, the horizontally sliding service window already open. She wore a headset; hair pulled back into a messy, frizzy bun. The voice, now not transmitted through a rusty speaker and coming from a plump face, repeated, "Two twenty-two."

The driver hesitated, speaking to the outstretched, open, palm-up hand that poked a bit through the window. "My friend Ben said he'd hook me up. Is he working?"

"Ben? Ben, who?" The hand clenched into a fist.

"Ah, Ben Porter. Buddy of mine."

"Hang on." The hand retracted, and the woman turned away. The driver could still hear the woman speaking; her voice now directed into the building. "Anyone know a Ben Porter?"

A second disembodied voice, this one also female, replied, "Not in today. Was here, I dunno, maybe yesterday."

Glancing to her right to see if any new vehicles had pulled up to the order station at the menu board, and seeing none, the woman pushed the microphone on her headset away from her mouth as she leaned toward the sliding window. "Assistant Manager says he's not here today. It's gonna be two twenty-two."

The driver offered three partially crumpled dollar bills. "No problem. Keep the change."

The woman brushed her forehead with her left hand as she accepted the bills with her right hand, saying, pleasantly, "Thank you. Hang on." A moment later, a lidded, white Styrofoam cup was wordlessly passed through the window.

The driver took the cup and slid his right foot from the brake to the accelerator. Rain dripped through the still-open driver's side window. The car stopped at the sidewalk apron at the street, the right side of the vehicle illuminated by a double-lantern streetlight.

Engaging the button to slide the window up, the driver jammed the cup into the center console dual cupholder at his right thigh, almost dislodging a second, mostly empty, identical Styrofoam cup in the process.

Checking the rearview mirror again to confirm that he was not holding up another early-morning coffee patron, the driver consulted a printed map, barely legible in the glow from the streetlight cast through the passenger-side window. Placing his forefinger on the yellow high-lighted notation numbered six, he traced a route, narrating to himself, "Location nine—opposite courthouse. No drive through. I'll have to go in."

As the driver checked the street for oncoming traffic, he squirmed in the cloth-covered seat, his bladder now uncomfortably full of the coffee from his first stop.

Third time's a charm, he thought, proud of himself for thinking in an English-language idiom.

The Fiesta inched forward, then accelerated into a right-hand turn onto Broadway, just as a smartphone chimed with an incoming call notification. The driver swiped to accept the call, then jabbed the speakerphone icon. "Da?" *Yes?*

A deep, male voice sounded from the tiny speakers at the base of the device. "Anything?"

"Departing the Broadway and Pleasant Street location. Number six. Assistant manager claims the target was here yesterday. Already checked location four. That one said he was there last week." The driver began to slow the Fiesta as it approached a red-lit traffic light.

A grunt was the reply. The connection remained silent for a beat, then the deep voice added, "Very well. You keep missing him. It's odd. But our source says he is part-time and works where needed or assigned. It seems to check out. Do another circuit today, then send a full report through the usual channel."

"Da." The driver tapped the *END* icon as the traffic light turned green, signaling him to continue his search for the American named Ben Porter.

CHAPTER
11

THURSDAY, DECEMBER 5, 2019 – NEW YORK CITY

FOR THE SECOND MORNING in a row, I woke up next to Anastasia Volkov.

Well, "woke up" might not be technically correct, because I didn't get much sleep. It's very difficult to sleep with one eye open, lying beside a person who once tried to kill you.

Outwardly, I'm pleasant and easy-going, doing my best to begin our new partnership in harmony and with cooperation.

Inside, I am stressed. *Is this a honey trap? She'll kill me with kindness and then . . . kill me. It won't be her first time.* That was the question that had kept me awake, while I lay beside her, listening to her even, soft breathing.

✳ ✳ ✳

After our tiff on Tuesday night, outside the Apple store on Fifth Avenue, we walked a block or two south in silence when I grunted, attempting to use my tone to take charge. "Neat trick at the Apple store. Now what? Where are we going?"

She giggled. "So many questions, Ben. First things first. We need a place to stay, but like I said earlier, I'm famished. I know a place that can take care of both."

We checked into a hotel just off Fifth Avenue, south of the magnificent New York Public Library and Bryant Park. At the reception desk, she gave her name as Ann Karin and requested a large room with a king-sized bed.

I watched with fascination when the reception clerk requested a credit card and, without hesitation, Volkov pulled out her newly acquired iPhone. She tapped it on the card reader. Magically, we were in.

After dropping our Apple bags in the room, we headed for the hotel's rooftop restaurant and bar, where we wined and dined under the stars—sort of, or at least under a clear plastic roof to ward off the chill. The dinner charge went on our room tab, but not before I asked, finally having the courage to be blunt, "What's with the king-sized bed? What are you up to?"

"Two people traveling together, with no luggage, requesting two rooms? That would look odd, don't you think?"

I couldn't think of a reason to object, though I would have much preferred my own room. Or at least my own bed. I ordered a chocolate cake and double shot of espresso for dessert. As, you know, a precaution. To help me stay awake.

After dinner, we rode the elevator down to our floor. Once inside our room, she had been quiet, washing up and then laying down on the bed, clothed, whispering, "Tomorrow, Ben, we shop. But now, we sleep." She fell asleep in an instant. I, as we've established, did not.

The following day, Wednesday, was a blur of shopping, hitting store after store where we bought luggage and clothing, with periodic trips back to the hotel to drop bags. Most of our purchases were for her; a few items for me to tide me over since I'd left my stuff in the trunk of the Kia.

After an early dinner at a nearby café, we returned to the room, where Volkov asked, "Okay, Ben, it's your turn. Who do you want to be?"

"That's a loaded question."

She laughed. "Let's just start with a name."

I had considered that already, and knowing how I'd conduct my mission, I had thought an esoteric reference would be fortuitous as I replied, "I'll be John H. Godfrey."

Wednesday evening passed as we unboxed the second set of Apple gizmos in order to create an email account and Apple Card account using that name. Trying to show her that I was useful with computers, I managed to somehow freeze the brand-new MacBook Air. Shaking her head dismissively at my incompetence as I flailed trying to undo whatever my error was, she took over, jokingly advising me, "It's a computer. If you get stuck, sometimes it's more effective just to pull the plug." She pantomimed yanking an electrical cord out of a wall receptacle while saying, "Of course, this one is a laptop and has a battery, so there are other ways," as she restarted the MacBook by holding down the power key.

With the electronic tools in place and with Volkov's wizardry in New York obviously complete, when the Thursday morning sun brightened the room, I decided it was time to act like my alter ego and to take command. I sat up in the king-sized hotel bed, and I shook Volkov's shoulder. "I've had enough of New York. Detour done. Time to move on."

Volkov mumbled sleepily, "Sure."

"Let's pack up, get some breakfast, and go get the car."

Volkov reached her hand out and touched my arm. It felt like a caress. I ignored it as she purred, "Where are we headed?"

I smiled, for I knew what lay ahead, and I answered, "To meet an old friend."

CHAPTER

12

I TRIED OUT MY NEW IPHONE—John Godfrey's iPhone—at the garage where we parked the rented Kia. I doubled-clicked the right side button, and the Apple Wallet app instantly appeared, waiting for me to look at the phone. Recognizing my face, the app unlocked, and with a tap of the device on the credit card terminal, we settled up the exorbitant two-day charge for parking in the city. Here's a pro tip: if you're using your own money, avoid leaving your car in a New York City parking garage for a couple of nights.

But we weren't using our own money, and as soon as we were clear of the city and driving south on Interstate 95, with the vastness of Newark Liberty International Airport to our right and the industrial clutter of Port Newark to our left, Volkov pulled out one of the MacBook Airs and linked it to a mobile hot spot, announcing, "Let's open the taps."

"The taps? I'm not sure I follow."

She laughed. "Like, as in, tap the account."

"Oh, right," I replied. "Your father's bank account."

She was typing on the MacBook as she replied, "Exactly. As you know, my father has many bank accounts. Or to be more accurate, he *had* many bank accounts. When he was apprehended by the FBI in 2017, and then interviewed for months before his, um, escape, he disclosed several relatively small domestic bank accounts before leading investigators to what he claimed was his largest account, an offshore account in

Switzerland holding about four hundred million dollars. That account was, of course, frozen, and contrary to pop culture, the Swiss bank privacy laws do not exempt criminal action."

"Oh? And where's that money?"

"Gone. The United States government took it."

I took my eyes off the road for a moment as I asked her, "But Macallister said that we were going to be using your father's money. You're saying the U.S. government already has control of it."

She paused her work and returned my gaze. "The government took only the portion of his wealth that they knew about, that he had deposited in Zurich. But he had another hidden account in the Cayman Islands, which he used to fund the last project. The project where I got cold feet and got out." She paused, took a deep breath, and continued in a subdued tone, "That account was his rainy-day money. About two hundred million dollars. Maybe two-fifty."

"Ah," I confirmed, "so that's the account we use."

"Nope. Because he knows that I know about that account, and if I drain it or lock him out of it, he'll logically guess that I had something to do with it and therefore conclude that I am alive. However, I gave those details to Macallister, and the FBI can and will be monitoring it from afar. If my father tries to tap into those assets, we'll find out. And, possibly, we can see where he is located."

"I think I'm getting a headache," I complained. "This is getting complicated."

"Not really," Volkov disagreed. "Those two accounts held under half his wealth. There's a third account."

"Dare I ask how much?"

"In U.S. currency, a bit more than three-quarters of a billion dollars."

I whistled.

That was more than we had imagined or discovered. After a team of FBI Critical Incident Response Group (CIRG) agents captured Petrikov from his 235-foot expedition-style yacht in 2017, the oligarch who dodged the FBI for so long finally was exposed. During the subsequent investigation, we determined that Petrikov had amassed a great deal of wealth, initially by buying precious metals from unsuspecting

Russian immigrants and then reselling those jewels at a comfortable profit. Not satisfied with that trade, however, Petrikov became involved in the Brighton Beach, New York, arm of the Russian mafia, sometimes known as the *Bratva*. As he rose in the chain of command, eventually reaching the top as the *vor v zakone*, the crime boss also known as the *vory*, Petrikov balanced between two worlds: a public one as an outgoing, charismatic, self-made Russian immigrant in the jewelry trade, and a private one as a ruthless mobster who traded in extortion and bribery.

It was in the latter realm that the immigrant had made the bulk of his fortune—one earned not in the genteel, respectable world of diamond merchants, but one greased by blood in the backrooms and basements of Brighton Beach and beyond.

With the *vory* in custody, FBI investigators assembled a profile of Petrikov's criminal dealings and potential profits, comparing the tally to the Zurich account balance of four hundred million dollars. The amount passed the so-called "smell test;" a tally of about a half-billion amassed over a fifty-year trajectory in crime seemed reasonable enough. I mean, like reasonable in a clinical sense, once you get over the distastefulness of it all.

Adding it up in my head and realizing that the FBI had grossly underestimated Petrikov's assets, I asked, "Does Macallister know about the third account?"

"He does now. I traded the knowledge of the account with him as part of my deal."

"Where is it? Does it matter where it is as long as we can access it?"

"To answer your second question, no, it doesn't matter. We can tap money globally using electronic means. However, we don't want to call attention to it, either, from banks or other watchdogs who are tasked to keep an eye on the money flowing around."

I started to laugh. I couldn't help myself. Here I am, driving a Kia rented in my sister's name, with a crime-boss billionaire's daughter, who once before tried to kill me but now who was educating me on offshore banking accounts, as we both traveled under assumed identities. I mean, you can't make this stuff up.

Volkov was looking at me, quizzically. "What's so funny?"

"Never mind. Nothing. Anyway, how do we—you—get at that third account?"

"That's our next step. We form a United States company, like people do every day across the country like we're some little startup. We open a U.S. bank account, and then I link that domestic account to the offshore account. Which, by the way, is in Nevis."

"What's Nevis?" I asked. "And why wouldn't your father do the same thing?"

"Nevis is an island country in the Caribbean. It has robust banking laws for companies. And that's why my father will find it difficult to access, unlike his Cayman Islands account. In Nevis, you have sharehold-ers, directors, officers, titles like that. In other words, you need multiple signatures to transact business. And I doubt my father trusts anyone enough wherever he is now to confide in them, to have them co-sign something, especially when he thinks he still has some two-hundred million dollars hidden away in the Caymans."

I put two-and-two together and concluded, "But he trusted you enough to disclose the account?"

"Exactly. Father and daughter, to take on the world. Except it didn't work out as he planned." Her voice faded, and I stole a glance at her. She was absently looking at the headliner of the car. I remained quiet, letting her reflect, wondering what she was thinking about but not daring to ask.

Volkov returned to the matter at hand and continued, in a stronger voice, "My guess is that he will use the Nevis account as a last resort. It is the most cumbersome to access, due to the corporate protections that Nevis has in place that are difficult to work with."

"But you can work around those restrictions?"

"Certainly." She paused, and once more, I took my eyes off the road. She was looking at me with a smile as she said, "And the best part is that once I'm done, he will assume that the corporate protec-tions that Nevis has in place are preventing him from accessing the account, should he try to use it. I doubt that he'll suspect that the daughter who has been issued a death certificate has a hand in locking him out of the account."

"I've still got a headache," I complained again, tired of the banking talk. "We've got, like, five more hours to drive. Is this what we're going to talk about for the rest of the trip?"

Volkov chuckled and cracked her window slightly, letting some fresh air into the car. "No. We're pretty much done. We can go over it some other time. But I have one last question. I'm forming our United States-based shell company. What's it going to be called, Ben?"

"I get to name this enterprise?" I had thought up my cover name, but it hadn't occurred to me that we would have, well, an enterprise. A business.

"Yep. Come up with something bland. If this ever shows up anywhere, especially at the FBI level, like on an email or something, it has to look innocuous. No flair."

"Gimme a sec to think."

"Okay," she replied, and we lapsed into silence.

After we passed three more exit signs on the New Jersey Turnpike, it came to me. At one time, working through the intricacies of an investigation, I drew a circle divided into four parts on a yellow pad to divide and organize my thoughts. I glanced to my right at Volkov, who was waiting patiently, and I stated, "We're going to call it Quadrant Procurement Group."

Volkov grinned her approval, "Mmm. I like it. Quadrant Procurement Group. What, exactly, are we going to procure?"

"You asked for bland. Something like that looks like nothing. It's dull. So, it passes that test. But, anyway, I'll tell you what we're gonna procure. We're gonna procure Anatoly Petrikov. Using his money. And using one other thing that used to belong to him."

"What's that?"

I said teasingly, "You'll find out in about five hours."

CHAPTER
13

FIVE HOURS LATER – PORTSMOUTH, VIRGINIA

A BIT OVER FIVE HOURS after Anastasia Volkov explained more than I ever wanted to know about offshore bank accounts, it was my turn to show her something new.

Following Interstate 95 south through New Jersey and into Delaware, we exited the highway just past Wilmington and headed south on Route 113. Volkov had offered to spell me at the wheel, but after she boasted about the progress she'd made with our banking, I suggested that she continue that task. I was planning enough work for us over the next few days, and frankly, I was more useful driving. Mostly because I'd be useless tapping at a laptop trying to link bank accounts. Not only would I have no clue what I was supposed to do, if I was bent over a laptop computer in a moving vehicle, I'd probably also get car sick. Some secret agent I am.

The highlight of the trip—for me as driver, at least—was crossing the engineering marvel known as the Chesapeake Bay Bridge-Tunnel. As we dipped under the water for the southernmost tunnel crossing, I had a moment of inner panic, imagining the countless tons of water pressing down on the tunnel ceiling, not to mention the many tons of large ships sailing overhead.

Bursting back into sunlight on the Virginia side of the entrance to the Chesapeake Bay, I followed the directions shown on the screen of my new iPhone, winding our way westward into the city of Norfolk. Finally, after one last tunnel under the Elizabeth River, we exited to surface streets in the town of Portsmouth, Virginia. I stopped the Kia in a marina parking lot which, curiously to me, was almost above the tunnel through which we had just passed.

Volkov pried herself from the passenger seat, and, standing next to the sedan, stretched, forgoing a coat bought for New York City weather thanks to the slightly balmier temperature of Virginia. "Nice view," she commented, admiring the boats of all sizes docked in the marina. "Rest stop? Picnic?"

"Nope," I replied. "Home. For now, at least."

She looked around, presumably scanning the area for accommodations, but finding only commercial buildings, quizzically asking me, "Huh? Where?"

I began walking toward the docks, calling over my shoulder, "Follow me. We can grab our stuff later."

On the outermost dock, I stopped next to a behemoth yacht, its massive, white-painted bow towering above my head, and said, "Welcome home."

I'd never seen this particular yacht in person, but I had studied it in photographs and on blueprints, and I would know it anywhere. It had been my revelation, on the waterfront in Bristol, that a boat would be the perfect place to stage my operation to find Petrikov. The bigger the boat, the better. Bonus points to actually use Petrikov's boat.

Volkov was putting it together, looking at the giant, 235-foot-long white hull as if it could speak, but instead asking me. "I'd say you're kidding, but it's brilliant. This is the *Almaz*, isn't it?"

"You don't recognize it?"

"No, of course not. I've never seen it in person. My father told me all about it when we were together. He loved this yacht more than anything. He lived on it, you know. How did you get your hands on it?"

"First off, it's not an *it*. It's a *she*. Boats, yachts, ships. They're traditionally referred to as *she*. I learned that already."

"Right," Volkov nodded. "I really don't care. How did you get it? Her?"

"When the Bureau apprehended your father, we took possession of the boat. The yacht was moved to the U.S. Navy yards across the river, in Norfolk, and moored there. I requested use of the vessel just before Thanksgiving, and Macallister agreed. The Navy recommissioned her and brought her to this marina. She's all ours to use."

"Well, that's great, Ben. But there's one thing."

"What's that?"

"Neither you, nor I, have any clue about boats. How are we going to operate it? Her?"

I laughed. "I'm way ahead of you. Let me introduce you to our captain."

CHAPTER

14

ANASTASIA VOLKOV AND I CLIMBED the gangway to our yacht.

Well, not *our* yacht, in the collective sense, but the yacht that we were going to take possession of. No, that sounds so dry.

Our new home.

No, that sounds so domestic. Whatever. You get the idea.

The six-and-a-half-hour drive from New York City to Portsmouth, Virginia, seemed like ancient history. Atop the gangway, I felt invigorated. The mission was about to begin. And the view was amazing. The yacht dwarfed the smaller boats below; not only that, the yacht reeked of opulence. The Navy had maintained the yacht beautifully, and it—sorry, she—was spotless. A highly varnished wood rail stretched both forward to the front of the yacht and back to the rear, the paintwork was glossy without any imperfections, and the metal bits here and there were polished to a mirror shine. The decking below my feet was oiled teak, and I immediately wondered if I was supposed to remove my sneakers.

I glanced at Volkov who apparently had the same question, and she verbalized it even as she lifted one foot up. "Do we take off our shoes?"

A male voice from a doorway rang out. "No need!"

Both Volkov and I turned, bumping our shoulders together on the relatively narrow side deck as we faced the voice. A man emerged from the doorway. He was fair-skinned with medium-length, dark-ish blond hair and two day's-worth of salt-and-pepper stubble on his chin,

He didn't look boyish, but he was not old, either. His hazel-green eyes glinted brightly, a smile visible in those eyes, as he said enthusiastically, "Good to see you, Ben."

Turning to Volkov, he offered a handshake. "Hi, Anastasia. Not sure if you remember me. I'm Miles Lockwood."

A caricature artist would have had an ideal subject in Volkov at that moment. Her face was tilted up, her eyebrows raised and eyes wide, and her mouth drooped open in legitimate surprise. "Of—of—of course I remember you, Miles," she stammered.

An accomplished offshore sailor, Miles Lockwood was a key player in the 2017 case that brought me to prominence, and he'd met Volkov during the course of that investigation. I'd learned through the case that Lockwood had an intuitive and quick mind. His day job was in real estate sales, a role where his memory for faces and names together with his outgoing personality were well suited. I had called Lockwood on the charcoal-gray flip phone before Thanksgiving, and he readily agreed to take a leave from selling houses in exchange for running a 235-foot yacht.

After Lockwood and Volkov shook hands, she turned to me with questioning eyes. I explained, "When I thought of using the boat for the operation, I knew we needed a captain. I reached out to Miles."

Lockwood picked up the story. "I immediately said yes, and I flew in from Boston a few days ago. I've still got a lot to learn about the *Almaz*. And Ben tells me you guys have a lot to set up, too. I'll figure it out soon enough."

Volkov touched his arm, looked up into Lockwood's hazel eyes, and said, "Oh, I'm sure you will." Her fingers remained on his arm, and they held the mutual eye contact for a moment. *Fascinating*, I thought. *Volkov appears, well, happy. And relaxed. Maybe I've misjudged her. Maybe it's she who is insecure. Maybe it's she who is looking for trust. For a friend.*

Breaking Volkov's gaze and spreading his arms widely, Lockwood warmly announced, "Welcome aboard *Almaz*. As I'm sure you know, she was designed by the world-renowned naval architect Topher Drake. Cruising speed of fifteen knots with a trans-Pacific range. Her expedition-style design is suited for exploring any ocean in any weather, and with her reinforced steel hull, she can easily take on Arctic ice."

I laughed scornfully, "The Arctic? No way. Not on my agenda."

Lockwood grinned, "Yeah, warmer would be way better." He led us into the vessel while he continued to narrate, "There are four decks. This is the main deck, deck three. There's a master suite forward on this deck, and aft are the living and dining areas, and a bar. Above us, on the top deck, there's an office and the bridge. Below is the galley, which is more of a commercial kitchen. Guest accommodations are also on the deck below. And finally, the lowest level, deck one, has crew quarters, stores, and machinery. I'll give you the full tour."

As Lockwood guided Volkov and me through *Almaz*, the look that I saw on Volkov's face began to change, and aboard her father's yacht, she appeared, well, determined. It was as if she could sense his presence.

I couldn't decide if that was a good or bad thing, though. Was she on the hunt, like I was, for Petrikov? Or was she playing an intricate game of double cross, and was my decision to utilize her father's yacht a massive mistake?

I would get a clue to her intentions that very night.

CHAPTER
15

HAVE YOU EVER SLEPT ON Italian-made, 100% Egyptian cotton sheets?

Neither had I until I moved into my new digs. Say what you want about Petrikov's megalomaniacal tendencies, I gotta hand it to him. He's got excellent tastes in boats and bedding.

Upon arriving aboard Petrikov's yacht earlier in the week, Lockwood did a provisioning trip, and following our tour of *Almaz*, our new captain served us a nice dinner before he retired to the captain's quarters on the top deck of the yacht, just aft of the bridge. Volkov and I got to pick from any of the several guest bedrooms—er, they're called staterooms, on the yacht—on the second deck.

I was delighted—and relieved—that Volkov quickly selected a room for herself. After two nights together but apart with Volkov in a New York City hotel room, I desperately needed a good night's sleep. And happily, my stateroom had a heavy, polished mahogany door—with a lock.

I woke with the dawn, and having learned already that the yacht was soundproofed, I didn't worry about waking Volkov when I swung open my stateroom door and padded by her latched door, my bare feet tapping softly on the dark wood flooring as I began to explore the yacht, taking my time and taking it all in.

Using the word "opulent" to describe *Almaz* would be an understatement. If the exterior of the four-deck yacht was imposing, the interior of the yacht was simply astonishing. The main deck living area was furnished with comfortable-looking sofas and chairs, a big flat-screen television, and, to my delight, a fully stocked bar with actual barstools. There was an indoor dining area with seating for twelve and, through sliding glass doors, an outside table overlooking the teak-decked helipad.

Working my way forward on deck three, I checked out the master suite. Instead of opulent, I'd choose "garish" to describe the master suite. A giant bed dominated a space that looked over the bow of the yacht through five-foot-tall windows. Beyond the bow of the north-pointing vessel, I could see the downtown waterfront of Norfolk.

I made a decision. During yesterday's tour with Lockwood and Volkov, we had imagined that Petrikov's former lair, the topmost, fourth deck office, would be our command center. The oligarch's original works of art still hung on the walls, and the carpet was a thick pile. The view outside the windows of the office, from that upper deck, were awesome, and the space was adjacent to the high-tech bridge, cluttered with glass-fronted displays and radios and navigational gizmos.

This morning, I decided otherwise. We would need more space than that office. I'd have Lockwood get some shipwrights in to rework the main deck master suite to my purposes.

Besides, it was Petrikov's old bedroom. Bad luck to sleep there, with his ghosts, right?

I wandered below to the second deck, located the kitchen—er, sorry again, galley—and brewed a pot of coffee, then took my hot mug outside to enjoy the solitude of the dawn. I found a place to sit near the empty, vast helipad, and as I watched the steam curl and twist from the shimmering, hot coffee in the chilly morning air, I mentally finalized the details of my plan.

$$* \quad * \quad *$$

"Okay, are you both ready?"

With breakfast plates cleared, Lockwood and Volkov simultaneously uncapped their pens, ready to write notes on the pads in front of them. They both nodded dutifully. And so, I began the first meeting of the Quadrant Procurement Group with our assignments, starting with my own, "First. Organizational chart. I'm in charge of the team. So far, the team is just the three of us. I will recruit two or three more people. Operations, logistics, transportation."

Neither one of them wrote a single note on their pads. Undeterred, I continued, "There's too many people for us to work effectively in that upper deck office. Miles, I need you to have someone gut the master suite. That will be our command center."

"That's a big job," Lockwood replied. "What do you have in mind?"

Volkov perked up. "That's perfect, Ben. Great idea. Miles, I'll get you a plan. We need computer terminals, video and voice conference ability, and screens."

"Exactly," I confirmed. "Volkov, you buy the gear. Get the specs to Miles. Let's fit this out in the next few weeks."

"The communications gear on the boat is pretty good, but I'm going to upgrade it to higher speed satellite data links," Volkov said as she started scribbling on her pad. "What else?"

"I can help with that," Lockwood offered, now also making notes. "Those two domes above the bridge deck are satellite dishes; the dome protects the dishes from the elements. We can upgrade to a larger, more robust system. We can install a bigger system on the helipad."

"Nope," I countered. "Volkov, second task for you. Buy us a helicopter."

Her eyebrows raised as she asked, "Who's gonna fly it?"

I answered, "My transport manager. My problem. I want a chopper, so Miles, find another place for the satellite gear."

"Got it," Lockwood said. "What else?"

"Provisions. Food, water, booze. Plus, you'll need to hire any crew you need to operate the vessel." I paused and added, "Any outline on that?"

"Yeah. Assuming you all will help stand watches if we go anywhere, I need three people. A mate to help me run the boat, an engineer to maintain the powerplant, and a steward who can also be a deckhand," Lockwood replied.

Volkov leaned toward Lockwood, batted her eyelashes, and purred, "May I make a suggestion?"

"Sure," he grinned.

"Get us a chef."

Lockwood chuckled, acknowledging that the dinner and breakfast he had prepared for us were adequate, but, well, not great. "Got it," he said again. "And what will you be up to, Ben?"

"I have two tasks. First off, we gotta rename the boat. We can't have Petrikov's name on the boat. What does the name mean, anyway?"

Volkov answered, "Diamond. *Almaz* is the Anglicized spelling for the Cyrillic characters of the Russian word for diamond."

Lockwood was shaking his head back and forth. "No, no, no. It's terrible luck to rename a boat. You risk the ire of the gods of the sea. Neptune, Poseidon, pick one. Doesn't matter which. If you have to rename a boat, and that's a big *if*, there's a lot of ceremony required in order to ensure the gods of the sea accept the new name."

Volkov and I looked at each other, and I asked, "Seriously?"

"Oh, yes," Lockwood said, without the slightest hint of sarcasm or humor. "It's quite involved. Incantations, rum, champagne. Oh, and we have to appease the wind gods, too. And—we have to do a purge."

I couldn't believe this. He *was* serious. With an effort not to roll my eyes and insult him, I repeated, "A purge?"

"Yes. Any item with the boat's name on it, we need to get rid of. The name *Almaz* is all over the place. On the plates. On the glassware. On the towels. On the sheets."

"Whoa." I stopped him. "We're not touching the sheets."

Lockwood stubbornly crossed his arms on his chest, leaning back in the chair, "Then we're not renaming the boat."

Thinking of those sheets that I had slept on last night, I yielded to Captain Lockwood. "Right. The name stays. Onward."

Lockwood exhaled, clearly greatly relieved. Volkov shook her head in wonderment at the exchange as I continued, back on mission. "Okay, now that my first task is off the table, onto my second task. Personnel. I have to do some recruiting. And I know exactly who I'm going to bring to the team."

CHAPTER

16

AVENIDA DE LAS LOMAS, CARACAS, VENEZUELA

WHILE THE VIEW FROM THE WINDOW in the bedroom assigned to him in the Russian Embassy remained, of course, static, Anatoly Petrikov's perspective had changed. Through the thick, bullet-resistant glass, he now saw not a forbidden city to avoid, but instead, a teeming metropolis to disappear into. He idly fingered the Canadian passport folio on the desk in front of him.

A most successful opening move, he gloated, thinking back to the meeting two days ago with Vitaly Nikolaevich Rodionov.

To be certain, receiving the passport was a surprise in a discussion full of surprises. But that was a start, and Petrikov felt, for the first time since arriving in Venezuela, that he was back in the game.

He heard a sharp rap on the door, yet another surprise. "Who is it?" he demanded.

A muffled reply. "Rodionov."

Petrikov ambled to the door to open it; he would take his time. Establish authority.

Casually, he swung the door open, and without so much as a nod, returned to his seat at the desk overlooking the window to Caracas. His visitor selected the small sofa and sat without invitation, a subtle power play. As Rodionov placed the medium-sized hard-sided briefcase that he carried onto the Kazakh rug, Petrikov sniffed, "What is it?"

"Our operative in New York has made several additional inquires. His conclusion is that the death certificate issued to your daughter has a high probability of being falsified."

Petrikov shrugged. "Meaningless. You told me that two days ago."

"Not exactly," Rodionov disagreed. "We had suspicions. Those suspicions are resolved. Now we have confidence. Yet, with all things, it is better to receive confirmation from a variety of sources. Wouldn't you agree?"

Rodionov didn't wait for an answer. Instead, with two successive *snaps*, he clicked open the latches on the briefcase. Raising the lid, he withdrew a charcoal-gray laptop computer, and, standing, he handed the device to Petrikov. As Rodionov returned to the sofa, he announced, "A gift. But one with purpose."

Petrikov made no move to touch the computer. He merely raised his eyebrows slightly and said, "Oh?"

Not intimidated by the cold reaction, Rodionov continued, "I know you have access to your banking accounts. Neither I, nor Mother Russia, have any interest in those accounts. You earned it; you keep it. Isn't that the capitalist way?" The Unit 29155 man sniggered to himself before adding, "However, you told me before that your daughter also had access. Isn't that correct?"

Outwardly, Petrikov showed no reaction, only saying, "Yes." But, inwardly, he mused, *This might be the opportunity to continue my opening move.*

Rodionov explained, "We suggest that you check your account, or your accounts, plural. To determine if someone else has accessed them, perhaps made withdrawals. It stands to reason that the only person who could do that is your daughter. And, if that's the case, it would be—"

Petrikov finished the sentence. "A second way of confirming that the death certificate is false. That would be true. There is one problem, though."

"What is that?"

"I don't trust you."

"You made that clear two days ago. My gesture with the passport was not enough?"

Petrikov inclined his massive head to the right just slightly, agreeing. "It was a start. But how would I know that you have not installed a key logger on this machine? And as soon as I enter my credentials, I've shared them with you."

"You don't."

"Pardon?"

Rodionov reclined into the sofa, crossing his right leg casually over his left leg as he said, "You don't know that I haven't done those things. It's immaterial, though. I could also be watching your actions through the wired network or through the wireless network. Or perhaps there's a screen recorder running invisibly in the background. That would be entry-level work for my Unit," he scoffed. "But why would I do that? Let's say the Unit swept your account. You'd know it was us, or your daughter. It really does not matter. At the end of the day, your money is meaningless. Your knowledge of your daughter's methods, if she is still alive, has value to us. You, perhaps as bait for her, has value to us. But, if she's truly gone, we'd have no more use for you, and we'd consider terminating you."

Petrikov guffawed loudly, cackling, "For once, your message is clear, Vitaly Nikolaevich. I respect that." The big man turned to the computer, and his fingers worked the keys faster than one would have expected, given their size. For a few moments, the room was silent, until Petrikov announced, "My account in the Cayman Islands has not been touched. My account in Zurich is inaccessible. But that is not unexpected."

"Why not?"

Petrikov explained, "I confessed the existence of the Swiss account to the FBI. I would assume they seized it."

"And the Cayman account?"

"I did not disclose the existence of that account to the FBI. My daughter and I used it for the previous project. She left me at the end of August, and the most recent transaction in the Cayman account was in June." Petrikov assessed Rodionov's reaction as he added, "It has not been touched since."

Rodionov stood, asking, "There are no other accounts?"

"No."

"Very well. Then, unfortunately, this has been inconclusive. You may keep the computer. Use it for whatever your purposes, but please check the account periodically. Also—in the interest of trust, know that the connection is monitored. My Unit can see what you access with that machine."

Petrikov snorted as he closed the lid on the computer, "I would expect nothing less."

Rodionov smiled thinly, "Our operatives will continue to do their research work in New York."

"Good," Petrikov agreed, as if he had a say in the matter.

As he swung the door open, Rodionov said conversationally, "And of course, please continue with those chess games that you play on the smartphone. On the social network. What is it called again? Trampoline? The matches are enjoyable? You are winning?"

"I am very good at chess. I usually win. But sometimes, I lose intentionally. You know, you can learn a great deal about your opponent in a loss," Petrikov replied evenly.

Rodionov did not comment as he closed the door gently behind him. The mastermind of Unit 29155 made his way to the elevator, where he selected the lowermost, subterranean floor, and he pressed his palm against a palm-and-fingerprint reading pad in the carriage wall.

When the doors slid open, Rodionov crossed the compact information warfare suite and stopped at a small counter, pulling a stainless-steel carafe from the coffee machine and pouring a cup of black coffee into a paper cup. Turning, he carried his beverage to a desk at which sat a similarly built, dark-haired, pale-skinned compatriot, who offered, "Unhelpful. And he's made no move to reopen the computer."

The two men watched the monitor in front of them in silence; on-screen, Petrikov remained seated in the desk chair, immobile, looking out the window. Rodionov spoke, "Did you hear his little lecture to me, Fedor? About learning about your opponent from a loss?"

"I did," Fedor replied, scratching his pale chin. "And?"

"He's arrogant, that one." Rodionov paused. "Arrogance can be blinding."

"Agreed."

Rodionov leaned down slowly, placing his paper coffee cup on the desk as he said, contemplatively, "I've been arrogant, Fedor." After a brief pause, Rodionov continued, "It's time I take charge of this search for Volkov and Porter. Personally."

"Personally?"

"Yes. We had operatives doing this work. But they are lazy. They don't understand the stakes. I'm going to do this myself. And you're coming with me. We're going back to America."

Fedor's eyes went wide. "To America? Where"

"To Boston," Rodionov replied, as he began walking toward the elevator. "We're going to start in Boston, and we are going to find Ben Porter."

JANUARY

MONDAY, JANUARY 6, 2020 – GLOUCESTER, MASSACHUSETTS

SITTING IN A FREEZING COLD, rented Ford Explorer, the engine long turned off and the cabin cooling to the outdoor ambient air temperature of twenty-eight degrees Fahrenheit at two o'clock in the morning on the sixth of January, Vitaly Nikolaevich Rodionov waited patiently for the part-time, night security guard to finish his lackadaisical circuit of a one-story, stucco-clad office building situated amongst similar architecturally uninspired structures.

Rodionov was not the slightest bit uncomfortable. Instead, he was pleased. He felt that he finally had a solid lead to follow. Besides, the most difficult part of his journey was behind him, for once he was on United States soil, he would operate unfettered. Once, of course, the security guard departed.

Late in December, amongst the throngs of year-end and holiday air passengers, Rodionov and his compatriot flew from Caracas to Rome, traveling with Russian passports. Then, utilizing Italian passports, they took an Air Canada non-stop flight from Rome to Montreal, Canada. They spent a few days in Montreal, then rented a car and driven across the United States border.

This was Rodionov's second journey into the United States by that method, and like the prior trip, it went without the slightest hitch.

Unfortunately for Rodionov's objectives, the travel arrangements were his only real success thus far, though he had a very promising lead to follow, thanks to a tenuous electronic trail discovered only days ago, back in the cavernous command center of Unit 29155 in Moscow.

As he traveled from Venezuela, to Europe, to Canada, and finally to the United States, Rodionov tasked his team of hackers in Moscow with a sole focus not on an elusive target in New York, but to a target that was presumed to be alive and well. In Boston.

Ben Porter.

Which, circuitously, was how Rodionov found himself watching as the hired security man started a non-descript SUV and pulled away from the single-story office. Looking across the darkened interior of his vehicle to his passenger, he announced, "Now, Fedor."

The front doors of the Explorer opened simultaneously; the interior overhead dome light had already been set to remain unlit. The two men approached the side door to the building at an oblique angle. As Fedor aimed an intensely bright, narrow-beam, LED flashlight directly at the black lens of a camera above the door, Rodionov focused on the electronic lock on the door itself.

Rodionov was carrying a small, black box, which he placed against the electronic lock. Operating on a wireless frequency, the black box would create a magnetic field and erase the lock's programing, restoring it to the factory settings. A light on the box changed from amber to green, and the lock itself beeped. Rodionov entered the default code of 1-2-3-4, and the lock beeped again. He could hear a slight whirring sound as the mechanism within spun the deadbolt to the open position.

With a curt nod to Fedor, Rodionov yanked the door open. Once inside, Fedor extinguished the flashlight just as a wall-mounted alarm panel began beeping, demanding a code. Both men ignored the warning, guessing that they would have between thirty and sixty seconds before the code entry time expired.

Aided by the dim, red exit lighting, they also ignored the night vision goggles strapped around their skulls as they split—Fedor heading left into what appeared to be a workroom, and Rodionov trotting straight down a hallway.

Twenty-six seconds later, both men returned to the door. As they crossed the threshold, Fedor relit the flashlight, holding the beam steady on the camera. Crossing the camera's field of view under the glare of the light, neither man rushed, instead walking steadily to the rented Explorer, where Rodionov turned on the ignition and piloted the SUV into the Gloucester darkness.

Nine seconds after the taillights of the Explorer disappeared on Exchange Street, the building's external klaxon alarm sounder began to wail.

It would be several minutes before the alarm company contacted the local police and the building owners. They would examine the building and discover nothing amiss—if the men from Unit 29155 had done their work properly.

And, if that was the case, and if Rodionov's intel proved correct, Bradford Macallister's fears about Ben Porter's cover legend would be realized.

CHAPTER
18

PORTSMOUTH, VIRGINIA

"IT'S 7:19 A.M. Oh-seven-one-nine hours," Miles Lockwood announced. "Sunrise on the sixth day of January. Sunrise is a fortuitous time to begin a journey."

I watched, faintly amused by the pageantry and superstition, as Lockwood started the two engines of *Almaz*. He had explained that the engines would need to warm up, so we were not actually leaving the dock at sunrise, only starting our preparations for departure.

What. Ev. Er, I thought, thrilled to be almost underway. We had spent the past month tied to the dock in Portsmouth, with shipwrights and technicians crawling all over the yacht, making the modifications that we planned back in early December. Lockwood recruited a crew, and I summoned my team. And now, days after the New Year, my vessel was ready, my people were ready, and I was ready.

It was Lockwood who made the suggestion, three days ago as we watched the final member of my newly formed team arrive in our shiny, new, single-pilot-rated Eurocopter EC155B1as it touched down on the helipad atop *Almaz*. As the rotors wound down, Lockwood said, "Well, that's the last piece of the puzzle in place. The comms gear is installed and tested, the situation room is up and running, and that's the last person we're waiting for. Let's get outta here."

I wasn't sure if I heard him correctly, so I inquired, "Huh?"

"Ben. We've got a two-hundred-plus-foot yacht, a chopper, a crew, plenty of food, and full fuel tanks. Why sit still? Let's go someplace warm."

Let me just say that Miles Lockwood might be a genius. I mean, I know, it's obvious to me now. But the thought of just casting off the lines and heading to sea had never occurred to me. And there was no need to tie our search for Petrikov to those dock lines. With the communications gear that Volkov ordered, now housed in a giant, almost round bubble just behind the yacht's main antenna mast, we had an always-on, super-high-speed connection to the terrestrial phone and computer networks coupled to a sea-water-cooled supercomputer that Volkov installed in the lowest deck of the yacht.

Even with all that, we barely made a dent in the Nevis account. The eleven-million-dollar Eurocopter was the biggest expense; the rest of the gear and modifications to the ship came in at under nine million dollars, a sum bloated by the premium we paid to have the refit work completed in only a month. Want another financial tip? If you're doing construction work on a deadline, don't tell your contractor. You'll pay out the nose for speed.

An hour after sunrise, we were underway, headed slowly north, past the U.S. Naval Yard in Norfolk, and then turning east to follow the channel out of the Chesapeake Bay. As we passed over the southern crossing of Chesapeake Bay Bridge-Tunnel, I thought back a month ago, when Volkov and I had driven a perpendicular route, under the waves, and I turned to look at her, standing on the bridge next to Lockwood, their bodies barely, or possibly, touching. I hated to interrupt the moment, but it was time to get to work. I barked, "Okay, let's get to work. Team meeting in the situation room. Miles, can Hector take the watch so you can join us?"

"Yessir," Lockwood replied professionally, and Hector Alverez, a stocky, brown-skinned, almost gray-haired, affable mariner slid into Lockwood's position at the helm of *Almaz*.

Alverez was grinning from ear to ear as he alternated his field of view through the reverse-angled bridge glass and down toward the high-tech, digital, flatscreen-filled bridge of *Almaz*. "I have the conn," he announced. With glee evident in his voice, he added, "This view sure as shit beats looking at dials and gauges."

I asked, rhetorically, "Happy to be above the waves and not under them?"

"Oh yeah. Fifteen years in submarines was enough. *Shee-yit*. This is one hell of a boat."

As Lockwood, Volkov, and I descended from the bridge to make our way to the situation room, I complimented Lockwood, "Alverez is a standout."

"Absolutely," Lockwood agreed. "Graduated with honors from the U.S. Naval Academy in Annapolis and did three five-year tours of duty, rising to the rank of lieutenant commander. He knows his stuff."

We reached the situation room, newly completed in what would have been Petrikov's main deck master suite. It was a work of art and tech. The centerpiece was a polished, black horseshoe-shaped table with seven black, executive-style chairs. Each seating location was equipped with a small console of switches and buttons as well as a recessed computer monitor, keyboard, mouse, and headset. The gently curved interior aft wall was dominated by three giant screens, currently blank. Above the screens, a series of red-numbered digital clocks indicated times in locations around the globe, with our local time shown at the centermost display.

The left and right edges of the outermost giant screens were each flanked with three slightly smaller screens. On the right, the top small screen displayed a view of the bridge, the middle showed an electronic chart that moved with our position, and the third, lowest screen was cluttered with numbers indicating our speed, course, outside and sea temperatures, our fuel states, and several other data points. On the left, we had forward- and aft-facing camera views from our antenna mast plus an interior view of the engine space. Naturally, all those image feeds could be changed to whatever was mission-critical. For example, any screen could show the feed from the camera that Volkov would be installing in the nose of the Eurocopter.

I took the seat at the head of the horseshoe, my back to the expanse of forward-facing windows. Lockwood took his position to my left, picked up the headset in front of him, toggled a switch on the console, and announced, "Team meeting in the situation room. All hands, please. Immediately."

Volkov's seat was to my right, and I chided her, "How come your console is so big, and you have two screens and two keyboards?"

She laughed. "You might be at the head of the table, Ben. But I get to run the show."

"Well," I replied, "we've set the stage. It's all yours."

Volkov nodded. "Let's wait for the team, then I'll start in with an overview, and then you reveal the plan."

I dipped my head in affirmation, exuding confidence. After all, I'd spent a month preparing the vessel and putting a team together. Only one little problem remained. Well, maybe not so little. I still had no clue where my prey, Petrikov, was hiding.

But with this—this boat, his former boat—I swore I would find him, even if I had to circle the globe to do so. And now, underway on *Almaz*, I began to do just that, unaware yet that my journey on *Almaz* would take me far, far beyond the mouth of the Chesapeake Bay.

CHAPTER
19

"**WELCOME TO THE** inaugural mission briefing for Quadrant," I proclaimed.

That sounded pretty good, right? Like I knew what I was doing.

I didn't wait for a response from the nodding heads of my team, assembled for the first time and seated around the table in my situation room, and I barreled on. "I expect that this will be a cooperative effort. We all have jobs to do, but, at the same time, let's not limit ourselves to those tasks. If you have an idea, a critique, a comment, say it. Be prepared to back it up. And remember, what we've got here is unlike anything else. We are no longer the FBI. However, we'll damned well act like it, with respect, integrity, and honor, to each other, to our country, and to our mission."

I felt pretty good about myself. I *owned* that speech. There was a moment of silence, and I imagined my teammates absorbing my words, my wisdom, my—

"That was somethin' else, bro. I mean, inspirational. In. Spur. A. Shun. All. You nailed it. You ever think about doing some motivational speaker gigs? YouTube videos? You could—"

"Thank you, Abdul. You're too kind," I said, my voice laced with as much snarkiness as I could manage as I tried to keep a straight face. Seated to the right of Volkov, the swarthy, bulbous-nosed, dark Middle Eastern skinned Special Agent Abdullatif al-Hamid was my roommate during FBI New Agent Training in Quantico, Virginia. After graduation, he'd been assigned to the Bureau's Albany, New York, office. We'd stayed in touch, and he was my first recruit; his casual, joking attitude belied an observant eye, an incredible recall, and a great deal of intelligence. I grinned and prompted, "Now that you've taken the floor, perhaps you might give us a quick update on your work?"

"Operations, man. Ops. And in our case, *black* ops. Lemme tell you what we got. Off the books, natch. We got protective body armor gear, night vision gear, earpieces with transponders and encrypted linking, that sorta thing. Tactical gear. You name it, we got it. And we got a pile of armaments. Sig Sauer P226 and Glock Model 22 handguns. M4 carbines with suppressors. For distance work, I stocked us with Barrett M82 sniper rifles, and for the work that may require a bit less accuracy, I got us Heckler & Koch MP5 sub machine guns. Finally, I have an assortment of fragmentation grenades, flash bang devices, smoke generators, and even a bit of C-4 plastic explosive. I'm sorry to say, though, I got nothing to give that sweet-looking chopper any teeth."

With an exaggerated tilt to his head, Hamid batted his eyelashes across the table at former Special Agent Heather Rourke, a pale-freckled, green-eyed, redhead whose sarcastic spunk could easily go toe-to-toe against Hamid's bluster. Rourke snorted, "I'm not worried. I can fly that helo in circles around you while you're fumbling around with your cock. I mean, Glock."

"Ohhh-kay," I interjected. There really was no need for me to intervene, though, as both were laughing good-naturedly.

Rourke collected herself and prodded, "Abdul, remind me again, how did you make the team? I mean, I got shot at in the line of duty and got put on a desk. Which was boring. Bore-ring. I retired and perfected my flying skills. But aren't you still a Special Agent?" There was concern in her eyes and on her face as she asked her question.

Hamid grinned, "A little paperwork, and I was assigned from Albany to Boston. The SAC in Boston, Jennifer Appleton, then assigned me to undercover work. I'm on the payroll, but there's really nothing that would link me to this little adventure."

"And," I added, "I thought it might be helpful to have an actual badge on the team. You never know what opportunities might arise."

"Speaking of opportunities," Volkov said, "what's the plan, Ben?"

"A moment, please. Rourke, your update?"

"Hopefully Abdul will let me get a few words in," Rourke sniffed.

Hamid quickly shot, "Maybe in a sec. Why's he calling you Rourke? Can't we use your first name, Heather?"

"I prefer not. Keep it professional. You can use my last name, but thanks for asking," Rourke replied. "Anyway, I got logistics and transport. The yacht used to carry enough water for a full crew, plus it has a desalination watermaker, so I had one water tank converted to carry aviation fuel for the helo, and one tank converted to gasoline. In the garage, forward of the fantail, we've got four motorcycles, and we've got two four-door, four-wheel-drive Jeeps. They can be lifted onto a pier with the aft crane. Or, that crane can launch one or both of the rigid hull inflatable boats. Mil-spec. Top of the line, top speed for each is sixty knots. And, under the helo deck, I've parked two Aston Martin DBS V12 coupes."

Lockwood's head swiveled to look aft, to Rourke at his left, as if he had been electrically shocked. He blurted, "What? Where?"

Rourke laughed, "Just kidding. What, you think this is something out of a Bond movie?"

"Damn," Hamid whistled. "That woulda been sweet."

Volkov rolled her eyes, "Enough of the toys, boys. What's the plan? You're stalling, Ben."

I grinned. "Stalling? Me? No way. Here we go."

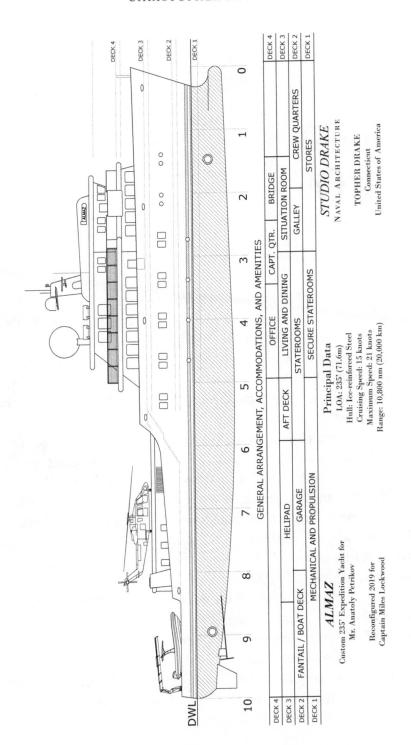

GENERAL ARRANGEMENT, ACCOMMODATIONS, AND AMENITIES

	DECK 4		OFFICE	CAPT. QTR.	BRIDGE			DECK 4
	DECK 3	HELIPAD	LIVING AND DINING	SITUATION ROOM	GALLEY	CREW QUARTERS		DECK 3
	DECK 2	FANTAIL / BOAT DECK	GARAGE	AFT DECK	STATEROOMS		STORES		DECK 2
	DECK 1		MECHANICAL AND PROPULSION	SECURE STATEROOMS				DECK 1

STUDIO DRAKE
NAVAL ARCHITECTURE

TOPHER DRAKE
Connecticut
United States of America

Principal Data
LOA: 235' (71.6m)
Hull: Ice-reinforced Steel
Cruising Speed: 15 knots
Maximum Speed: 21 knots
Range: 10,800 nm (20,000 km)

ALMAZ
Custom 235' Expedition Yacht for
Mr. Anatoly Petrikov

Reconfigured 2019 for
Captain Miles Lockwood

CHAPTER

20

"RIGHT. LET'S GET DOWN TO business," I stated, pushing one of the buttons on the console mounted in front of my seat on the black table. Behind me, electronic shades slid down, covering the tall windows that looked forward over the towering bow of *Almaz*. The room was silent, save for the brief whir of shade motors and the constant, distant thrum of the diesel engines far below deck. Pressing another button, I dimmed the room lighting.

"Our target, please," I said, looking at Volkov. She punched at her keyboard, and an image of Anatoly Petrikov filled the giant, middle screen. "And," I added, "his last known location, please." The right screen lit with a map and a larger map, like the picture-in-a-picture on a television. The smaller inset showed the town of Morristown, New York, on the Saint Lawrence River and the Canadian border. The primary map indicated Morristown's location in upstate New York State against the larger continental United States.

I had prepped Volkov on my desired infographic set-up prior to the meeting, and as I was saying, "Finally, let's review our investigation thus far," the left screen was filling, line-by-line, with a bullet-pointed list. I read the entries out loud, "First, an ongoing scan of all facial recognition imagery and border crossings into the United States from Canada, which continues to this day, for any close or exact match to our target. Second, a similar comprehensive facial recognition analysis, with assistance by Canada Border Services, of all air travelers departing Canadian airports for any international destination since the date of the last known sighting."

Volkov interrupted, adding, "Which has also been ongoing since then."

I continued, "Yes. And third, an analysis of all private aircraft traffic departing Canada for any international destination since then."

"Dat's a lot of data," Hamid said, wide-eyed.

"Indeed," agreed Volkov. "It's been a national security priority, and as such, the Bureau has full cooperation from all relevant agencies. There has been a great deal of manpower assigned to this task."

I stood from my seat, saying, "Yet, despite that manpower, the search has been fruitless." Crossing to the right-side screen, I tapped the display and concluded, "This points to one of two likely conclusions: either Petrikov remains in Canada, or he departed the country by boat."

Returning to stand behind my seat, I asked Volkov, "Delete the inset map and zoom out, please." Her fingers tapped and the display changed as I requested, to show the vastness of the Atlantic Ocean. "The fourth arm of the investigation was maritime. This, as we all know, is much more difficult to track. Nevertheless, we initiated an analysis of all marine traffic departing Canadian ports; those vessels that returned to Canada, we discarded, but those vessels that sailed to an international port, we examined as best we could."

Lockwood was shaking his head. "I'd imagine that investigation was fruitless, as well."

"Correct." I sat. "We're going to take a different approach. We are not going to look for Petrikov. We are going to look for links."

Hamid blurted, "Whadya mean, links?"

"You actually gave us an example a moment ago. You said that there is nothing that *links* you to this investigation. There are several links, in fact. You were assigned to Boston, where Volkov and I worked. Our former SAC assigned you to undercover work. And you and I were roommates at Quantico. If someone looks deep enough, they might put one and two and three together, and conclude that there was a link between us."

I paused to make sure they were all paying attention before continuing, "What we need to do is exactly that type of analysis. We need to look *next to* Petrikov, so to speak, and back our way to him. Volkov, you're on his personality. His habits, what he likes, what he doesn't like. His vices. Rourke, you're on his travel. Where has he gone in the past? How has he traveled? Any patterns during travel? Hamid, you're on his relationships. Who did he talk to regularly? Who were his friends? His enemies?"

Unlike the mocking reaction to my introductory speech, this time I saw agreeable nods as I wrapped up. Even Hamid knew to keep his trap shut. *It's go time*, I thought.

Lockwood raised his hand, as if he was in class. "I have a question. Got anything for me?"

"Actually, yes," I replied. "Where are we going?"

Lockwood chuckled, "There's no need to hang around any place where we can't wear flip-flops. We're headed to the Bahamas."

There were grins around the table, and Lockwood reached his hand skyward for a high-five. I laughed as I responded in kind, but my gut was doing flip-flops, thinking about what I had just said to the team. *I'm supposed to be in deep cover, and yet I brought Abdul Hamid onto my team. How could I have been so foolish to create such an obvious link for the Russians to follow?*

As the team filed out, looking forward to a visit to the Bahamas, I began to sweat, despite the perfectly tempered air circulating through the yacht's ventilation systems. *It's too late to undo my mistake. But there's no telling if and when the Russians make that connection.*

I realized, finally, that my cavalier attitude toward the passage of time was just as much my enemy. The clock was ticking against me, and unbeknownst to me or pretty much anyone, there were two completely different storms brewing.

The first storm, in fact, had already begun to swirl, thousands of miles away and halfway around the planet in Asia. We would eventually learn that Lockwood's decision to take us offshore on the yacht would remove us from the imminent threat of a respiratory pathogen that would soon consume the world.

The second storm would not become apparent to me for months.

Through it all, the Russians would persevere, and little did I understand just how close behind me they were.

CHAPTER
21

BOSTON, MASSACHUSETTS

JUST AFTER LUNCHTIME, only hours after their successful intrusion into a Gloucester office building, Vitaly Rodionov and Fedor had checked into a luxury suite at the Four Seasons Hotel Boston. Sipping a cup of black coffee, Rodionov stood at one of the suite's many windows. A light snow had been drifting down from the leaden clouds, yet by mid-afternoon, none of the flakes accumulated on the barren trees and plants that dotted the Boston Public Garden below.

"A tranquil afternoon. Like Moscow. But not enough snow," Rodionov observed idly.

"I'm afraid I am going to interrupt your moment of peace," said the man seated at a small worktable behind Rodionov.

"You have something, Fedor?"

The man named Fedor replied, "Oh, yes."

Rodionov took a seat in one of the leather-wrapped chairs at the worktable and demanded, "Explain."

"Allow me to recap. This morning, we each plugged a device that resembles a USB flash drive into two of the computers at our Gloucester target. Each drive installs a small software program that allows us to gain access to any computer that is connected to the local network. The drive you planted happened to be on what appears to be an accounting office computer."

Rodionov grinned, "Just my luck. Finally."

"It gets better. The computer has payroll records. This makes my task far, far easier. And faster, I might add."

"Good. And what have we learned?"

"Our source was correct. As we knew, the office is used by a real estate property management firm, which operates seventeen Dunkin' franchise locations in and around the greater Boston area. The payroll records are on this very computer."

With a modest tone to his voice, Rodionov said, "Well, that may have made your task faster, but we would have found those records regardless, yes?"

"Of course. Planting two devices doubled our chances, but also gave us two chances to hack the network. It would have taken much longer, but we would have eventually gotten to the payroll data."

Leaning forward in his chair eagerly, Rodionov asked, "And does our Ben Porter appear in those records?"

"Indeed, he does."

"And do we have the benefit of his schedule in these records?"

"Indeed, we do. He worked just this morning at a store in Medford. It appears he is off tomorrow. On Wednesday, he is scheduled to work at a location in Chelsea on Everett Avenue."

Rodionov tapped at the screen of a smartphone, bringing up a map and grimacing. "That particular Dunkin' is almost across the street from the FBI field office. Even for me, that seems risky. Where will he be scheduled on Thursday?"

"Back in Medford for the evening shift," Fedor replied.

"I believe we will pay him a visit," announced Rodionov.

Fedor shook his head ever so slightly, daring not to contradict Rodionov, but still offering, "Why not just go to his home address?"

"It's a valid question. We have had our operatives go past, by car and on foot. Lights on occasionally, lights off occasionally. But oftentimes, there's what appears to be an unmarked car in the area, as if the FBI also have an eye on them, as they should. If our intel is correct, he was terminated for insubordination. Perhaps he is unstable. In any event, our personally going to the home address would be a last resort as we might risk attracting the attention of someone else who might be watching. I would prefer to see him at work, when we would be mixed in with many anonymous customers."

Accepting the explanation, Fedor turned back to the data streaming from the hijacked payroll computer in Gloucester. "The sooner the better. At some point, someone in that office is bound to notice the flash drives. Certainly, they've noticed that there was a break-in attempt this morning due to the alarm being triggered."

Prefaced with a drawn-out, "Hmmm," Rodionov confirmed, "Yes, that's of course a concern. The fail-safe on the flash drives is guaranteed?"

"Certainly. There are two self-destruct protocols embedded in each device. If the drive is extracted from the machine, and loses contact, a tiny charge within melts the contents. There may be a wisp of smoke and a tiny bit of heat, and if the device is turned into the police or FBI, any competent technician will recognize the purpose, but will not have any clue as to the intent. The programming within will be destroyed."

"What if one drive is extracted, the office people call the police, and they send someone to investigate? And then the authorities attempt to access the other drive while it remains in place, so that it does not self-destruct upon removal?" Rodionov asked.

"That contingency is covered in the second protocol. If someone attempts to access the USB stick, the same type of fail-safe activates; it will melt itself. In the meantime, even if one drive is removed, we continue to enjoy the benefit of the data stream from the remaining device."

"Excellent," replied Rodionov. "This is coming together. In three days, on Thursday evening, we will have Ben Porter in our sights."

CHAPTER
22

WEDNESDAY, JANUARY 8, 2020 – PARADISE ISLAND, BAHAMAS

CRUISING AT A STATELY fifteen knots, *Almaz* made the seven-hundred-and-fifty-mile trip from the mouth of the Chesapeake Bay to the Commonwealth of The Bahamas in about fifty hours. Having left Virginia on Monday morning, we were in a totally different world by mid-day on Wednesday. And what a way to travel. If you have the means, of course.

Thanks to Anatoly Petrikov's money, we did. And his daughter had no reservations about putting that money to use.

Lockwood had not only hired first mate Alverez, but he also brought on board two more crewmembers. Frankie Dunn, a lanky, tanned, blond from Tampa, Florida, became our deckhand and steward. And, local from the Navy service yards in Norfolk, Lockwood found Warren Parnell, a short, bald, dark-skinned, cigar-chomping fireplug of a man with an innate aptitude for engines, motors, and machinery.

Responding to Volkov's suggestion to retain a chef, Lockwood also snagged the kitchen hiring equivalent of a brass ring in the plump, France-born Julienne Jacquard, who wore her brown hair in a head-topping bun, and who was a graduate of L'Academie de Cuisine, once one of America's most prestigious culinary schools, located near Washington, D.C., in Gaithersburg, Maryland.

Let me just say that it is very difficult to focus on work when you keep this kind of company, while cruising the ocean waves aboard an opulent yacht.

Most of us, however, tried to maintain that focus. Well, three of us.

Rourke tackled her assignment to track Petrikov's travel with gusto, pinning two actual printed maps—one of a globe, and one of the United States—on the wall of the situation room, and using string and pins to create literal connections. We had potential leads to follow in the northeast United States, with tentacles connecting New York to four cities in Europe: London, Rome, Paris, and Bodrum, Turkey, and one city in Asia, Singapore.

I was impressed. But I was also daunted by the sheer scope of the task, and by the knowledge that the FBI had done much of this work already in the course of the investigation. Rourke, however, had no answers when I asked, "How would he get to those places?"

Volkov updated me on Petrikov's habits and vices. "Vodka is his number one vice. He can get that anywhere, and he drinks it like you drink coffee. Any time of day is appropriate."

"Habits?"

She frowned. "Well, that part is interesting, if not manipulative. He carries himself, despite the intake of vodka, very carefully. If he loses his temper, he explodes. But that is rare. And, deadly. The rest of the time, however, he is polite. He prides himself on being very well-spoken. He wants his words and his demeanor to portray civility and sophistication. I think that's because he knows that he is simply an evil person, and he likes that polished outward veneer."

"What about hobbies?" I asked.

"Other than lining his pockets with ill-gotten gains? Other than killing people, dogs, or whatever gets in his way? Chess," she stated.

After his own enthusiastic start, Hamid's efforts declined from weak to poor. He gave me a succinct summary. "Current or recent business relationships? None. He hasn't been active in the New York gem trade for years, and I'm definitely not gonna be able to penetrate the Russian mafia from here. He sold off his businesses about five years ago, and he lived on this very yacht, very much alone. Solo."

I wondered, "What about family relationships?"

"None," Hamid said. "He killed his own wife. And we know quite well what happened to his only child. His daughter."

My plan to find Petrikov through links to his past was off to a poor start.

Frustrated by the lack of progress during our two-day trip, I morosely watched from the bridge as Lockwood expertly docked *Almaz* at a swank marina on Paradise Island, my mood definitely not matching the spectacular weather and equally spectacular surroundings. Best known for the sprawling Atlantis resort, Paradise Island is slightly removed from the Bahamas capital island of Nassau, and with that slight separation comes exclusivity. The east side of the island was a haven for the rich and famous.

Almaz would fit right in.

Lockwood, Dunn, and Jacquard headed ashore for supplies, and I wandered the yacht, eventually finding Hamid lounging on a chaise perched on the towering bow of *Almaz*. He was fiddling with a smartphone.

"What are you doing?"

Hamid barely looked up. "Good, clean fun, man. Trampoline."

I had heard of Trampoline, a newish social network, optimized for mobile use, but I didn't really know much about it as I repeated, "So, what are you doing on Trampoline?"

"Ah, man, you can do anything. Messages, scroll through forums, watch videos, play games. Dat's what I'm doing right now. Got a game going. It's called President."

"You're playing a game?" I settled into the chaise next to him, to look over his shoulder, and instantly I knew what link I could follow.

CHAPTER
23

FROM THE TALL BOW of *Almaz*, the high-end villas that dotted the southern waterfront of Paradise Island, with a lush, green golf course beyond, would be a captivating view for a normal person.

I'm not normal, apparently, as my attention was instead focused on Abdul Hamid's smartphone screen. "Tell me more about Trampoline, please."

Hamid caught the serious tone in my voice and shot me a look that acknowledged that playtime was paused. "Okay," he started, "it's called Trampoline dot Live. Their slogan is *good, clean fun*. I kinda quoted it earlier. It's cool. It's a platform for posts, chat, photo and video exchange, and games."

"I gotta admit. Social media is not really my game. How's Trampoline any different from the other networks and apps?"

Hamid laughed. "It's like a little bit of each of Instagram and Facebook rolled into one. It's got the levity of TikTok without the brevity and anger of Twitter."

"Levity and brevity, huh? That's some pretty impressive wordsmanship for you, Abdul," I mocked.

"Flash of brilliance. It happens," he replied sarcastically.

I laughed and then returned in a more even tone to the topic, "That anger part. How does it not have that?"

"Great question, bro. That's their hook. The platform is robustly censored. They make that very clear. Politics are taboo. Cyberbullying is inexcusable. Profanity is limited."

"That last one must be tough for you," I remarked, poking at my old friend once more.

"Yeah, I gotta keep it civil. And clean. But it makes for a nicer conversation."

"Conversation?"

"Yeah," Hamid confirmed. "That's part of the hook, too. I'm playing a silly card game called President. I can play against people around the globe, all on the app. You find a group that you like, and you play. The cool thing is that it goes beyond the game as you make virtual friends. The online chatter is amusing, and we're getting to know each other through the app. It's harmless."

Hamid turned his attention back to the smartphone, signaling that he was done with our real conversation as he turned back to his virtual conversation. I guess he was ready to start another round. I was not.

I touched his arm, inadvertently causing him to slide a finger on the screen as he protested in a moaning tone, "Hey, man, I just played a two by accident. I didn't wanna do that, yet. Man, now I'm gonna lose this round."

"Too bad," I said, without the slightest bit of sympathy in my voice. "I think it's time to pause the game."

"What's up, man? What's buggin' you? We're on a yacht, we're in the Bahamas, we can head to that casino tonight, maybe. It's time to chill, man!"

Perhaps it was the cold stare in my eyes that got his attention because he suddenly realized I was serious. Dropping the whine, he added in his normal voice, "Ben. What's up?"

I asked, hoping, "Does that Trampoline thing have any other games? Like, for example, chess?"

With credit to his sharp mind, so often distracted, he picked up on it immediately as his eyebrows shot skywards, and he exclaimed, "Why, yes, it does have chess."

I allowed a corner of my mouth to curl into a tiny, knowing smile. "Excellent. Let's go find Volkov. And then, let's find Petrikov."

CHAPTER

24

IN THE BRILLIANT, EARLY-EVENING, long-shadowed sunlight—a gorgeous time of day by any standard—Hamid and I found Volkov in the situation room, shades drawn, and lights dimmed.

She looked up from her computer monitors as I asked, "You do know that there's a really nice world outside, right?"

"I do know that," she answered sadly, her eyes lidded. "This is personal to me. He is not only a criminal, but he is a traitor to his family. To me. And we're not getting any closer to finding him."

There was frustration evident in her voice, and I didn't want to contrast her somber tone. Careful to keep the excitement out of my voice, I offered, "We have a new idea."

"Dish," she exhorted, with the slightest touch of enthusiasm in her tone.

"Have you heard of Trampoline dot Live?"

"Yes, of course," she replied. "Obviously, given my status as someone who has no identity, I'm not on it. But I know quite a bit about it."

I took my usual seat at the head of the horseshoe-shaped table and sank into the deep chair, saying with some relief, "Good, then I don't have to explain it to you. Abdul gave me the run down. On the Trampoline app, he's been playing a game called—"

"President," Hamid interjected, settling into the chair to the right of Volkov. "And I'm damned good at it, too. There's a lot of stratergery in that game."

Volkov rolled her eyes at Hamid as I regained control of the discussion. "What I'm more interested in, beyond Abdul's card-playing prowess, is another game on the app. Chess."

This time, Volkov rolled her eyes in my direction, chiding, "Ben. Really? You don't think that I've already gone down that road? There are dozens upon dozens of online chess sites, not to mention dozens and dozens of smartphone apps, both on the Android and IOS platforms. I've checked a lot of them out. It's really difficult to zone in on individual players amidst all the noise and chatter and static."

"Exactly," I agreed. "That is why we need to check out Trampoline. No noise, no static. Just chatter, which, by the way, is censored. Remember, you told us that Petrikov carries a veneer of civility. *Sophistication* was the word you used. This platform is right up his alley. He can be an erudite, polite chess player, and find other erudite, polite chess players to compete against."

"Probably using fancy words like *erudite* over and over again in their in-game conversations," Hamid said dryly. I extended my middle finger upwards slowly in response.

At first, Volkov showed no enthusiasm. "It's a stretch, you know. Like finding a needle in a haystack."

"Or, maybe, like mining for diamonds?" I argued. "This should be the strategy. You chip away at the rock until you find the jewel. Right? And what's the downside?"

Volkov nodded. "Okay. You're right, of course. I've looked elsewhere, but maybe you're onto something. I gotta sift through the noise." She turned her attention to her computers and began to mumble to herself. "I can run an emulator on this, make it look like I'm on Android, and set up an account on Trampoline. Then I gotta parse the chess games. I can build a bot to watch them. I can monitor conversations. Look for keywords. Look for phrases that he would have used. . ." Her voice trailed off as she became more and more absorbed into her work.

Hamid and I both rose silently and tiptoed from the situation room, leaving Volkov behind, muttering to herself as her fingers blurred over the keyboard.

✳ ✳ ✳

Thursday morning dawned and, per my custom, I stopped in the galley for my coffee. Jacquard had really stepped up the java offerings on *Almaz*, and as our chef cheerfully bustled around the shiny, stainless-steel cloaked, restaurant-quality kitchen area, I asked whether she had served dinner to Volkov in the situation room.

"Ah no," Jacquard replied in her lilting French accent, which I won't dare try to imitate, "but she did request a snack at about nine in the evening. I was about to bring up a breakfast plate to her."

"I'll take it," I offered.

In the situation room, I set a tray down next to Volkov, who, by the look of the bags under her eyes, had pulled an all-nighter. "You should eat. Take a break," I suggested.

"Thanks, but no. Breakfast looks good," she said, eyeing the plate of freshly cut fruit and scrambled eggs, as she helped herself to the silver carafe of coffee, which, of course, bore the yacht's name engraved on its sides.

"Any progress?"

She sighed. "No. Nothing definitive. Maybe a couple of leads."

As the daylight hours passed, my mood soured. Volkov had yet to reappear, and I began to worry that the task of finding Petrikov would be far more difficult than anyone imagined, even after putting a great deal of his money to work and, just as critically, having his very own daughter on the hunt—even as I assumed that I was being hunted by Petrikov's accomplices.

I toyed with what should have been an absolutely delicious meal of yellowtail ceviche with homemade flatbread, my thoughts consumed by worry, when Volkov stumbled out onto the aft *al fresco* dining area. All eyes turned to her as she inhaled deeply through her nose and exhaled with a whoosh through pursed lips, even as she stretched her arms above her head. Meeting our stares, she finally announced, "I think I found him."

CHAPTER
25

MEDFORD, MASSACHUSETTS

JUST OVER ONE THOUSAND nautical miles to the north, darkness had settled over the greater Boston area hours ago, the sun setting well before five in the afternoon this time of year, and with the sun's disappearance over the western horizon, typically, the temperature would drop, too. This evening, though, was anomalous, in that the thermometer remained steady, making for a warmish night by the time a rented Chevrolet compact SUV pulled to a stop in the brightly-lit parking lot adjacent to a Dunkin' store in Medford, Massachusetts, with garishly orange awnings.

Vitaly Rodionov had dropped the previously rented Ford Explorer back at the agency as Fedor picked up the Chevy from a different rental outfit. As they exited the newly rented SUV, Fedor commented, "If we must stay in Boston much longer, we'll need a vehicle more appropriate to the Four Seasons. Otherwise, we'll call attention to ourselves."

"A valid reason to spend Putin's rubles, I think," Rodionov sneered as the two Russians walked toward the building.

Pulling open the door to the Dunkin' store, Rodionov scanned the interior for threats. There were none. At a table in the far corner, two older men with bushy beards conversed quietly. *Locals*, Rodionov thought. Closer to the door, a table had a single occupant, a young woman in a light blue hoodie sweatshirt who pecked at a laptop computer, tethered to her machine with a cord dangling from white earbuds. *College kid,* assessed the Russian, recalling that Tufts University sat atop the hill across the street.

Fedor was second in line at the counter, waiting behind a tall young man sporting a tight-knit cap pulled down below his ears. *Another student*, assumed Rodionov as the young man stepped aside to await his order. Fedor stepped forward, and Rodionov joined him abreast.

It was Rodionov who spoke. "Two large black coffees to go."

The stocky, mildly overweight clerk behind the counter asked, "Anything else?"

"Just the coffee. Say, my friend said he was working here tonight. Ben Porter. Is he here?"

The clerk shrugged as he turned to the coffee machine, "Never heard of him."

"Porter, huh? He's on the schedule," offered a bespectacled, matronly, brown-skinned woman from the other end of the counter.

Rodionov sidled her direction, leaning in with a smile. "Really? He's a good friend of mine. That's unlike him. You know, to be unreliable."

The woman sniffed, "Coulda fooled me."

"What do you mean?"

"He was a no-show Monday, too."

At the opposite side of the counter, Fedor withdrew a twenty-dollar bill and passed it to the other clerk, settling up for the coffees and accepting change. Rodionov knew better than to linger and press the question, but he risked a quick follow-up. "You worked Monday? And my friend Ben was scheduled then, too, and didn't come in?"

"Yep. I dunno why they keep putting him on the schedule. I've never seen him." The woman crossed her arms, uncrossed them, and disappeared into the back of the store.

Rodionov followed Fedor out the exit door, and the two wordlessly made their way to the rental car. With the doors closed and the ignition turned on, coffee cups in the oversized console cupholders, Rodionov finally spoke, "That was fascinating. Did you hear what that woman said?"

"Yes. She didn't know why they kept putting him on the schedule."

"Exactly," Rodionov replied, the experienced spy quickly working through the variables. "When we sent our operatives to look for Porter in

December, they failed. But they did not have the benefit of the schedule. They reported, several times, that Porter wasn't working at those locations at those times. It all makes sense now. Now that we have his schedule."

"I don't understand," Fedor confessed.

Rodionov explained, "It was hit-or-miss. With seventeen locations, and who knows how many shifts and employees, the previous approach by our operatives was random. We, however, need not be random. Tomorrow, we are going to repeat the exercise. Where is Porter scheduled for tomorrow?"

Fedor scratched his neck idly as he responded, "I don't recall the address, but it's in Chelsea. Not the place next to the FBI office."

"We'll confirm it tomorrow," Rodionov decided. "We're going to drive by Porter's home right now. Maybe we'll see something, maybe not." He paused and then concluded, "I will tell you this. We are chasing a ghost. I think this is a cover operation. And our next task is to uncover that operation."

CHAPTER
26

PARADISE ISLAND, BAHAMAS

JUST OVER ONE THOUSAND nautical miles to the south, a dinner plate materialized in Julienne Jacquard's deft hands, and she slid it in front of Anastasia Volkov.

"Coffee?" I suggested.

Between bites, Volkov mumbled, "No. I'm gonna eat, I'm gonna tell you what I found, and then I'm gonna sleep." Even in the warm, dimmed overhead lighting of the aft *al fresco* dining area of *Almaz*, Volkov's face was pale and drawn, and her face sagged with obvious exhaustion. She paid no attention to the sparkling lights of Nassau across the bight, which reflected cheerily on the almost-still clear water.

"How 'bout a little pick-me-up? I can make you a drink. Whatever you want," offered Hamid, who, despite the overture, barely looked up from the smartphone, which he had only laid down while he ate dinner.

"No, thanks." Volkov leaned away from the table, having made short work of the ceviche. Picking up a piece of flatbread, she cracked it in half, then into quarters. Nibbling half-heartedly, she sighed and began, "Now that I've stepped away from the computer, I'm not nearly as excited as I was. This is a really tenuous lead."

I smiled and said reassuringly, "At the moment, it's the only lead we've got, so I think it's probably pretty good."

"We'll see," she muttered. In a clearer voice, "I'll run you through it. You be the judge. I wrote a script. In the jargon, it's a bot. A robot of sorts. I wrote several, in fact, to explore the Trampoline platform, focusing in, of course, on the chess games that are embedded in the app."

I held up a hand and snuck in a question. "Is this something anyone could do?"

"Maybe. Probably not. As you might recall, I had a supercomputer installed on the boat. That gives me the ability to run queries on hundreds of accounts per minute. Not everyone has that kind of brute force computing power. I used that power to analyze millions of accounts using several criteria."

"Criteria?"

She shot me a look, her eyes angry as she barked, "If you stop interrupting me, Ben, I'll explain." She closed her eyes for a moment. I thought that was a bit harsh, but I chose to keep my mouth shut. Finally, she sighed and spoke more gently. "Sorry. Long night."

I merely smiled, not daring to speak again, as Volkov continued, "I have a bit of an advantage because I am, of course, looking for my own father. I was too young to play chess with him before he and my mother sent me away to hide me from the *Bratva*, and my contact with him was limited during those years. However, when we were on the run a year ago, we played a handful of games. He's got a very distinct opening move style."

Pausing to take another bite of the flatbread, she chewed, swallowed, wiped her lips with a napkin—embroidered, of course, with the yacht's name—and went on, "There are countless books and primers on chess and the cascading effects of opening moves. Matches by grandmasters are excruciatingly analyzed, replayed *ad infinitum*. My father studies these. He'll play a game against himself just to replicate opening moves in historic matches. And, more often than not, he chooses a slightly unconventional opener in order to project strength but also to signal unpredictability. If he is playing as white, his first move will be to send his left knight to the left edge of the board. That is the most distinctive criteria that I searched for."

The table fell silent. Slowly, all eyes rotated to me. After I got shot down for my question earlier, I was a little reluctant to speak, but I thought, *Well, I'm the boss. This is my team. Use it or lose it, Ben.* I gathered my courage and said, my voice as sincere and as complimentary as I could make it, "That sounds really promising. Fantastic work. Really thoughtful. I—"

Volkov laughed, "Sorry, Ben, for snapping at you earlier. You don't need to lay it on so thick. But I appreciate it."

Dropping the last crumble of flatbread on her plate, she announced, "I found a player whose profile was created only in November. Two months ago. Plays all the time, like all hours of the day. Like the player has nothing else to do. That player does not banter with others except to politely discuss moves. Dare I say that the player is *erudite*. No trash talk, no humor, just chess."

She scanned the table and concluded, "And, this player, of all of the millions of them that my bots searched, satisfied the most important criteria. The player has a very consistent opening move, as described. But occasionally the opener is different, and then the player is chattier. Friendlier. Clearly experimenting. Testing. All of this fits the profile."

She dragged her fingers through her hair, attempting to smooth it, and added in a tired tone, "The next step is going to be much more difficult. The profile claims the player is in Kalamazoo, Michigan. But that's meaningless; you could enter Timbuctoo, and that would be your location. Therefore, to figure out where the player is located, I have to hack the platform. But for now, I'm done. Spent. I need to get some sleep."

Without another word, she disappeared inside, into the main deck living area, heading in the direction of the stairs to the stateroom deck. Lockwood rose from the table and rushed to follow Volkov to the stateroom deck. *They're getting closer and closer,* I thought. *Back when we set off from Danbury in that rented Kia, I made a mistake, being so cold. Volkov is as committed to this as I am. She's just as vulnerable, too. She wants a friend. She wants someone to trust.*

I looked around the table to see if anyone else picked up on Lockwood's abrupt departure. Jacquard and Dunn had stood and were clearing the dinner plates, and Hamid was fiddling with his smartphone while Alverez and Parnell watched. Only Rourke caught my eye, albeit only briefly. I couldn't tell if her expression was bemused or amused.

What does that *signal?* I wondered. I glanced back at Rourke, and she immediately looked away with a wry grin.

I was happy for Lockwood and Volkov. And I was happy for myself, my mood greatly improved since that afternoon. We *finally* had a lead to follow.

FRIDAY, JANUARY 10, 2020 – BOSTON, MASSACHUSETTS

VITALY RODIONOV CLOSED THE lid of a laptop computer and announced, "This past week, I've come to quite enjoy the accommodations at the Four Seasons and the view of the Boston Public Garden, but I would prefer a view of Ben Porter."

From what had become his usual seat at the small table within the exquisitely appointed suite, the man called Fedor merely grunted.

Rodionov paid the man no mind as he continued a monologue. "The fact that Porter appears on the Dunkin' payroll records, and the fact that the devices we planted are confirming that he is being paid to be there at the very time that we visited two locations, one yesterday evening, and another just this afternoon, and he was not at either location, smells like a cover-up. Something that the FBI has cooked."

Fedor added, "And throughout the course of yesterday, we drove by, walked by, and I even jogged by his residence in Chelsea this morning, and there is no sign of him there."

"Yes, Fedor, you jogged by. I'll have to make certain that it appears in the report. No one in our Unit will believe it. And yet you did it. Did you stop for a smoke on Porter's doorstep?"

Fedor coughed. "No. But jogging is not good for me."

"Americans, running around in the cold weather of winter," Rodionov mused. "What are they running from?"

"I do not pretend to understand," Fedor said, as he crossed the room to the balcony doors. The talk about smoke made the Russian crave a cigarette.

With a cold breeze tickling the interior of the suite from the open balcony door, Rodionov reopened the laptop computer and began typing, alternating between a secure email program and an equally secure connection to a Unit 29155 portal.

He had worked for almost five minutes by the time his compatriot, refreshed with nicotine, clicked the balcony door shut. Rodionov grumbled, "I do not believe that Porter is in Boston. That I am quite certain of. Therefore, the question remains, where is he?"

Without waiting for an answer, Rodionov offered, "According to the research that our team in Moscow compiled, that I've just reviewed again, Porter's parents live in a place called Quahog, Rhode Island, outside of Providence. His brother's name is Joseph; this person has recently relocated to New York City. And Porter has a sister named Grace who resides in Bristol, Rhode Island."

"That is an impossible area for only the two of us to surveil," Fedor moaned.

"Indeed. Our resources here are limited at the moment," reflected Rodionov, envisioning other Unit operations elsewhere around the globe.

"Before they were re-tasked to the other operation, we had men in New York. The men who made the inquiries about Petrikov's daughter," Fedor reminded his boss.

"True. A logical place for us to begin. New York, then Rhode Island."

"Very well, I'll make travel plans," Fedor suggested. "I will find us a place to stay in New York, and I will also arrange for another vehicle."

"Good idea," agreed Rodionov. "Oh, and speaking of travel, there's some sort of warning that the Unit has posted to our portal. Dated today, Friday, the tenth of January, from the World Health Organization. Please review it. Something on advice for international travel due to a pneumonia outbreak as a result of a virus in China. Make sure that does not limit our options to return to Venezuela or to Mother Russia."

"Certainly," replied Fedor.

Rodionov continued, "It has nothing to do with us. I do not think it is of any concern. The person who should be concerned, however, is Ben Porter. Because Fedor, I assure you . . . he is up to something. We're onto him, and we are going to tighten the net."

CHAPTER
28

PARADISE ISLAND, BAHAMAS

"RUN IT BY ME one more time," demanded Deputy Assistant Director Bradford Macallister, his inexplicably out-of-summer-season tanned face dominating the center screen in the situation room on *Almaz*.

The encrypted video feed showed Macallister seated at an ornate wooden desk in his new office within the J. Edgar Hoover Building in Washington, D.C. Behind him, hung on the wood-paneled wall, the round FBI logo was flanked by two American flags draping from floor-mounted staffs. It was quite the imposing set-up. As another reminder of the importance of Macallister's position, I noted that he his private office was wired with secure video teleconference capabilities—back in the Boston field office, we had to use our operations center for this type of high-tech, high-security communication.

Earlier today, just after lunch, I had called Macallister with the super-secret, plain-vanilla flip phone to schedule the emergency secure video teleconference (SVTC in FBI jargon), when Volkov had announced to me, "We're going to Venezuela. I'm convinced I've found him."

Getting on Macallister's schedule would be simple, I assumed, incorrectly. In the balmy weather of the Bahamas, the days blended together. I had forgotten it was Friday. Friday afternoon, to be specific. Macallister would be thinking about the weekend.

He relented, however, because this was the first SVTC that I requested since putting the "Quadrant Procurement Group" operation into motion. Macallister's curiosity got the better of him, even at the expense of starting the weekend a tad late. Besides, as I had pointed out during our brief phone call, his time log would show that he was putting in the hours with a Friday afternoon meeting covering boring procurement work. If anyone ever checked his schedule, they'd be impressed by his diligence and dedication to the job.

"Let me recap, sir," I said, careful to look at the eye of the camera mounted above the big center screen. "Two days ago, Volkov identified a chess player on the Trampoline social network platform who had both a pattern of play, and also of conversation, similar to Petrikov. Admittedly, that was a very tenuous lead. Therefore, Volkov took it a step further. She'll take it from here."

To my left sat Lockwood and Rourke, and to my right, Hamid and Volkov. Our computer expert appeared haggard after hours of computer work, but she composed herself and asked, "Are you familiar with Trampoline, sir?"

"I've heard of it. But I don't get into that social media stuff. Not for me," Macallister replied haughtily.

Not surprising, I thought. *Macallister can barely work a computer.*

"I'll take that," volunteered Hamid. "I've spent quite a bit of time on the platform, researching it." I could barely contain a laugh as Hamid quickly shot me a look before going on to explain, to my surprise, that he had actually done some research in between games. "The platform was formed in July of 2018, by a Stanford University graduate named Melissa Zhao. Her goal was to create a better social network. A platform that would take the best of the competition, and include a community-based system of intelligent censorship, to make it friendly and—"

"Do I give a flying fuck about this? Move it along," barked Macallister.

Hamid seemed put out, not yet familiar with Macallister's distaste for commentary. As slow as he was with computers, Macallister had a knack for quickly seeing the aspects of a case that deserved attention. Volkov took over. "No, sir, the history of the platform might not seem relevant, at this time. What Hamid was explaining, taking the long way around, is peripherally relevant, though, because the coding of the basics of the platform is fairly amateurish. Dig in, and it gets very complex, as if it got a lot more attention as it expanded, which does match Hamid's research. It appears that Melissa Zhao got some private venture capital to expand her utopian vision soon after she created the network, and the platform got quite a bit more sophisticated."

"Again, interesting, I suppose, but why do I care?" asked Macallister, in a slightly gentler tone, as he knew first-hand how good Volkov was at coding.

"You care, and I care, because it was relatively straightforward to crack the first layers of security, which were presumably created early on, and to hack the platform. I mean, it still took a couple of days, but that's pretty fast. Anyway, I could get specific user data."

Macallister leaned toward his camera and nodded. "Now it sounds like we are getting somewhere. From our conversation before, the first run-through, do I guess that this specific user data points to Petrikov?"

"Indeed, it does, sir," confirmed Volkov. "We have the date of profile formation, which matches our pattern of Petrikov appearing, or rather, not appearing on our radar, so to speak. And as of a few hours ago, we have a location. I isolated the IP address—the internet protocol address—to Caracas, Venezuela. And then, I created a series of tests to try and zero in on that particular IP. There is a very high likelihood that the address is in, or significantly near, the Russian embassy in Caracas."

Macallister hedged his response as he cautioned, "That might be a strong coincidence, but it is far from definitive."

It was my turn to lean toward the camera. I guess that's how you signal earnestness in a video conference, which I was already hating for its impersonality. "Sir, we all agree there, but this is the first lead we've ever developed that has a shred of credibility. We will continue to work other avenues, just as we continue to monitor this one. However, it is my decision that we will pursue it."

Macallister said dismissively, "I think it is potentially of very little value, but I can't think of any reason to stop you. Do you have a mission profile developed?"

"Not completely, sir," I replied. "We will develop a mission profile and a plan over the next—" I turned to my left before finishing my sentence, imploring Lockwood to jump in.

"Eighty-two hours, give or take," Lockwood said. "We've already refueled and reprovisioned. I've plotted a course that takes us north of the island of Hispaniola, instead of cutting through the Windward Passage and getting too close to Cuba. That's probably not a risk, but the route north of Haiti and the Dominican Republic adds only about six hours."

"Nice vacation in the Caribbean, huh?" Macallister grunted. He looked away from the camera for a moment, probably imagining, if I knew him well enough, tanning in a chaise lounge chair on a white sand beach, sipping some sort of fruity cocktail with a tiny umbrella poking out of it, before he stared back into the camera coldly to warn, "And what do you do when you get to Venezuela?"

"Sir, we have not completed formulating that part of the plan yet." That was a bold-faced lie I just told.

Macallister thought he was on to me, seeing right through my posturing. "I think that's bullshit, Porter. You better come up with a real plan in the next eighty hours. I can't stop you from taking Petrikov's boat, using Petrikov's money for gas, on your little cruise. That was our deal. But I sure as hell can caution you from putting American boots on the ground in another country. Because, in that instance, what little cover and protection I can offer you currently would become zero. Zilch. Got it?"

"Yes, sir," I confirmed.

Macallister was not going to let me off the leash. "Brief me before you execute *any* plan. Got it, Porter?" His voice was sternly uncompromising.

"Yes, sir," I repeated.

As Volkov terminated the SVTC connection, I couldn't help but think, *There's no chance I'll brief Macallister on the plan. Because I know what we're going to do, and he'll never approve it.*

CHAPTER
29

MONDAY, JANUARY 20, 2020 – SIMÓN BOLÍVAR INTERNATIONAL AIRPORT, MAIQUETÍA, VARGAS, VENEZUELA

"PASSPORT, PLEASE."

Go time, I thought. *And this better work. Otherwise, Macallister is going to have my head, after warning me ten days ago to brief him before I would "execute" any plan." Because this excursion definitely counts as that.*

With the outward confidence of a brash American tourist, I slid my blue-bound passport folio across a scratched Formica countertop, passing it to the uniformed Venezuelan border official at the Simón Bolívar International Airport. He accepted my passport book and flipped through it casually. Then, carefully, he slowly examined the blank pages, devoid of visa or immigration stamps. Pausing at the one page that displayed a stamp, dated just last week on Thursday, he asked, "Your first trip abroad, Mr. Godfrey?"

"Yes. Well, of course, this is the second leg of *our* trip. A honeymoon dream trip come true." I squeezed Anastasia Volkov's hand, which I'd been holding, as I said "our." She did not squeeze back, probably because my hand was really sweaty, and she was probably really grossed out. I didn't care. I was more worried about the immigration official's scrutiny of my passport than what Volkov thought of my damp palms.

John Godfrey's passport had been accepted the week before, but under much different circumstances, when we entered the tiny country of Trinidad and Tobago. When a pristine, 235-foot yacht docks in Port of Spain, the capital city of the multi-island nation, Lockwood had assured us that the customs and border officials would be eager to dispense with the formalities. Lockwood alone had brought our documents to the port immigration official, who gave the passports a cursory glance before stamping them. It had been a non-event. In fact, I hadn't even seen it happen.

This border crossing was a completely different story. This was the real deal; we were in the high-ceilinged, warehouse-like customs and immigration area of an international airport.

After the SVTC with Macallister on that Friday afternoon, roughly two weeks ago, we departed the Bahamas. I disclosed my plan to the team in the situation room during our first morning at sea. "We're going to Aruba," I announced. "We dock in Aruba, and Volkov and I will fly to Caracas."

I explained to the team that Volkov and I would pose as honeymooners. "The names on our passports don't match, we're a little awkward together, and we can get in and get out without attracting attention. Ann Karin and John Godfrey only exist on the passports that we had fabricated for us prior to leaving Virginia. And while they are legitimate, United States-issued passports, those names do not exist in any border control database."

"They will after this trip," Volkov warned.

"Yep. And if we have to, we will manufacture new identities. It can't be helped. We are going to have a look-see for Petrikov. And you, Volkov, are the only one here who will recognize him immediately on sight."

Rourke, ever the former agent, asked, "What do you do if you I.D. him? Take him down? Take him into custody? Then what?"

"Not yet," I replied. "This first trip is confirmation, and also reconnaissance. Get the lay of the land. That's if we are lucky enough to find him."

"Gonna be a challenge," Rourke said.

I dismissed her concern rudely. "It will be. We know that. Do you have anything helpful to add?"

"There's no direct flights from Aruba to Caracas," my logistics manager informed me, clearly taking a little pleasure in watching me squirm.

"Oh," was my lame response.

Rourke kindly bailed me out by suggesting we go a bit further on the yacht, to Trinidad and Tobago, from where the honeymooners could find a direct flight to Caracas. In the meantime, I sent a brief email to Macallister, from my Quadrant Procurement Group address, that read in part, "We are seeking new opportunities in Trinidad before we enter the Venezuelan market. More to follow."

That had been my last communique to Macallister. And now, here we were. Boots on the ground in a foreign country. Against his direct orders. Palms dripping, I began to second-guess myself, thinking, *If John Godfrey gets stopped by a Venezuelan immigration official, Ben Porter will be truly screwed.*

A moment later, my passport was slid across to me. I hoped my sigh of relief was not obvious.

"Enjoy your stay in Caracas, Mister Godfrey. Congratulations on your wedding," the officer said, without a hint of sincerity in his accented voice.

Volkov replied sweetly, flashing a wink, "Oh, thank you. We're *so* excited to be here. Lots to discover!" She tossed her hair and broadcast her most ingratiating smile, getting a grin from the official in return.

Outside the terminal, in the warm late-January air, I chided her, "I thought we wanted to be inconspicuous."

"We also want to play the part—you with the dead, sweaty hands. You look guilty," she countered. "Listen, we have a mission. Think like an operative. Act like one. This is theater, and you're on stage. Don't forget that."

I nodded my understanding as she flagged a taxicab, remembering that Volkov had far more experience than I in the field. Though, to be fair, not as an operative, but as an enemy. I had convinced myself that she was truly and legitimately working with me. But that nagging thought still remained, and now, here in Venezuela, I couldn't help but wonder what would happen if and when she saw her father.

Pushing those thoughts aside and focusing on the moment at hand, we clambered into a cab. From memory, I recited the name of the hotel to the driver, "InterContinental Tamanaco Caracas."

"Si, senor. Mi nombre es Rómulo," the cabbie replied cheerfully, probably thinking about the fare to charge the wealthy American tourists, as he added in English, "There is a lot of traffic. We take back roads."

Volkov grabbed the opportunity, answering, "Oh, that's wonderful. We get to see more of your country. Maybe I'll sit in front with you so I can see better." Without waiting for a reply, she hopped out of the backseat and jumped in the front passenger seat, flipping her hair and grinning a wide smile.

I put my head back and closed my eyes, listening to her chatter. Little did I know that I would need the nap. The next two days would require every bit of my energy, observational skills, and focus. *Your boots are on the ground in a foreign country, Ben,* I lectured myself. *With a woman who once tried to kill you. DO NOT lose your focus.*

I sighed to myself, *I should have listened to Macallister.* There were way too many ways that this could go south.

CHAPTER

30

I EXPECTED THE CAB RIDE from the airport to the hotel to run in the neighborhood of sixty U.S. dollars, about six hundred *bolívar soberano*, or Venezuelan sovereign bolivars. By the time we got to the hotel, it was quintuple that, thanks to Volkov's pitstops and detours.

Rómulo and Volkov made quite a team. With his swept-back, curly, white hair, white mustache, and sun-tanned brown face, our cabbie became part tour guide and part personal shopper. During the several-hour drive, we stopped four times to acquire various hats and a number of garish shirts. By the time we pulled up to the entry at the apex of the V-shaped, eight-story, vaguely mid-century modern hotel, our purchases were scattered about the taxi, and we checked in with a flurry of items and much laughter from Rómulo and Volkov.

The king-sized bed in our nicely appointed room reminded me of our hotel stay in New York, and my mood darkened. *More nights of sleeping with one eye open*, I thought, already dreading the prospect.

Volkov reprimanded me as soon as the door to the room closed. "What the fuck, Ben? Happy couple on honeymoon? Or morose, pain-in-the-ass entitled American? You're doing a hell of a job playing the second part."

I couldn't explain to her, obviously, what was bugging me, so I deflected. "What was the point of all the shopping? All the detours?

We're not here to round out your closet, you know," I spat back. "Not to mention, you've been anything but inconspicuous."

Volkov laughed. "Well, I'm impressed. I thought you'd cower a little. Nice to see some spark."

Her response surprised me, and I refocused. "I'm just not sure what you're up to." I meant that in two ways. I wondered if she would understand.

"It's late. Let's grab dinner. I'll talk you through it. By the way, I'm also impressed that you got us here. However, now that we're on the ground, I'm taking over."

I didn't like how that sounded.

✳ ✳ ✳

I slept poorly that night. I stressed about sharing a bed with Volkov, and I was also nervous. This would be my first field operation, ever.

Volkov slept soundly, snoring peacefully. Once more, I began to second-guess myself. *You're overreacting, Ben*, I told myself. *She's on your side now. Let it go.*

When Tuesday dawned, Volkov put us to work. At dinner the evening before, she had explained the rationale behind her shopping spree yesterday: she had bought us disguises to use as we did reconnaissance laps of the neighborhood. And by disguise, we're talking simple changes of shirts, hats, sunglasses, and so forth, to dress as tourists or as gringo ex-pat locals. "It's all in how you carry yourself," Volkov advised. "Look the part, dress the part, and you fit in. Own it."

In my sleep-deprived state, I had forgotten part of the dinner conversation. "It's how far to the Russian embassy, where the IP address is located that our chess player is using?"

Volkov reminded me, "A tad over a mile. An easy walk."

"Round trip?"

"No. One way."

I raised my eyebrows as I looked down at my gut. "A two-mile walk, then. And how many times are we doing it?"

"Five each. I have four disguises, plus one pass undisguised. Oh, and Rómulo will be picking us up at 4:30 this afternoon. We can do a drive-by then before hitting town for dinner, and then he'll drive us back to the hotel via the embassy."

"Our cab driver is now part of the op?"

Volkov giggled. "Yeah. I think he's handsome, though he's a little old for me."

I took a deep breath as she began to outline the route, the disguises, and the timetable.

By Tuesday night, I was exhausted from all the walking and riding and spying. Volkov had scheduled us to pass by the embassy at twelve different times during the day and evening on Tuesday. It was far from a perfect surveillance plan, and we had no success getting a sighting of Petrikov.

The day did establish, however, that Volkov was an excellent partner. Her dedication to the mission was evident in her eyes, in her voice, on her face, and in her actions. This was good news to me on two fronts: one, of course, for the op, and two, because I could get some sleep. Recalling her composure and attitude on *Almaz* and reminding myself that my initial reservations were most likely unfounded, I finally slept Tuesday night.

Waking early, we dressed in the darkness, getting ready for Wednesday's reconnaissance plan before sunrise. This morning's disguise was of an energetic, sporty, honeymooning couple dressed in athletic attire appropriate for a pre-dawn workout. We planned to walk past the embassy downhill, toward town, and then get breakfast. Then we would split up, change into another one of the disguises in Volkov's cavernous bag, return to the hotel, change yet again, and do another lap. Then another. Then another. Rinse and repeat.

In the relative cool of the early morning air, I steeled myself for a long day, happy that our first trek was downhill, not so happy to antici-pate the uphill return trip on a full stomach.

We had just passed the embassy gate, paralleling a tall concrete wall topped with a metal fence, when Volkov grabbed me suddenly, enveloping me in an embrace. With her right hand behind my head, she pushed my face toward her own, and our mouths met. After the briefest pause, her lips opened, and our tongues touched. *Wait, what?*

Her hot breath, her probing tongue, her soft lips . . . I closed my eyes and savored, feeling my groin bulge. *Not now, Ben,* I chastised myself. *Not on a street in Caracas.*

She was pressed against me, our mouths mashed together, no air between our bodies. *Think about something else, Ben. Distract yourself . . . think about anything but this. Um. Baseball. Baseball!*

I realized, barely, that it was only her right hand touching me, as she backed into the chain-link fence that abutted the sidewalk, pulling me with her, her tongue darting and probing, the growing erection in my shorts being squeezed between us. *Baseball!!*

And then it was over.

She pulled her mouth away from mine and inhaled deeply. I held my breath for a moment, unwilling to let the moment pass, ignoring the tent below the waistband of my shorts, feeling the sweat all over my skin, trying to refocus my eyes. She whispered urgently, bending toward my ear, "Ben. Ben."

I stood stock-still, unsure what to do, as I heard her say, "We got him."

THURSDAY, JANUARY 23, 2020 – DIEGO MARTIN, TRINIDAD AND TOBAGO

ALMAZ WAS "MED-MOORED," or stern to the dock with an anchor off her bow, at the Trinidad and Tobago Yacht Club, less than a mile west of the capital city of Port of Spain. Given the forward-facing windows in the situation room, there was no possible way for anyone quayside to spy on the giant flat screens—but the shades were drawn against the glare of the Thursday afternoon Caribbean sun as Volkov and I debriefed the Quadrant team.

"I can't believe how close you got to him," exclaimed Hamid. "I mean, that's not a zoomed-in photo. He's like, right next to you on the sidewalk, almost touching you."

I remained mute, not yet ready to address that word, "touching." Volkov reported to the team, "We did quite a few reconnaissance passes by my father's expected location. In this instance, he was walking by, and we were disguised along the fence line adjacent to the sidewalk. Good tradecraft, I guess. Besides, I was careful with the phone as I took the photos. Shooting from the hip, as they say. I didn't aim the camera; I merely moved the camera around and hoped my subject was in the frame."

"In the frame" was, quite possibly, the driest way to describe the photos. One picture after another of Anatoly Petrikov dominated the frame on the giant, center flat screen, as he walked uphill on Avenida de Las Lomas in Caracas, Venezuela, his head down, and his cheeks red from the exertion.

With her free left hand, Volkov had snapped almost twenty photos of our target.

What Volkov was doing with her right hand, naturally, became the next question posed by Hamid. "Where was Ben during the Petrikov photo op?"

Volkov and I eyed each other. We had discussed this at the hotel in Caracas, and we decided to be transparent with the team. I replied to Hamid, using a clinical, matter-of-fact tone, "I was kissing Volkov." As eyebrows raised around the table, I hurried on. "Volkov spotted Petrikov first. He was walking uphill on the sidewalk, directly toward us. She reacted quickly and used my body to not only shield the phone, but also to hide her face."

I scanned the room, mostly for show so that I could steal a glance at Lockwood. I did not want my old friend to think that I had imposed on what was obviously developing as a relationship between Volkov and him; fortunately, he appeared nonplussed. I elaborated, now with more enthusiasm in my voice. "Volkov said to me, quote, we got him, unquote. I didn't understand at first, but I followed her gaze uphill. We both watched Petrikov amble from the sidewalk to the gate of the Russian Embassy."

Taking turns, Volkov and I relayed the rest of the story to the team. Petrikov had disappeared from view, but he had been memorialized in Volkov's camera work, and captured by her instincts as she recognized her father walking up the hill toward us and disguised herself—using my mouth and my body.

We had returned to the hotel, and after confirming our flight for the following day, late morning Thursday, from Venezuela to Trinidad, we spent the remainder of Wednesday lounging in the shade by the pool, where I first saw Volkov's photos. I told the team, "Volkov and I figured it would be too dangerous to email the pictures, and that we'd show them to you when we got back onboard *Almaz*."

Rourke observed, "Okay, so we know where he is. The Russian Embassy. Exactly as the IP address suggested. But not exactly a soft target."

"We did a second recon run, early on Thursday morning, before checking out and settling our room tab," Volkov remarked. "We took a final walk together, lingering in the shadows of a scrub of bushes at the apex of a dark intersection downhill of the embassy. As if on cue, my father walked by, his shirt already sweat-stained and clingy. He's a creature of habit. I think that's something we can use to our advantage."

I added, "After that final recon, once Petrikov disappeared up the hill, Volkov and I dropped shirts and hats and glasses in various trash receptacles in a one-mile radius of the hotel. We left Venezuela with exactly the same items we arrived with."

"Not exactly the same," Volkov chuckled happily. "We departed with the twenty-odd photos of one of America's most-wanted terror suspects on my phone."

That was new, I thought. *Volkov referring to Petrikov as a terror suspect. Not her father.*

"Why didn't you nab him?"

I looked over to Hamid, who was grinning at the absurdity of his suggestion. The grin faded as I stared back, considering his words.

Directing my gaze to my right, to Volkov, I said, "That's not a bad idea. Why not?"

Volkov grunted. "Well, for starters, we were undermanned. He's a big guy. He's not going to just follow along."

"Sure, he will," I suggested, without elaborating. "The problem is exfil."

"Exactly," agreed Rourke. "Once you have him, how do you exfiltrate him? And how do you get the team out? The Russians are bound to notice that their guest has disappeared."

"We're going to need reinforcements," I decided. Turning to my left, I said, "Miles. Get us out of here. Let's get some sea room and go someplace less visible."

"Done," Lockwood replied. "While you were in Caracas, we've refueled and reprovisioned. We can get off the dock tonight. Anything else?"

I thought for a moment. "Not now. We will set up a conference with Macallister tomorrow."

Hamid chuckled. "He's gonna be pissed. Weren't we supposed to check in with him before we went to Caracas?"

"I'd rather beg forgiveness than ask permission. And I think the ends justified the means. Besides, what's Macallister got to object to? The deed is done. We have our target." I scanned the room and decided the meeting was over, and I adjourned it by saying, "That's it for now."

Lockwood rose and said, "I could use some help with preparations and with the dock lines and the anchor, if we're departing so quickly. Anyone available?"

Volkov shot to her feet, followed by Rourke and Hamid. "We're in," they chorused. There was a new sense of excitement in the team, and I felt it, too.

We had our target in our sights.

I remained seated, reclining in the black, executive-style chair, resting for a moment. Putting my feet on the floor, I felt the big engines rumble to life as I leaned forward to my console, touching a button to activate the television feed. Selecting CNN's global satellite news channel, hoping that the background noises of the talking heads on-screen would become white noise as I organized my thoughts, I couldn't help but listen to the broadcast. "There is a rush to get out of the city. Train stations in Wuhan were packed early Thursday morning as passengers scrambled to leave the city before the lockdown began."

I wondered, *Lockdown?* Using the computer terminal at my seating position, I quickly Googled "Wuhan lockdown" as the newscaster's voice continued, "The outbreak and lockdown have been announced at a time certain to cause disruption. Three days from now, we will expect to see the beginning of a major travel season, as millions of people gather throughout the Asian continent to celebrate the usual carnival-like celebrations that ring in the Lunar New Year."

That's it, I realized, and in a flash, I knew how and when we would have the perfect opportunity to apprehend and seize Anatoly Petrikov.

FEBRUARY

CHAPTER

32

MONDAY, FEBRUARY 24, 2020 – BRISTOL, RHODE ISLAND

SEATED ON A BENCH in Walley Park on a late winter Monday morning near the close of February, overlooking Narragansett Bay, Vitaly Rodionov complained, "In Moscow, this would be the beginning of a balmy, spring-like day. Here, it is still cold and gray. I have tired of this place." He sniffed at the plastic lid of the paper to-go cup half-filled with black coffee.

His compatriot Fedor concurred, "It is the raw salt air. The humidity. Moscow has a proper winter. Rhode Island has nothing but cold dampness." He checked his watch—ten in the morning.

Rodionov, who was in an especially contemplative, dark mood, finally spoke, "Did you hear the news about Italy?"

"Yes. They announced a lockdown yesterday. Airports and train stations closed. Citizens told to shelter in place because of the virus. The Americans are growing concerned, too, it appears," Fedor commented.

"I am unaccustomed to failure," mourned Rodionov, changing the subject yet again. The talk of the so-called coronavirus bothered him. It was something vague, beyond his control. He could neither hack it, nor spy on it.

The virus was as invisible as Ben Porter, the elusive, former FBI agent.

Rodionov pulled his coat tightly against the pervasive chill and made his decision, announcing, "While I might be unaccustomed to failure, we have failed. We have wasted our time for over a month. Volkov might be in New York, she might not be. But I'm certain that Porter is not in New York, at his brother's residence. Nor is Porter at his parent's home, or at his sister's house here in Bristol."

Standing, Rodionov grumbled, "We are running in circles, like an American out for a jog. Porter has gone underground. For what reason, we have failed to find. And this virus has become a concern to me, too. They are locking down Europe. We cannot return via Rome, as we arrived. What's next? Where is next? I do not want to stay here any longer." He paused, looked out on Narragansett Bay one last time, and said firmly as he stood up, "We are returning to Moscow."

His compatriot followed suit, and, in silence, the two men puttered back to their car, this one a rented Hyundai sedan with Rhode Island license plates. Clambering into the sedan and turning the heater on full blast to rid themselves of the humid chill, Rodionov explained his orders to his associate in the driver's seat, "Book us a direct flight to Europe. Rome is obviously out of the question. Find a nearby European airport, just as any Italian traveler might do, and we will travel overland back to Russia. There will be a mass of people traveling to get ahead of these lockdowns. We cannot afford the delay by departing, as we arrived, via Canada."

Fedor offered, "Perhaps we might return directly to Venezuela. The Americans are distracted by this virus. There may be little risk."

"Hmm. That's an interesting thought. I wonder if Ben Porter has disappeared in order to seek out Petrikov." His voice faded.

After allowing thirty seconds for his superior to think, Fedor offered, "That would be an unlikely coincidence. Perhaps Porter has gone undercover as an FBI agent. Yet, if that's the case, he would have no jurisdiction to pursue a suspect beyond the borders of America. That would be a job for the Central Intelligence Agency."

Rodionov nodded his head. "That's a good point. Besides, Petrikov was spirited into Venezuela by me personally. There is little chance the CIA, or the FBI, would be able to discover his location."

"True," Fedor agreed.

With a more confident tone, Rodionov decided, "No. There is no need for us to return to Caracas to babysit Petrikov. I am told he has not varied his routine since we left. A walk, a vodka, his games, more vodka. Order our men at the embassy to step up perimeter surveillance at the compound and confirm that the only time Petrikov is allowed to leave the grounds is for his morning walk. Have him tailed."

"Understood."

"There is little of value to us in returning to Venezuela," Rodionov concluded. "We will return to Moscow. We have other work to do there."

So jaded were the Russians by the monotony of their mission, and by the promise of returning home, neither operative noticed the white Chevy Tahoe with darkened windows that trailed their Hyundai, hanging two or three vehicles behind, matching their route turn-by-turn. And, with such a simple oversight, the hunter would become the prey.

CHAPTER
33

TUESDAY, FEBRUARY 25, 2020 – CARACAS, VENEZUELA

IT HAD TAKEN THE Quadrant team, and me, a month to prepare.

Thirty days.

That seems like a long time, looking back on it, but for the people, the travel, the negotiations, the mission planning—well, it had gone by in a flash.

At this exact moment, however, the minutes ticked by in agonizing slowness, made even more difficult to bear because it was dark, and because I was crouched under a bush.

The city of Caracas was as silent as it would be for the day. Once the sun rose in two hours, citizens would wake lethargically, shake off the cobwebs and the hangovers, and prepare to party. Tuesday, February 25, would be the final day of *Carnaval*—the two-day Venezuelan national holiday of parades, dancing, and drinking that I had seen advertised and promoted literally everywhere when Volkov and I made our successful recon run a month ago in January.

Venezuelans would make Tuesday a day of excess, since Wednesday would bring Ash Wednesday, the beginning of the Season of Lent: a time for simple living, sacrifice and fasting, or forty days for the predominantly Catholic population of Venezuela to recover from the festivities of *Carnaval*.

My earpiece clicked, and I heard Volkov's voice whisper, "Porter. Are you in place?"

"Affirmative," I hissed, from my position hidden in a scrub of bushes adjacent to the three-street intersection of Calle la Cinta, Carretera de Baruta, and Avenida de Las Lomas. Whichever of the two former streets Anatoly Petrikov chose for his early-morning walk, it wouldn't matter, since he would start the uphill trek back to the Russian Embassy at this point. I was the spotter.

About a third of a mile uphill of me was the intercept team. Special Agent Jackson Robinson, a giant of a man with a dark-chocolate-colored polished scalp and a tidy, meticulously trimmed chin goatee, slumped behind the wheel of a beat-up, blue-painted and rust-speckled Chevrolet Silverado pickup truck, parked on a dusty lot adjacent to a soccer field. In the bed of the truck lay Special Agent Leroy Havens, an ebony rock of a man who was pretending to be asleep, cuddled in a pile of festively colored blankets.

Both agents were featured in the case file that put me on the map, and these men were my picks to enhance the capabilities of my team. Robinson and Havens were members of the elite Critical Incident Response Group (CIRG). The Navy has its SEALs, the Army has its Delta Force, and the FBI has the CIRG: a relatively small group of exceptionally well-trained agents that are kept in a ready state to respond to any crisis—hazardous device interception and disruption, surveillance, behavioral analysis and negotiations, and, relevant this early morning, tactical operations.

Upon Deputy Assistant Director Macallister's top-secret orders, Robinson disappointed his two boys at home once more, cancelling a planned President's weekend trip when he hopped a flight from Chicago to New York. There, he met up with Havens, who was Heather Rourke's former partner. The two men boarded a JetBlue direct flight to Barbados, where *Almaz* lay at anchor, and the Quadrant team plotted our plan to nab Petrikov.

Any good plan requires a catalyst, or a trigger, to set it in motion. That would be my role. Upon my command, the plan would set the bait for a trap, in the form of Anastasia Volkov, now waiting on a house stoop about three hundred feet uphill from my position, and about the same distance downhill from the embassy. She was wearing a flowing white dress accented with red, blue, and yellow ribbons. If the residents within the house awoke from their alcohol-induced slumber, to them, Volkov would look like a passed-out parade participant, and in their genuinely friendly, South American way, they'd probably offer her coffee.

Coffee, I thought, salivating. We had taken our positions an hour ago, having mobilized early the previous evening. I was famished, tired, and bored. Another hour to wait was likely, and I whispered, "What would I give for a cuppa coffee right now. Anyone want me to grab them one?"

My attempt at humor fell flat, as Robinson spat, "Radio silence."

Chagrined, I rustled deeper into my bushy hideaway. *I shoulda known better*, I thought. *These guys are pros. Just do your job, Ben.*

I was not off to a good start. I hoped that was not an ominous omen.

CHAPTER

34

AN HOUR LATER, I was miserable. My legs were stiff from immobility, my hands were sweaty and hot from the gloves that I, and the rest of the team, were wearing, and my stomach was growling. And my ass was damp from sitting in the soil. I was idly thinking about important stuff, like, what kind of waterproof underwear do the cool spies rock these days? I mean, Jason Bourne never seems to be uncomfortable. When he's on a stakeout, waiting in the snow for the bad guys, what is he wearing, you know, down there, to stay dry and comfy?

I didn't know how much more of this wretchedness I could take when I saw Anatoly Petrikov at the intersection.

This area of Caracas, called Chula Vista, was dotted with embassies—Russia, of course, but also Turkey, Syria, and the United States of America. The latter was the biggest, a sprawling compound with a commanding view of the hills and the city.

It was the hills that forced the roadways to wind and twist, and Avenida de Las Lomas was not a shortcut to anywhere. In order to do a loop for his morning walk, Petrikov would cut through a tight band of trees uphill from the embassy. If he chose the longer route and returned downhill via Carretera de Baruta, he would pass by Robinson's and Havens' Silverado. Robinson would inform the team if he saw the target.

He did not, and therefore the expectation was that the target had selected the shorter route for today's excursion, cutting through the trees to intersect Calle la Cinta before reaching the soccer pitch. Indeed, true to form and habit, he turned right and began plodding uphill.

"Target acquired," I whispered.

"Copy that," hissed Volkov.

After we had eyeballed Petrikov a month ago, Volkov was grimly determined to work out every possible eventuality with this operation. Reflecting back months ago, when I was worried that she might turn against me, I now worried, a bit, that she might snap, and attempt to even kill her father, so deep ran her anger. Indeed, that possibility had been discussed during the mission planning process. As the calm heads on the team, Volkov's included, checked in, I gained a newfound confidence.

"Copy," Robinson said, adding evenly and precisely, "Going to standby mode."

I imagined Robinson turning the ignition key, firing up the big V-8 motor in the truck as Havens' deep voice also affirmed, "Copy." In the bed of the truck, Havens would be tossing off his blanket, sitting up, and dropping the truck bed's tailgate.

"Pace?" Volkov's voice, questioning.

"Slow steps," I replied. "A bit faster than one per second."

I knew both Volkov and Robinson would be doing the math. Given Petrikov's height and stride, we estimated that he moved about three to three-and-a-half feet per step, especially when he began to climb uphill. One hundred seconds to Volkov's position.

I extricated myself from the bushes, which I had become familiar with for the past several hours, my knee joints popping and complaining from the sudden movement. My new role was sweeper: if Petrikov reversed course, he was my responsibility, and I followed him slowly, hanging well behind and out of sight as the road curved.

"In sight," Volkov announced. She would be making her way from the stoop to the roadway.

In the pickup truck, Robinson and Havens would be rolling downhill. *Thirty seconds to go.*

CHAPTER

35

ANASTASIA VOLKOV SMOOTHED HER white dress, a reflex, as she stood from the stoop, dusting the fabric with quick hand movements as she walked to the edge of Avenida de Las Lomas.

Her father, head down, plodded uphill on the narrow sidewalk.

Toward her. Toward a reunion.

Anatoly Petrikov must have sensed the figure in white standing before him, and he raised his head in annoyance at the inconsiderate woman blocking the sidewalk.

Grunting, he began to push by the woman, but he stopped dead in his tracks as he saw her face in the dim, pre-dawn light, gasping, "Anastasia?"

Volkov chirped a cheery, "Good morning."

As he heard the voice of his daughter, Petrikov's face clouded, and he muttered, "But . . . but, they told me you were dead. Then alive. And . . . you're here?"

Momentarily confused, Petrikov didn't notice a beat-up, blue-painted, and rust-speckled Chevrolet Silverado pickup truck, tailgate down, as the vehicle rolled to a stop on the street with a light squeal of worn-out brake rotors under very little load. The engine of the truck ticked as a giant, dark-clothed, ebony man leaped gracefully from the bed of the truck. Feet planted on the pavement, the giant shape enveloped the equally big Russian immigrant in a giant bear hug, lifting him off his feet.

Stunned by the sight and sound of his daughter, and taken by surprise by the attack, Petrikov barely resisted as he was thrown into the bed of the truck, landing on a pile of festively colored blankets.

Volkov agilely hopped into the bed of the truck as, behind her, Havens slammed the tailgate closed and then clambered over it, landing with a thump beside Volkov.

With the transmission shifter in neutral, Robinson removed his foot from the brake pedal, and the truck began to roll downhill. Seconds later, the passenger-side cab door was opened, and a somewhat stocky, somewhat overweight figure dove into the passenger seat.

Robinson shifted the transmission to drive and stomped on the gas pedal, the sudden acceleration swinging the passenger-side cab door shut.

In the open rear of the pickup, the big Russian was coming to his senses. Crushing Petrikov into the steel bed floor, Havens used surprise and his own body weight to subdue the struggling and squirming Russian. "A little help, please," Havens grunted.

"Almost there," replied Volkov, trying to time her motions with the swaying of the elderly pickup truck. While Havens was pinning the target to the truck bed, Volkov had reached into a small satchel and withdrawn a syringe. Flicking the cap from the needle, she drove the device through her father's pants and into his fleshy left buttock. With a sense of satisfaction, she pushed on the plunger with her thumb, injecting 300 milligrams of Ketamine, a potent, fast-acting dissociative anesthesia, into her father.

With the rapid-onset drug taking effect in sixty seconds, Petrikov's movements stilled. Havens rolled Petrikov's nonresponsive mound of a body onto its back, and then the CIRG agent shoved the target into a slumping sitting position.

"Pass me the bottle," Havens commanded. Volkov reached into the satchel and pulled out a dark bottle of rum, handing it over to Havens. Twisting off the cap, he dribbled the liquid onto Petrikov's lips, letting it run down his cheek, dripping into the blankets. Not quite satisfied with his creativity, Havens poured a bit more of it onto the front of Petrikov's button-down, tropical-weight shirt.

His prep work completed, Havens assumed a more comfortable position, sitting much the same way as Petrikov with his back to the cab and his legs outstretched in the bed. Examining the rum bottle, Havens tipped it to his own lips, gulping a shot.

Crawling to a similar pose on the opposite side of her father, Volkov scolded, "Drinking on the job? Before sunup?"

Reaching over Petrikov's inert body, Havens passed the bottle to Volkov, explaining in a serious tone, "For cover. If we get stopped, we all need some rum on our breath. Take a slug."

"Yeah, maybe," Volkov replied, taking a tiny sip from the rum bottle. "I think that was the easy part, though. The Russians are going to notice that their guest hasn't returned. Probably, if I could guess by our prior recon runs, by sun-up."

"What time is that, again?"

"Six forty-four," Volkov answered.

"What time is it now?"

Volkov consulted her watch. "Six twenty-eight. We have at best, by my guess, sixteen minutes before the Russians get concerned. Maybe twenty or thirty minutes by the time they've reviewed all their perimeter security camera footage and zero in on this truck."

Havens stretched his hand towards the bottle, asking, "And then what?"

"And then the Russians call their friends the Venezuelans, and we have two countries after us."

Havens examined the bottle of rum, hesitated for a second, and swigged another mouthful of rum, swallowing and saying, "That might make it a fair fight."

Volkov added, "Well, don't forget that the Ketamine will begin to wear off in about twenty minutes. Then we'll have one delirious, pissed-off Russian in the truck with us, while other pissed-off Russians are looking for us."

With a barely evident, thin grin, Havens snorted, "Now, *that* sounds like fun." He wiped his lips and readied for action.

CHAPTER
36

FROM THE PASSENGER SEAT of the Chevy pickup truck, it was difficult for me to decide what to watch—the building traffic which slowed us at each intersection, the confusing map on my phone, or the pavement rushing beneath my feet, visible through a watermelon-sized rust hole in the footwell.

Robinson glanced over at me, looking at the floor, and warned, "Sorry, forgot to mention the hole. Don't drop your phone through it. Then we will truly be fucked."

I refocused on the phone and yelled, "Shit! Left!"

Robinson hit the brakes and veered the truck as we turned onto the surface road that paralleled the highway, the Autopista Francisco Fajardo. Our route out of Caracas would not utilize the highway; even during the excesses of *Carnaval,* having three people in the bed of the pickup, including one who we expected to be unruly any moment now, would attract attention. And, as we had planned the mission, we decided that switching vehicles would be not only time-consuming, but difficult to stage with precision. The pickup truck was our chosen steed, and therefore we adapted the route accordingly.

By 7:15 a.m., I had no doubt that the Russian embassy had discovered that Anatoly Petrikov did not return from his customary morning walk. The security staff were probably already scouring their surveillance systems and combing the area on foot. However, we were clear of the stop-and-go traffic in the city, and in our unremarkable pickup truck, we were beginning the long descent, via rural roads with lots of switchbacks and curves, down to the coastline, following roughly the same route that Volkov and I had taken by taxicab a month ago.

To my left, I could see the embankment leading up to the *autopista*, and out my passenger side window, to the right, the red-roofed buildings were less and less dense. Ahead lay open road and valley. I could feel the truck accelerating slightly, and I was glancing over at Robinson when Havens, from the rear bed, banged on the cab roof and shouted, "Pull over!"

Tapping the brakes, Robinson slid the truck into a roadside parking lot, and before the pickup's tires stopped rotating, Havens jumped from the bed and trotted toward a farm-type truck, with high wood sides enclosing its load area, parked in front of a non-descript building; the sign above the door read *Bodega*.

My language skills stink, but I knew what that meant: it was a kind of general store. I watched Havens jogging back to our Chevy, aiming for my window and informing Robinson and me, "We searched Petrikov, per the plan. He had a phone on him. In case they can track it, we ditched it in that farm truck." As he spoke, two men exited the bodega and climbed into the cab of the truck. Its engine sputtered to life in a cloud of hazy, blue-gray exhaust, and the truck pulled onto the road, headed into Caracas.

"Nice work," I said in a complementary tone.

"Thanks," said Havens, "but the work has just begun. Our passenger is starting to wake up from the tranq shot."

He climbed aboard the Chevy, and as Robinson pulled out of the lot, I peered through the flat glass rear window of the truck cab. Sure enough, Petrikov was stirring.

"Just poke him again," suggested Robinson, returning the truck to the speed limit as we began to descend into the valley.

"We can't. Too much of the Ketamine, and he'll stop breathing. We would need medical help to resuscitate him, which, obviously, we cannot risk."

Robinson grunted. "Hell, it's not gonna matter. Petrikov is no match for Havens. One punch in the face from Leroy, and it's lights out."

* * *

The sun was high in the sky an hour-and-a-half later, most likely creating a great atmosphere in the city of Caracas for the final day of *Carnaval*. I was feeling good. We had almost reached our interim destination in the sprawling, congested village of Quenepe, on the hillside overlooking the container and ship terminal at Port of La Guaira, when a motorcycle-riding policeman pulled in front of Robinson and came to a halt.

"Oh, shit," I moaned.

Apprising the uniform, Robinson muttered, "Local police. Not one of the *Policía Nacional Bolivariana*. I got this. Just keep your mouth shut."

El policía ambled to the driver's side door, his right hand precisely resting on his sidearm, a signal to project authority. His brown face was stern and unsmiling, and his dark eyes were clear and sharp. In rapid-fire Spanish, he barraged Robinson with questions, pointing at the back of the truck repeatedly, where Volkov, Petrikov, and Havens remained. Robinson sat mute and immobile, his hands at the ten and two o'clock positions on the steering wheel.

As the policeman, still talking, began to walk to the bed, Robinson broke out in a stream of Spanish. The officer stopped and returned to the window. I knew Robinson was fluent in the language, which was one of the many reasons to request him to the team.

I followed Robinson's instructions perfectly. I didn't say a word, and I hoped that my pounding heartbeat was not visible through my shirt, and that the sweat on my face would be written off to the heat of the day.

With his left hand, Robinson reached up to the battered sun visor and tipped it slightly, carefully keeping his motions slow as he allowed his right hand to casually drop to the lower rim of the steering wheel.

I knew that was a deliberate choice, for his pistol was at his right hip, tucked discreetly out of sight. With his CIRG-trained reflexes, I had no doubt Robinson could draw his gun faster than the Venezuelan policeman.

Robinson extracted the small bundle of folded papers tucked above the visor and handed the registration documents to the officer, who inspected them cursorily before carrying the bundle back to his motorcycle.

I inhaled sharply and whispered, "What did you tell him?"

Barely moving his lips, Robinson hissed, "The cover story. Shut up."

Keep your cool, Ben, I chastised myself. Robinson and Havens were pros. *Let them do their job, and you do yours, Ben. Zip it.*

If I had thought the minutes had ticked by slowly when I was hiding in a bush in the pre-dawn morning, hours ago, well, now those clock hands moved glacially. Sweat literally dripped off my nose and onto my lap. It took everything I had not to move. To follow orders.

I watched with concern as the officer raised a radio microphone to his lips, and from the corner of my left eye, I watched with dread as Robinson's right hand dropped off the steering wheel and onto his right thigh. His body remained rocklike in the driver's seat.

I didn't dare turn around to see what the trio in the bed were doing, behind me, but for the absence of creaking in the old truck's suspension, I figured they were as immobile as Robinson and me.

Finally, after perhaps three minutes—which felt to me like thirty—passed, the officer returned to Robinson's window, and as the policeman passed the papers back to Robinson, he asked in slow but passable English, "You are returning the vehicle now, yes?"

"*Sí.* Yes," Robinson replied calmly.

"I will escort you." It was not a question. It was a demand.

Robinson restarted the engine of the Chevy and pulled forward, and as he passed the motorcycle, *el policia* gunned the bike's engine and began to follow us. I finally dared to breathe, "Can you tell me what just happened?"

Robinson's focus was intense. "I did what we planned. I told him that I had borrowed the vehicle to retrieve our friends in the back. The fat guy had too much to drink. He passed out."

Still using my phone, I kept my cool as I continued to give Robinson directions, all the while hearing the buzz of the revving motorcycle engine behind us, but not allowing myself to look. Turning onto a side street, the houses hemming in the hill-climbing road, we found the address, and as he brought the truck to a halt, Robinson ordered, "Stay put."

He switched off the engine of the Silverado and leaned his head out of the window, aiming his gaze at the still-saddled motorcycle cop. Without acknowledging Robinson, but after a slow scan of the surroundings, obviously confirming that the address of the residence matched the registration documents, the officer twisted his right hand and fed gas to the motor. With a whine of engine noise and the churn of a rear tire on gravel, *el policia* astride his machine disappeared back down the hill.

I exhaled. Robinson celebrated, too, by allowing the thinnest of smiles to just barely show on his face, commenting dryly, "It's a relief the officer didn't want to search the property."

That's an understatement, I thought. This two-bedroom residence high in the hills of Quenepe, which Volkov had found on Airbnb for twenty dollars per night, had been our safe house since we landed on a remote beach some eleven miles to the east, under the cover of darkness seven days ago. Lockwood and Hamid had piloted one of the rigid inflatable boats that rested on the fantail of *Almaz,* dropping Havens, Robinson, Volkov, and me on the rocky beachline, only one hundred feet from a lightly traveled roadway, where a cab driver, now accomplice, with swept-back, curly white hair, picked us up.

Volkov had convinced our friend Rómulo to help us, his enthusiasm greased by a handsome fee paid in Petrikov's dollars. Rómulo not only gave us a ride, but also identified the truck for us to buy. Rómulo even helped Robinson manage the registration process for the truck. The cab driver was our only loose end, and I figured that he was well-compensated while being well-isolated from any future investigation.

Isolation was important for us, too. We had the rest of the day to kill at the safe house, and as soon as the police officer was out of sight, Robinson and I hopped out of the cab to check on our cargo. Petrikov's eyes were closed, and he was breathing deeply, almost panting, through an open mouth.

I repeated my earlier question, in awe of the CIRG agents. "What just happened?"

Havens raised a bottle of rum and said sternly, "Good thing we had these rations."

"But what happened to him?" I asked, pointing at Petrikov.

Waving the empty bottle, Havens explained, "Well, when Robinson stopped for the police, I forced the remainder of the emergency rations down his throat, and then maybe he hit his head on this empty bottle."

"Hmmph," Robinson grunted with skepticism. With sarcasm heavy in his tone, he added, "It's a shame that his head hit the bottle so hard. I bet you had nothing to do with it."

"Nope," Havens deadpanned.

Havens and Robinson picked up Petrikov and carried him into the safe house. Volkov and I followed. It was time to hide, and yet, with *el policia* knowing where we were, what we had planned as a discreet hideaway had most likely been exposed on the policeman's radio.

Our time to hide was on borrowed time.

CHAPTER
37

BOSTON LOGAN INTERNATIONAL AIRPORT, BOSTON, MASSACHUSETTS

"HE'S BEEN MISSING all day?" Phone cupped to his ear, Vitaly Rodionov hunched in a plastic-covered chair in the international departures lounge at Boston's Logan International Airport. Listening to the response, he snarled, sotto voce so as not to be overheard, "It is just now that I am being informed? This is outrageous!"

Over the lounge public address system, a cheery voice announced, "Final call for Air France flight 333, non-stop service from Boston's Logan Airport to Paris, with an on-time departure at 5:20 p.m. Eastern Standard Time. All passengers should be on board."

Without disconnecting the call, Rodionov ran to the mouth of the jetway, where Fedor had his tickets waiting, and as the duo passed the threshold of the doorway, a uniformed attendant closed the door behind them. Rodionov took his time pacing through the jetway tunnel to the plane, barking order after order, "Inform our security forces, notify the Venezuelan National Police, the Caracas police—"

There was a pause as Rodionov listened and then shouted, "If they've already been notified, you would have found him by now!" He dropped his voice to a less noticeable level and continued through clenched teeth, "A fat Russian who does not speak the local language wandering around *Carnaval?* He must stand out. He has no money. He has no passport—"

Fedor elbowed his superior. Taken aback, Rodionov turned his ire momentarily to his accomplice before understanding the message, and Rodionov said, in a more controlled tone, "He has a Canadian passport. Dig up the name from our records and notify the airports. And what about the Venezuelan military? Army, navy?"

Another pause, and Rodionov, standing at the jet's door, hissed, "Authority? I'll send a message to President Putin himself. The military will heed an order from Putin, I assure you. Find him. Find Petrikov!"

He jabbed the *End* icon as Fedor led him to his seat in the first-class cabin of the Boeing 787. Rodionov was already pecking out a message. Slumping into the wide, leather-appointed seat, Rodionov exhaled miserably as Fedor questioned, "How did this happen?"

"He took his usual walk and never returned. He's gone."

"Your instructions yesterday were to have him tailed if he left the compound. I passed those orders on *yesterday*," Fedor said defensively.

"I know. The fools there told me that they were planning on starting the tail tomorrow morning. They claimed that they didn't have anyone scheduled for this morning. I can assure you that someone's head will roll for that lapse in command," Rodionov growled.

"Security cameras were reviewed, of course?"

"Yes. But useless. They're tracking every vehicle that passed the gate from the moment Petrikov exited the compound to twenty minutes past his usual return time. Given the early hour, not that many vehicles, but all the same, enough. We just do not have the kind of camera network in Caracas that we would need to effectively track a fugitive."

"Enough eyes looking, we'll find him," offered Fedor hopefully.

"It's been ten hours. He could be anywhere. But yes, perhaps the military will be helpful, especially at the air terminals. There's really no other way to get out of Caracas unless you had alternate transportation. Which, for Petrikov, would require someone else to help him."

Rodionov accepted a glass of fizzy, bubbly champagne from the smiling flight attendant, and he downed it in a single gulp, burping. He cursed, "Dammit. *I* gave him that fucking Canadian passport. I never believed he would have the audacity to try and escape."

As a French-accented voice from above droned, "We are preparing to back away from the gate; all passengers should be seated," Rodionov snagged the flute of champagne from his partner's hand and sucked down the golden liquid as he stared out the window, his mood as dark as the Boston airport beyond the porthole. Catching his scowling reflection in the plastic inner window, Rodionov relaxed his face and inhaled. He'd faced worse problems. The operative would work out his options during the trans-Atlantic flight. Because, after all, the reach and ambition of Unit 29155 went far beyond Anatoly Petrikov.

One hour later, plus one time zone to the east, and two thousand, two hundred statute miles to the south, a fax machine whirred in the sparse, tile-floored, and drooping drop-ceiling duty office of the Coast Guard Command of the Bolivarian Navy of Venezuela, in the coastal city of La Guaira, some eight miles north of Caracas and only three miles east of the Simón Bolívar International Airport.

At the sound of the machine, a bored enlisted man with the equivalent rank of an Able Seaman, *Cabo Segundo* Alejandro Zavala, blinked his eyes. His watch had begun at noon, and he had forty minutes more to suffer, the pounding headache from the previous night's *Carnaval* celebration still lingering. He may have, in fact, begun the watch while still drunk, after only a handful of hours of sleep after the sun rose that morning. He wasn't sure.

Listlessly, Zavala pulled the paper from the machine.

Seconds later, after scanning the sheet, and shaking his head to clear the cobwebs, Zavala rushed unsteadily to seek his superior, the on-duty lieutenant commander *Teniente de Navio* Jorge Garica.

Zavala knew, of course, that Garica would be in the darkened radio and radar control room, from where the Coast Guard monitored the territorial waters of Venezuela. Indeed, Zavala should have been there, too, not hiding his hangover in the adjacent duty office. Brandishing the paper, as it would be his excuse for leaving his post at the radar, Zavala handed the sheet to Lieutenant Commander Garica, who was on the telephone, his face furrowed.

Zavala breathed a sigh of relief. His superior officer, normally cold, emotionless, and demanding, was distracted by something else. Examining the sheet quickly, the Lieutenant Commander continued to speak into the phone handset, "Yes, we have received the fax as well. It is in my hand. We have no suspicious or unidentified traffic in the area." There was a pause, and then the officer added, "Understood. And likewise, if you see any air traffic, inform us immediately."

Placing the handset in its cradle, Garica explained to his enlisted man, "Air Command. There's a notice for a fugitive Russian, last seen in Caracas this morning. That's what's on the fax. It's not our concern, and even if it was, there's little we could do."

As they spoke, neither man noticed the blip that appeared momentarily on the radar display, ten miles offshore, then disappeared, then reappeared seconds later.

CHAPTER
38

QUENEPE, VARGAS, VENEZUELA

AT 7:20 P.M., ROUGHLY AN HOUR after dusk, we took our positions as we reboarded the beat-up, blue-painted, and rust-speckled Chevrolet Silverado pickup truck, and we rolled downhill from the densely built hillside community of Quenepe, overlooking the port area of La Guaira.

From the bed of the truck, looking rearwards, I watched the route that we had driven earlier that day in reverse. I wasn't just sightseeing, though. Propped between Havens and me, and sprawled on a pile of festively colored blankets, was America's most wanted terror suspect.

Our operations outline presumed that the early morning dose of Ketamine would have dissipated in Petrikov's system by evening, and we dared a second dose for this evening's mission. Volkov had administered the shot, and Havens tossed Petrikov into the truck cargo area like a giant sack of flour.

The next twenty or thirty minutes would be crucial, and we would require every second. We couldn't be slowed by a recalcitrant Russian.

Up front, out of my field of vision, Robinson was at the wheel of the pickup. Next to him sat Volkov, who would have a more delicate role than me. She relaxed in the passenger seat, her caramel-blonde hair flowing in the breeze from the open truck window. I envied Volkov's comfortable seat, but I should have warned her of the hole in the foot-well. It wouldn't do to have the communications transmitter pack that was strapped around her left thigh slip out through the hole or, worse, have her drop the backpack that she carried onto the pavement rushing by below. That pack would be crucial for our salvation.

My comms transmitter device—which paired my wireless earpiece to each of my team member's identical, tiny, voice-activated earpieces—was duct-taped to the small of my back, and I squirmed, the sticky tape pulling at my flesh. Havens glowered at me. *Suck it up, Ben.* I withered under Havens' glare and focused not on my comfort, but on my mission.

The truck wound its way downhill to Avenida Soublette, and as the truck carved a right-hand turn, I caught a glimpse of the sign at the intersection of the Avenida, barely lit by the dim headlights, that cautioned "Authorized Entry Only — Restricted Area of the Bolivarian Navy of Venezuela."

We drove past the Port of La Guaira, to our left. Less than ten minutes after beginning the journey, Robinson reversed the truck's course at a roundabout, and he piloted the Chevy into a tiny parking lot. To my dismay, a policeman caught sight of us immediately and began furiously waving the truck on to proceed.

As *el policía* accosted Robinson, Havens grabbed Petrikov's limp body as I unlatched the tailgate. I could hear Volkov chirping in English, "He is very drunk, but he'll wake up for the party!" From my position at the back right quarter of the truck, I watched as Robinson conversed with the policeman, passing him an American bill that he had ready in the event of this type of occurrence.

I heard the policeman say, "Gracias," as Robinson successfully executed the bribe, allowing us to leave the truck parked. *El policía* shook his head as Havens and I, walk-carrying Petrikov, did our best to play the part of clearly intoxicated tourists, weaving our way into the throng of revelers celebrating the final hours of *Carnaval* at the beachside Plaza Soublette.

* * *

"Traffic, sir," exclaimed *Cabo Segundo* Zavala, pointing at the radar display, the throb of his hangover still dulling his senses.

Bending to examine the radar display data, *Teniente de Navio* Garica shook his head, commenting without concern, "Fishing boat. Seven miles out, to the north, making only thirteen knots. She is just headed for port."

"The fishing vessel port is five miles to our west, sir," objected Zavala.

Garica laughed. "It is *Carnaval*, even at sea. The boat will make a course correction as soon as they clear their heads and realize they're headed for the wrong port."

As the lieutenant turned his back to the display, the seaman reexamined the radar, not believing what his clouded eyes saw. Hesitating at first, he stuttered, "Sir. Sir! *Sir!* The boat sped up. It's showing thirty knots of speed."

Garica spun to the screen. "That cannot be correct."

His eyes widened as the tracked target speed increased with each sweep of the radar, from thirty to fifty and then to seventy knots. As Garica and Zavala watched, dumbfounded, the target raced closer and closer to the coastline, and then suddenly veered east, away from the port.

I pushed the tiny earpiece deeper into my ear, hoping to block out the cacophony of the raucous *Carnaval* celebration two hundred feet behind me, but still I could barely hear Volkov's voice through the device as she announced, "Homing device active . . . *now!*"

"Acquired," Heather Rourke's voice confirmed calmly over the earpiece. I was thrilled to hear her voice as she asked, "Ell Zee clear?"

"Affirmative," replied Volkov. "Landing zone clear. But not for long, so make it quick." She had activated the portable homing device within the backpack that she carried, using it to guide Rourke to the LZ that we identified on the beach, slightly removed from Plaza Soublette and from the *Carnaval* partiers.

Robinson menacingly approached a couple who were staggering toward the beach, hand in hand, no doubt seeking solitude but intimidated by the shape of the big man blocking the way to the beach. The heads of the couple swiveled westward and skyward as they heard the whining whistle of the twin Turbomeca Arriel 2C2 turboshaft engines as Rourke flared the EC155B1 helicopter to a fast and hot landing only fifty feet from Volkov.

The instant the wheels of the chopper touched the rock-strewn area, Havens and I—well, mostly Havens—dragged the still-drugged Petrikov through the sand pelting our faces. Abandoning his LZ perimeter protection role, Robinson raced to the craft and to our assistance.

Climbing into the chopper, Havens lifted, and from below, Robinson and I pushed, and together we unceremoniously shoved the obese once-oligarch through the space where the door would have been. With Havens securing Petrikov, Robinson jumped on board and pulled Volkov, who was struggling with her dress snapping about her body in the rotor wash, up and in through the chopper door.

Robinson reached out to me. I grabbed his outstretched hand and was yanked off the ground. Feet airborne, I yelled, "Go!" and Rourke applied full power. The five blades had not stopped spinning, and it was only two seconds before the wheels lifted from the ground, as I collapsed to the floor of the chopper's cabin.

My heart was pounding, and my eyes were tearing from the sand and gravel whipped up by the chopper blades. As I struggled to collect myself, Rourke spun the Eurocopter to the left, put its nose down, and headed out to sea.

Lieutenant Commander Garica had the telephone handset to his ear as he spoke defensively, "No, sir, I don't have an explanation. The target was on the radar and was of no concern. It was merely a boat headed to the port. Then it accelerated to almost one hundred knots, then came to a stop on the point of land near Plaza Soublette."

There was a pause, and Garica said strongly, "No! You call the police. Or your commander. I am reporting a target as required. It is on land and not my concern. It is clearly not a vessel. It may even be a bad return on the radar."

Garica slammed the handset back into its cradle, the noise of the impact causing Zavala's headache to return in earnest. Rubbing his

forehead, Seaman Zavala backed away as Garica reconsidered, order-
ing, "Call the police. I better cover myself on this one. Tell them to—"
he thought for a second and decided, "Tell them to investigate a vessel
aground near the Plaza."

✳ ✳ ✳

I dared a peek. The water's surface was skimming by as the helicopter
raced so close to the waves that it left a wake on the surface, the rotor
wash trailing the chopper's swerving course.

I felt sick. I dared not vomit. Not in front of Havens and Robinson,
both of whom were sitting calmly, flanking Petrikov while he stirred,
ready to subdue him if the Ketamine produced deliriousness as he regained
the use of his senses. I gulped a deep breath of the humid, salty air, and
kept my focus on the barely visible dials and displays in the cockpit at
the nose of the chopper.

"Hang on," I heard Rourke's voice say, for the third or fourth time.
The chopper banked hard left as she jogged our course again.

"Airspeed?" It was Robinson's voice.

Rourke replied, "One hundred and fifty-seven knots."

My gut churned. The pre-mission planning had established that the
"never exceed speed" of the airframe was one hundred and seventy-five
knots, but that was at a reasonable altitude. And given the view outside
the doorless cabin, I didn't think that this was a reasonable altitude.

Rourke is going to be exhausted, I thought with concern. On the
inbound approach leg, she would have maintained a one-hundred-foot
altitude and a crawling, almost hovering, thirteen-knot speed to fool any
radar watcher into assuming that the return blip from the chopper was
a vessel. On this outbound, exfil leg, Rourke would keep the machine
"on the deck," below the sweeps of an air search radar, and she would
confuse any ground-based radar returns by flying an erratic course. *This
flight can't be over soon enough.*

A long forty-two minutes later, my throat was desert-dry, and I
had stopped sweating, perhaps because I was so dehydrated that sweat
was impossible. The black night and the black sea melded into one, and

I came to terms with my fear, taking strength from the composure of my teammates.

One hundred miles north of the Venezuelan coastline, exactly where the yacht was supposed to be, Rourke found *Almaz* plodding northeast at three knots, with barely enough momentum for steerage, and pointed into a twelve-knot northeasterly breeze. The yacht's radar and Automatic Identification System would both be switched off, and every cabin light and running light would be unlit. Only a series of green glowsticks, adhered to the helipad with duct tape, would mark Rourke's landing zone.

With a graceful flare, Rourke touched the wheels directly over the capital H painted in black on the teak-decked helipad. Her feet remained on the brakes, and through the door cavity, I could just barely see Hamid and Dunn trotting from the sides of the pad with wheel chocks. As soon as they were clear of the chopper, Rourke began the shutdown procedure, and I caught a glimpse of Alverez as he dashed forward, toward the bridge.

Only seconds later, *Almaz* shuddered slightly. On the bridge, Lockwood would have applied power to the engines, and the yacht accelerated slowly as it turned to the north.

On unsteady legs, I dropped to the helipad, thankful to be back aboard *Almaz*. Robinson and Volkov jumped down to join me on the pad to receive Petrikov as he was lowered from the door opening by Havens. The Russian immigrant was awake, the primary effects of the Ketamine gone, but he was manacled with zip ties at his wrists and somewhat unsteady from the lingering delirium of the drug.

Supported by Robinson, Petrikov swayed slightly as he scanned the helipad and his surroundings. His eyes widened as he realized where he was, and he turned to Volkov and snarled, "You insolent bitch. How dare you? This is *my* boat."

Regaining my confidence and composure now on the stable deck of *Almaz*, I stepped between father and daughter. "Not anymore. And I apologize. It was too noisy on the flight to introduce myself properly. Plus, you've been so sleepy. I think you've had too much rum."

As I was addressing Petrikov, Havens had lowered himself silently from the chopper. Placing a warning hand on Petrikov's shoulder, Havens observed, mockingly, "It would appear that the big guy can't hold his booze."

Looking Petrikov directly in the eye, I continued, "Well, now that he's awake, let's welcome our guest aboard *Almaz*. Anatoly Petrikov, my name is Ben Porter. And you are now in the custody of the United States government."

Petrikov sneered at me. "So, you're the Ben Porter I've heard so much about. You forget, Mister Porter, that I have some very good friends in Russia. You're no match for them."

"Perhaps," I countered, "But here's their problem. The United States government doesn't know where I am, and if they don't know, I'm guessing the Russians don't know either."

As Petrikov's expression dimmed, I leaned toward the big man's left ear and whispered, "In chess, I believe they call that *checkmate*."

CHAPTER
39

I COULDN'T BELIEVE what I was hearing. "I think it's a non-starter to bring Petrikov back to the United States," Deputy Assistant Director Bradford Macallister mused.

The Quadrant team had gathered first thing in the morning to report to Macallister that we successfully intercepted and apprehended Anatoly Petrikov, and I knew that we were all surprised at Macallister's less-than-enthusiastic response. It was clear that he had other things on his mind as he added, "This virus, they're calling it Covid-Nineteen, is gonna be a problem. The Centers for Disease Control and Prevention just issued a warning to United States citizens. Infection reports are popping up all over the globe. Hang on."

Macallister shuffled some papers on his desk as we watched in stunned silence. We had been consumed with planning the mission from the confines of the yacht, surrounded by balmy Caribbean weather, and we had little interaction with the news cycle. We had only each other, and as I looked around the table at my team, I was pleased.

After landing last night, Havens and Robinson confined Petrikov in a secure stateroom on the first deck. Back in Portsmouth, two of the lowest deck staterooms, previously used for crew when the yacht was fully staffed under Petrikov's ownership, had been configured as makeshift cells. The interior of each stateroom was sparse, and each had only one round, ten-inch diameter, non-opening porthole to the outside world.

The staterooms included tiny, en suite, porthole-less bathrooms. Our work had been limited to securing any loose furnishings, adding steel doors to separate the cells from the corridor, and installing cameras so that occupants could be monitored from the situation room.

With Petrikov detained, it had been time to celebrate. Jacquard prepared an outstanding meal for the team, and we kicked back with beers and food, telling and retelling the tale of the intercept over and over. Volkov asked, "Ben, what did you say to him on the helipad when you whispered in his ear?"

I grinned and announced, "With an emphasis on the last word, I said," as I raised my fingers to air quote, "In chess, I believe they call that *checkmate.*"

The team gave me a standing ovation. Volkov laughed as she and I high-fived, and Rourke enveloped me in a hug, whispering, "Well played, Ben, well played," as she kissed me on the cheek.

My recollections of a triumphant evening were interrupted when Macallister found the paper he wanted and read aloud to us, "These are the reports from yesterday, February 25. First virus cases reported in Algeria, Austria, Croatia, and Switzerland. Both Jamaica and the Cayman Islands denied permission for a cruise ship to dock in their ports. Here in the States, the CDC warned that spread of the virus is likely, and the city of San Francisco declared a state of emergency due to Covid-19. It's getting worse. You're better off where you are. Where are you, anyway?"

"For operational security and deniability, let's not share that information," Hamid suggested, quite lucidly. Macallister nodded his consent as Hamid directed his attention to Lockwood, asking, "How long can we stay out at sea?"

Lockwood didn't hesitate, "Three more weeks. Possibly four if we conserve fuel and food. We can desalinate seawater to make our own potable water, so that's not an issue."

"Lemme make some very discreet inquiries," Macallister offered. "In the meantime, go in circles or something."

"Sir," I quickly said, fearing that Macallister would terminate the connection, "Do we have permission to speak with Petrikov? Interview him? Ask questions?"

"Yeah, sure," Macallister replied. "I doubt he'd talk but do whatever you want—just no interrogation or torture. The FBI does not do that sort of thing, as you know. Once I can find a place for you to bring him, we can arrange for the interviewing professionals and debriefers to meet with him."

"Understood, sir," I said.

My worries about Macallister ending the call were unfounded. He fidgeted for a moment, and then spoke, this time in a quiet and concerned voice. "Hey, Porter. One more piece of intel that you need to know, and this might also factor in you not hurrying back to the States. Now, before I get into it, let me assure you that we have this as a top security priority." He paused and then stared carefully at the camera. "As you know, we've had surveillance on your cover legend. We believe your cover has been blown."

That got my attention as I asked, "How so, sir?"

"We discovered two devices at the donut franchise offices. Very sophisticated little gizmos. Our technical people said that these things can be used to infect malware, or they can be used as relays to harvest data from the source machine. One of the flash drives self-destructed when it was removed from the computer. The other one is still there. That computer was turned off, obviously, as our tech team works on it."

"I'm familiar with those things," Volkov interrupted. "When did you find them?"

"Yesterday," grunted Macallister, "The company had a building alarm incident on the sixth of January. They said it was a false alarm, but they neglected to tell us about it then. We learned about the alarm, and we found the devices, when we were prompted to check out Porter's cover integrity due to another . . . *incident.*"

I didn't like the way Macallister hesitated, and I blurted, "What incident?"

"As you know, we've been keeping an eye on your family members, Porter. On Monday, two days ago during a routine patrol, our agents tailed two men who had been lurking by your sister's house."

My heart sank. "Is Grace okay?" I couldn't believe my sister had been sucked into my work. Again.

Macallister was quick to reassure me. "We quadrupled our security. We've actually seen nothing since Monday. It's possible it was coincidental but given the discovery of the devices at the offices, I think that's *too* much of a coincidence."

"Agreed," I said. "Out here, on the boat, I'm not at any risk. But I hate to hear that. Promise me you'll do more than keep an eye on my family?"

"Yeah. We've stepped up the protection operation, and it's being run by none other than the Boston SAC. By Appleton. You trust her, I assume."

"Absolutely." That was a relief. Jennifer Appleton was the real deal, as good of a Special Agent in Charge as they came.

Macallister was leaning back in his chair, steepling his fingers as he did when he wanted to look thoughtful, and he concluded, "Porter. Team. This is a historic moment. I apologize that I'm distracted by this virus thing. Don't let that diminish my congratulations. But as you know, we're not done yet."

"What do you mean?"

"Outside of that boat, there are four people who are fully read into this operation—the Director, the Attorney General, Appleton, and me. Now that you've succeeded, it's going to take time to disclose that, well, you succeeded. And, of course, the question will come up: how did they do it? With what resources? With who's authority? It will have to be handled delicately and deliberately."

"Understood, sir,"

"I gotta hand it to you. Nice work." Macallister flashed a thumbs-up, and with that, the screen went blank.

Havens and Robinson had taken the last two seats at the seven-person horseshoe-shaped table, and it was Robinson who asked, "Did I understand that correctly? We're stuck out here?"

"It appears that way. I'm sorry you'll be away from your families, but that's the deal until Macallister decides where he wants Petrikov."

"What's the problem?" Havens wondered. "High-value terror suspect, and Macallister doesn't know what to do with him?"

"You heard him. The problem," I explained, "is us. Quadrant. Very limited need-to-know circle and the United States government intelligence and justice organization doesn't know about us. Macallister can't waltz into an office and say, *hey, we got Petrikov,* without the logical question of *how* we got him in custody coming up."

Havens, a man accustomed to action, shook his head glumly. "Man, this boat is nice and all that, but what are we gonna do while we wait for Macallister?"

Hamid casually waved his smartphone. "Well, I'm gonna play some cards."

Havens rolled his eyes, but he visibly perked up when I said, "Well, I'm gonna torture Petrikov."

"Ah . . . wait a sec," Havens grimaced, "Didn't Macallister just say that we couldn't do that?"

"Let's just say I'm not using the word *torture* in a literal sense," I replied. "Listen, I've been chasing this guy for over two years. Now he's on *my* boat. I'm gonna talk to him."

It was Volkov's turn to grimace. "He's not going to talk, Ben. He's not going to spill his guts. And don't take this the wrong way, but especially not to you."

"I disagree," I said with confidence, repeating, "He's on *my* boat. You saw his reaction when he put his feet on the helipad. I'm just going to take advantage of that and add in a few theatrics. You'll see."

CHAPTER

40

"MY CHEF WAS FAR better," Anatoly Petrikov grumbled petulantly.

I laughed as I poured the last of the 2015 Château Lafite Rothschild Bordeaux Pauillac into Petrikov's empty glass. "You might complain about the food, but you can't complain about the wine. This is your bottle, after all." I paused for dramatic effect and snickered, "*Was*, that is. Was your bottle."

Petrikov snorted. "Is this supposed to be some sort of torture? Two days after you bring me aboard, you serve me dinner on *my* yacht, on *my* dinnerware, while drinking *my* wine?"

"That's correct. I might add, too, that I'm sleeping on *your* sheets. And no, not *some* sort of torture. In fact, I hope it *is* torture for you. Enjoy it while you can. Where you're going, you'll never see anything like it again, for the remainder of your breathing days," I bluffed, careful to keep my voice casual and even, but firm. I mean, I didn't know where Petrikov would be going, except for guessing that Lockwood would take the yacht on several laps of the loop from Montserrat to Martinique and back before we'd hear from Macallister. But Petrikov didn't know that.

"And what do you expect from me, Mister Porter? A confession? Remorse?"

That's my opening, I thought as I pushed the tiny transmitter button that Volkov had embedded under my chair a few hours earlier, and as planned, the door to the elaborate dining area opened. Havens strolled through the opening.

"Humility would be a nice change of attitude, for starters," the big CIRG agent suggested, having listened to the conversation that was broadcast to the exterior of the room by the microphones and cameras Volkov had also installed in preparation for our show. Standing beside the table, Havens asked, "You do remember me, don't you, Tony?"

Petrikov's eyes narrowed to a malevolent slit a moment later as he realized that the giant man was the very same CIRG agent who had arrested him, on this very yacht, over two years ago. Havens added, "You managed an escape last time, but only thanks to your daughter. Who, you've learned, is now quite clearly on our side. And, for what it's worth, I'm not letting you out of my sight."

Havens slid into a chair at our table and sat, while scowling the whole time at Petrikov, daring him to break eye contact. As Petrikov blinked rapidly, I pressed the hidden button under my chair for a second time, and on cue, the door reopened to reveal Lockwood.

Lockwood crossed the space to me and handed me a slip of paper covered in gibberish. I examined it and returned it to Lockwood, saying formally, "Thank you, Captain. Oh, Mister Petrikov, I don't believe you met our captain in person. But of course, you must remember his name. This is Miles Lockwood."

Petrikov blanched. "You're . . . you're Lockwood?"

"The one and the same," Lockwood grinned. "And, as I'm sure you remember, I don't give up easily. Nor does Ben Porter, as you're learning."

It was almost impossible for me to keep a straight face. This was pure Hollywood, Broadway theater. Havens and Lockwood had delivered their lines with the aplomb of seasoned actors who had memorized their scripts and then added their own personal touch for authenticity. And it was time for the finale.

I pressed the button for the third time, and Volkov glided into the space. This, of course, was the predictable move, perhaps made a tad more dramatic by the uncorked bottle of Château Lafite and the three empty glasses she carried.

Selecting a seat at the table, Volkov settled primly, with Lockwood formally pushing in her chair for her and then taking a seat for himself. No one spoke as Volkov emptied the bottle into the three glasses she had carried and into the two empty goblets already on the table in front of Petrikov and me.

The message had to be clear to Petrikov—he was surrounded, four against one, in the middle of nowhere, having been told that the operation that recaptured him was outside the supervision of the United States government, and therefore facing dismal odds. Furthermore, as he must have accepted, the sole reason he was able to escape his first capture was due to his daughter's help.

However, she was no longer his ally, and now she held the keys to his kingdom, so to speak. And less lyrically but no less importantly, to his wine cellar aboard *Almaz*. Therefore, it was Volkov, not me, who got to deliver the closing soliloquy of our little one-act play, her voice cold and her eyes narrowed. "You, father, are a traitor. To everyone, but perhaps most importantly, to my mother. And to me. I will *never* forgive you. I will never forgive your cheating, duplicitous ways. Those days are over. *Your* days are over."

Petrikov blinked, taken aback by the obvious venom and fortitude in her voice. With her pitch rising just so, Volkov continued, "You're not worth the time that it will take for an investigation. You haven't earned the right to the formalities of a trial. You deserve to be coldly executed, just as you've done to so many others. An eye for an eye. And for that reason, it was my strong suggestion to toss you over the side after chumming for sharks. But Ben Porter here has agreed to let you live."

She looked at me, and I recited the final line, "To be clear, I'll agree to that only if you tell us *everything* about Unit 29155."

MARCH

CHAPTER
41

WEDNESDAY, MARCH 11, 2020 – MOSCOW, RUSSIA

FOR THE FIRST TIME IN THE two weeks since departing Boston's Logan International Airport, Vitaly Rodionov felt that Unit 29155 was on the cusp of a breakthrough. And, given the setting, it was difficult for Rodionov to imagine any other outcome as he reclined in a comfortable swivel chair in the loft-like Moscow command center of the Unit. With its gleaming hardwood floors, impossibly high ceilings, modernist artwork, and sleek table after sleek table of monitors and keyboards and printers and telephones, the command center could have easily been in Silicon Valley, or in a trendy New York City building,

"Timeline it for me, Fedor. From the beginning of Tuesday, February 25, to the end of the day," Rodionov ordered, holding a glass mug of black coffee.

The centerpiece of the space was a story-high curved screen of Imax proportions. Using a touchscreen tablet, Fedor swiped photo after photo onto the screen, building a visual timeline as he spoke. "Petrikov left the embassy grounds at his usual time, well before sun-up. We searched his room, of course, and reviewed the security tapes of the cameras in the room." Swipe. Photo of Petrikov in his room. Swipe. Photo of Petrikov's back, departing the embassy gate, as Fedor continued, "No unusual behavior. He only took his phone; he did not take the laptop computer that you allowed him to use, and the Canadian passport was in the desk drawer."

Images of passing vehicles at the embassy gate; swipe, swipe, swipe. Stop. A still photo of a pickup truck as the narrative restarted, "Embassy security camera footage of one of the many vehicles that passed the gate during the examination time. A dark-colored pickup truck. An American brand. However, there are thousands of these trucks in Caracas. Tens of thousands in Venezuela."

"What makes this one special?"

"You'll see." A swipe, and a new photo, this one of a non-descript bodega, and then another swipe to reveal a map. "We found Petrikov's phone in a random farm truck. Our men from the embassy interviewed the farmers, and their story matched the location history from Petrikov's phone. The route that the phone traced had done a one-hundred-and-eighty-degree turn at the bodega, where the farmers had stopped before heading to their work for the day. The theory is that the phone was dumped into the truck, by Petrikov or by one of his accomplices. The bodega is on a route out of the city."

"Theory," Rodionov repeated with a dismissive wave of his hand.

Swipe. A photo of a policeman. "This officer claimed he stopped a dark-colored pickup truck, driven by a dark-skinned man, in Quenepe. A coastal village just south of the Port of La Guaira."

"Coincidental," spat Rodionov. "And we learned this when?"

"Four days ago. The *Policía Nacional Bolivariana* are not known for their expediency. And this particular report was from the local police. They took their time relaying it to the *Policía Nacional*. But it is the last two photos that we received from them just yesterday that are the most interesting."

"Continue."

Swipe. A photo of a different policeman. "This second officer claimed he saw a dark-colored pickup truck, driven by a Black man, and carrying a woman and three other men, parked near Plaza Soublette, on the last night of *Carnaval*. The vehicle was abandoned. It was traced to an address in Quenepe. It was registered to that address on the Friday before *Carnaval*."

"To whom?"

Fedor didn't have a swipe for that, and he explained, "The address is a simple home, high in the hills above Quenepe. The home is owned by a local. Ariadna something. She rented it through Airbnb to an American named Akmal Sayed. The truck was registered in the American's name. We have no records of the American."

"Find that person. And continue," Rodionov demanded.

A swipe later, and all of the photos on-screen disappeared and were replaced by a single, blurry, black-and-white photo of a fair-skinned woman, in a light-colored dress, carrying a backpack, her body partially blocking a figure of a dark-skinned man. Obscured behind them was what appeared to be a trio of men. Further in the background, a parked dark-colored pickup truck was barely visible.

Rodionov put his feet to the floor, abandoning the reclined mode of the fancy chair as he blurted, "I've already seen that picture, as you know. Useless. The problem is that this is all disparate evidence, cobbled together. There is absolutely nothing definitive. We have a truck that passed the embassy in the city, and possibly the same truck reappeared at the coastline. We have nothing unless you tell me you've got a better photo than this."

Fedor was nonplussed by his superior's reaction. "This is the only security camera at Plaza Soublette, on the beach near the Port of La Guaira. And, while we don't have a better photo as you've requested, we do have the technological capabilities to enhance and colorize it, which our technicians have been working on since we received the image."

A final, triumphant swipe transformed the photo from a blurry image to a supercomputer enhanced masterpiece, and Rodionov shot to his feet, exclaiming, "The woman is Volkov! In Venezuela?"

With two fingers, Fedor zoomed the photo closer, and one of the faces of the trio of men in the background came into focus. Instantly recognizing the bloated middle face, Rodionov yelled, "Petrikov!"

"Yes, but additional intel has come to our attention from the Venezuelans. The story gets worse from our perspective," Fedor said, quietly and cautiously. "Eyewitnesses told the police that the five of them boarded a helicopter that came in for a fast landing on the beach, and took off equally quickly, headed out to sea."

"And the Venezuelans missed this? How is that possible? How is it possible to miss a fucking helicopter landing on your beach?" Rodionov's booming voice was hoarse with ire and frustration.

"We've asked that question many times. The usual excuse is *Carnaval*. The naval base at the Port Coast Guard station was understaffed. The radar operator was allegedly hung over and was not keeping a close watch on the radar. The eyewitnesses at the beach were drunk. They assumed the helicopter was part of the entertainment. And so on. Regardless, it was reported that the radar operator at the Port Coast Guard station claimed to observe what appeared to be a boat, but which then sped up to a very fast speed as it went to what was obviously its landing point near the Plaza. Then it disappeared."

Rodionov sank into his chair, muttering, "How does it disappear?"

"The Coast Guard station radar is designed for sea-level vessel surface intercepts. It's not a tall antenna, which limits the range. Furthermore, it is a slow-sweep antenna intended for slow-moving marine targets. A fast-moving helicopter, flying low, will disappear quickly into the surface clutter from the radar returns, especially as it gets further and further from the base antenna."

Shaking his head, defeated and disappointed, Rodionov grumbled, "Fine. And who is the man next to Volkov? Who are the men on either side of Petrikov?"

"We don't know."

Rodionov was shaking his head, saying, "On one hand, I marvel at the audacity. Volkov is creative. And aggressive. I must say, I respect that. But she's made one mistake."

"What's that?"

"She has revealed that she is alive and well. She has revealed that she has help. Look at these assets. She has access to a helicopter. To men. Where does she get them? How does she pay them? With promises? With IOU's from Petrikov's accounts?" Rodionov shot to his feet and began to pace, growling, "Or is the American government involved?"

Spinning on his heels, Rodionov faced the giant screen, announcing, "We're going back to America. We have people there. We will dig. We will—"

Fedor held up a cautionary hand, interrupting, "Sir, there's a problem, as you must know. The World Health Organization has labeled the outbreak of coronavirus as a global pandemic. The Americans have placed a ban on any travel to or from Europe. International flights are being canceled. Travel is becoming more and more difficult."

Rodionov snorted. "That is true, and that will create some friction. But you forget. We are Unit 29155. We report to no one but President Putin. We'll find Anastasia Volkov, pandemic or not. Enough tiptoeing around, Fedor. Volkov has invaded Venezuela and rescued her father. It's our turn. And as they say in America, now the gloves are off."

CHAPTER
42

FRIDAY, MARCH 13, 2020 – 14° 20' N, 061° 33' W

ALMAZ HAD BEEN LOAFING through the clear, tropical blue waters of the Caribbean Sea for sixteen days since we brought Anatoly Petrikov aboard. To conserve fuel, and because we had nowhere to go, Lockwood kept the engine revolutions low. In fact, he shut one engine down for several days so that our engineer, Warren Parnell, could service it, and then Lockwood reversed the process for the other engine. The crew aboard *Almaz* were professionals. Even Petrikov was impressed that Lockwood was taking such good care of the yacht.

I was beginning to understand how Petrikov had been so successful, operating as a legitimate businessman and, at the same time, as a mobster. He had a certain charm, I hated to admit. But I remained carefully removed, even as we met for lunch almost every day for the past two weeks.

I had not done this cavalierly, of course, and ensured that we were joined by at least one other member of the Quadrant team. Jacquard would deliver a scrumptious meal, I would carefully pour Petrikov glass after glass of chilled vodka, and Petrikov began to talk.

It hadn't happened immediately, naturally. He was reserved and dismissive at our first lunch, but I think he eventually realized, after I explained just the bare minimum of how the Quadrant operation came to be, that he had no options. I told him transparently that we were merely marking days, that the virus was holding us up, and that he might as well enjoy what little time he had left on the yacht. After a couple of lunches, he began to open up, and once the deluge began, my main concern was that we would run out of vodka. Lockwood assured me that wouldn't happen.

I know it might sound strange, but I got the sense he was relieved to confess. Relieved, and proud—Petrikov bordered on boastful, and my time with him generated a trove of national security intelligence.

"Vitaly Nikolaevich Rodionov. He's the mastermind of Unit 29155," Petrikov had explained a few days ago, during one of our long lunches on the aft *al fresco* dining area of the yacht. He sipped his vodka contemplatively before adding, "Fedor and Gregoriy. His two assistants at one time. Those two never used last names."

"Anyone else?"

"Eventually, yes. But he was careful, of course, not to introduce me."

"He?"

"Rodionov," Petrikov explained. "Not only did he run the Unit, but he was also my handler."

I sniffed with scorn, "*Your* handler? I thought *you* were in charge."

I knew I had baited him, almost insulted him with my tone, and Petrikov scowled. "I *was* in charge. But I needed technical help, which I received from Rodionov. He, however, played me."

The malice was evident in Petrikov's voice and on his face, and I dared not push further, fearing that I would trigger the rage that Volkov warned me about. I took a new tack by asking, "He played you? When did that happen? Or when did you become aware of that?"

Petrikov took a sip of his vodka, and I watched as his eyes clouded while his scowl faded. "Yes. I was unaware, at first, but you're correct. His intent was evident, and I missed it. In fact, that blunder has cost me dearly."

"Blunder?"

Crossing his arms over his chest, Petrikov clarified, "It's a chess term for a very bad move. An oversight in overall tactics. I finally realized my mistake in Venezuela."

I began to put it together, and I asked to confirm, "In Caracas? Rodionov was in Caracas?"

"For the most part, yes," Petrikov replied. "At the beginning. Then I saw less and less of him. He took what I had to offer, but in return, gave me only promises. To bring me to Russia. To give me asylum. But in fact, all he gave me was a device to play chess on. To pass the time. Which, as I came to discover, was so that *he* had the time to decide if I was disposable," Petrikov concluded, grumbling.

From the tale that he had told me, I tended to agree. He had been used and then stashed in Venezuela until they figured out whether he still had value.

And that tale! I could write a book if it ever became declassified. I'd call it *Threat Bias*. I finally understood what I was up against and how I completely misjudged the threat because of my biases. It was an important lesson.

It took me a full day to summarize my discussions with Petrikov in an email, which I had sent to Macallister yesterday. He confirmed receipt without comment, and also replied that he would give us further instructions on what to do with our guest today. Seated in my usual spot in the situation room, I waited for Macallister to connect our scheduled secure video teleconference.

The Quadrant team members were all in place around our table, trying to forecast what Macallister would say. "We're going back to Portsmouth," wagered Rourke. "They'll stash him in a CIA safe house in Virginia."

"Nah," countered Havens. "Miami. Plenty of agents there with facilities for interviews due to the drug trade. The D.C. area is too obvious."

Robinson remained quiet. I think he just wanted to go home.

He would be disappointed.

The screen lit, and Macallister's face appeared. In the two weeks since we'd seen him last, he'd aged. His face was pale and drawn, and his eyelids were heavy. He looked like shit and sounded worse when he began speaking. "This is unprecedented. The President just declared a national emergency. Sporting events and concerts are being canceled. Schools will close. Non-essential businesses will close. Travel is shut down. Planes and trains are empty. The stock market is way down. There's talk of shutting down the nation."

Aboard our 235-foot yacht, we were speechless. Macallister continued, "I'm afraid this is just the beginning. People are scared. They are stockpiling food. You can't even find toilet paper in the stores."

Robinson's head sagged as Rourke asked, "What's the status of our stores?"

As a rule, Lockwood monitored our consumables carefully and thoughtfully. He cupped a hand under his chin and said, "We're good for two more weeks. We could start rationing and stretch that out. Petrikov eats and drinks a lot. Can we cut him back?"

I wasn't sure if Lockwood was joking, but I didn't have to ask because Macallister said, "You can cut him loose. Porter's email yesterday was helpful and gave us a great deal of information, and we can get more with trained interviewers."

"That's a little unfair." I was offended. I was proud of myself; my tactic to wine and dine Petrikov had been successful. He had wanted a taste of his old life, and I had given it to him. He had repaid the favor by talking. I considered it a win/win.

Macallister was blunt. "I appreciate the work, Porter. But Petrikov is no longer a threat. This virus is the current threat. I have to focus on that for the moment. In the meantime, I've arranged for custody for Petrikov. You're taking him to Gitmo."

I asked, "Guantanamo Bay?"

"Yeah," Macallister confirmed. "But you can't dock that boat in Cuba. Someone will see if for sure. Nor can you fly him in. I haven't disclosed that you have a helicopter. And, anyway, an air approach will attract too much attention. We gotta keep it subtle. We gotta keep this under the radar. Can you do that?"

"Of course, sir," I replied. "We got Petrikov out of Venezuela. We can get him into Cuba."

"Good. I don't know how far from Cuba you are, so get there as fast as you can. Lemme know your arrival time, and I'll handle the receipt. You figure out how to get him to the beach. Send me an Ops Order with the details. I gotta go. The world is ending here."

He abruptly terminated the connection, and I realized that we were within days of completing our mission. Or so I thought, in error.

43

MONDAY, MARCH 16, 2020 – 19° 15′ N, 075° 44′ W

DURING THE TWO-AND-A-HALF days it took to travel to our mission commencement point, we had started to pay much closer attention to the news feeds that we could get through the yacht's high-tech comms systems. As we motored into position during the late afternoon of Monday, March 16, we learned that the nation would be effectively closed in an attempt to contain the contagious coronavirus. "Fifteen days to slow the spread" was the refrain on every news channel. We were shocked.

Well, most of us. Hamid played his games on the Trampoline app, claiming that it was his breakthrough that got us to Petrikov. Meanwhile, Robinson paced the decks, worried about his family back home in Chicago, as Havens attempted to console him. "From what I'm seeing in the news, the virus is concentrated in the northeast. New York, New Jersey, New England."

"I gotta get off this boat," Robinson muttered.

"I can't get you home, but I can get you off. At least, for a short while," I offered. "Mission planning recap, situation room. Macallister has confirmed that go-time is tonight. Let's run through the mission one more time. Let's roll."

∗ ∗ ∗

At one in the morning, Havens barged into Petrikov's cell and jabbed him in the ass with somewhat less than the usual Ketamine dose. As soon as the potent anesthesia took its effect, Havens and Robinson carried the obese Russian immigrant to the aft deck.

Our mission outline called for redundancy where possible. We planned to send two teams out into the night; we would have a transport boat with Petrikov, and, as a contingency, we would send a second boat with extra hands, gear, and weapons. Lockwood's crew had already launched both of our military-specification rigid hull inflatable boats. Each RIB was equipped with two Yamaha XF425 outboard motors, and with the combined thrust of 850 horsepower, each boat topped out at sixty knots of speed. Naturally, the boats and motors were painted flat black.

Petrikov was lowered into one of the boats, and Havens and Robinson flanked him in order to restrain him when the tranquilizing agent wore off. Rourke was behind the wheel, grinning, her white teeth and the whites of her eyes the only parts of her black-clad body reflecting any light.

Similarly dressed, Lockwood and I had already cast off from *Almaz*, and we floated aboard our boat about fifty feet away, invisible in the dark, overcast, moonless night. *Almaz* herself was also unlit, every light extinguished. Even the screens on the bridge, where Alverez conned the yacht, were dimmed. The shades were tightly drawn in the situation room, where Volkov and Hamid would monitor the mission on the big screens, each of them responsible for tracking one RIB each.

My earpiece clicked, and I heard Rourke's voice softly say, "Engaging engines. First leg, on my mark. Three . . . Two . . . One . . . *Go*."

Lockwood advanced the throttles, and our RIB lifted immediately onto a plane, water whishing by as the boat accelerated effortlessly to a cruising speed of forty knots. The only visible sign of Rourke's boat was its wake, just to our left as Lockwood maintained a position off Rourke's back-right quarter. The boats would run in tandem for ten miles before separating in order to present an even smaller target on any shore-based radar sweep.

It's not every day that you get to do a nighttime run, at sea, into communist Cuba.

Like Rourke's exfil from the beach in Venezuela, we plotted a zig-zag course toward the shoreline. From fifty miles offshore, the course that was pre-programmed into each boat's GPS system would total sixty miles due to the turns, and we would run for an hour and fifteen minutes at speed, then slow for the final, short leg to the target, a small stretch of beach east of the United States military base at Guantanamo Bay, Cuba.

✳ ✳ ✳

Click. Click. Click.

The first signal. Havens and Robinson, dressed in black, full-body wetsuits, would have tossed Petrikov over the side of their RIB. Volkov had given us a key piece of intel: Petrikov could barely swim. He'd built *Almaz* because he liked to be *on* the water, not *in* the water. He'd be panicking, disoriented, and splashing about, his reaction times also slowed by the recovery trajectory of the Ketamine. Havens would swim to his side and offer a flask of vodka while Robinson helped keep him afloat. The vodka was laced with a mild sedative.

A mile offshore, engines quietly idling but ready to race to shore if required, Lockwood and I could do nothing but wait as Petrikov was swum to the beach, where, if Macallister had done his job, four Marines would relieve us of our charge.

I was chewing on my fingernails when I heard a *click*, and I began counting, saying to myself, *Only three. Not five.* Five clicks would mean a problem, and Lockwood and I would be en route to Cuba.

My earpiece clicked two more times, and I exhaled. Havens and Robinson were back aboard Rourke's RIB, and she was headed out to sea. I poked Lockwood and whispered, "They're off the beach." Lockwood pressed a button on his watch to start a timer. Ten long minutes began counting down as Rourke would slowly work the RIB away from the beach.

As Lockwood's watch neared the end of the countdown and displayed 1:56, 1:55, 1:54, it happened.

Click. Click. Click. Click. Click.

CHAPTER
44

THROUGH HIS EARPIECE, Lockwood heard the emergency clicks, too, and to my surprise, he turned both ignition keys to the *Off* position. Removing his earpiece, the sailor cocked his head toward the water and began to turn his body in a slow circle. The only noise that I could hear was the gentle lapping of waves against our RIB.

In the pitch-black at sea, there was no frame of reference except for the dim glow of our GPS screen. There was nothing. My heart raced. I was scared. I chided myself, *Pull it together, Ben.*

Lockwood had stopped spinning and was facing to the left of our boat when my earpiece clicked again five times. I hissed, "They signaled again."

"Yeah, I got 'em," whispered Lockwood. Without moving his head, he reached his right hand for the right-most ignition key, and he turned it. The big Yamaha whirred to life, and again without looking, Lockwood notched the right-hand throttle into the forward position. The RIB began to turn left, and as the boat's direction swiveled to match the aim of Lockwood's stare, he used the steering wheel to counteract the off-center thrust of the starboard engine to straighten our course. With almost casual, unhurried motion, he removed his right hand from the throttle and reinserted his earpiece without moving his head, his left hand making tiny adjustments to the steering wheel as he stood immobile.

I wanted to date him. Well, no, not really. But I could see what Volkov saw in Lockwood: his absolute calm and his overwhelming, instinctive confidence. Just watching him made me, in fact, feel that confidence. I matched his stance, leaning my head just slightly forward and cocked imperceptibly to the right, my feet planted, my body swaying gently with the movement of the boat.

Looking forward with a focus that I had never experienced before, I felt that my senses were as intensely tuned as they'd ever been, and I caught a glimpse of movement in the waves. I jabbed Lockwood in the ribs and commanded, "Stop."

Lockwood clicked the throttle to neutral as I knelt on the RIB's right-side tube, saying with as much composed coolness as I could, "Pardon me. Have you any Grey Poupon?"

In the water, Havens snorted, and mimicking a London accent, said, "Sorry, old chap. I'm afraid I've run out."

"Oh, dear," I breathed, asking, "Well, what brings you to this part of the world?"

"Seems we've hit a spot of trouble. Ran over a floating fishing net. Both propellers are hopelessly fouled. Don't go any closer," he warned, ditching the goofy voice and replacing it with one that was dead-on serious.

Lockwood leaned over my shoulder and wondered aloud, "And you thought you'd swim our direction and hope to be rescued?"

"I was about to signal you with my light, but Porter spotted me. Nice going, Ben. Pull me aboard with this towline. Rourke and Robinson are cutting as much of the net free. Maybe we can pull the boat away from the mess and clear the props."

Lockwood and I dragged the big guy aboard and secured the towline. Starting the second engine, Lockwood carefully applied throttle pressure as the towline came taught. The RIB began to move through the water.

The weight of the tow was evident by the bar-tight towline and the straining propellors, churning angrily and frothing the seawater as Lockwood increased power until the boat plodded at only ten knots, but at the same revolutions that had previously driven us at forty knots. After only two-and-a-half minutes, Lockwood shook his head, "This is futile. We must be dragging way more net than boat. The engines are beginning to overheat, we're making too much noise, and going too slow."

I made a decision, channeling my newly discovered inner Lockwood, and I said evenly, "Lockwood, cut the throttles. Havens, follow the towline back to the other RIB. When you get there, sink the boat and use the towline to pull yourselves back to us. Got it?"

"Yep," he replied without emotion, and with one hand lightly gripping the towline, he disappeared into the night over the back of our RIB.

We waited several minutes. Lockwood kept examining the instrument panel gauges and reported, "Engine temperatures have returned to normal."

He was shaking his head morosely, and I asked, "What?"

"These engines are like forty-five thousand bucks *each*. And Havens is out there somewhere, scuttling a RIB with two perfectly good engines on it. What a shame."

"Petrikov will buy us a new RIB," I reassured him.

"Petrikov is not gonna be happy with his new accommodations."

"No, I don't think he will be," I agreed. We remained silent until the towline splashed, and Havens, Robinson, and Rourke clambered aboard. Lockwood pushed the throttles down, and the RIB flew over the waves as we raced to our rendezvous with *Almaz*.

It was my turn for moroseness. I was ashamed of myself. I had the team knock out Petrikov, and they dumped him at Gitmo. Despite our differences, Petrikov had been polite and respectful with me. He had been forthcoming with information. The least I could have done was have the courage to speak with him directly, to let him know what his fate would be, and to look him in the eye. I had taken the easy route, a cowardly route.

It was a bitter pill to swallow, and yet we'd accomplished our mission, and our target was in custody. I could sense that the team was ready to celebrate as our sole remaining RIB was hoisted aboard *Almaz*. Alverez engaged the yacht's engines to drive us away from Cuba as wetsuits and black night ops gear were exchanged for t-shirts. The yacht's lights remained extinguished, but a constellation of tiny, red flares glowed as the team gathered on the aft deck to puff cigars and to pour the first of many rounds of drinks.

With one of Petrikov's fine cigars in one hand and a cold, longneck bottle of beer in the other hand, I promised myself that I would never again cave to the easy route. On the next mission, if there was one, I'd be as confident as Lockwood, as graceful as Havens, as energetic as Rourke, and as mindful as Robinson.

Little did I know then that a new mission had already begun and that I'd soon get a fresh chance to prove myself as a leader.

CHAPTER

45

MOSCOW, RUSSIA

AT THE REAR OF THE loft-like Unit 29155 command center, in a glass-enclosed office raised ten feet above the floor, Vitaly Rodionov oversaw, quite literally, the teams of programmers that parsed through the endless stream of data collected from around the globe.

Once one of the best-kept secrets in the world of espionage, the Unit was first exposed in 2019 by the French daily afternoon newspaper *Le Monde.* Instead of dooming the Unit, outing it caused the opposite effect; the Unit was elevated in stature with a shady gravitas. On the rare slow day like this one, Rodionov amused himself by sipping black coffee while combing the Internet for news articles about the Unit to see just how wrong outsider's observations were of reported assassinations, destabilization campaigns, or political coups attempted by the Unit.

The details, Rodionov was pleased to see, were always incomplete, and often suggested failure. Even the Wikipedia entry for the Unit described its operations as "sloppy."

"Never underestimate what you do not understand," Rodionov muttered to himself, his scrolling interrupted by the hiss of the glass door to his office opening.

The normally composed Fedor was panting, perhaps from the climb up the modernist glass stairs to the office, or perhaps from excitement, as he breathlessly announced, "We've identified Ben Porter."

* * *

Fedor Ilin, with his pockmarked, pale, white face, punctuated by dark eyes and topped by a mop of dark hair, appeared entirely unremarkable. But he was remarkable.

A programming prodigy, as he completed the final year of his senior term, or his eleventh year of schooling at the customary graduation age in Russia of seventeen years old, he was recruited by a recently formed, clandestine arm of the Russian military. For the next eleven years, he coded, first working out of the eastern Moscow headquarters of the 161st Special Purpose Specialist Training Center, and then transferring to the newly constructed loft-like command center in 2018, where he was assigned to work directly with Vitaly Rodionov.

Fedor had spent the entirety of his teen and adult life behind a keyboard until Rodionov plucked him from the ranks that manned the sleek tables in the command center, deciding that the remarkable man would have value as an operative, not just as a programmer. Fedor had certainly proved Rodionov's instincts to be correct in the past, and therefore Fedor was his superior's first choice to lead the newly invigorated search for the American Ben Porter.

Fedor and his five-man team had started, five days ago, with the supercomputer enhanced and colorized photo from the beach in Venezuela, and what they discovered was critical.

Like every snowflake is unique, the number of permutations of human facial structures approaches infinity. Cheeks, eyes, ears, chins, mouths, and foreheads all differ, and therefore, if quantified as measurement points, can be used as identifiers. Enter: facial recognition technology.

By identifying eighty nodal points common to all faces, and by analyzing the arrangement of, and distance between, those nodal points, a computer can quantify a face as a mathematical formula. This is colloquially called a "faceprint." Like fingerprints, faceprints can be stored and retrieved at will. They can also be compared.

The sheer quantity of photographs available online is staggering; one study in early 2020 suggested that 1.4 trillion pictures would be taken in the 2020 calendar year alone, and a 2019 analysis estimated that 250 billion photos have been uploaded to Facebook, which is where Fedor Ilin tasked the computers and technicians of Unit 29155 to begin searching for matches to the faces found in an enhanced Venezuelan beach surveillance camera image.

Five days after that painstaking and tedious search began, Fedor was ready to triumphantly reveal to Rodionov that they had an image to match a name, first explaining, "Facial recognition technology often has difficulty with incomplete profiles, and therefore we first isolated one of the men in the background, who had the most complete, visible facial structure, and who was next to Petrikov in the picture from the surveillance camera. We created a faceprint and then began running comparisons, starting with Facebook."

Fedor passed over the tablet that he had carried to his superior's office to Rodionov, whose eyes narrowed as he examined the device. Fedor narrated, "The image on the tablet is a screen shot of a Facebook page. The date of the post is May 2012. The caption reads, 'Me and my little Benbro.'"

"What does that mean? And who are these two people? The man and the woman in the Facebook photo?"

"Allow me to finish, please," Fedor pled. "That Facebook page belongs to the woman in the photo. She lives in Bristol, Rhode Island." Rodionov's eyes went wide as Fedor added five words: "Her name is Grace Porter."

Rodionov made the link quickly. "Grace Porter? The same Grace Porter we attempted to surveil?" Fedor nodded affirmatively as Rodionov guessed, "Am I to conclude, I hope, that the person in the photo, with Volkov, on the beach in Venezuela, is Ben Porter?"

"Yes. It's a definitive match to the faceprint from the beach photograph. It's even roughly the same angle."

"Expand the search," Rodionov ordered excitedly. "I will get authorization to use as much computing power as we can get. There could be more photos of Porter online, now that we know what he looks like. Find them. And work on the other individuals in the beach photo. Find more links."

"Yes, sir."

Locking eyes with Fedor, Rodionov breathed, malice in his voice, "Porter took Petrikov. Porter *and* Volkov." He closed his eyes for a moment and then snapped them open. "Ben Porter did this. I'll have Putin put a bounty on his head out to the entire Russian intelligence and military apparatus. From this moment on, Porter and Volkov shall be considered as enemies of the Russian state."

APRIL

CHAPTER
46

FOR IMMEDIATE RELEASE

APRIL 19, 2020

CONTACT: GOODCLEANFUN@TRAMPOLINE.LIVE

SAN FRANCISCO, CALIFORNIA, UNITED STATES.
Melissa Zhao, founder and Chief Executive
Officer of Trampoline Inc., announced
today that the company's Trampoline.Live
social network platform has reached the
milestone of 500 million subscribers,
with users located in every country on
the planet. With characteristic modesty,
Zhao acknowledged the happenstance of
the coronavirus pandemic in the success

of the platform, saying humbly, "I dare
not say Trampoline went viral, but that's
what you're all thinking, so we might as
well acknowledge it. And while I wish it
happened under different circumstances,
at the same time, I hope that our
platform of 'good, clean fun!' has been
a gift of simple pleasure in such dark
days for all of us, a way to connect us
together during a time when we all must
be apart."

The user base of the platform grew 500%
since the beginning of the year. Howard
Weatherstone, a nationally recognized
Wall Street analyst specializing in
social media companies, noted that
"the speed of subscriber growth is
unprecedented, and it demonstrates not
only how reliant the consumer has become
on mobile platforms for entertainment and
connection, but also that these types of
platforms have become a significant core
of the online user experience."

In terms of scale, Trampoline is roughly
30% larger than Twitter and 50% smaller
than Instagram. However, based on
current rates of user adoption, which
have been increasing on an exponential
curve, CEO Zhao expects that Trampoline
will match and then exceed Instagram's
one billion users by the end of August
2020. Zhao added, "Keeping size in
perspective, even then Trampoline will

still have less than half the reach of
Facebook at 2.7 billion users. However,
as I've done since founding the platform,
I remain committed to my promise to
our users that we will never abandon
our morals and integrity in pursuit of
growth. That growth is only a means to
be more inclusive and to connect each of
us to more of our fellow global citizens.
We're not about making money. We're about
making connections."

As a privately held firm, Trampoline
does not release revenue or profit data.
However, summary subscriber data,
including daily usage, user engagement,
conversions, response rate, and time on
platform, are all available to accredited
media organizations or interested
advertising or commercial partners by
application to the contact email address
above.

###

CHAPTER
47

APRIL 19, 2020 – MONTEGO BAY, JAMAICA

I ASSUMED THAT THE REST of the team felt as stir crazy as I did.

Since dumping Petrikov in Cuba almost a month ago, we had retreated to the only harbor where we could find both fuel and provisions—and who would not turn us away, perhaps due to some high-up diplomatic work by Macallister. Jamaica was accepting no visitors due to the Covid-19 pandemic, but we were permitted to tie off at the empty cruise ship terminal where a bunker truck came alongside to fill our fuel tanks, provided we departed the dock immediately thereafter and dropped anchor in the harbor. Lockwood and Jacquard were permitted to go ashore, under escort, to shop for supplies. However, even though they had the foresight to stock up on local beer and rum, the evening cocktails on *Almaz* were clouded due to the tempest that we knew was swirling back home.

If the drumbeat of news via our high-tech comms system was depressing for us, quarantined on a luxury yacht in a beautiful Caribbean harbor, we could only imagine what it was like in the States and elsewhere in the world. Each evening, at seven, we'd raise our glasses northward, hoping to feel solidarity with the ceremony that would be taking place thousands of miles away, that we would watch on television, as people from all walks of life and in cities and towns around the globe banged on pots and pans and clapped for first responders.

By day, we had little to do. Our instructions from Macallister were to wait it out. I was beginning to understand that he, and, well, everyone else, may have underestimated just how long the wait would be. We filled our time with mindless maintenance on the yacht, hoping every morning that we would have clarity. That day had yet to arrive as I wandered the decks of *Almaz*, finding Hamid lounging on the helipad.

"Bro, you ever take a break from that thing?"

Hamid risked a glance away from his smartphone screen to glower at me, grunting a blunt, "Huh?"

"Take a break, man. Let's launch the RIB, head out of the harbor, and throw some fishing lines in the water. Have a few beers. Have some laughs."

"Nah. That's too much work."

I gave up and meandered forward, finding Robinson leaning against the high-gloss varnished, wood-topped rail, facing the colorful shoreline of Montego Bay. A gentle, warm breeze tickled his t-shirt, and his feet were bare against the teak decks of *Almaz*. I repeated the proposition that I had just made to Hamid, "Hey, man. Wanna go fishing?"

Robinson cracked the slightest of grins. "Yes and no. No, because it's gonna remind me of my kids. Yes, 'cuz I got nothin' better to do. Maybe a distraction will be good for me."

"That's the spirit," I cheered.

Together, we walked further aft toward the crane that would launch the RIB. I was guessing we'd find someone else there, Dunn or Alverez or even Lockwood, to help us. And maybe go with us.

Robinson and I coerced Dunn into lowering the RIB into the water, but he declined the invite to our little expedition. Not that it would be much of an adventure—the local officials had little else to do other than keep an eye on the strange, foreign, 235-foot expedition-style yacht, so we knew we'd be watched. Just puttering a few hundred yards from *Almaz* felt like an escape, though, and the officials turned a blind eye to our fishing trips. And by "blind eye," I mean they probably shielded their vision with the image of Benjamin Franklin on the bills that Lockwood "tipped" them with, thanking them for their hospitality in Montego Bay.

Lines in the water, with "Oracabessa Moonshine" by UB40 playing softly in the background from the RIB's stereo speakers, Robinson and I relaxed, assuming that there was little to no chance that we'd catch anything. I knew he was hurting, and I chose to keep my mouth shut, waiting for him to talk. After a sip from a sweating bottle of Red Stripe beer, Robinson finally muttered, "Thanks, Porter. I needed to get off that boat, even if it was to trade for a smaller boat. I can't believe we're stuck here."

"Yeah, I'm sorry, man."

"I didn't sign up for this."

"I know," I said, with what I hoped was a reassuring tone to my voice. "I emailed Macallister from one of the dummy accounts. It was a cryptic note, but he got the gist. He promised to look into alternatives."

"It's ridiculous," Robinson sighed. "We infiltrated a prisoner into Cuba. *Cuba!* Can't you just drop me off in Florida? Key West, maybe?"

"No need for the Ketamine, I presume?"

Robinson laughed heartily. "Are you kidding? No way. I'd go willingly."

It was good to hear him laugh, and I replied, "Tell you what. That's not a bad idea. I'll propose it to the team tonight at cocktails."

Robinson turned to me wide-eyed. "Really? I might get to go home?"

I picked up my stubby, brown-glass bottle of the local beer, and we clinked bottles in a toast as I said, "To home."

Robinson nodded solemnly and repeated, "To home."

As I sipped my Red Stripe, I asked myself, *I'm an American, working on behalf of the American government, and yet I'm considering infiltrating the United States? Has it come to this?*

48

THE QUADRANT TEAM GATHERED in our situation room on the afternoon of Monday, April 20 with a renewed sense of energy. We had outlined the mission the night before and reviewed it that morning. It would follow the model that we'd already once executed successfully. I figured it was a slam dunk to sell it to Macallister.

Turning to Volkov, who was, as usual, seated to my right, I asked, "Did you download it yet?"

"Yeah, but why? We have a secure comms link. This Zoom platform is anything but secure," she complained.

"Macallister emailed and said he was working from home today. They're rotating staff in and out of the headquarters building to keep the number of people inside down," I explained.

She shook her head. "Whatever. Anyway, I created an account, and I emailed him a link. All he has to do is click the link."

We sat in silence, waiting. Hamid's face was lit with the glow of his smartphone screen as usual, while Robinson and Havens stared at their reflections in the polished, black table. Lockwood leaned back in his chair and closed his eyes while Rourke fidgeted.

Accompanied by the *ding dong* trill of a simulated doorbell sound, the center screen lit with an image of Macallister. It looked like he was sitting at a table in his kitchen, wearing a white button-down shirt and a loosely knotted red tie. His hair, normally perfectly trimmed, was shaggy. His cheeks were puffy, and it also looked like he'd eaten whatever once filled the empty Styrofoam and paper take-out-type containers that littered the countertops behind him.

His lips were moving, but there was no sound. I shot a look at Volkov, who said, "All my settings are correct. We've got sound. But we can't hear him." She fiddled a moment longer and then yelled at the screen, "Macallister! You're on mute. You have to unmute yourself."

I don't read lips, but clearly his response was "What?" as he shrugged, his face leaning in and dominating, uncomfortably, our giant screen. I could see his pores and . . . *gross!* . . . his nose hairs.

Rourke chuckled, "He's a hot mess. What's up with that?"

"You're on mute," Volkov repeated. She pantomimed as she spoke, "Move your mouse arrow to the bottom left. There's an icon with a red microphone-looking-thingy with a diagonal line through it. Click there."

"This is a horror show," Rourke giggled.

"CAN YOU HEAR ME NOW?" Macallister's voice boomed from the speakers flanking the big screen and from surround-sound speakers built into the perimeter of the situation room.

Through Rourke's peals, Macallister yelled, "WHAT ARE YOU LAUGHING AT?"

"You don't need to yell," Rourke gasped. "We can hear you just fine now. Use a normal voice, please!"

"Oh," he said, finally pulling his face away from the eye of the camera on what had to be a laptop because the angle kept changing as he adjusted the tilt of his screen. "We good now?"

"Yes, sir," I stated, trying to be professional, as Rourke examined the table to regain her composure and as Volkov rolled her eyes in disbelief. "Sir," I went on, "thank you for connecting. I won't take too much of your time. We want to propose a solution to get Robinson and Havens back home."

"Alright. Make it fast. I got another meeting soon."

"It's a simple plan, sir. A quick outline starts with an easy, 1,000-mile journey at sea, leaving Jamaica, jogging west around Cuba, and then turning northeast to Key West. Then, we'd parallel the islands of the Florida Keys, leaving them well to the north but within range of the RIB. All we need is your approval, and an FBI car to meet Robinson and Havens somewhere along a desolate stretch of Route A1A, maybe at one of the ends of the Seven Mile Bridge."

"No way. I can't authorize that." Macallister crossed his arms defiantly across his chest.

Robinson faced the camera and protested, "Sir. With all due respect. I commenced this mission on February 15. It was supposed to run for two weeks. I was assigned to stay with the mission, and we successfully disembarked our target into Cuba a month later. Now we are past the middle of April."

Macallister didn't back down. "I'll remind you that you are assigned to the Critical Incident Response Group. You follow orders, Special Agent Robinson."

Robinson shook his head back and forth and lowered his gaze, demurring, "I know. I know—apologies, sir, for my outburst. But, again, with respect, sir, I don't think it is too much to ask to have a car meet us and to pull some strings with Immigration. Sir."

Softening, Macallister conceded, "I understand the uniqueness of the situation, but I cannot authorize a clandestine entry into the States without compromising the secrecy of your group. It's just not possible. And it's a damn good thing that you didn't try this stunt on your own. I wouldn't put *that* past you, Porter."

"No sir, of course not," I agreed pleasantly, thinking, *It had occurred to me, though.*

Macallister barreled on, saying, "Nevertheless, I understand the concern. I'll put some effort into a resolution. But you are not to leave Jamaica. Understood?"

There were nods at the table, but no one verbalized a response. Macallister didn't notice or didn't care as he changed the subject. "A new development came to light over the weekend. It seems that someone talked at Gitmo. I was informed that there is a, quote, high probability, unquote, that the Cubans have discovered that there is a new, very large, very surly prisoner who curses out the guards in Russian and who is now residing in the Guantanamo Bay camp. I have no doubt that the Cubans will tell their friends, the Russians, this piece of news."

Volkov's voice rose as she asked, "I might be jumping to a conclusion, but are you saying that the Russians will try to get him back?"

"I dunno," Macallister confessed. "It's a possibility, though. And for that reason, you need to be on standby in Jamaica. How long does it take for you to get back to Cuba?"

"Even accounting for engine start-up and mobilization, we could be there in less than eighteen hours," Lockwood declared.

"Okay, good to know. You're not going yet. They are going to move Petrikov from the camp to a new, secure location at the naval base," Macallister said, looking to his left as we heard the *ding dong* of a doorbell, this time from Macallister's audio feed. "I got another meeting. Gotta go."

Abruptly, Macallister stood, revealing that below the shirt-and-tie combo, he was sporting athletic shorts. He disappeared off-screen. Faintly, we heard the sounds of a door opening and Macallister's voice saying, "What do I owe you?"

Rourke, unable to contain herself, snickered, "He's getting another take-out delivery!"

"I don't think he understands that the connection is still live," I realized.

"I better turn it off before he sits back down and realizes that we are all still watching," Volkov offered. Her mouse arrow hovered over the *End Meeting* icon, but she didn't click, and we heard rustling noises as Macallister reappeared, bearing a brown paper bag. With his back to us, he set the bag on the counter, showing us the hairy backs of his pale, white, untanned legs.

"I can't watch any longer," choked Rourke, and Volkov ended the show with a click.

The team remained in mute astonishment, having had a look into the boss's home and lifestyle, until Robinson broke the silence, "Well, if I can't go home, maybe I get to go back to Cuba."

"Yeah, and we put Petrikov back in *our* custody, on *our* boat," Havens suggested. "That will keep him away from the Russians."

As the team's voices rose around the table as they debated options, I, for once, remained quiet. I couldn't imagine that the Russians weren't having a similar conversation, and that a once-powerful oligarch would not be the only target that they wanted.

No, I thought, *the oligarch's presumed accomplices would also be targeted. The Russians wouldn't know if Petrikov was captured or if he escaped. Either way, they'd probably first assume his daughter was involved. But since she's dead, on paper, they'd likely turn their attention to . . . to me. If, that is, they could identify me.*

I was naïvely unaware that they had already done so, and I was unaware that would be the least of my upcoming challenges.

49

"NOT GONNA LIE. This is a better alternative than goin' back to Cuba."

"I think so," I agreed, smiling at Robinson, who stood with me as we patiently waited for Havens to join us on the aft deck. A day after our Zoom call with Macallister, he had emailed me with a solution, which was complicated by the virus. I reminded Robinson, "It's gonna be a long trip, though."

"Yeah, I get it, but I don't care," Robinson grinned. "Nice of Macallister to get both Havens and me on a State Department plane from Jamaica to Washington, D.C. Havens goes to New York by train, and I fly to Chicago. We both gotta do a virus test, and we both have to stay home for two weeks. No problem for me. Once I get home, I'll be happy not to leave."

"What are you gonna do with your time?"

"I can tell you what I'm not gonna do. What he's doing." Robinson inclined his head toward Hamid, who had come to see the CIRG agents off, but, as usual, who was engrossed by his smartphone.

"It's a real problem," I grumbled dejectedly. "Abdul is not himself. He's been completely sucked into that thing. I don't understand how something like that phone completely enthralls a smart, outgoing dude like Abdul. I mean, this is not him. Now he just mopes around, head down, tapping and swiping."

"I saw that with my kids. There was a time, when I gave them access to phones and tablets, that they did the same thing. They retreated into a virtual universe," Robinson said. "It was an addiction for them. And like any addict, Abdul doesn't know he's also addicted."

"You said there was a time, inferring that was in the past. How did you solve it?"

"I made 'em go cold turkey. Broke the habit, and then once they learned that they could live without the constant use, I figured out a way to wean them back in. You can't avoid social media and all those instant connections, so you gotta manage them."

Havens slung his duffel bag into the RIB, where Lockwood was ready to ferry the CIRG agents to shore, where they'd meet a member of the U.S. State Department staff and be escorted to Kingston for the flight. Havens and I shook hands, and as he released his grip, he grinned, "It was fun working with you, Porter. Let's do it again sometime."

He spun and dropped his big frame into the RIB.

I turned back to Robinson. "You know, back home, everyone has stopped shaking hands. Have you seen it on TV? The elbow bump?"

"Yeah," he laughed, angling his elbow toward mine. "And then there's the foot tap. Like you're dribbling a soccer ball or something." We both looked down and attempted to do the two-step move that we'd watched on television and failed, almost tripping each other.

I got my balance and asked, "How 'bout just an old-fashioned handshake?"

"Nah," Robinson murmured, as he embraced me in a bear hug. "I owe you more than that." Straightening, he looked me in the eye and said, "Porter, you got potential. Keep it up, man. It was a real pleasure to be on your team."

I could only smile as the compliment washed over me.

Robinson followed Havens' path to the rail but paused. Turning to Hamid, he said casually, "Hey, Abdul, whatcha doin'?"

"Uh, nothin'," Hamid muttered.

"Yep. Exactly," Robinson laughed as he yanked the smartphone from Hamid's hands.

"Hey . . ."

"Sorry, pal, but you'll thank me later." Gracefully, Robinson vaulted into the RIB, and Lockwood touched the throttles. As the RIB pulled away from the lee of *Almaz*, Robinson shouted two final words, "Cold turkey!"

Hamid stood still, stunned, his hands still cupped in front of his body, as he watched the RIB, with his phone, disappear to the Montego Bay waterfront.

I didn't realize until much later that this was a turning point.

CHAPTER
50

THE TWINKLING LIGHTS of the homes that dotted the hills beyond Montego Bay, with the glow of the city beneath them, were a festive backdrop to a somber dinner on the aft *al fresco* dining area of *Almaz*. The Quadrant team had lost two big personalities, and a third personality petulantly toyed with his fork, pushing food bits around his plate like a scolded boy.

It was difficult not to laugh at him. Indeed, a laugh would have certainly lightened the mood.

When Hamid scraped his chair back and left the table without a word. Rourke caught my eye and winked, then broke the silence with a giggle. "He's such a man-boy! What the fuck?"

Volkov smirked. "Right? The boy lost his toy, and now he's gonna brood and pout."

"You sure this was a good idea?"

I turned to Lockwood, who had directed that question at me, and I objected. "Wasn't my idea. Robinson just did it. He said, you gotta go cold turkey. You heard him."

"Not just that," Lockwood explained. "What if we need to go back to Cuba? We just lost two of our guys, and the third one is, well, what'd you say? Pouting."

"We're not going back to Cuba," I said confidently. Volkov nodded her agreement as I elaborated. "We've talked about it. And we could be wrong. But we both think it's very unlikely that the Russians will want

Petrikov back. First off, that would signal that he's important to them, which would only add to our interest. Second, they don't know we took him. And by we, I mean the FBI. Could have been CIA or military. Could have been his former *Bratva* accomplices. The Russians might try to put the coincidences together, but at the end of the day, that's all they'll have."

"I don't follow," interrupted Rourke. "If he was an asset, they're not going to care who took him. They'll want the asset back."

"Sure," I agreed, "but that asset will be compromised. They can't know if he has talked or if he has stayed quiet. Besides, if they try to get him back and fail, they've tipped their hand."

"And furthermore," Volkov added, "for what purpose? He had no value to them. His value to them was his connection to me. Frankly, I wonder why they kept him around."

"That's it, then?" Lockwood scratched his chin and said, "Now, what do we do?"

"Good question. We got the bad guy, so now what?" I asked rhetorically, before continuing, "Petrikov told us that he told the Russians my name. Macallister already told us that my cover has been compromised. I think it's time to turn the tables. I think we should chase down Unit 29155."

"That's a tall order," Rourke countered. "Search for Putin's cyberwarfare team? How do you plan to do that?"

I grinned. "I was reminded of something, watching Abdul moaning and groaning at dinner. Remember that Petrikov told me that the Russians gave him a device to play chess on, to pass the time. The Russians know just as much about this stuff as we do. So, how about we draw them out using social media?"

Foolishly, I didn't imagine that the Russians could do exactly the same thing.

CHAPTER

51

MOSCOW, RUSSIA

INFORMATION ONLINE IS information forever, and Fedor Ilin and his team began to dig up link after link from a single photo. After making a connection to Ben Porter's sister in order to identify Ben Porter himself, Fedor had two leads to follow, and he began scouring faceprints to match either Porter sibling.

Ben Porter had apparently been diligent in minimizing his digital footprint, but his sister had no such reservations. Fedor's team created faceprints for every single person in every single photo on Grace Porter's Facebook and Instagram accounts and then drilled down through those new faceprints to identify them. Like following the twisted roots of a tree, this exercise had innumerable variations; for example, if a photo that Grace Porter posted to her Insta feed had four new faces in it, each of the four new faces was faceprinted and then identified, usually through publicly available photos on social media.

It was six weeks after the painstaking and time-consuming exercise began when Fedor rushed to Rodionov's office, carrying a tablet and breathlessly announcing, "Not only have we identified Ben Porter, we've found a credible link to him."

"Explain," demanded Rodionov, focusing his attention on Fedor's tablet.

"We started with Grace Porter's accounts and created thousands of faceprints and leads. One of those leads so far has borne fruit. Look at this," Fedor instructed, as he swiped the tablet to bring up a selfie photo of Grace Porter in the foreground, standing beside a vehicle with an open trunk and luggage. In the background, also near the open rear of a car, was a figure with a darkish complexion. "This photo was posted to Instagram in early 2018. The caption reads, 'A long drive for Grace's jitney service!' I took an interest in this particular photo because of the caption. What is a jitney?"

"This isn't a trivia quiz," Rodionov objected gently.

"Apologies. A jitney is a bus. But this is not a bus, of course. This caption confounded me. In the course of our analysis of all of Grace Porter's photos, we came back to this particular one, because it was one where the caption seemed opaque, and my team zeroed in on the figure in the background."

"And who is that?"

Fedor ignored the question as he continued his explanation. "The figure in the background posts prolifically, but often cryptically, to Instagram. In late December of 2019, he posted this image of himself." Fedor angled the tablet toward Rodionov to show a selfie image of a swarthy, bulbous-nosed, dark Middle Eastern skinned man. In the background, a low, picturesque pedestrian bridge was dotted with lights strung from suspension cables.

"I've seen that bridge," Rodionov exclaimed. "I could see it from the window at the Four Seasons hotel. That's in the Boston Public Garden."

"Exactly," confirmed Fedor. "And just after this photo was posted, what had been a constant stream of posts stopped. Which, as you might recall, is when we determined that Ben Porter was not in Boston."

"Circumstantial. You must have more."

"Indeed. Further inquiries reveal that the man in question is a Special Agent with the FBI. His name is Abdullatif al-Hamid. He had been assigned to the Albany, New York, field office, and he was transferred in December to the Boston field office, where Porter worked before he was terminated. And then he ceased posting."

"Still circumstantial."

"Except for this. Here is a post on Instagram, captioned 'First day of training,' which was posted in early 2018. In fact, a day after the post by Grace Porter." Another photo on the tablet, this one of al-Hamid in a sparsely furnished, concrete block-walled room. As Fedor pinched and dragged his fingers on the touchscreen, he zoomed to the extent of the photo, where a partial face was visible. Then, with a tap on an icon, he joined the Instagram photo to the Venezuelan beach photo, completing the partial face.

Rodionov stared intently at the screen as he exhaled. "Well done. That's our Ben Porter with our new target, this al-Hamid. And this al-Hamid is another FBI agent."

"Precisely."

"Can you find him?"

Fedor grinned. "We already have. We found Mister al-Hamid on another social network, one that you're familiar with, of course. Trampoline. We tracked his device to the cellular networks in Jamaica. He traveled from Kingston to Washington, D.C., and now our new target is in Chicago."

MAY

CHAPTER
52

MONDAY, MAY 4, 2020 – 25° 07' N, 079° 22' W

AS *ALMAZ* MADE A LEFT TURN well off the southeast tip of the Florida penin-
sula, about halfway through the journey from Montego Bay that began
two days ago, on the morning of May 2, I began to get nervous. The
yacht's new course would be northward, and soon our fishing expedition would begin.

Unlike the excursions tootling about the shallow waters at the
perimeter of Montego Bay, this expedition would be far more serious.
We would be fishing for a shady Russian quasi-military operation—using
me as the bait.

The team gathered in the situation room for a final planning session
with Macallister, and I realized that my palms were sweaty. *Chill, Ben,*
I thought, *You're not on the ground. Yet.*

With a *ding dong*, Macallister's face filled the screen. He looked
pretty good; he had slicked his growing, untrimmed hair back with
gel, shaved, and dressed in a suit coat over a dress shirt and tie. He had
clearly spent some time outside in the warming early May weather; his
skin had a more tanned tone to it.

He'd also clearly mastered the Zoom videoconference app since
we'd last seen him, and he had no trouble logging in—a marked departure from Macallister's usual incompetence with all things technical.
The Deputy Assistant Director was all business as he started in, "All

right. Here's an update. Virus cases in the northeast are declining, and the New England states are cautiously reopening. Rhode Island and Massachusetts are imposing a fourteen-day quarantine to any vessel arriving from out of state. Harbors in Connecticut are open. You should find a place to go there."

"A boat this size in a Connecticut harbor is bound to attract attention," Lockwood warned. "Let's go to Rhode Island. This boat could be accommodated in Newport."

Before Macallister could speak, I quickly picked up the conversation. "I know Rhode Island pretty well, too. And my cover story will be that I've been working as a crew member on the yacht, and that I need a new job on land. Newport will have more opportunities."

"Okay, then. That makes sense. But the rest of the plan? Put Porter on the ground, and to get him a job using his real identity? Seems weak to me." Macallister paused before adding, "You want to flush out the Unit, but you're assuming they have some robust intel to have real-time monitoring that will expose you immediately. Or is this an excuse for you to pick up a lazy summer job in some roadside lobster shack somewhere?"

I laughed and replied, "No, and I don't like lobster, anyway. You're right, of course. We have an angle that we think might work."

"What's that?"

"I'm gonna do something I've never done before. Never been comfortable with it. I will plaster myself all over social media. If the Russians are really looking for me, they'll be monitoring social media."

"Social media, huh?" Macallister was scratching his chin. "Like, Facebook?"

"Yes," I confirmed, "and we assume that they monitor, no differently than the US government, all the social media platforms. However, we are going to narrow our focus on only two: Twitter and Trampoline. The former, because it's sort of a free-for-all. And the latter, Trampoline, because you gotta figure that the Russians monitor that, if they allowed Petrikov to use it. It's new and it's small. Anyway, the idea is to focus our efforts on a couple of outlets, not all of them. Quality over quantity, if you will, for my posts and to build my following. To attract attention."

"I'm not sure how that's going to get you attention," Macallister warned. "You're not a, whatchamacallit, an influencer."

He laughed. I didn't.

"That's right. Ben's not. And I'm not either. But I have learned a few tricks," interjected Abdul Hamid.

Since being forcefully parted from his phone weeks ago, Hamid's externally visible emotions shifted from dismay and anger, to acceptance, and then to relief. He began to resemble his former persona, a bit goofy, but also perceptive. To reengage Hamid, Volkov and I had tasked him with an assignment: learn as much as he could about manipulating social media, with specific emphasis on the platform that had captivated him the most, Trampoline.Live.

"The fundamental key to social media is engagement," Hamid explained. "If you want attention, you need eyeballs. To get those eyeballs, you need to grab attention. It's a virtuous cycle, and it can be manipulated."

"How?" Macallister asked.

"It depends on the desired outcome. What we have here is a very targeted desire. We need to focus on Ben Porter. Which, on the surface, seems to be a tall order. He's an average-looking, unremarkable dude."

I played to Hamid's chiding, "And I'm kinda chubby, too."

"True dat," Hamid agreed, barely cracking a smile, "But he does have one redeeming quality. He's got a bit of a sense of humor. And we're gonna use that to get attention."

Macallister was shaking his head. "I don't follow."

"Lemme lay it out," Hamid said. "We're going to start with Trampoline. It's censored, which gives us an advantage because Ben can post with credibility as a former FBI agent. He'll join the conversations and user groups for former agents or for people interested in the Bureau or law enforcement in general. That alone will get some attention. Ben also sets up a Twitter account. He joins the relevant groups there, too, and he can post more freely. Like anti-government rants, for example."

"There's plenty of the latter on Twitter," Macallister laughed. "But Porter has said he's never done social media. How's he going to do all this while holding down the job at the clam shack?"

"I thought it was a lobster shack," I reminded him. "And I'm not. Rourke and Hamid are going to run the accounts for me, with Volkov investigating who connects with me or likes my posts."

Macallister was nodding, "This could work. It's dangerous, though. What prevents the Russians from coming to your hamburger stand with a Makarov?"

"Nothing," I confessed. "However, it's going to take some time to build the following on the accounts. I'll be invisible for a little while. We keep an eye on the number of followers and the activity, and at some point, maybe I need some protection."

"I think you're being cavalier, Porter. And while I agree this might be productive, I also reserve the right to stop it. Understood?"

"Yessir," I agreed.

Macallister grunted and disconnected.

With concern in her voice, Volkov said, "You know, Ben, he's right. With you on the ground, the risks go *way* up."

"I know, but this is a risk that I am willing to accept," I replied. "Here's how I see it. Either I spend the rest of my life hiding from Unit 29155, or I draw them out. It's gonna be the latter."

Soon, I would learn that bravado can be dangerous.

CHAPTER
53

TUESDAY, MAY 5, 2020 – NEW YORK CITY, NEW YORK

IN THE DARKENED control booth of the *Welcome to a New Day, America* morning news and variety program, broadcast live from New York City every morning from seven to ten, East Coast time, the unsung production team worked in silence, their faces eerily lit by the glow of computer and television monitors, mixing boards, and lighting control boards. Through their headsets, they followed the verbal instructions of the television director, who oversaw the production, selected the camera shots, and triggered the cues.

With the talent and the guest both in their seats, and as the makeup crews retreated off-stage after one last application of powder and one final hair adjustment, Vinay Panja slipped his headset on, aligned the attached boom microphone to his lips, and cleared his throat. This was Panja's five-hundred-and-seventy-eighth show in the director's seat. He was neither nervous nor excited. He was a professional, and he would run this segment like every other segment that he'd directed: with precision.

At this exact moment, Panja's attention was focused on two screens: one that showed the live feed, and a second that indicated a clock. He cleared his throat a second time, activated his microphone, and in his clipped voice, began.

Okay, folks. Here we go again. Quiet on the set. Coming back from commercial in five. Four. Three. Two. One.

Cue theme music. Cue graphic: 360° Deep Dive. Rotate graphic and fade to camera one. Slow trolly toward stage while panning to host. And . . . action.

"Good morning. I'm Cleveland Bauer, your host of *Welcome to a New Day, America*. I'm pleased to introduce my three-sixty deep dive guest for today. As you know, our dive-in guest is a new feature of the show, where we spend a full six minutes, or three hundred-and-sixty-seconds, exploring topics that deserve our attention. Today's guest hails from San Francisco, California, and she is the founder and chief executive officer of Trampoline dot Live, the social network that we've come to love. Please welcome—live from our studio in New York City—Melissa Zhao."

Cut to camera two. Slow zoom to close-up of guest.

"Thank you, Cleveland. It's great to be with you, in person. Six feet apart, of course."

Cut to camera three. Hold at full set view.

"Well, Melissa, they tell me it's more like ten feet. This, as I'm sure you're aware, is our first in-studio, live interview with a guest since, what, March?"

"That sounds about right. It's been a difficult spring."

Cut to camera one. Slow zoom to host.

"For many of us, yes. But for many of us, Trampoline dot Live, your new network, has been a place of refuge. An escape. Can you tell us about how it all came to be?"

Cut to camera three, full set, and pan to guest. Slow zoom.

"Sure. It's become my legend, if you will. I started Trampoline when I graduated from Stanford in 2018. I was a computer science major. I wanted to create a different kind of social network. One that would avoid the unattainable perfection on some existing platforms, and one that would discourage the prevalence of hate and negativity we see on others. That's the idea behind our slogan of 'good, clean fun.'"

Cut to camera one.

"That seems utopian, almost simplistic. I hope that doesn't sound offensive, Melissa."

Pan to guest. Zoom.

"Not at all, Cleveland. Instead, I'd call it a strategic decision, one that I made when I started the company. We are based on the concept of 'martial morality,' an idea and culture that I borrowed from my fore-bears in China. These are a combination of the five virtues of deed and the five virtues of mind adopted by the traditional schools of Chinese martial arts. And, in fact, we use those concepts to censor the platform. Rigorously."

Cut to camera three. Full set.

"Censorship, huh? That must take an extraordinary amount of work."

Cut to camera two. Focus on guest.

"Indeed, it does. And that's also where we are community driven. We oversee the platform with volunteers we call *sifu*, which is a word for a 'teacher' of *kung fu*, but in our case, a censor, a wise individual with a strong moral compass. Those who volunteer as *sifu* pass a thorough application and examination process. And then, in turn, they recruit a cadre of trusted members within the platform to help enforce the rules, some of which are written, but many of which are unwritten."

Cut to camera three. Full set. Pan from guest to host.

"And would I conclude that being appointed as a *sifu* or one of their associates is a great honor for a user of the platform?"

Pan from host to guest. Zoom.

"That's absolutely right, Cleveland. Those users hold themselves to the highest standards. They protect the integrity of the platform."

Cut to camera one.

"It seems to be working. Your user base expands daily."

Cut to camera two.

"I'm so grateful for that trust, the trust that users have placed in us. In fact, by the end of the summer, we project that we will be as big as Instagram. One billion wonderful users across this amazing planet, all linked together."

Cut to camera three. Full set.

"That's fantastic, Melissa. Exponential growth, in a very short period of time, and a dedicated and loyal user base. I'd imagine that you're fielding daily calls from Wall Street. Will you take Trampoline public?"

Pan to guest. Zoom out.

"Monetizing this has never been my goal. So no, I don't think so, Cleveland."

Cut to camera one. Focus on host.

"That's admirable, but some say disingenuous. Critics have said you won't go to Wall Street until you've satisfied the Federal Trade Commission, which, for our viewers, I'll clarify is the government agency that has oversight of social media practices and, lately, of privacy concerns. The FTC has launched an investigation of Trampoline. Let's get to the tough question: how do you respond to the FTC's very strong and serious allegations that your app is harvesting your users' private and personal information without their permission?"

Pan to guest. Close up zoom.

"We've been transparent on that, Cleveland. While, of course, I can't talk about the specifics of the FTC investigation in this setting, I can say this: our privacy policies are robust. Respecting our users' privacy is very important. It's part of the integrity of the platform."

Quick fade to camera three. Full set.

"But, with all due respect, that doesn't respond to the question."

Cut to camera two.

"Listen, we've told the FTC that profit is not our motive. We want to keep the platform free to use, and of course we do allow advertising. We've told the FTC that, indeed, we sell your anonymized in-app usage and out-of-app browsing and location history, in order to serve ads that are relevant to you. That's covered in our usage agreements."

Cut to camera one.

"I see. I might add that one of the other criticisms of the platform, by both the FTC and by users, is that Trampoline uses a lot of data, and drains a user's battery. It's been called a data hog. A battery hog. How do you address those complaints?"

Cut to camera two.

"Yes, Trampoline uses a lot of data. But let's be honest with ourselves. Trampoline is appreciated by our users for long stretches of time, and that screen time uses data and battery. We've made it clear these are the tradeoffs for all the functionality you get while you're enjoying our platform. I think users respect that."

Pan to center. Zoom out. Full set.

"Well, it would appear from your numbers—what did you say, one billion users by the end of the summer?"

"That's correct, Cleveland. That's our prediction."

"Well, I'd say, Melissa, that your user growth indicates that your users respect you, and they respect your personal accountability and transparency in this ongoing FTC investigation. And that kind of personal accountability, in the face of such stunning growth and success, Melissa, is a wonderful story, in what has otherwise been a troubling time. Thank you for joining us today. And best of luck."

"Thank you, Cleveland. It's been so rewarding to be here with you."

Cut to camera one. Zoom to host.

"And that's six minutes of dive-in with Trampoline's Melissa Zhao. We'll be back after these brief messages."

Cue theme music. Fade to graphic: 360° Deep Dive. Rotate graphic and fade to black. Cut to commercial. And . . . folks, we're clear.

CHAPTER

54

IT WAS THE MORNING after our Zoom call with Macallister, and Volkov, Hamid, Rourke and I watched a New York-based television news station picked up by the sophisticated comms systems aboard *Almaz*, curious to tune into a much-advertised and hyped interview with the CEO of Trampoline, given that the app had not only been critical to us in locating Petrikov, but also would play a significant role in our new operation to bait Unit 29155.

In the living area of *Almaz*, I set down my morning coffee cup and picked up the television remote control. Stabbing the *mute* button, I wondered, "Where'd she get the money?"

"You're so cynical, Porter," Hamid scolded me. "She's optimistic, kind, and bubbly. No wonder celebrities and influencers are signing up for accounts on Trampoline. They see an opportunity to burnish their own images while riding the wave of Melissa Zhao's popularity."

"I hate to be a cynic, but that all seems too good to be true. This thing has become massive. And yet, you heard her. There's no talk of an IPO. Of raising sacks of cash by taking it public," I snorted.

"That is odd," agreed Volkov. "And did you hear Zhao's defensive answers when she was asked about the FTC investigation? The battery usage? The data usage?"

"Mm-hmm," I hummed. "Why the FTC, anyway? Who do these social media companies have accountability to? What about the FCC?"

Volkov's expertise in tech was far-reaching, and she furrowed her brow as she explained, "Basically, the Federal Communications Commission deals with the infrastructure stuff. Frequencies and access. The Federal Trade Commission watches over general business practices. And this is relevant because, in Trampoline's case, or Facebook, or Twitter, if those companies do something other than what their policies say they do, then the FTC calls them out."

"So, that's why the FTC is investigating Trampoline?"

"Exactly. I know a bit about it, just from monitoring news in the tech sector like I like to do," Volkov admitted. "But it really hadn't caught my attention till now. The thing about the FTC is that its investigations are retroactive. They look back at what a company is doing. They don't anticipate what it will do."

I thought that over, looked at Volkov, and suggested, "You already dug into Trampoline to locate Petrikov. Could you use that as a head start and get ahead of the FTC? Could you use the Trampoline account that you're going to run for me to see why they collect all that stuff? Why they use so much data?"

Volkov nodded, "Sure. That's a good idea."

I turned to Hamid and reminded him, "Abdul, you looked into Zhao back when we used Trampoline to track down Petrikov. What's she all about?"

Hamid laughed. "She's a cipher. If I didn't see her on the news just now, I'd say she's a cheap face."

Rourke was slumped on the sofa next to me, our hips touching, and at Hamid's comment she abruptly sat up. "A what?"

"A cheap face. You know, one of those computer-generated things."

Laughing, Volkov tried, "You mean a deep fake?"

"Yeah, yeah, yeah. Whatever. If you didn't see her live on television, you'd assume she was made-up. A work of fiction. She's well-spoken and articulate, clearly intelligent, outgoing, bubbly, and cute. She even drives a cute car. A silver Mini convertible. With a manual transmission. She was quoted in some magazine that driving a car with a stick shift makes her feel connected, just like Trampoline makes us all connected.

Blah, blah, blah. Everything she does and says is like it was scripted by a public relations team."

"It's a helluva team because they've grown the platform exponentially," I said with a bit of wonderment in my voice. "What did she just say? A billion users by the end of the summer?"

"Yeah," Hamid confirmed. "Not me anymore, though. Thanks to you guys."

"What do you think happened to your phone?" Rourke asked.

Hamid smirked. "When Robinson took it, it was fully charged. But it was protected with my face as a log-in, so he wouldn't have been able to use it. I wonder if he turned it off or if it kept vibrating with more and more frequent Trampoline notifications until the battery died. I bet there are a lot of people missing me on Trampoline."

"Hopefully, I'll take your place," I offered with a grin, "when I burst onto the social media scene during my rediscovery of mainland America." I laughed, swallowing the remainder of my now lukewarm and flavorless coffee. *Yuck.*

✳ ✳ ✳

At the same time, in the heart of New York City, the right-rear passenger door of a black Cadillac Escalade clicked closed, and Melissa Zhao settled into the right-rear bucket seat with a sigh. She pulled her ponytail free of its elastic and then carefully, but clearly reflexively, gathered up the long, jet-black strands and fashioned a new ponytail before settling into the leather-appointed throne and closing her eyes.

A voice with a hint of a European accent of some kind spoke, "Very nice, Miss Zhao. A compelling performance."

Zhao opened her eyes and scowled at the figure in the front passenger seat. "And what did you expect? I think I've become quite adept at telling the story. Give me some credit."

"Ah, yes," the man in front whispered. "Credit where credit is due." Turning to the driver, the man barked, "Let's get out of here. How long?"

The driver consulted the in-dash display and said, "We'll be at Teterboro Airport in less than one hour."

In the backseat, Zhao leaned her head against the right window and closed her eyes once more, thinking, *One billion users. What have I done?*

A single tear rolled down her right cheek and dribbled onto the glass of the window as she wondered, *One day I'll stop telling the story. Because then, I'll be the story. I'll be the villain. Maybe it's not too late. Maybe I can find a way out.*

55

TWO WEEKS LATER – WEDNESDAY, MAY 20, 2020 – NEWPORT, RHODE ISLAND

TYING TO A PIER adjacent to a big hotel complex, *Almaz* had docked in the virtually empty Newport Harbor thirteen days earlier, flying the internationally recognized, yellow quarantine flag from the main antenna mast. Lockwood contacted the shipyard operators, the local health department, and the state health department, filing the appropriate papers and disclosing our last port of call as Portsmouth, Virginia. During the trip north, Lockwood even detoured into the Chesapeake Bay, leaving the yacht's AIS transmitter in the off position for almost twelve hours as he guided the yacht north, then south, meandering through the bay. The system was turned back on as the vessel traced a course out of the bay. It was a loose, not terribly sophisticated cover, but it would suffice if any of the health officials bothered to check the electronic records of the yacht's travels.

Even though the transit from Portsmouth would have counted against the required fourteen-day quarantine for arriving out-of-state vessels, we had decided to wait the full two weeks. Tomorrow, May 21, would be my first day on the ground, in the United States, since January. Tuned into the local news, I could not believe how much had changed in such a short time.

I would be required, by state mandate, to wear a face mask when in public. I'd have to be mindful of remaining six feet away from any other human. I'd have to remember to wash my hands frequently, and I was advised to sing the "Happy Birthday" ditty to myself, repeating it twice, to make sure I scrubbed for at least twenty seconds. I mean, seriously, people, we have to be taught how to wash our hands?

As we wrapped up my farewell dinner, I knew I was going to miss being on the boat that I had called home for almost six months. I was definitely going to miss the camaraderie, especially as more wine was poured, more beers were uncapped, and inhibitions evaporated.

It was my former Quantico roommate who started digging at me, "Hey, Porter, do you have any qualifications to get a job?"

"None," I laughed. "I did get a job, though. I applied online. I'll be working at the shipyard over by the Goat Island bridge. I mean, on the job application, I put down that I was a deckhand on *Almaz*. I figure that I can fake it until I make it."

"You can always call me on the phone for advice," Lockwood offered.

"Thanks," I said gratefully. "Can I call for take-out food, too?"

Jacquard smiled kindly and replied, "Anytime. Come on by, and I'll package up something for you."

"Sorry, no," Volkov objected. "That's a bad idea. You don't want to be seen on this boat."

That was a disappointment, but it raised another question. "Well, if that's the case, how am I going to get you my phone so you can set up my social media posts?"

"We'll work out a handoff plan," Volkov replied. "Where are you going to live? Maybe we can do a handoff there."

"I found a one-bedroom rental on Craigslist. It's walking distance, but not like right around the corner."

Rourke was sitting next to me and poked me in the ribs. "Ben, what are we going to do without you onboard?"

"I dunno," I replied. "I assume you'll figure out what to do. Hopefully, this ruse works, and the Russians will seek me out."

Rourke rolled her eyes. "And then what, big boy? You're going to duke it out with a couple of Russian agents? Intimidate them into submission? This is a weak plan. You're getting way out of your league, Ben."

I sensed concern in her voice, which I thought was unusual. Rourke was a risk-taker, and I slurred, after a gulp of beer, "When the Russians show up, I call you, and you fly in and save the day."

She shook her head. "What makes you so sure that the Russians are still looking for you?"

Volkov took that question as I sipped again at my beer. "Oh, they'll be looking. Someone went to the trouble of planting electronic devices at the office that oversaw Ben's fake job, and someone was surveilling Ben's sister. They're not going to give up. That's one thing about cold winters; they make you very tenacious."

"I think it's really dangerous," Rourke shot back stubbornly. "Because if you're correct, and if that's the case that the Russians are out for you, putting Ben on the ground by himself is foolish. We don't put people in the field alone."

I wanted to tune out, my mind worried about stepping back on land tomorrow and faking my new job, my gut burbling with too much beer, and my anxieties dwelling on Rourke's warnings. I pushed my chair back and stood, a bit unsteadily, announcing, "I'm done for the night. Early day tomorrow. Thanks, everyone, for the send-off."

It was time, and there were murmurs of "good luck" and "we'll miss you" from around the table, but it was Rourke who shot to her feet and declared, "New plan. We are *not* putting Ben out there by himself. I'm going with him. He's getting a girlfriend."

She grabbed my elbow, and we walked side-by-side to the stairs that led below to the staterooms. Normally, on the deck below, I'd go forward to my stateroom, and she'd head aft to hers.

Not this time.

At the base of the stairs, we paused, an almost simultaneous yet unspoken decision made by two separate minds. I looked into Rourke's green eyes—those eyes that showed such spark and humor, so many times before on this journey, and those eyes that could be fierce and focused, in the heat of a mission, at the controls of the helicopter, and at the wheel of a RIB on dark waters. Of everyone on the team, Rourke was, dare I say, an enigma: she was the most playful, but she was perhaps the most dangerous.

If there was anyone that I wanted by my side if, truly, I was to take on the Russians, to draw them out—it would be Rourke.

I grinned, maybe a bit tipsy, but with sincerity, and she smiled at me, those green eyes sparkling and bright. Not a word was spoken. It was all in the eyes.

We ended up together in my room. Let's just say that those sheets that I'd become so fond of ended up in a twisted, sweaty, wet mess, partially on the floor and barely on the bed. As I finally began to drift off into a satisfied sleep, Rourke's red hair splayed out on my bare chest, I grinned, now not the least bit anxious about heading to my new sho-reside job tomorrow morning.

Unfortunately, Rourke would be proven correct. I was going to be way out of my league.

JUNE

CHAPTER
56

TWO WEEKS LATER – WEDNESDAY, JUNE 10, 2020 – MOSCOW, RUSSIA

"I HOPE YOU HAVE something new for me," Vitaly Rodionov demanded as Fedor Ilin pushed open the glass door to Rodionov's raised office within the cavernous Unit 29155 command center. "Your last breakthrough was, what, two months ago? This has been a disappointment."

"There's nothing we could have done about that," Fedor replied with a defensive tone. "We isolated al-Hamid's device and tracked it to Chicago, but then it disappeared off the grid. Either it was destroyed, or the battery was removed, or the battery died. The accounts were never activated or used again. Al-Hamid's other social media accounts had gone dormant in December, and there has been no activity on them since. If I had to guess—and with my tools, rarely do I have to guess—my conclusion would be that al-Hamid gave up social media."

"Fine. Why are you here now?"

Fedor grinned widely, his pockmarked cheeks dimpling as he announced, "al-Hamid no longer matters. I can give you Ben Porter himself."

Rodionov choked on the black coffee he was sipping and blurted, "Porter?"

Taking a seat without invitation, Fedor reported, "Porter is in Newport, Rhode Island. This is a town only ten or twelve miles south of Bristol, where the sister lives and where we gave up the chase at the end of February. Porter has gotten a job. He is working in a shipyard. And he has a girlfriend. A redhead."

"Where are you getting this data?"

Fedor replied, "The usual sources. Social media. Specifically, Twitter and Trampoline."

"Is this another cover? A job like the one he had at the coffee chain in Boston?"

"We cannot know that until we can verify with our own eyes," Fedor suggested. "We made that mistake once already."

Rodionov wiped spilled coffee carefully from his metal and glass desk before asking, "Do we have any operatives available?"

Fedor nodded. "Yes. Even though we recalled most of our men when the pandemic began, we, of course, allowed a handful to remain in the United States. I have already made an inquiry, and we can utilize an agent who is with the GRU, Unit 74455, outside of Washington, D.C., in the state of Maryland. I have an order ready for your signature. It will take a day or two to make the arrangements."

"This is for reconnaissance only, correct?"

"Yes, that would be my approach. Let's first confirm that this is not another subterfuge."

Scratching the side of his face under his right ear, Rodionov said, "I agree, but I also believe that time is of the essence. Put a mission plan together to capture Porter—if this person in Newport is truly him."

"We'll need more than one GRU agent for an operation like that."

"Of course. Tell me what you need, and I will coordinate with the Directorate. I'll need permission to run an operation on American soil."

"Shall I include provisions to have you personally involved in America?"

"No," Rodionov said, "not at this time. As much as I would like to speak with Porter, that can wait. I have other priorities. Let's get him in our custody first."

Standing, Fedor confirmed, "Understood."

As the programmer-turned-operative began to take his leave, Rodionov reclined back in his chair, allowing himself a moment to dream about seeing Porter face-to-face.

He would get that opportunity.

CHAPTER
57

TWO DAYS LATER – FRIDAY, JUNE 12, 2020 – NEWPORT, RHODE ISLAND

TWO WEEKS INTO MY new job at the shipyard, my routine was comfortable. Monday through Friday, I worked, and honestly, I enjoyed it. They had assigned me to the carpentry shop, and though I had no talent for doing the exquisite joinery work, I was skilled in organization. I cleaned up the shop, inventorying various exotic woods, sorting fasteners, and creating bins for everything from hinges to biscuits. The shop foreman was impressed and allowed me to do a bit of rudimentary cutting.

I loved it. Working with my hands and seeing a tangible result at the end of the day was satisfying. And returning to the rental apartment and to Heather Rourke's body was also satisfying, albeit in a completely different way—if you know what I mean.

Rourke had gotten a job working the front desk at the hotel compound where *Almaz* was docked, and we established the operational procedures of the mission.

The key to my new social media presence was, of course, a smartphone: in my case, a new Samsung Galaxy A51, that Volkov ordered online and had sent to the yacht during our quarantine period in the Newport harbor. Volkov had plenty of time to set up the device for the mission. She disabled all the privacy controls, enabled location tracking, and configured my new Twitter and Trampoline accounts.

Because Volkov wanted to analyze the device daily, and because Hamid would be responsible for creating content, at the beginning of each workday, Rourke and I would walk from the apartment to the hotel, where I would turn off the phone and hand it to her. In the event that someone tried to track the phone even while it was off, Rourke would drop the device into a shielded pouch, and then she would meet up with one of the Quadrant team members somewhere in the complex who would take the phone to the yacht. Working within a Faraday enclosure that they'd set up on the yacht, Volkov and Hamid would do their work.

Volkov set up the procedure, explaining, "In the event that someone is tracking that particular phone, it will appear that you are dutifully turning it off before going to work. The pouch and the Faraday enclosure make it impossible for the cell networks to see it, even when I power it back on aboard the yacht."

At the end of the day, Rourke would retrieve the device. If there was something to be posted, I'd tap the icon as required—always posting from the apartment, always posting in the evening. It was a pattern, Hamid advised, that would be predictable.

As a backup, in case of an emergency, I kept the plain, charcoal-gray flip phone with me, too. If the Russians came for me at work, I could speed-dial a number, and the Quadrant team and the FBI, via Macallister, would be notified.

Macallister had derisively called the plan "Swiss cheese." "It's full of holes," he'd grumbled. And he was correct—if, indeed, the plan worked, and Unit 29155 was drawn out and located me in Newport, well, then what? Would they follow me? Would they abduct me? Would they take me out on the spot?

We had no idea, and Volkov, Hamid, and Macallister would be considering options, because we figured we had a bit of time. We didn't expect results immediately since it would, indeed, take time for Hamid to build and expand my online profile.

I figured I had a while before I needed to worry, and during those first two weeks of the op, I simply followed the protocol with the weekday phone handover. Weekends, however, were another story, and as Rourke and I walked back to our apartment from the hotel after the final

Friday afternoon phone retrieval, I knew we would have the weekend to ourselves.

Grabbing Rourke by the hand, I asked, "Want to get a drink? Maybe some clam chowder, too?"

"Yeah, sure," she exclaimed.

Normally busy, even in mid-June, Newport remained quiet, the tourists staying away due to the pandemic. A local waterfront restaurant that was famous for their New England clam chowder (not the kind with the clear or red broth, but the proper cream-based version, thank you very much) had reopened their outdoor patio, overlooking the docks, and we headed there for an early dinner and sunset cocktail.

Walking hand-in-hand over a cobblestone-paved, pedestrian-only street, neither Rourke nor I noticed, at the time, a blonde woman, her face mostly hidden by the required mask, who followed us toward Bannister's Wharf with a Nokia smartphone in her hands.

CHAPTER
58

SUNDAY, JUNE 14, 2020 – NEWPORT, RHODE ISLAND

HEATHER ROURKE'S PHONE pinged first thing on Sunday morning, a bit more than two weeks after we had stepped ashore in Newport, with a notification chime for a new text message, the content of which left little to the imagination:

    911. 3pm. Queen Ann Square.

At the appointed time, Rourke and I made our way to Queen Ann Square, a midtown Newport park where it would not be uncommon to see friends gather under partly cloudy skies to enjoy the early summer, 70-degree weather on a late Sunday afternoon.

Finding a bench, we sat closely together, perched at one end like a pair of birds, our bodies touching. We'd at least appear, from a distance, to be observing some physical distance from the bulbous-nosed, Middle-Eastern skinned, masked man that we shared the bench with, who chuckled, "You know, these masks defeat the facial recognition software. Doesn't work."

"No kidding," Rourke responded. "I have to use my passcode instead of my face to unlock my iPhone."

"And speaking of phones, and because we probably shouldn't dawdle here, you must have something for us. Otherwise, you wouldn't have called an in-person meeting," I said.

"Yup," Hamid confirmed. "I'll do my best to relay what Volkov told me to say. Do you remember the conversation we had after we watched the TV interview with the CEO of Trampoline? When you suggested to Volkov that she use your new Trampoline account to get ahead of the Federal Trade Commission investigation? She's made progress. She's learned that Trampoline gains access to the host device's camera, microphone, and storage."

"That's not unusual, though," I countered.

"Absolutely not," Hamid agreed. "Volkov says that just about every app of this nature does the same thing, and when you install it, the app is required to ask for your permission. It also asks to access your contacts. But that's where the similarity ends."

"What does that mean?"

"Trampoline is also skimming pretty much whatever it wants off your phone. It copies all your contact info, your texts, and your emails. It can copy your passwords. And it can copy your photos. However, it doesn't copy all the photos. It only copies photos with faces in them. She doesn't know why."

"What does it do with all that stuff?" I asked.

"It's copying it and then sending the copy back to its servers as you use the app. *That's* why the app tries to be so sticky and so addictive. While your screen time ticks up, it's sending data in the background. *That's* why the app uses so much data."

Rourke tilted her head slightly toward Hamid and wondered, "What does it do with the copy once it is sent to the servers?"

"Deletes it. Volkov figures that's so that the available memory on your phone doesn't show much of a change. Otherwise, it would accumulate, and you would start to fill the memory and maybe notice."

Rourke had been shaking her head. "I don't get it. Wouldn't all that data being transferred cause you to notice? Like if the battery usage was higher than other apps? Or if you blew through your cellphone service provider's data caps, and they billed you for some exorbitant excess data charge?"

As she asked her question, Hamid was nodding affirmatively. "Yeah, yeah, yeah. Those are exactly the types of complaints that have come up in parallel with the FTC investigation. Users have said the same thing. The platform has claimed the data usage was to make it more enjoyable because it offers so much. Volkov figured out what it's really doing."

What it's really doing. I repeated Hamid's words in my head, and then Rourke's word, *exorbitant.* That brought me back to a New York City parking garage when I used the iPhone that Volkov had set up for me to pay the ridiculous two-night tab, and I made a link, whispering, "Shit. There's a connection that we're overlooking."

Rourke and Hamid stared at me until I explained. "Abdul, you said it was copying only photos with faces in them. Heather, you said that your phone doesn't recognize you with a mask on. That's because it uses facial recognition to unlock the phone. And that facial recognition process also unlocks your banking applications. Like Apple Wallet. And Trampoline is collecting that info and sending it to . . . itself."

None of us spoke until I said, "We gotta call this in. Abdul, get in touch with Macallister."

"He's back at work every day," Hamid reported. "We can do a secure conference from the yacht. Maybe you sneak aboard some night this week."

"Not some night. Monday night. Set it up for tomorrow night," I demanded. "Say, eleven in the evening."

"Okay," Hamid agreed, and he stood, shoving his hands into the pockets of his oversized cargo shorts.

Rourke couldn't help herself, "Your shorts are ridiculous. They're hanging at your calves. They look like capri pants," she laughed.

Hamid shrugged, clearly offended, and he stalked away. Rourke buried her head in my shirt, giggling, and I watched Hamid hitch his short pants up a bit at the waist as he walked toward the waterfront.

With my attention on Hamid, I failed to notice a blonde woman, her face mostly hidden by the required mask, carrying a Nokia phone in her hand as she strolled the opposite direction, away from our park bench, and blended into the usual Sunday afternoon Newport pedestrian traffic.

CHAPTER

59

THE NEXT DAY – MONDAY, JUNE 15, 2020 – MOSCOW, RUSSIA

BEFORE VITALY RODIONOV could settle into his command center office on a Monday morning and begin a new work week, Fedor Ilin burst through the glass door just as Rodionov took his first sip from a mug of freshly brewed, black coffee. Thrusting a tablet in front of Rodionov, Fedor gasped, "Porter. And al-Hamid. Confirmed together, in Newport."

"This is new," Rodionov exclaimed, wiping the dripping coffee from his chin absently as he examined the photo. "That's the same redhead that our operative photographed Porter with on Friday night." Looking up from the tablet, Rodionov demanded, "When was this photo, of the three of them, taken?"

"Sunday afternoon. Yesterday afternoon. The time in Newport is eight hours different than in Moscow. That photo is only several hours old."

"Do we know who the redhead is?"

"My team has been scouring our facial recognition database since the first picture of the redhead and Porter was taken on Friday. We got a picture of her with her mask off as she and Porter were at an outdoor restaurant. Her name is Heather Rourke. She is a former Special Agent of the Federal Bureau of Investigation."

Hearing that, Rodionov sat bolt upright in his seat and, with his eyes closed, began to speak in an even monotone. "We started with Porter, an active agent who was terminated and then disappeared. We mix in al-Hamid, believed to be an active agent, who was on social media until December, popped up briefly in April, and then disappeared again. And now we have this Rourke, a former agent. What do we know about her?"

Fedor consulted his tablet and began, "From social media, we know that she is the divorced mother of two children who live with their father. She posted often that she is not fond of the ex-husband. She posted that she retired on disability from the FBI. She's a pilot. Helicopters. And most interestingly, at the end of December, she ceased posting to social media."

"End of December," Rodionov muttered. "Like al-Hamid."

"Yes."

"And did you say helicopters?"

"Yes."

Rodionov raised his eyebrows and murmured, "I'm finding all this too coincidental. Not only do these two, al-Hamid and Rourke, suddenly change their social media behavior at the same time, but also Rourke pilots a helicopter? Perhaps a helicopter that landed, briefly, on a beach in Venezuela?"

Rodionov tilted his head to the ceiling, speculating in an absent-minded tone, "Porter, with al-Hamid and this Rourke, together in Newport. Do we continue to observe? Or do we plan to intervene?" Scratching his chin, Rodionov decided, "Fedor, I think the latter. This is an opportunity that we cannot waste. Porter is in our sights."

CHAPTER
60

LATER THAT DAY – NEWPORT, RHODE ISLAND

ON A DARK MONDAY EVENING in Newport, *Almaz* lay alongside the pier, dimly lit, and somehow Lockwood or one of the crew managed to extinguish the handful of lights on the pier itself. It would have been really awkward if Rourke or I had tripped and fallen into the dark water. Fortunately, we made it aboard, reasonably certain that we were not spotted by the lazy security guard at the hotel complex who appeared to be asleep in his parked golf cart.

It was nice to be back in my black, executive-style chair at the head of the black, horseshoe-shaped table in the situation room, and even better to have my team assembled with me as we waited for the secure video teleconference to begin, precisely at 11:00 p.m. according to the digital, on-screen clock that ticked down the seconds.

The screen lit with Macallister's tanned face in the foreground and his office in the Hoover building as his background. He wore a white button-down shirt, and his tie was loose with his top button undone. A dark suit coat, navy blue perhaps, draped over the back of his chair. His hair was perfectly trimmed. The Deputy Assistant Director appeared to be all business, but that façade quickly disappeared as he began the discussion by belting out, "What the fuck, Porter? It's fucking eleven at night."

"Apologies, sir. But as you know, I have a day job too. And I thought it preferable to get back onto the boat under the cover of darkness," I said defensively.

"This fieldwork is going to your head, Porter," Macallister replied, in a somewhat calmer tone. "And with little effect, I'd add. You haven't been captured by the Russians. You must not be that tasty as bait. You're still alive."

"Don't sound so disappointed," I shot back.

Macallister laughed. "All right, Porter. Enough. What do you have that's so important? I have learned how to read emails, you know."

"We'll take you through it," I replied evenly. "First, the tradecraft. I hand off my phone to Volkov every morning, and I get it back every night. During the day, Volkov and Hamid set up my social media posts in a way to attract the attention of the Russians. But Volkov and Hamid have also learned something new. Something disturbing."

"Go on."

Volkov picked up the thread. "As you must know, the Federal Trade Commission is investigating Trampoline. The FTC claims that the app is possibly violating its privacy and user agreement policies. And users complain that Trampoline consumes a lot of data. The company claims that happens for two reasons, first because it offers so much on the platform, and second because users spend so much time on the app. Screen time, it's called. Hamid, take it from here."

Hamid faced the camera and nodded. "This is a concept that has been well-documented with Facebook, Instagram, TikTok, and the like. The user interface is built and programmed with a learning algorithm to feed you content, based on your prior preferences and usage. When you see stuff that you like, your brain produces dopamine—sometimes called the pleasure neurotransmitter—and you get a little high from that satisfaction. Your brain wants more. This is well understood, actually, but users choose to ignore what these platforms are doing, which is compiling all sorts of data about what you like and what you scroll past and then using an algorithm to feed you what you want to see. You get what you want, your dopamine surges, and you go back for more. It's how these things are so addictive."

"Moreover," I added, butting in, "that addiction feeds on itself. Those algorithms work to promote content to you that other users with similar tastes have liked. That's how stuff on social media goes viral. The algorithms create a wave of popularity not particularly for the best content, but for content that is 'liked.' That popularity begets more popularity, and users also get that dopamine high by being included in a viral wave."

Hamid leaned forward and said earnestly, "It goes beyond dopamine, though. Your brain synapses are stimulated by what we see and by what we think. Simplistically, if we think creatively, we are stimulating and training our brains. If we just consume visual content without thinking, we risk cell death, which to some degree is normal, but if we don't stimulate enough growth to counter that death, we slowly lose the executive functioning abilities of our brains. Ultimately, what happens is users spend more and more time on the platform, being sucked into a vicious cycle of wanting more dopamine highs, and not wanting to leave the platform, while their creativity and imagination for other outlets are being dulled."

Macallister clapped his hands gently. "Golf clap. That's some impressive research."

"Thanks," Hamid replied gratefully. "I was on the other side. I was addicted to the platform. I literally could not see my problem. But now, looking at it sorta clinically, my addiction makes sense."

"In fact, it is intentionally addictive. The entire premise is deceitful," I suggested strongly. "When Hamid started using Trampoline, he called it harmless. It is anything but that. It is subversive."

"Mm-hmm," Macallister hummed, "Under the guise of Trampoline's feel-good vibes, it's selling addiction. But for what?"

"For screen time," Volkov answered. "Macallister, here's the key to this discussion. I learned that while a user's eyes are glued to the screen, in the background, the app is copying *all* the data on the device and sending it to Trampoline's servers."

Macallister grunted. "How can you see that?"

"The key is that a phone has a flash memory system. Without boring you with the details, a simplistic explanation is that flash memory is basically storing ones and zeros in an electronic grid of cells, mapped in pages and blocks. A zero is a charged cell; a one is an uncharged cell. Accessing data, in binary form of ones and zeroes, can be very fast since the memory controller knows what cells are mapped for what purpose. There are no moving parts."

I could tell that Volkov was losing Macallister's attention when he snorted, "Simplistic, huh? Sounds pretty complicated to me."

"That's not even the complicated part," Volkov warned, ignoring Macallister's tone. "But at the risk of complicating it further, here's the good part. The main limitation on this type of memory is in the read, write, and erase cycle. It's very fast to read and write data. It's harder and slower to erase data because that requires a negative charge applied to a charged cell to turn a one into a zero and to clear its memory. This gets messy and requires a lot of power to do over and over, and so to speed things up, your phone, or any device with a solid-state type of drive, will do something in the background when it is idle called 'garbage collection,' which is when deleted data is reorganized into fresh pages and remapped. By comparing what has been remapped, I can examine what data on your phone is being copied and deleted without you knowing it."

Macallister's eyes had closed. I stepped in with a curt and loud, "Sir." His eyes snapped open at the sound of a new voice, and I continued more quietly, "The app is copying *everything* on your phone. Your emails, texts, contacts, photos. More specifically, face photos. There's a possibility that the facial recognition and possibly the fingerprint data that can unlock a device is being copied, along with saved passwords. And then, as you are using the app, under the cover of the screen time that the platform gets because it addicts you, Trampoline is sending as much of *your* personal information as it can find back to *its* servers."

"Why?"

Macallister got right to the point, and with one word, asked the question that we had no definitive answer to. "We have some theories, but, really, we don't know," I confessed.

"And one more thing," Macallister added. "What about the FTC? You think your investigation is more comprehensive than theirs? How come they haven't come to this conclusion?"

"That I can answer with more confidence," I said. "The FTC looks backwards. It looks at what the app does. Not what it's going to do. And they don't have Volkov, who started looking at the app back when we chased down Petrikov. They don't have her imagination to look outside the confines of some policy, and to look at the actual stuff happening on the device, and to reach the conclusion that screen time is being used for data transfer."

Macallister grunted, "Okay. I get that. And we've underestimated Volkov's skills before. So, Volkov, while I applaud you, neither you nor Porter know *why* this thing is doing this. If you don't know why, then why is it a threat? Hypothetical question. I don't deny that what you've found is suspicious. Play it out. Why is it a threat?"

"Take TikTok," I offered. "There's a ton of attention on TikTok now. That's a short-form video app that is based in China. There are rumors that it is a tool for Chinese spying."

"Yeah, I know," Macallister confirmed. "But there's no proof yet. Are you saying that Trampoline is also spying for China?"

Hamid jumped in. "It's a possibility. Trampoline was founded by an American of Chinese descent. Melissa Zhao. She's a computer science major from Stanford. Where'd she get the coding help? The money to build and maintain the platform? Possibly from China."

"I dunno," Macallister mused. "How about this claim that TikTok is allegedly spying for China? What's the point? So the Chinese can watch a bunch of videos? What's the end game? And in this case, it's Trampoline. It's fun. It's clean. There's nothing to it but fluff."

"It might be fluff," I agreed. "But it's a lot of fluff. Look at the growth. One billion users projected by the end of the summer. It blew up in size during the lockdowns. It's still growing, and all that time, it's been collecting user data and sending it somewhere."

Macallister may not have been adept with technology, but he was a good agent, and he immediately added, "And that's the big question. Where? Where is it sending all that user data?"

Volkov lowered her head slightly and admitted, "I don't know yet."

"Well, then, what do you propose?" Macallister crossed his arms over his chest and waited imperiously.

"I think this should be our priority, sir," I suggested.

Macallister shrugged, "Okay. How does that change anything? Porter, you know as good as I do that Volkov is driving this research. Not you. What, do you want me to put a body double in place for you at your job? Keep the bait out for the Russians while you do . . . what?"

My shoulders sagged. He had a point, and I had called this meeting with my usual bluster and without a plan. He had seen right through it. I fumbled, "Yeah, well, um, no, that's not what I propose. I think, um, as you said, we continue on the path that we're on, but in the meantime, I thought you should know that this Trampoline investigation might be more important than the Unit 29155 operation."

I thought I finished strong and recovered, but Macallister only laughed. "Whatever, Porter. Nice try. Come back to me with a plan. In the meantime, if the Russians come after you personally, or if Volkov can figure out where the data is going, well, that will get my attention."

We'd have both items checked off in two weeks. But, of course, we didn't know that. Nor did we know that we would soon have some unwelcome company.

JULY

CHAPTER
61

FRIDAY, JULY 3, 2020 – NEWPORT, RHODE ISLAND

TWO WEEKS AFTER THAT long conference with Macallister, our routine had not varied, and I questioned our operation. It wasn't going anywhere, and it seemed monotonous. Depressing, almost.

In normal times, we would all be looking forward to this first Friday night in July, which would be rockin' in Newport with parades, big parties, and spectacular fireworks shows. Instead, due to the coronavirus pandemic, this was going to be a subdued Independence Day holiday. And that was depressing, too.

At least I had Heather Rourke at my side. The spunky redhead and I had become inseparable. She was great for me; her wit, her positive, upbeat, can-do attitude was an antidote to my often-bumbling anxiety.

As we perched at what had become our favorite Friday spot in Newport, an outdoor dining patio on Bannister's Wharf, the sun's rays long since gone and the temperature dipping into the mid-sixties, I felt gratitude. And then I felt her hand, a light touch, crawling slowly up my inner right leg. "Let's go home, Ben," she whispered.

We settled our tab and began the long uphill walk from the gorgeous, festively lit waterfront, leaving behind the cobblestone streets and picture-perfect Colonial-era clapboard and brick buildings, dotted with lights that reflected in the still waters of the harbor, and we trudged up the winding, narrow, mostly one-way streets to our apartment.

Our apartment. I had been referring to the apartment as "ours." It was comforting.

The final leg of the walk home was a dark, unlit alleyway that cut between a three-story, Federal-style, clapboard-sided home with an overgrown side garden to our right and a plain three-family, two-story, pale brick home. But it wasn't really brick; it was a veneer of some sort of fake brick, plasticky material that had been tacked over shingled siding. I was reasonably certain that the shingled siding was also fake. *Probably asbestos*, I had thought in the past.

As we plodded by on this night, because of the darkness, I wouldn't have been able to examine the siding as I might have to see if a new section had begun to peel away, and frankly, I didn't care as I held Rourke's cool hand and thought about our—yes, *our*—bed.

The fist that connected with my left cheek was, therefore, a complete and not at all welcome surprise.

A man and a woman had appeared from the shadows on either side of the alleyway, the man to the left and hiding behind the end of the fake brick building, and the woman to the right, obscured by the bushes of the overgrown garden. The woman angled for Rourke, and the man, dressed in black pants and a black, long-sleeve t-shirt, jumped me.

I dropped Rourke's hand involuntarily, the stinging pain from my cheek clouding my vision, and I stumbled backwards.

The second hit came instantly, to the right side of my gut, and I doubled over.

The third punch was an uppercut to my lower left jaw. I felt a searing pain.

I dropped to the pavement, slamming my skull into the ground. With my ears ringing and my eyes tearing, I tried to focus. Tried to figure out how to protect myself. Tried to see Rourke.

I caught a brief glimpse. Rourke had the woman, who was clad from head to toe in black, in a headlock. With her free hand, Rourke was yanking off a black knit cap to reveal a flash of blonde hair. The man who jumped me, perhaps satisfied to see me curled in a fetal position on the scarred, black asphalt, was turning his attention to Rourke.

I tried to call out. I tried to warn her. I couldn't get the words out. I was dizzy.

My left eye closed to pain. Through a slit of my right eye, I saw another dark shape materialize, ghosting toward our melee in the alleyway.

Another attacker. We were outnumbered. It would be three against two. Or, three against one, because I was already on the ground. I couldn't move.

Rourke was struggling. She might have been able to subdue the woman, but the man . . . and the other new player who had appeared . . .

As my world went dark, I thought, under the pain of a crushing sadness, *We're done.*

CHAPTER

62

I HAD NO IDEA what time it was. Where I was. What happened. *One thing at a time, Ben,* I told myself. *Take inventory. One thing at a time.*

I was on my back.

My ears were ringing.

My brain . . . hurt. My head was pounding. It was like I could feel the pressure of blood coursing through my skull.

There was a cool weight of something covering my left eye.

I tried to open my eyes. I couldn't.

I lifted my left arm, and instantly, I felt pressure pushing it back down. A hand. A cool hand. I let it be for a moment, defeated.

My heart began to race. I tried to take a breath.

Inhaling through my nose was difficult. I couldn't get enough air. My mouth tasted metallic. Blood. Saliva. I probed my teeth with my tongue. They seemed intact.

I tried again to open my eyes. My left eye saw nothing. My right eye saw haze. Blurry. Dim light. Not the black of night.

"That's gonna be a helluva black eye."

The voice. That voice. It felt familiar. Male. Deep. Reassuring.

"The eye will heal. That cut on his cheek will scar."

A woman's voice—also familiar. I swallowed, bile and blood, and inhaled deeply. It was restorative. *I can do this.*

The woman's voice again, "The scar will add character. I like it."

Rourke!

It was Rourke's voice. My body relaxed, I inhaled again, and I forced my eyes open.

Left eye, still dark. Right eye, focusing. Rourke's face. The ceiling. *I know that ceiling. This is the apartment.* Our *apartment.*

Blinking rapidly, my heart rate increased as I realized I felt my left eyelid moving, but I had no vision. I tried to raise my left hand again and felt pressure, and I heard the deep male voice again, "Careful. Don't move it. Don't touch it. That's what you're trying to do, right? Your face is covered with a compress. Let it be."

It couldn't be. But it had to be. I knew the voice. Leroy Havens. *But how?*

I closed my eyes, and I lay still for a moment. Maybe it was longer. Maybe I slept. I don't know. When I opened my eyes, I could feel the weight of the compress on my left eye, and I could see clearly from my right eye; the haze and blur was gone, and the ringing sound had faded from inside my head. Rourke's face. I focused, licked my lips, and garbled, "What? Where? How?"

Swallowed. No blood. Blinked. Rourke spoke. "Relax, Ben. Just breathe. Can you sit up? Let's get some blood moving."

I felt strong hands slip under me, and I was slid backward, my upper body tilting and leaning against the headboard. The compress slipped off, and as I blinked yet again, I was relieved to be able to see out of my left eye.

Scanning the room, I took in a grinning Havens, a smiling Rourke, and . . . a body. Lying on the floor. Black sneakers. Tight black leggings. Tight black shirt. Black blindfold wrapped around a white-skinned face. Blonde hair. I mumbled, "Who . . . who is *that?*"

Rourke answered, "Well, we haven't formally met yet, but about forty-five minutes ago, I had her in a headlock. I owned her. Until the other dude decided to take me on, too, after he dropped you."

"You could have taken 'em both," Havens said, still grinning.

"Yeah, sure," replied Rourke, with sarcasm evident in her tone. "You showed up just in time to get in my way."

"Sorry. Shoulda held back. Let you mop up."

It was Rourke's turn to grin. "I'll forgive you. Nice of you to lend a hand."

"Wait—wait—wait," I stuttered. "First off, Havens, where did you come from? And second, where's the other guy? The guy who hit me."

Havens' expression turned serious as he said, "I've been tailing you two for about a month. Here and there. Mostly concerned with your movements after dark or before dawn. But, occasionally during the day, too."

"Why?"

"Well, Porter, Macallister called me in late May. He explained your shitty plan to me. That you'd use yourself as bait. Stupid, in my mind. Then he called me back and told me that Rourke had gone with you. Still stupid."

"Oh, yeah," Rourke objected. "What's so stupid about that?"

Havens laughed. "Oh, you got the chops to defend yourself, that's for sure. Problem is, and the problem we just saw, is that you can't defend yourself *and* Porter at the same time."

He paused, and Rourke, too, remained quiet. *I owe Macallister,* I thought. I had known that my plan was loose; even Macallister had ridiculed it as "Swiss cheese." But, true to form, I barreled on carelessly.

I felt . . . stupid. Amateurish. I closed my eyes, and the pounding in my head resumed. But this time, I knew the pounding was because of guilt. I promised myself that I would be more cautious. More deliberate. More thoughtful.

As I reopened my eyes, Havens continued, "Now, strategically, maybe if you were attacked, you could run and sound an alarm. Call in reinforcements. The problem with that is that no one knows what you are doing, and no one is on standby. It was a shitty plan," he repeated.

"CIRG planning and redundancies," Rourke hummed. In a stronger tone, she added, "You're right, of course. We had no contingency plan. No bolt holes."

"Yep," Havens confirmed. "Except for me. Macallister assigned me to be your contingency. To be your shadow."

Rourke was nodding, but it was me who spoke, softly, apologetically, "I get it."

I could tell from Havens' expression that he knew I had received the message, and I decided it was time to move on. "But, what about my second question? What happened to the big guy who took me out?"

Havens' mouth drooped in a frown. "Well, he took off. I saw him drop you, and I saw the woman attack Rourke. I was going to take him on, but after you fell to the street, and after the big dude made a turn to Rourke, I intervened. I couldn't do both things at once: help Rourke clear the woman and tackle the dude. He bolted."

I pointed at the black-clad woman on the floor of my bedroom. "And am I to guess that you decided not to let her follow her accomplice?"

Flashing a toothy smile, Havens smirked, "No way. I'd like to get to know her a bit better. When she comes to, that is. She may have bumped her head."

Rourke laughed, "Into your fist?"

"Might have been my knee. She'll sleep it off."

I grinned. It hurt my jaw. Clenching my teeth, I mumbled, "So, what's next? Who is she?"

"That, we don't know. I've seen her once before. She followed you before, but I didn't take much notice because you were in touristy places when I saw her, and if I started suspecting everyone walking up and down Bannister's Wharf, I'd go nuts. Now, however, I'm gonna guess from her movements and from the dude's fist work that they are not your everyday, run-of-the-mill local thugs," Havens replied.

"Well, I got a thought," I proposed. "I know the perfect place to stash our new friend so we can enjoy a proper introduction."

CHAPTER
63

AS THE CHURCH BELL several blocks away from the head of our alley rang with a single, mournful *dong,* marking one o'clock in the morning, Havens and Rourke picked up the unconscious woman, wrapping their hands around her waist. From behind, I placed the woman's arms across Havens' and Rourke's shoulders. It was a rudimentary disguise; any close exam would reveal that the woman was out. We dared not call a cab or an Uber; we hoped that due to the hour, we would not run into any other pedestrians.

Skulking through side streets, avoiding streetlights and main roads, we made slow progress downhill, and as we neared the wide, four-lane America's Cup Avenue, I whispered, "Guys, this is never going to work. We're moving so slowly that we are going to attract attention crossing the Avenue."

Havens grumbled, "What do you suggest?"

"Just carry her by yourself. Rourke and I can pretend to be drunk. Hell, I'm still so dizzy I can barely walk in a straight line."

"Yeah," Havens mumbled. "Probably less risky. Let's do it."

With Havens cradling the woman's limp body, our pace quickened considerably, and we darted across the wide Avenue without incident. Ducking around the hotel, we made for the water, where *Almaz* floated motionlessly in the still evening. Only her side deck courtesy lights were illuminated. Rourke dashed ahead of Havens and me.

Within moments, as Havens and I approached the gangway, a light just aft of the bridge within the upper deck structure lit, and it was Rourke who met us at the crest of the gangway, accompanied by a sleepy-looking Miles Lockwood and Anastasia Volkov.

Both of them looked briefly at me and then did a double take at the sight of Leroy Havens and his cargo. "This night just got quite a bit more interesting," Lockwood deadpanned.

"Yeah. I'll explain later," I offered. "For now, let's get our guest below."

"You know where you're going," Lockwood said to Havens. Turning to me, he added, "Ben, follow me. Your cheek is bleeding. Let's get that patched up before you drip blood on our carpets."

With the back of my hand, I wiped my cheek sort of clean, saying, "Miles, I'm happy to hear that your priority is the carpets."

He laughed, and I followed him to the stairs to the bridge deck as Havens, Rourke, and Volkov disappeared below, taking the woman to one of the two lower deck cell-like staterooms.

We all reconvened in the situation room, lights dimmed, with three of the smaller flatscreen displays on, displaying the camera images of the interior of the cell. The woman had been placed on the bed. Volkov wondered, "Hate to ask, but did you strip-search her?"

"Yeah," Rourke affirmed, "before we left the apartment. She's got a hell of a body. Very fit. No tattoos, piercings, or identifying marks. No capsules hidden in her mouth or in her, um, orifices. No jewelry, phone, or identification."

Volkov focused the view on the woman's face, and a small, red-outlined box appeared on screen. "Lemme get a facial capture. We can run the image through the Bureau's database. I've also got access to the National Security Agency data set."

Abdul Hamid slid through the door, clad in sport shorts and a ratty t-shirt, and in a startled voice said, "I was wondering why Miles called my room and woke me up. What the hell is going on?"

As Volkov worked, Havens, Rourke, and I told the story of the alleyway fracas, the escape of the big dude, and the detainment of the woman. As Hamid examined my wounds—the growing shiner around my left eye, and the gash on my cheek that Lockwood had expertly patched—we watched on-screen as the woman began to stir.

She moved slowly, at first, as she only tilted her head to examine her dimly lit surroundings. Finally, she stood, flexing what might have been a sore right arm, flipping her blonde hair with her left hand. Her movements were casual but clearly cautious as she explored the room, testing the door handle and peering out the porthole, where she would see nothing but perhaps the glint of dark water under the pier.

As the woman turned away from the porthole, Volkov gasped and then said in a clear voice, "That was quick. We got a hit. Several, in fact."

Our eyes swiveled as one from the screens to Volkov and then back to the screens. The woman sat, primly, on the bed, crossed one leg over the other, and stared into the eye of the camera, as if she could hear the voices in the situation room above as Volkov announced, "She's a pro. We got hits in the Immigration and the NSA databases. Her name is Nina Mishkin. Immigration records show her as a foreign service diplomat, based in Washington D.C., with a residence near the capital in Maryland."

Volkov paused and then asked, to no one in particular, "However, how are we going to explain to Macallister that the NSA database indicates that Nina Mishkin is a suspected agent of the Russian GU, which you would also know by its former name, the GRU? Or, as it might have been referred to in the past, the KGB?"

I stared at the screen, thinking, *GRU?* I whispered, at first, my voice rising ever so slightly as I addressed the team, "GRU. Unit 29155 is part of the GRU. It worked. The plan *worked*. We drew them out."

As Havens spoke, the emotions that I felt in the apartment flooded back. *Now what, Ben? You made yourself bait for the Russians. You drew them out. And now what?*

I had no answer for that, other than to realize, once again, that I had to do a better job planning out contingencies. To think like Havens or Macallister. To go that extra step.

However, the decisions that I had made thus far were about to drive our mission in a completely unexpected direction, both figuratively and literally. I wouldn't understand that, though, for several more days.

CHAPTER
64

MOSCOW, RUSSIA

VITALY RODIONOV GROWLED in a low, deadly tone, his face bent to the ear of his listener, "He said *what?*"

Cowering at a computer terminal, one of the many lined on the sleek desks under the giant, center screen in the loft-like office of Unit 29155, a technician bleated, "He said that their targets escaped. And that the operative that was tasked from Unit 74455 is missing."

With a clatter, Fedor Ilin rushed into the room from a side door, tablet dangling uselessly from one hand. As he ran toward his superior, he called, "I just heard. The operation failed."

"I know," Rodionov grunted, anger evident on his face and in his hunched shoulders. "This is unbelievable. A complete mess."

"What happened?"

Gathering his courage, the technician stammered, "It—it—it was an encrypted email. It has been decoded, and I am putting it on screen now."

The giant screen glowed with a handful of sentences:

```
Mission compromised. Both targets
escaped. Targets assisted by an
unidentified third party. 60937 subdued
and abducted by the third party. 50530
E&E. 50530 standing by for further
instruction.
```

Quickly reading the lines, Rodionov spat, "This is outrageous. He's evading and escaping while 60937 is being abducted? Abducted! By a third party? And he did not intervene? How is this possible?"

"I don't know, sir," Fedor confessed. "The mission profile was for our two operatives to be unarmed, in the event a local police authority got involved. Furthermore, the profile assumed that the two targets were soft. That they would be taken by surprise and easily subdued. We did not have intel that there would have been a third party." Fedor's face clouded as he uttered the final words, realizing that the same words had been used in the report.

Rodionov did not seem to notice, as his mind had already raced ahead, working out next steps. In a commanding, decisive tone, he ordered, "Recall 50530. I want a full statement from him. He will be punished, of course."

"Understood," Fedor said, as he tapped at his tablet, taking brief notes. "Do you want him sent back to Moscow? Or will that be too obvious in the event that the Americans are monitoring international travel? Which, I'd add, we are doing."

"Ah, yes, good point." Rodionov scratched his face under his right ear, a tik which indicated that he was thinking. "We're leaving Moscow next week and will be gone through the end of the month. Send him to meet with me. I'll meet with him on the tenth level. You understand?"

"Yes. Consider it done."

"That's fine," Rodionov agreed. "In the meantime, I will be forced to report to the Director. He will be very displeased, of course, but he will apply the appropriate pressures. The Americans cannot simply hold one of our operatives. Remind me; who is 60937?"

Consulting the tablet, Fedor disclosed, "Her name is Nina Mishkin. She is tasked to the Center for Russian Culture in Washington, D.C."

"This is an abject fiasco." Looking at the technician, Rodionov demanded, "Take that down. Off-screen. Send the entire file to me." As the tech clicked keys, Rodionov turned again to Fedor and, in a low tone, hissed, "We have underestimated Ben Porter once again. This man is very, very clever. He is wily. But I believe that he will now find that he has overstepped. He cannot take custody of a Russian citizen. His government will never allow it. In fact, his government may even punish him for us. This event *will* cause serious repercussions for Mister Porter. I can assure you that Putin himself will see to that."

CHAPTER
65

MONDAY, JULY 6, 2020 – ONE HUNDRED AND FIFTY MILES SOUTH OF NEWPORT, RHODE ISLAND

I KNEW I HAD LESSONS TO learn about planning and being mindful. Therefore, on Friday night, after learning the identity of our new guest as an agent of the GRU, I had sat with the team almost until sunrise on Saturday, talking through the options.

Havens cautioned both Rourke and me, "Don't return to the apartment. We know one of them got away. We don't know if he called in reinforcements, or if he was part of an advance team with others standing by. Really, we know nothing. And since that's the case, I think you should stay here, on the boat."

With that decision made, I called Macallister on the charcoal-gray flip phone to update him, waking him in the middle of the night. "Well, you've got my attention," Macallister declared, adding, "I can assure you, however, that very shortly, you will have some unwanted attention. This is a very, very dicey situation."

No shit, I thought, as Macallister requested that Volkov send the images of our guest to him for independent verification over the weekend.

I concluded I had done pretty well, all things considered, and given the still-throbbing bump to my head, by not reacting rashly.

That all changed late on Saturday after I had a conversation with Volkov. Returning to my usual ways, without consulting Macallister, I ordered Lockwood to cast off the lines. *Almaz* headed out to sea, and I headed to yet another confrontation with my boss.

First thing Monday morning, I confessed what I'd done to Macallister. He was, to say the least, pissed off as he glared at me, staring straight and seriously into the eye of the camera in his office in the J. Edgar Hoover building in Washington, D.C. "Porter, you fucked up. You have no business taking a suspected Russian agent offshore."

From my seat at the head of the table in the situation room on *Almaz*, now making a leisurely eight knots of boat speed in a generally southerly direction, I defended my actions. "Sir, I made the decision to leave the dock in Newport for two reasons. First, if there are additional Russian operatives in Newport, they'll be looking for me. We know there's at least one. The one that got away. We don't know if there are more. Now, of course, we think it's very unlikely that a Russian operative would put two-and-two together and link the disappearance of Nina Mishkin to the superyacht once owned by Anatoly Petrikov. But it's possible. Now that we know the Russians are in Newport, we can't hide *Almaz*."

"That's weak, but I agree," Macallister admitted, as he picked an imaginary spot of lint off the lapel of his suit.

I didn't want to let him take over the conversation, and I continued. "Furthermore, if we remained in Newport, and we turned the GRU agent over to the FBI locally, we would be revealing the existence of Quadrant to a much wider circle. I believe that you need to keep us compartmentalized as much as possible. With the GRU agent onboard, you and you alone can manage the disclosures."

I had hoped that Macallister's ego and career ambitions would mollify his annoyance that I had directed *Almaz* to leave Newport, and I was correct. Macallister's face relaxed as he said, "Yeah. What do you think the reaction will be here in D.C. when the U.S. government realizes that a sub-rosa arm of the FBI has taken a Russian agent into custody?" He whistled softly. I think he was happy that he would get the opportunity to take credit for that big reveal.

"Furthermore," Volkov added, "We've proven that the Russians are interested in Porter. Remember, this all starts with my father. As far as we know, there's been no attempt to remove him from Cuba. Instead, they went after Porter, which means that they believe he is a threat. If they didn't go after him, we could have concluded that they were satisfied with the outcome. That's not what happened. You don't understand Russians. Sometimes it's just about revenge. Payback."

"What's your plan, then?" Macallister asked. "You're going to go in circles or something while I deal with all of this?"

I shook my head back and forth. "No. Actually, I see this as an opportunity. Look at it this way. Quadrant successfully apprehended Petrikov and delivered him to the custody of the U.S. government. In addition, we defended our team from an attack by Russian agents. We have a very good track record," I said proudly, before concluding, "With that basis, now it's time for you to carefully reveal the existence of Quadrant."

Macallister scowled. "Reveal Quadrant to who?"

I turned to my right, to Volkov, and said, "Your turn."

CHAPTER
66

ANASTASIA VOLKOV FACED THE camera and Deputy Assistant Director Bradford Macallister's waiting stare. His eyes narrowed to slits. He didn't like surprises. And, of course, we knew that Macallister disliked technology, and as we prepared for the secure video teleconference, I asked Volkov to keep the discussion as simple as possible, even if it meant glossing over the technical details.

Volkov began, "While Porter, Havens, and Rourke were capturing foreign spies, I was continuing my work on Trampoline. Let's do a quick recap. We've established that the app is copying user data and, while the app is running and keeping a user's eyes glued to the screen, it's sending that user data back to Trampoline servers."

"Yeah," Macallister grunted. "I remember all that. The question that we were left hanging with two weeks ago was *where*. Where is it sending data? I assume you're going to tell me."

"Norway."

Macallister leaned back in his chair, his eyebrows hoisted, and repeated, in a questioning tone, "Norway?"

"Yes," Volkov confirmed. "There's more, too. I've—"

"Wait," Macallister commanded. "What about the talk of China before? Didn't Hamid tell me that he thought that Zoo got her money and her programming from China?"

Hamid stepped in, saying, "It's Zhao, sir. Not Zoo. And yes, I said that, but in the context of a theory. Which, I might add, would be no different than assuming that I was a terrorist because I'm of Middle Eastern descent. I apologize, and I should have known better. Assuming Zhao's backers are Chinese just because she has an Asian complexion is a form of racism."

"Certainly," Macallister offered, "and I applaud that apology. But that's not the point, is it?"

"No sir," Hamid explained, "my reference was intended to be nothing more than an example. All that's important is that Zhao did not have the money or programming experience to create this herself. I've done more research on this. There is no question in my mind that she had significant outside help."

"From Norway?" Macallister asked.

Volkov quickly corrected him, "No. We don't make that connection. All we know, and can prove, is that the data is transmitted there."

Macallister fired back, "Not a place that immediately comes to mind. Why there?"

"Temperature," Volkov answered. "Cold water and cold air. That combination is excellent for cooling servers, which generate a lot of heat. One of the biggest expenses in running a server farm is electricity for air conditioning, in order to keep the racks upon racks of servers and switches from overheating. A Nordic climate is exceptional for this purpose."

"Huh," Macallister grunted.

Unfazed, Volkov continued, "It's not just climate. It's also cheap power to keep those servers running twenty-four/seven. Much of the electricity generation in the Nordic countries is hydroelectric. None of this is really new. It's just that users don't typically think of where they are connecting to, as long as the web page or app loads. Facebook, Microsoft, Google, and Apple all maintain server farms in the Nordics. Sweden, Finland, and of course, Norway."

"Well, knowing where it goes is helpful. But you still don't know why," cautioned Macallister.

"Sir, we have a suspicion," I interrupted. "It is tenuous, to say the least, and I hinted at this when we last spoke. It starts with something that seems fairly innocuous. The app is copying your photos. Our theory is that Trampoline would try to use your face in order to unlock your phone, using facial recognition derived from photos—"

Volkov interrupted, "But, it's not just photos. It's the *actual* faceprint data. When you set up a phone that is secured by facial recognition, you expose your face at various angles to the phone during the setup procedure. The phone measures eighty nodal points and converts those dimensions to a formula. To a faceprint. If your phone is equipped with a fingerprint reader, it does basically the same thing with your fingerprint data. Trampoline has harvested those two security items, and it has copied your passwords. Potentially, we believe that the app has the ability to spoof your faceprint, your fingerprint, and your passwords, and to gain access to whatever is protected or secured by those methods."

Macallister leaned forward and summarized, "Oh? And it's sending all that information to Norway?" His voice had a note of incredulity.

"Yeah," Volkov confirmed. "It's sending that identity information, along with your location, your IP address, your phone number, and way more. Trampoline does all that and then some. It's sending your device identifier, serial number, usage patterns, and more. Basically, Trampoline has unfettered access to your device and everything on it, including your identity."

I knew I had to wrap it up, so I butted in and stated, "Sir, Trampoline has become the most talked-about social media platform on the planet. It bills itself as a refuge from the pandemic and from the political fray. It applauds itself for its robust censorship. And yet, there's clearly a dark side to the platform, which goes hand-in-hand with the FTC investigation. But what the FTC hasn't realized is that Trampoline is very deliberately creating an addiction, so that you keep your eyes glued to the screen while in the background, it collects a vast amount of information about you: your identity and what are presumed to be on-device security measures, including your faceprint, your fingerprint, and your passwords. In theory, we believe that the app has enough data to pose as, well, you. Or as any of its one billion users. And it's sending all of that data to a server farm in Norway."

"I got it," Macallister nodded. "What do you propose?"

"We're going to Norway to check it out."

Macallister laughed. "No, you're not. Don't forget you have a Russian spy on board. We need to clean up that mess first." He paused, "Listen, this is all great work. And very concerning. I'm going to brief the Director of the FBI immediately. He and I will escalate this as quickly as possible."

With that, Macallister terminated the call.

I turned to Lockwood, and I asked, "How long to go transatlantic?"

"A couple of weeks, at our usual cruising speed."

"Do we have the fuel and the provisions for that distance?"

Lockwood replied confidently, "Oh, yeah. More than enough. Fully fueled and fully stocked. We could go for a month, easily. Maybe a month and a half."

"Let's go then." I looked around the table, first to Volkov, then to Rourke, then to Havens, then to Hamid, and finally back at Lockwood, as I asked, "Any objections?"

The faces at the table remained silent. I looked at Lockwood and ordered, "Plot a course to Norway."

CHAPTER

67

MONDAY, JULY 13, 2020 – WASHINGTON, DC

TAKING UP A FRACTION OF the 2,800,000 square feet within the J. Edgar Hoover Building, the FBI's Strategic Information Operations Center (SIOC) is a 40,000 square foot, hi-tech command center that is the hub of the Bureau's ongoing, everyday crisis management and event monitoring work. The SIOC is built as a Sensitive Compartmented Information Facility, and within it, adjacent to the Global Watch Command Center, there are a number of executive briefing rooms. Deputy Assistant Director Bradford Macallister had reserved one of the rooms that was rated for Top Secret discussions, the highest of the three levels—Confidential, Secret, and Top Secret—within the United States government's information classification system.

Since the SVTC with the Quadrant team, it took Macallister a full week to brief the appropriate power players in D.C., and then to coordinate and assemble an in-person meeting with this always-busy group—people who represented the very pinnacle of the United States intelligence apparatus.

Only four other individuals were seated with Macallister around the polished oak conference table. To his right, with an empty chair between them to achieve the prescribed measure of physical distancing, was a tall, white-haired, fair-skinned man, Director Walter Toffer, the highest-ranking official of the Bureau. Seated to the right of Toffer, again with a vacant seat between, was Toffer's counterpart, the Director of the Central Intelligence Agency, Hazel Ginachere, her pale face partially obscured by large, black-framed eyeglasses that matched her jet-black, shoulder-length hair.

Ginachere was removing her glasses and absently polishing them as she scolded Toffer and Macallister in a cold, harsh tone, "I am going on record that I am extremely troubled to learn that the Bureau has been operating in the international arena. I've read your report of an operation conducted in not only Venezuela, but also in Cuba, and now on American soil, which involved a suspected agent of the Russian government. If this was ever disclosed, it could have disastrous consequences." Turning her attention to address the woman seated opposite her, Ginachere demanded, "Wouldn't you agree?"

That woman, Genevieve Sullivan, whose white-haired, white-skinned face barely peeked above the table due to her short stature, turned to Macallister and continued the rebuke, "I absolutely concur. I've already received inquiries on the whereabouts of that suspected Russian agent. This places me in a very, very difficult position. As Under Secretary for Political Affairs, and here representing the interests of the Secretary of State, the actions of this team—Quadrant, as you've called them unless I'm mistaken—have been absolutely unsanctioned by the United States."

Macallister may have called the meeting, but he was the lowest-ranking official at the table. And yet, while his appearance was polished, even he knew that his words were sometimes not as well constructed as these more experienced bureaucrats, and the Deputy Assistant Director knew when to keep his mouth closed.

Fortunately, one of the individuals responsible for Quadrant stepped in. "That is not accurate," said Bart Williams, the Black man seated to Macallister's left. He ran a hand through his curly, short, gray hair and continued in his deep baritone voice, "Macallister received approval from not only me but also from Director Toffer to conduct this operation. It was necessary to keep it compartmentalized. As Attorney General of the United States, I have sanctioned the work of Macallister's team."

"And I might add two points," Toffer said, choosing his words carefully and speaking slowly. "First, the team was authorized for a limited scope of work only, to locate and apprehend Anatoly Petrikov. Second, their work was exceptionally successful. I recognize that the approach was unconventional, and I acknowledge that I've stepped on toes within this room. However, now that the operation is complete, it is important to disclose so that we may work collaboratively going forward."

Ginachere fake-laughed. "Bullshit, Toffer. You're disclosing it because your team overstepped their operation, which you just tacitly acknowledged, by taking a Russian agent into custody. Like the Under Secretary, I'm hearing chatter about that agent. You've created quite a quandary for yourself, and let's be honest, that's the only reason you're coming clean now."

Toffer stood his ground. "I disagree. The apprehension of the Russian agent was a happenstance that should be considered as an extension of the original mission. You all were read into the history prior to this meeting. You all know that Petrikov was assisted, as he has admitted under questioning not only by the Quadrant team informally but also by trained investigators who have been meeting with him in Cuba, by the Russian Unit 29155. You all know that is an arm of the Russian GRU, their military intelligence. You all know that the Russian agent now in our custody is, without question, a GRU agent. I don't give a damn what unit number she might be from."

Toffer paused to inhale and attempted to continue before anyone in the room could offer an objection, but instead, the Attorney General stepped in. "Those are all acceptable exigencies of the operation. Petrikov is considered an unlawful enemy combatant. He is a terror suspect. I am comfortable with the Bureau's actions leading to this point. We can agree to disagree on who should have known and when, but we have more pressing issues to discuss. Let's move on," suggested Williams. As the highest-ranking lawyer in the land, his word was final, and the others, having staked their positions, knew that he was correct.

Ginachere, no stranger to power plays, moved quickly. "Very well. Macallister's pre-read on Trampoline was compelling and concerning. However, I don't trust your methods nor your team. I will not agree to move forward unless the CIA has management of the team."

"That's impossible," Macallister blurted, finally adding to the conversation, unable to remain mute any longer. Macallister's rise from Supervisory Special Agent, to Acting Special Agent in Charge, and to Deputy Assistant Director was meteoric in the context of FBI promotions, and he was unafraid of diving into the fray with a direct contradiction to the Director of the CIA.

"Deputy *Assistant* Director," Ginachere hissed, emphasizing the second word, "Your team is untrained in these matters. You would do well to benefit from my organization's expertise, I think."

"The personnel count of *my* team is currently sufficient," Toffer countered, pointedly taking ownership of Quadrant, before offering an olive branch. "How about we link you in electronically? Give you full access to the data collected and the systems we have in place."

With Toffer himself backing the Quadrant team, the CIA Director knew better than to press the matter, and she hesitantly agreed. "I can live with that. But, with a proviso that I reserve the right to include an agent, or better yet, to take over management of your team if you propose to conduct operations on the ground."

Before Toffer or Macallister could object, Sullivan squeaked, "I'll require full access as well," her high-pitched, bird-like voice belying the power that the tiny woman held in the Department of State. "You will report to me at every opportunity. I will choose to brief the Secretary of State, as well as the President, as conditions warrant. If the Quadrant team is operating in foreign states, I will be the liaison to the Executive Branch."

Sullivan placed her hands flat on the table in front of her, pushing her shoulders up as far as she could. "You're treading on thin ice, Director Toffer and Deputy Macallister. This is a high-risk proposition. Your team has proven its effectiveness, but as we all know, if there's one tiny misstep and this goes public, you're on the front page of every newspaper and website on the planet. The Executive Branch will be fully informed at all times. Is that clear?"

First looking at Sullivan and then turning to Ginachere, Toffer said smoothly, "Of course. The Quadrant team will be fully accountable to both you, Madam Under Secretary, and you, Director." Glancing to his left at Macallister, Toffer asked, "Is that clear?"

"Of course," Macallister agreed. "Perfectly clear, sir. And ma'am," he added, looking first at Sullivan and then at Ginachere. *I can play the game at this level,* he thought.

Macallister was savvy enough to recognize that Sullivan's words were for her self-interest only. A successful mission would be credited to the Secretary of State and possibly to the President. A failure, and it would be solely the FBI's problem. And if it was the FBI's problem, it was Macallister's problem.

I'm risking not only the standing of the United States of America, but also, selfishly, my career, on Ben Porter, Macallister thought, keeping his face blank as the group began to wrap up a meeting that pulled in some of the highest-ranking members of America's intelligence community and government—and had authorized an international investigation.

I wonder if Porter truly understands the stakes.

CHAPTER
68

45° 34' N, 053° 01' W

"THERE'S NO QUESTION whatsoever. Carole Baskin killed Don Baskin." As the big flatscreen television went black, I sat back, lifted the longneck, dew-dripped beer bottle to my lips, and took a deep, long swig, putting my feet back up on the coffee table in the sumptuous living quarters of *Almaz*.

"I don't know, man. I think she's innocent. She's played off as the villain to the hero," Abdul Hamid objected.

We had just wrapped up an almost seven-hour, binge-watching marathon of *Tiger King: Murder, Mayhem and Madness* on Netflix. We all knew about the eight-episode series that launched in March, and as *Almaz* cruised slowly east over the Atlantic Ocean waves, Hamid, Havens, Rourke, and I decided to indulge in the much-talked-about show as Volkov continued her coding conjuring in the situation room.

Rourke laughed. "I agree. Joe Exotic is kinda cute. Hamid's right. They make him their hero and almost into a victim, and they needed someone to balance that. Ergo, Baskin." Her face clouded as she added, "What's really sad is the animals. What happens to them, once all the people get over their petty squabbles?"

We didn't have a chance to continue our critique because the intercom buzzed, and Volkov's disembodied voice announced, "Situation room. Macallister has called for an SVTC in ten minutes."

En masse, we rushed below, changing t-shirts for more appropriate videoconference attire—only required from the waist up, as we'd learned. A refreshed Quadrant team gathered in our usual seats around the horseshoe-shaped table.

The big center display brightened, and a room that we had not seen before was imaged on-screen: blue-painted walls, white ceiling tiles, and at the center of the view, a polished oak conference table. Of the seven black chairs visible, only two were occupied. At the head of the table, glaring at the screen, sat Macallister. To his right was a tall, white-haired, fair-skinned man. Volkov mouthed, "Walter Toffer." I shot back a glare; I knew full well what the Director looked like. Good thing I changed my shirt.

Macallister wasted no time getting started, saying, "Okay, you've got approval to investigate Trampoline. I've explained the parameters of the mission that you've emailed me, and I've explained the objectives—which, at this time, remain limited to determining why the platform is collecting identity data. What are they doing with that data? That's the question to answer, that question, and that question alone. You're going to be on a tight leash."

"Let me elaborate on that," Director Toffer quickly added, leaning his upper body toward the camera with earnestness. From the look in his eyes to the body language, I knew I had better pay attention. Toffer's command of the room was palpable. I felt that he was addressing me, personally, even though I knew he was talking to the eye of a wall-mounted camera. "You're going to link in the CIA so they can observe. If you go on the ground, they might want to be there with you. You're also going to be supervised by the Secretary of State. I want a detailed report of what you're doing, no less than every day or, better yet, constant communication. Got it?"

I probably should not have had a few beers while watching *Tiger King*, and had I not done that, I might have been more reserved. Liquid courage, I guess, as I objected, saying, "Sir, I understand, but I'd like to point out that we've been successful largely by being invisible. The more people that know about this, the more opportunities to leak it."

"You're Porter, right?" The Director glared at the camera, and this time I knew he was most definitely talking to me. I nodded as Toffer continued, "I'll compliment you with reservations. You have managed to pull off a neat trick. However, I for one believe that luck is not infinitely sustainable. At some point, you need to learn accountability."

"Yessir," I replied. "I understand."

Toffer leaned back in his chair, his message delivered, as Macallister demanded, "Where are you, anyway? How long to cross the ocean?"

Oops, I thought. After that lecture from the Director, was now the time to come clean? Or maybe a little white lie? I considered my options and made my choice. "I made the decision to pre-position the team so we could save some time." I saw Macallister's face beginning to redden noticeably as his eyes narrowed, and I rushed on. "We headed east but at a very slow speed. We're still on the western side of the Atlantic."

Lockwood, seeing my discomfort, specified, "We're about one hundred and fifty miles south of the south-east tip of Newfoundland, Canada. We have plotted out the mission, and we have about twenty-one, twenty-two hundred miles to go. Approximately six days at our normal cruising speed."

Macallister's expression softened. I figured he heard only "Canada." He wouldn't have grasped that we had already traveled almost one thousand miles from Newport. And it appeared to me that he was trying to impress the Director when he said, "Good, good. Good to be proactive. Pre-positioning and all that."

The Director, however, was not as accommodating. He did not have the history that Macallister had with me, and the Director was not so quick to applaud me. "That seems reckless. You've still got a Russian agent aboard. Isn't that correct?"

"Well, yes," I admitted, "but frankly, I don't think it makes a difference whether she's on board and we are in the middle of the ocean or we are at a dock somewhere."

Toffer turned to Macallister and asked in a startled tone, "Is he always this objectionable?"

Macallister chuckled. "As you know, on paper, I had to terminate him for insubordination. It's part of the package. And, by the way, he's right. We've gamed this out, and there's really no option open to dis-embark their, um, passenger."

As if the entire Quadrant team was not visible on what had to have been a big screen facing them, the two high-ranking Bureau executives continued their conversation, with Toffer outlining to Macallister, "You know that both the CIA and the State Department have received inquiries from the Russians. Along the lines of, what happened to Nina Mishkin?"

"I'm aware. And their answer should remain the same: we don't know."

I interrupted, "They do know, though." I think it was the beer talking.

Toffer faced the camera, scowled at my impertinence, and said, "Pardon?"

Yikes. I better dig out of this one, fast.

"Mishkin had an accomplice. A burly dude. Surely, he has reported to his superiors. But here's the rub. The Russians can't come to you and say they are missing an agent who was tasked to take me down. And now we have something they want back. I think *we* hold the strategic advantage." *Damn,* I thought in angst, *I should not have had so many beers while watching "Tiger King."* I had slurred "strategic." *Shra-tee-shick.*

"That's an excellent point," Toffer agreed. Relieved, I realized that the Director would be unaware that I don't normally speak like Sean Connery in a Bond movie. "Have we had any success with identifying or locating the accomplice?"

Macallister shook his head. "No. Unfortunately, there are no cameras in the alley where the attack took place. We had Havens, Rourke and Porter each describe the accomplice to our artists. Needless to say, we don't have a lot to work with."

"Long shot, I suppose," Toffer observed. He stood, adjusted his tie, and buttoned his suit coat. "Very well. Carry on, but remember: constant communication."

The video went black, and Rourke exclaimed, "Great. Now we're gonna have the State Department, the FBI, *and* the CIA watching our every move."

I turned to Volkov and asked, "Is it really necessary to share our comms links?"

She eyed me. "Well, we can decide what we want to share, I suppose."

"Exactly," I suggested. "They don't need to know our *every* move. Just the ones we want them to know."

Havens leaned forward. "Really? What do you have in mind?"

I leaned back in my chair and began to outline the plan.

But I forgot, for a moment, that while Rourke correctly concluded that three arms of the American government would now have oversight on Quadrant, the Russian government would also be even more interested in me, and in the fate of my guest who was below deck, currently residing in a cell-like cabin once occupied by Anatoly Petrikov.

And there was something else. In my excitement to hear the Director himself approve my operation to travel to Norway to investigate Trampoline, I had forgotten the principle cautionary lessons that Havens had taught me, and the plan that I would outline would drive the team carelessly into peril.

In a stark space with smooth, white, polished concrete floors, two men were seated on plain, gray, metal folding chairs that had been placed three feet apart, and a third man stood beyond, motionless.

Vitaly Rodionov occupied one of those chairs, his stare boring mercilessly into the eyes of the man seated, almost knee-to-knee, opposite him in an identical chair. Through clenched teeth, Rodionov hissed, "For your failure, operative 50530, you would normally be assigned to perimeter security at a camp in Siberia. This, however, has become your salvation."

Rodionov waved the black, rubber-encased smartphone device that he was holding, tempting the man to speak. Knowing better, he did not, and Rodionov continued his monologue, "A useful tactic, to prop your device on the curb, or whatever, and record the scene on video. Thus, we've been able to identify the third party. His name is Leroy Havens. He is an agent of the FBI. Is that a surprise to you?"

The operative knew that it was time to speak, and he replied, "Nyet." *No.*

"Why not?"

"He was very well trained. That was obvious by his movements and his combat skills. And by his appearance. He attacked from ahead, not from behind. He knew where the targets were going, and he didn't trail them. He advanced them."

"A reasonable analysis," Rodionov agreed. "I'd also compliment you, despite your failure, for having brought the device to us, rather than attempting to transfer the video file. I'll concede that was a smart thing to do, given the subject matter of the video."

The man merely nodded as Rodionov called, "Fedor!"

"Sir?"

"Make arrangements for our guest to return to Moscow. And send this video file via the usual encrypted channel."

"Understood. Anything else?"

"No." Rodionov smiled wickedly and stood, signaling an end to an interview that was conducted in what was a most unusual interrogation space. The mastermind of Unit 29155 concluded, "This will no doubt place a great deal of pressure on Ben Porter. We now have concrete, incontrovertible evidence that the FBI was involved with the apprehension of our operative. The question becomes, what does the United States government do in response? I suspect we will soon find out."

TUESDAY, JULY 21, 2020 – 61° 56' N, 003° 15' E

EVEN MILES LOCKWOOD had been impressed when the GPS displays on the bridge of *Almaz* changed from showing West longitude coordinates to East longitude coordinates as the yacht crossed the Prime Meridian soon after ducking south of the Faroe Islands. "A few hundred miles further north, and we would cross the Arctic Circle," Lockwood advised us, explaining, "That's why it's light until almost eleven at night, and the sun rises before five in the morning. Not quite at the land of the midnight sun, but close."

"More like the island of misfit toys," Hamid observed, taking in the Quadrant team as we covered the final miles of our journey. "Rourke, Volkov, and Porter. A retired CIRG Agent. A disgraced Intelligence Analyst. And an insubordinate, fired Special Agent," he said, mocking us. "The only people on this boat with a badge are Havens and me."

His attempt at humor fell a little flat, and the laughter was reserved. It was almost go-time, and our journey had been slowed by bad weather, Lockwood pulling back on the throttles to lessen the loads imposed on the vessel by the Atlantic waves and a fierce summer gale. Maybe our nervousness was also a remnant of seasickness, or maybe it was just, well, nerves.

By two in the morning on July 21, eight days after getting the go-ahead from Director Toffer, we were at our staging location, about fifty miles to the west of the Norway coastline, the yacht now steady on the flat seas and motoring at idle speed in a due north direction. The RIB was launched from the aft deck crane on *Almaz*, and Rourke, Volkov, Havens, and I climbed aboard, carrying, among us, two black, anodized aluminum cases containing laptops and networking gear, two backpacks that held climbing harnesses and rappelling equipment, and a final duffel filled with lights and weaponry.

Advancing the throttles of the twin-engine RIB, Rourke piloted the craft due east, aiming for the mouth of the Vågsfjorden, between the seaside villages of Vågsvåg and Husevåg.

I looked at the speed indicated on the screen in front of Rourke and saw that we were making, as planned, twenty-five knots. Not too fast, not too slow. Goldilocks speed.

The RIB carved a straight and true course, bouncing gently over the low swell. Two hours to landfall, and my stomach was churning.

An hour into the ride, the hairs on the back of my neck prickled. *This is wrong*, I thought to myself.

I heard Havens' voice in my head, and for a moment, I thought he was actually talking. *The problem with that is that no one knows what you are doing.*

And then, it was Rourke's voice sounding in my head. *No contingency plan. No bolt holes.*

My eyes blurred. I blamed the windswept salt air, the speed, but as I wiped my eyes, I knew what I had to do.

Touching Rourke on the shoulder, I said, in an unsteady tone, "Turn back. We're turning around."

She pulled her eyes from the controls and gauges and compass and asked, "What? Really?"

"Yeah. Back to *Almaz*."

"Okay," she said, drawing out the word with obvious skepticism. Pulling back on the left-hand throttle slightly and rotating the steering wheel counterclockwise, the RIB carved an arc north and then west, eventually retracing our wake.

"What's up?" Havens and Volkov chorused.

I blinked, my eyes suddenly clear, my convictions strong, as I answered, "This plan is flawed. I'll explain back on the boat. We're aborting the mission."

CHAPTER
70

CUPPING A MUG OF freshly brewed coffee in my hands, I examined the steam drifting from the dark liquid as I waited for my team to take their seats in the situation room. One by one, they sat, staring me down, waiting for my explanation. I kept my head down, though not as they might expect from shame, but simply so that I could make sure they all were settled.

Rourke was the last to arrive, having changed out of the black night ops gear and into jeans and a sweatshirt. As she gathered her red hair into a messy ponytail, she glared at me, her green eyes clouded, so it was in her direction that I looked as I started in, "First off, my apologies. This is a team, and we work as a team. I understand I do not have totalitarian authority. However, our plan sucked."

I let that sink in and then continued. "Really, it was my plan. I called an audible days ago, thinking about the success of our incursion into Cuba. I figured if we moved fast, and we got into Norway before the suits back home could second-guess us, we'd be better off. But as the Director cautioned, luck is not infinite, and attempting to repeat that playbook was a foolish error on my part."

To my surprise, Rourke was the first to say, "I agree." She chuckled and smiled, "I thought you just got cold feet."

I nodded. "Well, honestly, I did, but for the right reasons. Cold feet from a lack of planning. Cold feet from carelessness. Cold feet because I'm not going to repeat the mistakes I've made in the past." I glanced to my left, to Lockwood, who always seemed to exude confidence, and I took some strength from him and from Rourke's apparent acceptance as I asked Volkov, "Run down the target again."

"We've done this ten times, Ben," she admonished in a gentle tone.

"I know. Turn it up to eleven. Let's do it again."

Volkov shook her head back and forth but recited, flatly, "Our target is inside the Lefdal Mine Datacenter. About fourteen nautical miles east from the mouth of the Vågsfjorden. The data center, as its name suggests, was built in a former olivine mine. The subterranean tunnels of the mine were converted to a server farm in 2017, and it is currently utilized by several multinationals, including Trampoline dot Live. There is high-speed, redundant fiber connectivity, and the center boasts round-trip data connection to London in seventeen milliseconds and to the United States in twenty to twenty-two milliseconds. Within its six or seven, depending on how you count them, sloping levels, it is about 1.3 million square feet, though there's a rumor that there are possibly up to ten levels total, the deeper ones awaiting development."

"Right," I added, "and as the crow flies, the secondary entrance to the mine is only about 300 feet from the banks of the fjord, which would appear to make it a perfect target for infiltration by water."

"You said, 'would appear,'" Havens said. "Wasn't that the plan?"

"Yeah," I replied. "The plan that sucked. By the time we ran the fourteen or so miles up the fjord, it would be well after sunrise, which is really early in the morning this time of year, given our latitude. The security of the center is, of course, twenty-four-seven, so we'd be making a daylight incursion, and by the time Volkov got what she needed, the place would be fully staffed, making our exit all the more dangerous."

"When you lay it out like that, it does suck," Hamid agreed.

"Oh, there's more," I laughed. "In the meantime, while Volkov is working her magic—which, by the way, assumes that we've found the Trampoline servers within that one-point-three million square feet on six or seven levels—and while Havens and I are watching her back, Rourke is puttering around the fjord in a matte-black-painted hard-bottomed inflatable boat with two giant engines, and Lockwood and Hamid are watching our collective backs puttering around the Norwegian coastline in a superyacht."

"Truly a masterpiece of deception," Lockwood deadpanned.

"Ah, sadly not," I admitted. "But that, my friend, that is exactly how we should approach this. A bit of deception."

CHAPTER
71

THURSDAY, JULY 23, 2020 – MÅLØY, NORWAY

THE WATER AHEAD OF *Almaz* changed from the deep, dark gray of the Atlantic to the characteristic turquoise of a Norwegian fjord as Miles Lockwood guided the vessel into the Vågsfjorden. Our captain explained that the spectacular color of the water was due to the sunlight reflecting off blooms of a single-celled phytoplankton, but our bioscience lesson ceased as Lockwood focused on passing under the Måløybrua Bridge, above the Måløy-Husevåg vehicle tunnel, leaving us to gaze in admiration upon the bright green trees that clung to the rising, steep, hillside banks of the Måløystraumen, an offshoot passage from the Vågsfjorden.

Nineteen days after departing Newport, Lockwood deftly maneuvered *Almaz* into a berth at the commercial shipping pier in Måløy, Norway, a picturesque town of red, yellow, and white-painted buildings and houses with just over 3,000 residents that nestled into the foothills of the Måløystraumen.

The moment the dock lines were secured, the crew used the aft deck crane to unload our two four-door Jeeps, top-of-the-line models which were custom painted in matte black, of course.

Fortunately, despite her protestations, CIA Director Ginachere had been overruled, and we were allowed to proceed with my newly created operation. Our liaisons at the State Department had sold our cover story perfectly, and we were welcomed, our passports barely examined, and our vessel uninspected. After a cursory explanation of Norway's current Covid-19 policies, which seemed unrestrictive and did not require face masks, we were offered ground transportation, but we declined, pointing out that our Jeeps would not be out of place since Norway drives on the right side of the road. And by right, I mean "right hand;" certainly, I don't mean to infer that if you drive on the left side of the road, you're not right and you're wrong.

With that exhausting explanation out of the way, and with the maneuvering and docking and unloading concluded by ten in the morning, the convoy of two Jeeps set off for our thirty-minute drive, following the scenic Rv15 road, which hugged the northern banks of the fjord. Rourke, dressed in a loose, long-sleeve black t-shirt and black leggings, was driving my Jeep, and I ogled the view out the window, occasionally ogling the view of Rourke's shapely legs. In the backseat, I hoped Hamid would be doing only the former.

Behind us, Havens, clad in a black mock turtleneck shirt and black pants, drove the second Jeep, with Volkov riding solo in the backseat.

"This is it," I announced, and Rourke slowed the Jeep and turned left off Rv15. "Check it out," I added, pointing at a paved helipad at the edge of the fjord. "That could be useful."

Rourke nodded as she braked the Jeep at the security gate to the Lefdal Mine Datacenter. Rolling her window down, Rourke smiled cheerily as the guard said, "Ah, yes, the Americans. Welcome. Please proceed."

"That was easy," Rourke said as she engaged the button to roll up the window and pressed the gas pedal.

"Getting in will be the easy part. Getting what we need will be substantially more complex," I replied.

We parked inside the mine's cavernous mouth, the second Jeep pulling alongside, and we assumed the roles of our deception. Rourke and Havens would pose as our drivers and assistants, each hefting a black, anodized aluminum briefcase from the rear of the second Jeep. Volkov and Hamid would be the technicians. And I got to be CEO.

"Welcome to Lefdal," said a chipper, tall, blonde woman, with a slight accent. "I'm Eva Sigmund."

"John Godfrey. A pleasure, Miss Sigmund," I boomed.

"No, no, it's my pleasure. Such a surprise," she said, with a hint of questioning in her voice.

"For us, as well," I replied. "We were on vacation, holiday, if you will, enjoying the coastline, when it occurred to us that this would be a good side excursion for our business. Plus, now the whole trip will be a tax write-off," I laughed. I hoped it didn't sound too insincere, though I did want to come across as a slightly obnoxious American.

"I don't know what that means," chirped Sigmund, "but all the same, I am happy to show you the center. What, again, was your business?"

"Procurement. We set up bulk buys of commodities, materials, and natural resources." I didn't want to dwell on the topic because I was making it up, so I segued, "Allow me to introduce my associates, Ann Karin and Akmal Sayed." I could see Hamid smirking; he had picked his own cover name months ago, and his first name meant "perfect" in Arabic. "Sayed" was a derivative of "lord."

Without giving Sigmund a chance to ask for further identification, Volkov enthused, "This is *perfect*. Stunning, really. Show us around, please. I'll explain our specifications."

We climbed into an extended golf cart-type vehicle. With Sigmund behind the wheel, the electric motor engaged, and the cart whirred into the heart of the mine.

Volkov was correct. It *was* stunning. As Volkov rambled tech-speak, sitting next to Sigmund, I stared, slack-jawed, at our surroundings. The wheels of the cart rolled on a smooth, white, polished concrete floor, a stark contrast to the rough-hewn rock walls, which were lit with green, red, and blue lights that created an otherworldly ambiance as the cart glided deeper and deeper into the earth. Above, shiny metal ductwork ran alongside dull metal latticework, which was punctuated by bright white lights and the occasional black dome of a security camera. Resting on top of the lattice tray were bundle after bundle of thick wires. And, nestled into indents created in the rock walls, hundreds of white shipping containers were stacked on yellow-painted racks.

Sigmund explained, "Those are our container servers. One of the features of the facility is the ability to provision a standard-size shipping container with servers. We can move them easily within the mine. And, if you need to scale, we can simply add a container to your rack. We offer unparalleled expansion speed."

Volkov saw her opening and hurriedly asked, "Can you give me an example? Of clients who have needed to scale?"

"Of course," Sigmund replied. "One of our highest-profile clients is a social network called Trampoline dot Live. I'm certain you've heard of them." Volkov nodded agreeably as the Norwegian continued, "Given their massive user growth, they've had to add server after server. They've actually grown into being the sole occupant of one of our three-story data halls."

I couldn't believe our luck that Trampoline was the first client Sigmund referenced, but before I could say anything, Volkov reacted perfectly, purring, "Fascinating. Can we see that data hall? Scalability is very important for our operation."

"In fact, it's right here." A wide, metal roll-up door stood to our right, and as Sigmund halted the cart, we waited as she swiped an access card at a smaller, metal, standard-sized door. Above was a black dome, and she pointed at it, explaining, "Our security is quite complex. What I can tell you is that everything is monitored, twenty-four/seven, by a closed-circuit camera system. We have personnel watching the feed, and we store that feed for one hundred and eighty days. Because, after all, we have no shortage of data storage facilities." She giggled at her own joke as she led us inside.

A massive, almost hangar-like room lay ahead, with yellow racks stretching at least thirty-five feet above our heads. White containers were stacked on the racks, and only a few empty slots remained. Sigmund waved at those spots and said, "Still a bit more room for growth. They'll need it, I suspect."

Hamid sidled next to the blonde and pretended to shiver, asking flirtatiously, "How does the cooling work in here?"

Our guide giggled again, "Oh, yes, it's quite chilly. The cooling is seawater based. We circulate the water from the fjord, which is fed by glaciers and which remains just above freezing, around a closed freshwater cooling circuit. And our primary power supply is ninety-eight percent hydroelectric. Together, our power and cooling systems are very friendly to the environment."

As she recited her sales pitch, I caught Havens' and Rourke's eyes. Havens, composed as ever, barely moved; Rourke gently rotated her eyes to the ceiling, where she had spotted yet another camera. My call to abort the infiltration attempt had been justified. We would never have made it this far into the facility without being intercepted.

Volkov smoothly played her final move as she wondered, almost absently, "I'd love to test the system latency. From within the data hall. Mind if I plug in?"

"That's an unusual request," Sigmund responded. She pointed at a computer that was perched on a workstation at the base of one of the towering server container racks. "I can use one of the network management terminals to demonstrate connection speeds, if that's helpful. But for security reasons, I can't let you connect a machine."

My heart sank. From what Volkov had explained to me, and from what I could understand—admittedly, not much, given the technical jargon she used—the critical step in the infiltration plan was to be able to connect one of Volkov's computers within the Lefdal complex.

I blinked rapidly, trying to think up something to say to Sigmund, in order to convince the Norwegian to allow Volkov to proceed. Meanwhile, Havens was tugging at his shirt, and Rourke narrowed her eyes. *We may need to use force,* I thought with dismay.

Volkov nodded and addressed Sigmund, saying, "No problem." I, in turn, nodded at Havens. It was time to trigger the contingency plan, and I wondered what kind of mess we would make on the smooth, white, polished concrete floors deep within the Lefdal Mine Datacenter.

CHAPTER
72

ANASTASIA VOLKOV PUSHED her right hand outwards, at her waist, palm facing down. It was a subtle gesture that went unnoticed by Eva Sigmund—but not overlooked by trained CIRG agents. Havens and Rourke both paused, staring back at Volkov, who repeated, "No problem. But . . ."

Her voice trailed off as she made eye contact with Sigmund. Volkov spoke in a bright voice, "While I certainly understand the security issue, I wonder if I might explain. And demonstrate. What I'd like to do is nothing that you'll find objectionable."

Without waiting for the Norwegian to respond, Volkov motioned to the black, anodized aluminum briefcase that Rourke was carrying as Hamid retrieved an identical-looking case from Havens. I stood there with my hands in my pockets, pretending to admire the towering rock walls behind the stacks of containers housing server after server for Trampoline.

Volkov snapped the two latches on her case to the open position, and, lifting the lid, revealed two silver-colored MacBook Air laptops. Selecting one, she addressed Hamid, "A patch cable, please. And a USB-C to Ethernet dongle."

As Sigmund watched carefully, Hamid handed Volkov a bright blue Ethernet cable and a small white box with a short, white cord attached. Volkov snapped one end of the Ethernet cable into the receptacle in the dongle and then plugged the white cord into one of the two ports on the left side of the laptop.

Then, to my surprise, Volkov handed the lightweight, silver computer to Sigmund. "Listen, I know you're doing me a favor. You're more than welcome to take over. Then you know for sure I'm not doing anything fishy," Volkov concluded with a sincere-looking smile.

I watched the scene unfold in slow motion, wondering how Volkov would pull off her heist while not even touching the computer.

Sigmund lifted the lid of the computer with hesitation and the screen lit. Volkov explained, "I'm most curious about your connection speeds. All I'd like to do is to send a series of data packets back to our server. The application will time how fast those packets are sent and received, and it will also show us if there is any data loss."

Sigmund eyed the screen, which remained unchanged, and then directed a question at Volkov, who kept an innocent grin plastered on her face, "Do you have a specific application that you'd like to run?"

"Oh, no," Volkov demurred. "I wouldn't ask that of you. You'd never be able to verify if it's secure. Use Apple's native Terminal app."

"That's reassuring," Sigmund replied. "And hardly a security issue. I'm not connecting to the Trampoline servers, only to the outside link to the cloud." The Norwegian exhaled as she accepted the machine in one hand, and with the other hand, took the untethered end of the Ethernet cable. Carrying the laptop, she snapped the Ethernet cable into one of the several empty receptacles on a black, multi-port switch adjacent to the network management computer.

With Volkov looking over a shoulder, Sigmund clicked open the Finder application, then clicked Applications, then Utilities, and finally clicked on the word "Terminal." A white box appeared on screen. Volkov narrated, and Sigmund typed:

```
ping 181.51.91.523
```

In a fraction of a second, the screen responded, showing one line after another:

```
64 bytes from 181.51.91.523: icmp _ seq=0
ttl=51 time=63.654 ms
```

```
64 bytes from 181.51.91.523: icmp_seq=1
ttl=51 time=67.294 ms

64 bytes from 181.51.91.523: icmp_seq=2
ttl=51 time=67.707 ms

64 bytes from 181.51.91.523: icmp_seq=3
ttl=51 time=57.876 ms

64 bytes from 181.51.91.523: icmp_seq=4
ttl=51 time=70.365 ms

64 bytes from 181.51.91.523: icmp_seq=5
ttl=51 time=61.021 ms

64 bytes from 181.51.91.523: icmp_seq=6
ttl=51 time=64.523 ms

64 bytes from 181.51.91.523: icmp_seq=7
ttl=51 time=65.174 ms
```

"That's plenty," Volkov said. "Control 'c' to stop." Sigmund tapped the two keys, and a final line appeared:

```
--- 181.51.91.523 ping statistics ---

8 packets transmitted, 8 packets
received, 0.0% packet loss

round-trip min/avg/max/stddev =
57.876/64.702/70.365/3.697 ms
```

Raising her eyebrows and reviewing the summary statistics of the latency test, which showed no data loss and an average round-trip transmission speed for a 64 byte data packet at 64.702 milliseconds, Sigmund stuttered with some dismay in her tone, "That's—that's quite slow."

"Not unexpected. That's our third-party hosted public server. It's not going to be as fast as a direct connection to our private server, and for security reasons, I'd rather not share that IP address quite yet. I'm sure you understand," Volkov said gently.

"Oh, absolutely," our host replied, her relief evident. "I'm happy to know that you take security as seriously as we do here at the data center."

Responding to a wave of Volkov's hand, Hamid leered as he accepted the laptop from Sigmund before disconnecting the Ethernet cable, packaging up the computer and dongle, and snapping the briefcase catches closed. We departed the hall single file, Sigmund the last to leave as she closed the heavy, metal door behind her and took her seat in the cart.

Winding our way out of the mine, Volkov carried on a technospeak conversation with Sigmund that baffled me as we glided silently through the stark but somehow gloriously fascinating tunnels, finally seeing daylight as we stopped next to our Jeeps.

"Thank you, Miss Sigmund, for accommodating us on such short notice. This has been extremely helpful. We are grateful for your hospitality," I enthused, trying to sound sincere.

"I'm so happy to help," she replied as she offered me a business card. "Call or email with any questions. Anytime."

"I'm sure we'll be in touch," I grinned.

As we climbed back into our Jeeps, Volkov whispered to me, "We got it."

I didn't know what she meant, but I was about to find out.

CHAPTER
73

BY SEVEN IN THE EVENING, the Jeeps were craned back aboard *Almaz*, and Lockwood put us out to sea. With the postcard-perfect town of Måløy well behind us as we steamed out to the open waters of the Norwegian Sea, with full fuel tanks and replenished stores below our feet thanks to Lockwood's proactivity while we were at the mine, the team gathered in the situation room. Havens and Rourke had both removed the weapons harnesses that were concealed beneath their oversized black shirts, the unused guns packed away securely for a future battle.

Fortunately, a battle had been averted and, frankly, the entire afternoon had seemed anticlimactic to me. I knew, however, never to underestimate Volkov.

"You know," she started, relaxing in the big chair to my right, "if you hide in plain sight, exploiting the false assurances that we all take for granted, that if something looks like whatever it is supposed to look like, it is invisible."

"Sounds very mythical," Hamid laughed. "I like it."

"Mythical is a good analogy. You all know, of course, the legend of the Trojan horse." No one said anything, and Volkov rolled her eyes with a bit of condescension as she explained, "The Greeks constructed a massive wooden horse, a desperate last tactic of trickery to break the stalemate of a ten-year siege of the city of Troy. As one of the stories goes, the Greeks left the horse behind as an offering for a god and sailed away. The citizens of Troy opened the gates of their city willingly and rolled the horse inside as a trophy. Of course, in the belly of the horse, ten men were hiding, including Odysseus, and under the cover of night, Odysseus and his men reopened the gates, and the Greek army invaded the city. Miss Sigmund plugged my cable into the Trampoline servers and figuratively rolled my horse inside."

"A lovely story," I said, before adding impatiently, "Kindly explain."

Volkov chuckled. "The Terminal application that she ran was not the native app on the computer. It was a decoy, meant to look and feel exactly as it should. During my conversation with Sigmund in the cart as we rode to the data hall, I learned that she was not just in marketing and sales but was also a competent computer operator. She would be familiar with the application and comfortable using it. She typed in the appropriate commands, and the Trojan horse, my decoy Terminal program, downloaded several lines of code from the MacBook into the Trampoline servers connected to that network switch. However, from what Sigmund saw on the screen, the Terminal application was doing what it should, pinging an IP address and timing the response. It actually never did that."

Volkov's face was painted with a look of self-satisfaction. "When I set up the decoy, I had no idea how fast it should have connected. Sigmund caught on when she noticed the latency was slower than she expected. I thought I covered myself quite well with that comment about a third-party hosted server."

Havens, always concerned with contingency plans, asked, "What if she had you run the test again?

"I would have leaned over her shoulder and given her one of the four other IP addresses I had prepared within the decoy program. Each address would have appeared to return the data packets at various speeds, either faster or slower. Knowing by then what she was looking to see, I could have managed it. Worst case, I would have taken over and, with two keystrokes, pulled up the *real* Terminal application, if, for example, she wanted to ping an IP address that was familiar to her."

"Very nice," Havens complimented, "I admire that you had more than one backup plan."

"There were other backup plans, but I won't bore you with them," Volkov said. "What's important is that the task that we would have performed by sneaking in and risking exposure was completed in plain sight."

I was anxious to move on, so I said so. "I'm anxious to move on. What's next?"

Volkov grimaced. "The Trojan horse was the key to access, and through it, I sent a second program that will allow me to index the Trampoline servers. Like drawing a map, it will take time, and since it is important that the activity of my bot crawling the servers remains unnoticed by the host, it's not efficient. Unfortunately, Ben, what's next is a wait."

"Are we talking minutes, hours, or days?"

"Days. More like at least a week. Maybe more. It's impossible to know at this moment because, frankly, we don't know how big or complex that map will end up being."

"Okay," I said. "What's the end game? What do we learn from this map?"

"We will be able to see exactly what data Trampoline has been collecting. We'll be able to see how they index that data. And we should be able to infer what they could do with it."

Volkov's voice brimmed with confidence, but I didn't share that sentiment. I didn't like that word "infer." I looked at Havens. He didn't "infer;" he planned, one contingency after another. I reclined in the big, black chair, steepling my fingers as Macallister did, finding that the gesture almost centered me, and allowed me to collect my thoughts. *I have no choice but to let Volkov do her work. But I'd like to come up with a contingency. Another angle. Some other way to dig into Trampoline.*

The problem was, it wouldn't be until Lockwood took *Almaz*, chugging along at a stately, lumbering ten knots, for two laps of the Faroe Islands, and then guided the ship north to the Arctic Circle, that I would dream up another angle. There's nothing like a deadline to spur your mind into action, but I didn't have that deadline. Yet.

CHAPTER
74

TUESDAY, JULY 28, 2020 – 65° 23' N, 004° 00' E

OVER THE WEEKEND, since our departure from Måløy late on Thursday, *Almaz* meandered toward the Arctic Circle while Volkov's Trojan horse program parsed through the massive amounts of data that Trampoline was amassing on its servers buried deep beneath the earth in the Lefdal Mine Datacenter.

On Sunday evening, I had decided to reach back out to Eva Sigmund, but, frustratingly, she was off on Monday. I called again on Tuesday morning, and in my mind's eye, I could visualize the blonde Norwegian woman as she pleasantly said, "Mister Godfrey. So nice to hear from you so soon after your visit to our facility. What was it, just last Thursday?"

"Indeed, Miss Sigmund. Thank you for taking my call." I tried to sound smooth, professional, but non-committal.

"I do hope you are calling with good news. Will your firm be represented within the Lefdal Mine Datacenter?"

Sigmund, I'd imagine, was hoping to close a sale, and I hated to disappoint her. "I suspect so, yes. I hope that's good news. However, I'm not ready to commit to the firm yet, even though my technical associates, Miss Karin and—and—and—"

I paused, trying to remember the name Abdul had given himself, when Sigmund interrupted, "Mister Sayed?"

"Sayed. Yes. He's new to the company," I rushed, hoping to alleviate my lapse. "My associates were quite impressed. As they complete their due diligence, I'd like to check a reference or two. I was wondering if you could connect me directly with a representative from one of the firms that uses the center. Trampoline, for example."

"I suppose so, yes. I'm not permitted to discuss technical matters, of course, and I don't think it would be appropriate to introduce you to the people we work with directly. I can tell you that the vast majority of our work is coordinated with Trampoline's European offices, not with their headquarters in San Francisco. You should reach out to London."

"London?"

"Yes, the Trampoline office in the United Kingdom. In London. You're familiar with it, yes?"

"Of course," I lied. *Why London?*

"Wonderful. I'm certain that they will speak highly of us. And I do hope to hear from you soon. Please let me know if there's anything specific I can help you with."

"Of course," I repeated. "Thank you, Miss Sigmund. I'll be sure to be in touch."

I disconnected the call and pulled off my headset. Around the horseshoe-shaped table, Rourke and Hamid, who listened in with their headset microphones muted, did the same. Hamid had already begun tapping keys on the computer at his station and reported, "When Volkov and I started our research on Trampoline, I remember seeing a London office listed as the base for their European operations. I can't say I paid much attention. Hang on."

Hamid worked in silence and then announced, "Gotcha! Here's the address. It's . . ." He paused, his lower lip drooping as he leaned closer to his screen. "What in the fuck is that?"

"Put it on the big screen," Rourke requested.

With a few key presses, the left big screen lit and filled with an image of a cylindrical building, with a tapered cone top, and wrapped in a spiraling pattern of light and dark glass panels framed in a whitish colored metal. Hamid narrated, "That's a funky looking building. The locals call it the Gherkin. Cheeky British wit, 'cuz it looks like a pickle." He looked up at the big screen and said, "I dunno. It looks kinda phallic to me. Anyway, it's forty-one stories tall. And, regardless of what it looks like, that building has some A-list tenants inside. A global insurance company. A big media outlet. And Trampoline is listed as a tenant."

"Where? What floor?" Havens had entered the situation room silently and was examining the screen, his CIRG-trained mind already considering potential mission options.

"The building directory on the website says that Trampoline is on the tenth and eleventh floors," Hamid replied.

I asked, "Any names? Who's in charge?"

"Um, let's see. Here it is. Title listed as Vice President, Global Operations. The most impressive title on this webpage. Dude's name is Karl Roddick."

I ordered, "Start a dossier on Mister Roddick, and on the two or three people who you think report to him. Let's learn more about Trampoline in London. I'd like to be able to call them and see if we can get more information about who's in charge of the Lefdal operation."

"I've already Googled the dude," Hamid reported. "One point one million results, most of them on a tennis player with a different first name. Hang on; let me put in quotes." He changed the parameters of the search by adding the two punctuation marks and said, "That's interesting. Less than two hundred results. Nothing that seems to relate to Trampoline. No LinkedIn page or news links or anything."

He looked up at me, confusion on his face, and added, "You'd think a high-ranking executive of a multinational social media company would have a bigger footprint on the Internet."

I laughed and reminded Hamid, "We can do better than a Google search. Run him through the FBI database. And don't forget, we're cooperating with the CIA and the State Department. Contact Director Ginachere with the CIA, and—" My mind blanked on a name for the second time today. *What was the name of the woman from the Secretary of State's office?*

Hamid remembered and said, "Sullivan. The nice lady from the Sec State's office. For sure, they can run him down, too. Karl Roddick can't hide from us, or from the collective investigative power of the United States."

Soon, Hamid would be proven wrong. We were about to learn that Karl Roddick did not exist.

✳ ✳ ✳

"Mister Roddick?"

"Yes?"

"Eva Sigmund. Lefdal Mine Datacenter. Thank you for returning my call from this morning."

"Ah, yes, Miss Sigmund. What can I do for you?"

"Yes. I received a call first thing today from a potential customer interested in the data center—an American company. Last week, I gave them a tour and showed them, among other things, the data hall that you lease. Today, their representative asked to reach out to our clients to check references. Now, naturally, I didn't share your name or any names for that matter, but I did infer that they could reach out to Trampoline for that purpose."

"I suppose so."

"Oh, thank you. So that you'd be familiar with it, the name of the company is Quadrant Procurement Group. A Mister John Godfrey."

"Hmm. I'm searching the web as we speak for such a company and name. I don't seem to find anything."

"Nor did I, Mister Roddick. They said they maintained a, what was it, a low profile. However, the visit was arranged by the Norwegian Nasjonal Sikkerhetsmyndighet. Sorry, the National Security Authority. That was a good enough introduction for me."

"Yes, I know the NSM, of course. That's fine, Miss Sigmund."

"Thank you for being so accommodating, as always, Mister Roddick. It's always a pleasure to work with Trampoline. Good day, sir."

"Wait! Miss Sigmund. This mystery company and its representatives. Might there be a chance that the cameras at the entrance were utilized to start your usual security dossier?"

"Of course, Mister Roddick."

"Would you kindly share a photo of this Mister Godfrey?"

"Of course, Mister Roddick. My assistant has left for the day. I'll have him review the security camera images and email some still photos. Will sometime tomorrow be soon enough?"

"That will be fine, Miss Sigmund. Tomorrow, please. Thank you. Goodbye."

CHAPTER
75

WEDNESDAY, JULY 29, 2020 – 68° 23' N, 006° 00' E

THOUGH HAMID AND I HAD requested that the search for Karl Roddick be given priority status, there was nothing we could do about the six-hour time difference between the Quadrant team, north of the Arctic Circle toward the Norwegian coastline on *Almaz*, and Washington, D.C. My team assembled in the situation room at five minutes before three in the afternoon, our time, or almost nine in the morning in the States.

In our situation room we found Volkov scrunched at her computer terminal, as she had been for much of the time since departing Måløy six days ago. Her portion of the horseshoe-shaped table was littered with three coffee mugs, two plates with unidentifiable food remains, and one small white pill bottle. "Ibuprofen," she muttered, tipping two brown-colored tablets into her palm and tossing them into her mouth, chasing the pills with a sip from one of the mugs. Making a disgusted face, she made a "blech" sound and explained, "Cold coffee. Ugh."

I dialed the extension for the galley and asked that a carafe of fresh coffee be brought to the room, and then, looking at Volkov, offered, "Do you need a break? We can handle this call."

"No," she replied flatly. "I think I might be near a breakthrough. I'm running another routine now to confirm. But I could also be chasing another dead end. There have been plenty of those so far." There was no enthusiasm in her voice. She was clearly exhausted.

Hamid repeated, in a questioning tone, "Dead end?"

Volkov sighed, "I'm trying to make sense of the Trampoline data collection. We know it is harvesting data that is not really applicable to the function of the app. You know, that 'good, clean fun' bullshit. Therefore, I've tried to explore the servers, delicately, of course, to look for patterns. In other words, what data is indexed to what other data? I mean, collecting and storing is one thing, because it's definitely not appropriate, but maybe it's not nefarious. Maybe they are just like the other operators of these networks, trying to harvest as much personally identifiable information as possible, and they'll use it for some other purpose later on."

There was a defeated tone to her voice, and I wondered, "What do you mean by *later on?*"

She laughed dryly. "Imagine some teenage kid posting a video on TikTok today. What happens in twenty years? That data will still be out there, even if the actual app fades away. Imagine that kid running for president? Or trying to get a mortgage? Or being charged for a crime? What happens to that video? What happens to all the data that these social media giants are harvesting?"

Before anyone could attempt an answer or a theory, the big center screen came to life with Macallister's face as he connected from his office in the Hoover building. He was impeccably attired in a gray suit jacket, white shirt, and red tie. I assumed that, because he was at headquarters, he was wearing pants.

His sartorial appearance did not match his weary expression as he began the secure teleconference. "I have discouraging news to report. Yesterday, at your request and with a priority tag, I forwarded the name to CIA, NSA, and Immigration. Naturally, we also used our own databases, including the Uniform Crime Reporting Program and the National Crime Information Center. This was a multi-agency search, encompassing millions and millions of records."

Pausing, Macallister finally verified what his expression already had disclosed. "Karl Roddick does not appear in a single record. He is a ghost."

I looked at Volkov, hoping that by some miracle, her face would brighten, and she would enlighten us with a breakthrough. Instead, her eyes were closed, and she appeared peaceful. It was that impression of composure that gave me an idea, and I did what we should have already done when I said, "Enough tiptoeing around. Let's talk to Melissa Zhao."

CHAPTER
76

THURSDAY, JULY 30, 2020 – SALEM, MASSACHUSETTS

GAMESMANSHIP. IT WAS SOMETHING that I needed to learn, to better understand.

In Newport, I had learned the value of careful planning, and I'd made good on that lesson when I aborted the first, ill-advised mission to the Lefdal Mine Datacenter.

But those lessons didn't make it any easier, or make me any less impatient, during the course of the day yesterday, after I had asked to talk to Melissa Zhao, and the suits in D.C. began playing their games.

The first roadblock was the Attorney General. In one of our several conferences yesterday, Macallister relayed Bart Williams' objections. "The AG says no way. The FTC has an open and ongoing investigation. They've talked to Zhao. They've been to Trampoline's head office in San Francisco. And all you have, Porter, is conjecture. You don't have evidence. The FBI does not have a case against the company."

"Sure, we do," I countered. "We have an application that collects data without a user's permission."

"Not so fast," Macallister objected. "The AG, and the FTC, have established that Trampoline *does* get user permissions, but it does so with complicated language, offered as a 'click here to read more about our privacy policies' in a way that most users, if not all of them, will just ignore."

I suggested, "That's borderline subterfuge."

Macallister shrugged his shoulders. "The AG agrees, but that's nothing new. In fact, that's a summary of the FTC investigation. He's not going to let us interfere."

Later in the day, I tried a new tack with Macallister. "Sir, the person that's listed as the head of their international office appears to be a ghost. Let's tell the AG that is our focus. Let's investigate Roddick, not Trampoline."

Macallister agreed with that approach, and Bart Williams relented. Putting the resources of the FBI to work, we easily located Melissa Zhao in Boston, Massachusetts, doing a publicity event. The location was fortuitous. We had the perfect person in mind to conduct the interview, arranged for Thursday morning, in Salem, Massachusetts.

As the Special Agent in Charge, Jennifer Appleton ran the Boston Division field office with a velvet fist. Kind and gentle were not words used to describe her; if you made the mistake of crossing her, the reaction would be swift, decisive, and most likely unpleasant—but usually well deserved. Appleton was fair, and for that, she was deeply respected within the Bureau.

She was also persuasive, and it was not a surprise that, with short notice, she was able to arrange an in-person meeting with Melissa Zhao, to be conducted in the innocent-looking setting of Appleton's pristine home in Salem. Zhao would have been impressed by the technology hidden behind the walls of Appleton's impeccably restored, colonial-era house; the residence had been wired by the Bureau to be used as a home office for the SAC, which included secure video teleconference ability. Zhao, of course, didn't know that, nor would Appleton be so foolish as to actually look at one of the three hidden video cameras that would record the conversation, as well as broadcast it in real time to us on *Almaz* and to Macallister in D.C., who would watch the interview alongside Director Toffer and AG Williams.

At first appearance, the setting was innocuous—two well-dressed and composed women having a friendly discussion. Zhao reclined comfortably into one of Appleton's white armchairs. The Trampoline CEO's jet-black hair was pulled into a ponytail, her medium brown skin was flawless, and she appeared relaxed and confident. Seated over six feet away from her guest, no strands of Appleton's conservatively styled, shoulder-length auburn hair were out of place, and her lightly tanned, unlined face looked relaxed.

Before the meeting, Volkov and I spoke at length to Appleton, briefing her on the matter at hand. We also successfully convinced the AG to allow a broad scope of questions.

Appleton, to my delight, immediately took advantage of that accommodation and wove way outside any discussion guardrails in an almost disarming manner. "Miss Zhao, we have a number of topics to cover. Let's start with generalities and set the stage. I don't want this question to come across as intimidating, but a number of agents within the FBI have begun to express concern about the operations of your company."

Zhao smiled, revealing perfectly aligned white teeth, and responded, "Please, call me Melissa. And your question is anything but intimidating. I think it's just a natural occurrence that we've attracted attention, given our rapid rate of growth."

Appleton disregarded the first-name informality, instead choosing to focus on Zhao's words. "Rapid rate of growth. It's been astounding. I've been told that you expect one billion users by the end of the summer."

"We're there and well past that milestone now. As of yesterday, we claim one point two billion users. We won't make that public at this time."

"Why not?"

Zhao tittered quietly, and to me, her laugh sounded a little nervous. "Oh, we've discussed strategy, and figure we will reveal that after Labor Day. In September. It's better for the news cycle."

"As I understand it, Trampoline is a private company. You don't need to report to investors or to Wall Street. Why report at all? And why then?"

"Yes, we are private. We report our user base for advertising purposes. The larger the base, the more opportunities we have to drive ad revenue. And, of course, we've always prided ourselves on transparency."

Appleton tilted her head at that opening and gently objected, "But you're not transparent. Actually, that's at the heart of the FTC investigation, isn't it? You collect a substantial amount of data that you don't really need."

"Oh, no, that's not the case," Zhao countered. "We have been totally transparent with the FTC, too. We only collect what our privacy policy allows us to collect."

"Photos? Emails? Text messages? Contacts?"

Zhao replied quickly, "Those items are covered by the privacy policy."

"Really?" Appleton replied with sarcasm evident in her voice. "Our people have combed through your privacy policy. That policy does not indicate that your application routinely sends not only those items, but also a user's location, phone number, device identifier, and other personally identifiable data back to your servers while the app is running."

"That's covered by the user agreement, so that we can provide user-specific services and content," Zhao said flatly. To me, it sounded like she was reciting the words. Her voice was uninflected and unnaturally even.

Appleton apprised her guest for a half-second, and then the SAC smoothly served a statement that Volkov and I had crafted, to expose a detail that we had guessed the FTC investigation would not have touched upon. "Neither your user agreement nor your privacy policy specifically discloses that you collect, and then store, and then send back to your servers, the eighty nodal points used in a smartphone's facial recognition process."

For a beat, Zhao remained silent, though her eyes, clearly visible on the giant flatscreen in my situation room, blinked rapidly, and her face flushed before she said, "That's very . . . specific. Our policy says that we collect personally identifiable data. I suppose it would include that." Zhao's voice trailed off.

"I doubt your users would agree. That seems to contravene your policy of transparency, wouldn't you think, Miss Zhao?" Appleton leaned forward and murmured, "And what's most interesting to me, Miss Zhao, is that I am unable to discern if that question bothered you because you are taken aback that we know about that specific data collection, or if you yourself are surprised firsthand to learn that your app collects facial recognition nodal points."

Appleton let her question sink in for a second and then concluded, "Which is it?"

Zhao remained mute and closed her eyes. Watching the scene, I counted to myself, *One Mississippi. Two Mississippi's. Three Mississ—*

"Both."

Appleton considered Zhao's single word response, perhaps selecting the right words or, if I knew Appleton, already knowing the right words but allowing the tension to build, before asking, somewhat coldly, "Miss Zhao, are you ready to tell me the story of Trampoline?"

CHAPTER
77

MELISSA ZHAO PULLED HER hair from the elastic at the nape of her neck and then carefully, but clearly reflexively, gathered up the long, jet-black strands and fashioned a new ponytail. I wasn't sure if she was buying time or gathering her energy, but something had changed regardless. The earnestness had left her face, replaced by something more akin to dejection. Or, quite possibly, relief.

Zhao finished with her hair and pushed herself deeper into the white chair, crossing one leg over the other. Appleton mimicked her movements, indicating that she, too, was ready for story time.

With a deep breath, Zhao began, "It was never meant to get this far. It all spiraled out of my control. It's like Pandora's Box, you know. It seemed like such a gift, at first. And then it became a curse. And now—"

Zhao paused and eyed Appleton with what might have been gratitude, adding, "And now, I think this might be my opportunity to talk about all of it."

"Start with the gift," Appleton suggested.

Zhao smiled, but bleakly. "I came up with the idea for Trampoline during my senior year at Stanford. You know, we've all heard the story about how Facebook was created. It even became a movie. What I saw, what I remembered, what influenced me, was the initial effort to build some innocent fun so that college kids could connect to each other with a virtual face book instead of a printed face book, and then it got bigger and bigger, and bigger, and—well, you know, it became about the money. I swore I would build my network differently. Ironic, right?"

"What's ironic?"

"That, ultimately, it did become about the money. You see, my ideals were pure. My idea was sound. I knew enough about coding to get the platform up and running. I recruited my first *sifu* to help manage and censor the platform. Trampoline would *not* be like Facebook, for example. We wouldn't allow hate speech or politics or bullying. We'd control all those things. It *was* fun."

Appleton recrossed her legs, a signal that she was engaged. "What do you mean, 'was'? What happened?"

"At first, the users on the platform were just me and my friends and family. And then their friends and family. And so on, now once or twice removed, but remaining connected by some link to someone else. We were all so earnest, so committed to the platform. It was like hanging out at a party of your closest friends, except that instead of twenty people, it was two thousand, and then twenty thousand. But it still felt close-knit."

Zhao's face drooped, and her eyes narrowed, "And that, I guess, is what attracted their attention."

"Who's that?"

Zhao held up two fingers and air quoted as she said, "My investors." Folding her hands primly on her lap, she explained, "I was living in San Francisco. I had maybe ten employees, and we had grown to about fifty thousand users in about six or seven months since launch. It was touch-and-go, financially, because while we were eking out ad revenue, mostly from local California businesses, I was not paying competitive wages. I couldn't. That's to be expected, of course. Anyone who gets into this has a dream of going public, raking in the dough with a stock offering, or getting an angel investor."

"I take it, since you have not gone public, that you found your angel?"

"That's what I thought. That's what we all thought. An international investor, not from Silicon Valley, wanted a toehold in the American market. They loved us, they told us, because we were small and nimble and, well, pure. They made me an offer I couldn't refuse."

Appleton smiled. "That sounds fantastic. What was the offer?"

"For starters, competitive salaries for all my people. A monster salary for me, plus the CEO title. They'd invest in the coding and the algorithms to really push up user counts, and they'd build the backbone to manage revenue and subscriptions and add-ons. Best of all, they were clear about wanting to leave the structure in place. The *sifu*, all the volunteers. That's the differentiator, they told me. That's what we want. They told me that I'd be the face of Trampoline. They wanted *my* honesty and charisma."

"There had to be strings attached," Appleton commented.

"At first, no. That's what made it such a dream come true. Gosh, I was so inexperienced. I should have asked more questions, done more analysis. Basically, the deal was simple: they took seventy-five percent of the profits, and I'd keep the rest, but I would have control. I never really thought it through. And by then, it was too late."

Appleton shook her head and said, "I'm not sure I follow."

"It was a hollow deal. They may have told me that I had control, but they owned three-quarters of the company. In the beginning, when I would question things, all they'd say was, 'no, you have to go along; we're investing in your company for your benefit,' or stuff like that. Little by little, and I didn't realize it because I was too busy trying to, well, be the face of Trampoline, they bought out my original staff members with golden parachutes, and they began introducing layer upon layer in the platform until it became a bloated version of how it started."

"When did you realize this?"

"Um. I started the company in July 2018. The investor onboarded in early 2019. And they were great, I guess, at first. So, it got to be November. The user base was growing nicely, and I had gotten pretty far removed from the actual coding. And then my second-to-last original employee called me, thrilled that he got a multimillion-dollar deal to retire. I remember the call exactly. He said, 'I'm never gonna be as rich as you, Zhao, so I'm taking it now while I can!' He was excited and happy."

She paused, obviously recalling the event, and Appleton asked, "How did that become an epiphany?"

"I went for a drive that night. Actually, it was super early in the morning. I couldn't sleep. I wanted to clear my head, and then I wanted to call my last remaining original employee, who I knew would be loyal to me. I'd work out a plan with her."

"What did she say?"

"I never made the call. Two of the programmers who worked directly for the investor followed me in their car. I thought someone was chasing me. I got scared. When they cornered me, I lost my composure. I never made the call." Zhao inhaled and added, "It wouldn't have made a difference, anyway. That last remaining original employee was let go that week. She got an offer she couldn't refuse from a competitor. I think it was a set-up. But I'll never know."

"I don't understand," Appleton said quietly, in almost a conspiratorial tone. "Why did you need her anyway? What was holding you back from telling your investor that you wanted to renegotiate? To use your power as CEO?"

Zhao's head hung as she muttered, "Shame. And ego, I guess. They had taken the coding to a level I couldn't understand or even penetrate. I didn't want to admit that I didn't know what my own platform was doing." She lifted her face and looked Appleton in the eye. "When you told me what you found, I wasn't surprised, though I didn't know they had gotten that far."

After the briefest moment, Zhao added, "But I can't imagine what they will do."

With the confession unfolding before our very eyes, not a word had been spoken inside the situation room on *Almaz* as we were enthralled by Zhao's story. It got our full attention, then, when Volkov suddenly spoke with earnest urgency, "She might not be able to imagine what they can do, but I can."

CHAPTER
78

100 MILES WEST OF THE NORWEGIAN COASTLINE

IN THE SITUATION ROOM aboard *Almaz*, when Anastasia Volkov had exclaimed, "She might not be able to imagine what they can do, but I can," I had never before seen her expression as wide-eyed and alert.

In complete contrast, on-screen, Zhao's face appeared exhausted.

I knew that we needed to hear from Volkov, and I barked, "Macallister, you're watching us on one screen and Appleton on another like we're doing here? Right?"

"Yeah," he said, turning to face the camera, just as Toffer and Williams did the same. "Why?"

"Volkov has something. We need to hear it. We gotta buy some time with Appleton."

Macallister nodded. On Macallister's conference table, there was a telephone handset, incongruously out of its cradle, and its purpose immediately became clear when Macallister lifted the handset and spoke one word, "Stall." On-screen, we watched as Appleton brushed a hand past her right ear, adjusting the auburn strands that hid the earpiece she was wearing.

Rising, Appleton said kindly to her guest, "Let's take a break. Can I get you some tea?"

"That would be nice. Thank you," Zhao gratefully replied, closing her eyes once again.

I was turning to speak to Volkov just as Appleton's disembodied voice came over the speakers in the situation room, ringing with annoyance, "What's going on? I'm in my kitchen, and I've got maybe four minutes."

"I got a breakthrough. I found a piece of code on the Trampoline servers," Volkov reported. "And that code might tell me what Trampoline is going to do."

"Make it a fast explanation, please. I've got Zhao in a confessional mood. It won't last," Appleton warned.

"I know," Volkov shot back. "First, a quick recap. We know what the app does. It collects all your passwords, your phone numbers, your email accounts. All that stuff. Trampoline has got all the info it needs to bypass two-factor authentication or any of your security measures because it's got access to your email and text accounts. It's put all of those things together. Trampoline can log into your account whenever it wants. You'll know, of course, since your phone or computer will get the authentication message, but Trampoline is ahead of you because, by the time you see the message, Trampoline has changed your password. You're locked out."

"What good does that do? All Trampoline would be doing is locking out their own user base," I suggested in confusion.

Volkov spat, "I'm not done. The piece of code that I found is incredibly clever. But it's also incredibly simple. All it does is monitor your phone, even when you are not running Trampoline's app, and waits for you to access any sort of banking service. Because Trampoline knows what app you've used to access your bank, it doesn't need a bank routing number. Those are public. So, when the code sees your phone access one of those apps, it starts a routine to copy your screen and to scrape your account number. It puts that number together with your bank. And that—knowing your bank routing number *and* your bank account number—that is a deadly combination."

AG Williams jumped in, booming, "Can you prove this? Can you establish that this is what Trampoline is doing?"

"Indirectly, yes," Volkov confirmed. She looked across the situation room table to Hamid, who had certainly put his time in on Trampoline, and stated emotionlessly, "Hamid, the last four digits of your bank account are 0810. And you bank at Chase. Correct?"

"Yeah," Hamid acknowledged.

Volkov wasn't finished, adding, "Your email password is 'FancyBear2019'. Your security code for your bank account is 'sexy-back'. Which, I might offer, is kinda weird. And your savings account balance is—"

"Enough," I commanded. I had put it together, and it was time to get to the point. "They've got your name, your face or fingerprint, your passwords, your bank app login, and your bank account information." I looked directly into the eye of the camera and concluded, "Trampoline is nothing but a Trojan horse. It glues your eyes to the screen. It addicts you so that it has the time in the background to collect all this information. It's not going to unlock the gates of a city like in the Greek myth. It's going to unlock bank accounts around the world."

"And guess who gets the blame?" Appleton had walked back into her living room carrying two merrily steaming tea mugs atop a polished silver tray. Her question grabbed Zhao's attention, and she reopened her eyes with a confused expression as she accepted a mug from Appleton.

The Boston SAC got straight to the point, sternly addressing her guest. "My people have outlined a potential nightmare scenario, and the target of the blame game will be one person. The face of Trampoline. Melissa Zhao."

Zhao's face paled.

Offering a small silver cup stacked with white cubes to Zhao, Appleton spoke sweetly. "Sugar? Then I'll explain that nightmare scenario to you, but first I'd like to know . . . are you with me, or are you against me?"

THURSDAY, JULY 30, 2020 – 65° 25' N, 007° 00' E

ABOARD *ALMAZ*, WE BROKE FOR a late evening dinner in the situation room as we marveled at the audacity of the Trampoline operation.

"How can we stop this?" Rourke wondered.

"Stop what?" Volkov asked rhetorically. "We can't stop the fact that Trampoline already has this ability to lock users from their communication accounts while unlocking those user's banking accounts. They've already collected that data. The question is: does Trampoline put that data to work, locking users out of their accounts and stealing their money?"

"That's right," I agreed. "And if they do that, when? We're missing a trigger. A catalyst."

All eyes went to Volkov, who shrugged, "You got me. I don't have a clue how they could pull it all together as, say, an attack."

"Then we need to expose it. Take it public," I suggested.

Hamid immediately replied, "No way, Ben. We need way more before it goes public. If it trickles out, who knows what Trampoline does. They could start draining my bank account."

"They could start locking people out of their devices, too," Volkov added. "He's right. There's got to be a coordinated effort to bring this to light."

"The hell with that," Havens suggested. "Let's storm the Lefdal Mine Datacenter and take the Trampoline servers by force. Then they can't do anything."

"Sounds like fun," Hamid agreed, "and I get to reintroduce myself to Eva Sigmund."

Volkov immediately discarded that idea. "There's a duplicate set of servers somewhere. I don't know where yet, but I do know that the servers are backed up. That would be the protocol for any platform like this. Redundancy. And while I can probably find the backup, there might be a backup of the backup. I don't see that as a feasible alternative at this time."

I gave up. Coding was far from my forte. If there was an electronic solution, Volkov would find it. If there was a public relations approach, well, that was up to the suits in D.C. I decided to focus on investigation, and I paged through the notes that I took during Appleton and Zhao's discussion, noticing that because of the manner in which the conversation unfolded, Appleton omitted a fundamental question.

While my colleagues strategized potential ideas, I put on a pair of headphones and replayed the interview in Salem, knowing that in the meantime, Zhao had willingly joined Appleton and the duo had been driven, in an FBI Suburban with red-and-blue strobe lights flashing, to my former workplace, the Chelsea, Massachusetts, field office. In Washington, Toffer and Macallister were assembling a team in the SIOC.

I realized that when the next round of videoconferences would begin, Quadrant would no longer be a secret. We would be broadcast onto the screens in the SIOC, and representatives for the FBI, CIA, NSA, and other acronymically named government entities would see our faces, in our swank situation room, on our yacht. They'd all be jealous. And the bean counters would go berserk, wondering how we paid for it all.

It was mid-afternoon Thursday, United States east coast time, and evening for us on *Almaz* when the SVTC began. On one of our big screens, we had the secure feed from the Boston Field Office, starring Appleton and Zhao, and on a second screen, an image of the dais in the SIOC where the bigwigs sat, currently occupied by only Toffer and Macallister. The foreground in the SIOC showed row after row of computer terminals with FBI analysts and agents bent to screens. What they were doing was a mystery to me, but whatever it was, they looked intent, as they should, with the boss looking over their shoulders.

I was relieved that Appleton had become a part of the investigation. Her cool, analytical mind would be the antidote to what was sure to become a frenzy in D.C. as the second-guessing, the wacky ideas, and the power-play positioning began. Indeed, it was Appleton who called the conference to order, introducing Zhao and picking up where they left off in Salem. "Miss Zhao, during the car ride here, I explained the scenario that my team gamed out. You were not surprised. It's about time we get to your angel investor. Who was that? Is that investor also a programmer? How much contact did you have with that person?"

That was the fundamental question that Appleton had not asked earlier, and I had begun to form my own suspicions. I interrupted, "Miss Zhao, my name is Ben Porter. Before you answer that question, let me toss a name at you. Who is Karl Roddick?"

Zhao was clearly caught off-guard, stuttering, "How—how—how did you know that? That's the name of the investor."

Around the Quadrant table, there were knowing nods, and even Macallister, who had run the search for Roddick, leaned forward in his seat in the SIOC. I continued, "Roddick is the top name listed in your London office. We've already run him down. He's a ghost. Wouldn't you have done the same before signing your deal with him?"

Defensively, Zhao answered, "I did that, of course. I was surprised that there was so little information publicly available for him, and I asked him why. Karl told me that he kept a very low profile. That, like many investors of his ability, he preferred not to have a bunch of tire kickers chasing his money and expertise. That makes total sense, you know. It's not like the deep pockets who back Silicon Valley advertise who they are."

I prodded on, asking, "How did he verify who he was? Or did you never ask?"

"I mean, I didn't exactly ask to see his passport. I felt like he was legit. Every wire transfer was on time, every legal document—and I had my own lawyers review the documents—was promptly delivered and professional. It all checked out."

"Okay," I replied, with some skepticism in my voice, "Where was he from?"

"London. He works out of our offices in London. He's there now. I spoke with him earlier today."

"Do you speak with him often?"

"At first, yes," Zhao said. "In the early days, I talked to him a lot. His involvement waned, as I guess would be expected, as his team took over the programming."

"When was that?"

"Oh, summer of last year, I guess. Then I talked to him much less frequently. But he told me he had other projects. I didn't think it was unusual."

I wonder what those other projects are, I thought, and then I came up with a more obvious question. "What does he look like?"

"He looked, like, normal. Medium-height, dark hair, dark eyes. He had, like, a little bit of an accent, but, you know, he's from London, so I never gave that a second thought. He spoke precisely, and he knew a lot about technology and computers."

"We need a sketch," I declared to no one in particular.

"Tell me more about what he looked like," Miles Lockwood asked gently.

Director Toffer immediately jumped in, "Who said that?"

"That's Lockwood, one of my team members," I spat back, outwardly annoyed at the interruption, but quickly recalling my first introduction to Lockwood, when he had said, "I'm in sales. I remember faces."

Zhao had apparently missed the moment of tension and was saying, "He's white but not super white or brown-skinned like me. Not tanned, but not pale."

"That's a start," Lockwood encouraged. "Tell me about his eyes."

"His eyes were, like, deep-set. And dark."

"Ears like Dumbo? Or covered by long hair? How about ear lobes? Connected to his face or hanging loose?"

Zhao perked up. "Yeah. His ears kinda stuck out because his hair was always cut pretty short. Not a crew cut, just a very trim haircut. He was always clean-shaven. No stubble. But occasionally, I saw, like, a hint of maybe razor burn—like he shaved a lot." She paused, thinking, and then blurted, "This is kinda weird, but he must have shaved a lot because he had, like, lots of nose hair. Bushy. It was *gross*."

Across the table, I noticed that Volkov's color had drained from her face as Zhao described Karl Roddick. Volkov said quietly, almost in a whisper, "Did he drink a lot of coffee?"

Zhao laughed. "Gallons. I rarely saw him without a cup."

"Never milk. Never sugar. Always black?" Volkov's voice strengthened, and she was staring fiercely at the screen as if Zhao were actually in the room with us.

"Yeah," Zhao confirmed, with a touch of hesitation, perhaps wondering how the woman that she could see on-screen knew this.

"I think I know who Karl Roddick is," Volkov announced. Her tone was surprisingly dejected, not triumphant as would be expected when coming to this sort of conclusion. I came to understand, however, when she elaborated, "It's all come together—cup after cup of black coffee and the blooming outgrowth of nose hairs. Karl is Vitaly. I worked with him, briefly, before running away from him and from my father's twisted ambitions. Summer of last year, in fact. Vitaly is a Russian programmer. He's part of Unit 29155."

"Yeah, I've heard that name, too," I blurted. "When I was speaking with Petrikov, after we—"

"Stop!" Macallister commanded. "We need to limit this. Reconnect in two minutes to the secure conference room. SAC Appleton, stand by."

Macallister stalked off-screen in the SIOC as my blood pressure rose, realizing the conclusion that had become evident. My mind raced as I wondered, *Is Trampoline being run by the Russians? But this Karl Roddick is based in London. Zhao says that Roddick is in London now.*

I turned to Lockwood and asked, "How far are we from London?"

"About nine hundred miles or thereabouts," Lockwood replied after consulting the GPS display before him.

I glanced up, above the screens, where a series of digital clocks indicated times around the globe. The center clock showed our local time in the Norwegian Sea at 9:03 p.m. and displayed a label, "Local—UTC+1." To the left, another digital display designated "Eastern US—UTC-5" and read 3:03 p.m. I asked Lockwood, "How long to go that far?"

"Well, we turned south earlier today, and we're still loafing along at ten knots, about a hundred miles off and paralleling the Norwegian coastline. If we push up to our cruising speed, give or take sixty hours. Two and a half days."

"I think we should head for London. At cruising speed, please." Lockwood stood and made for the bridge. I asked Volkov to set one of our clocks to London time, one hour ahead of us in the UTC-0 zone, or Greenwich mean time. The Quadrant team, less Lockwood, and I waited for Macallister to reconnect, not knowing that sixty hours would not be nearly enough time.

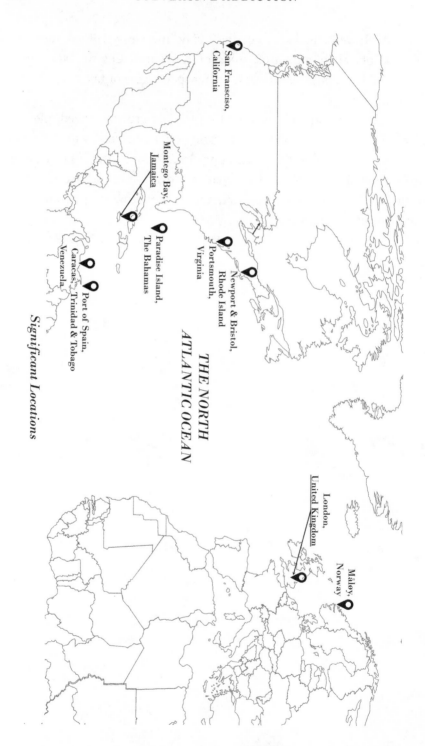

San Fransciso,
California

Montego Bay,
Jamaica

Paradise Island,
The Bahamas

Portsmouth,
Virginia

Newport & Bristol,
Rhode Island

Caracas,
Venezuela

Port of Spain,
Trinidad & Tobago

Significant Locations

*THE NORTH
ATLANTIC OCEAN*

London,
United Kingdom

Måloy,
Norway

CHAPTER
80

"PORTER, YOU GOTTA BE more careful," Macallister scolded, adding, "The Petrikov investigation is need-to-know only."

"Apologies, sir," I replied meekly, cursing myself for my clumsy breach of confidentiality.

Macallister, however, moved on, "It's a good point, though. Remind me what Petrikov told you about this Vitaly character?"

I looked at the screen; Macallister was seated at a polished oak table in what appeared to be within the blue-painted conference room that we'd seen before, and he was joined by Director Toffer and AG Williams. I asked, chagrined, "I assume I can speak freely?"

"Yeah. Come on. You're wasting time," Macallister barked.

I reminded the group, "Petrikov said that his handler was named Vitaly Nikolaevich Rodionov. This Rodionov was part of the operation when Volkov was involved, and later, he met up with Petrikov and helped him arrange asylum with Russia. Petrikov told me that Rodionov wasn't just a member of Unit 29155. Rodionov headed it up."

"Big fish," Macallister muttered.

"It seems awfully coincidental," Hamid pointed out. "With all respect to Volkov, we're jumping to a pretty tenuous conclusion."

"Agreed," Bart Williams boomed. "It's very circumstantial."

"No," I disagreed. "Petrikov also told me something else. Rodionov gave Petrikov a device to play chess with, to pass the time. And what app did Petrikov use to play chess? Trampoline, of course."

"Still coincidental," Hamid reiterated.

"Yet the coincidences add up," I countered, adding, "But it would be helpful to find another link to tie it together."

The conversation stalled until Volkov reminded us, "When I surrendered myself back to the Bureau, I described Vitaly to a sketch artist. Surely, you still have that document. Show that sketch to Zhao. See if it matches."

"No," I exclaimed, "but that's part of a great idea. Macallister, get Zhao with a sketch artist. Have her create her own image."

"Why, so we can compare them? See if there's a match? I think that's a weak connection, Porter," Macallister grumbled.

I laughed. "You could compare them, sure. But let's say we want to get a third-party verification. Let's show the sketches to Petrikov. Ask *him* who the subject of the sketches is."

Volkov's eyes brightened briefly, then dimmed as she asked, "Who's gonna do that?"

Macallister grinned as he said, "Me. Let's keep this information as tight as possible. I'll take a Bureau plane to Cuba with both Volkov's sketch and Zhao's sketch of the suspect." He turned to Williams and asked, "Can you set me up with access at Guantanamo Bay for a very private discussion with Petrikov?"

Williams nodded. "It's unusual, but I think the circumstances warrant it. I imagine we can pull the correct levers by tomorrow morning."

We hashed out the logistics quickly, and I sensed Macallister was excited to do fieldwork for a change as he rushed off the video conference.

Macallister would have an answer from Petrikov first thing tomorrow morning, Friday morning East Coast time, and Friday afternoon in the Norwegian Sea. I felt good. The circle was tightening. But we still weren't working fast enough.

✳ ✳ ✳

"It's been confirmed."

"Say again, Fedor?"

"We have positive matches on all six individuals in the security camera still photo that Eva Sigmund's assistant emailed to you yesterday," Fedor Ilin explained. "To be absolutely sure, we used our facial recognition procedures against the various photographs that we have collected during the course of this operation."

"Run the names by me," Vitaly Rodionov commanded.

"The blonde woman is Eva Sigmund, of course. The Black man is FBI Special Agent Leroy Havens, whom we identified with the video that our operative took of the botched takedown of Porter, in Newport. The Middle Eastern complexioned man is FBI Special Agent Abdullatif al-Hamid. The redhead is former FBI Special Agent Heather Rourke. And, most importantly, standing in the foreground, addressing Eva Sigmund, are Ben Porter and Anastasia Volkov."

Rodionov was shaking his head as the names were spoken. "Inside the Lefdal Mine Datacenter. How did they reach that conclusion?"

"Volkov's computer and hacking skills, presumably," Fedor suggested.

"Hmm," Rodionov mumbled, noncommittally, before asking in a louder, angry tone, "Where are they now?"

"We don't know. But there's more."

"More? How can there be more?" Rodionov raged.

"Porter gave his name to Sigmund as John Godfrey, of the Quadrant Procurement Group. That company does not exist in any form except as a United States company that was formed in December. However, I took the initiative to run John Godfrey through our databases." His face blanched as he paused, before revealing, "A man by that name passed through border control at the Simón Bolívar International Airport, outside of Caracas, on the twentieth of January. That information was provided by our friends in Venezuela."

Before Rodionov could explode, Fedor rushed on, "That man was accompanied by a woman named Ann Karin. Her passport photo is a very close match to Volkov."

Checking his emotions, Rodionov breathed deeply once, then twice, then a third time. "Porter and Volkov, first with Petrikov in Venezuela, then together at Lefdal. Petrikov didn't know of our involvement with Trampoline. How did they discover it?"

"I don't know. But. There's—there's one more item."

With venom, Rodionov hissed, "And what is that?"

"The driver and bodyguard assigned to Melissa Zhao reported that she went to a private home outside of Boston earlier today. Zhao departed that home with another woman. They got into a black car with emergency lights. The car drove to the FBI office in Chelsea."

"When was this reported?"

"Twenty-three minutes ago."

Steeling his voice, Rodionov grunted, "I spoke with Zhao earlier today. She made no mention of a meeting outside of Boston. Nothing like that was on her schedule." Rodionov pressed a palm against his forehead before concluding in a graveled voice, "We are running out of time. How long to complete the programming work if we wanted to accelerate the timeline?"

"Not long. A day, at most. But you said you wanted to wait for a catalyst. A time when the Americans and their allies would be in disarray or distracted. The American election, for example. Or the Christmas holiday."

"It can't be helped. I fear that Porter is closing in, and we don't have the luxury of time. We can start tomorrow?"

"Yes."

"Make it happen."

CHAPTER
81

FRIDAY, JULY 31, 2020 – GUANTANAMO BAY, CUBA

AS THE LOW, GRAY, OVERCAST skies began to brighten from an unseen sun at dawn on the final Friday of July, a Bureau Cessna Citation X jet lifted off a rain-slicked runway at the Ronald Reagan Washington National Airport and turned south for the one thousand, one hundred nautical mile flight to Cuba. Three souls were aboard the lightly laden aircraft: a pilot, co-pilot, and Deputy Assistant Director Bradford Macallister.

The two-hour flight was uneventful, and the white-painted, two-engine jet touched down at Leeward Point Field, the sole active military airfield within the Guantanamo Bay Naval Base, precisely at 8:05 a.m., Eastern Daylight Time. A military Jeep pulled up as the jet's staircase was lowered from inside the cabin. The pilots remained onboard the aircraft, having been advised that it would not be a long layover.

Only Macallister disembarked. He was casually dressed in a blue short-sleeved shirt and khaki-colored pants. He carried only a small, brown, canvas bag, more like a satchel than a briefcase, which he placed on his lap as he sat in the passenger seat of the Jeep.

The driver wordlessly guided the vehicle across the macadam to a waiting helicopter, painted a drab gray and bearing the logo of the United States Marine Corps Security Force Regiment on the tail boom. Buckling himself into a seat in the cabin and tightening the belt as the chopper gained altitude and dipped its nose, Macallister peered out the opening where a sliding door would have been, expecting to see the open waters of the Caribbean Sea to the right of the chopper, and the green and brown hills of Cuba to the left as the chopper flew to the Guantanamo Bay Detention Camp, located near the beaches at the south-east corner of the sprawling, forty-five square mile base.

Instead, the helicopter vectored in a northeast direction, flying over the bay itself, and ultimately touching down on a cracked asphalt area bordered by red, gray, and white shipping containers. As the rotors wound to a stop, Macallister dropped to the ground and was met by an unsmiling, heavily armed, body-armor clad Marine who uttered only two words, "Follow me."

Dutifully, Macallister tailed the soldier to a pair of silver, dome-roofed huts. Entering the door of the righthand building, Macallister realized quickly that this was no ordinary Quonset hut; the door jamb was at least ten inches thick, and the air inside was cool, dry, and well-lit with LED overhead fixtures. A second Marine stood in front of the only door visible within the interior of the building, and, with one hand brandishing a pistol, used the other hand to open the door as he instructed, "Knock three times when you are through. You'll be watched on camera."

Macallister nodded, stoically repressing his enthusiasm to be in the field. As he crossed the doorway threshold, he was calm, collected, and, frankly, eager to lay his own eyes on the elusive, megalomaniacal target that he, alongside Ben Porter, had chased for over two years.

The sight that greeted him was not, however, one to fear. Anatoly Petrikov's complexion was pale, and folds of skin draped from his face and jowls. He pushed himself up with a wooden cane as he laboriously stood from a metal chair, his weakened body clearly frail and thinning beneath a plain white t-shirt. His pants were ill-fitting and drooped at the crotch; Macallister assumed that the prisoner would not be afforded a belt.

Petrikov cast a wave about the sparsely furnished but spotless room and said, politely, "Welcome to my quarters. Visitors are rare. My name, as you must know, is Tony Petrikov."

The door latched behind Macallister, who replied, "Deputy Assistant Director Bradford Macallister, Federal Bureau of Investigation."

"I recognize the name. You are based in Boston. My daughter knew you."

"Was based in Boston. Now I'm in D.C. You have excellent recall."

"Thank you," Petrikov exhaled, sinking back down to the metal chair. Leaning the cane on his right hip, he breathed, in a weak voice, "To what do I owe the pleasure?"

Macallister remained standing as he extracted two sheets of paper from the brown, canvas satchel. Handing the sheets to Petrikov, Macallister asked emotionlessly, "Who is this?"

Petrikov accepted the sheets and balanced each of them on opposing thighs. He squinted at the pages for a moment before announcing, "That is Vitaly Nikolaevich Rodionov."

"Are you certain?"

Petrikov's face creased with a weary smile as he confirmed, "Oh, yes, very much so. Mister Rodionov is a traitor to his friends and accomplices. Much like I was. Much like I remain."

"I take it that you've met him in person?"

"Oh, yes."

"When did you meet him?"

"Summer of last year."

"When and where did you last see him?"

Petrikov didn't hesitate with his answer. "Late December. In Caracas. At the Russian Embassy to Venezuela."

Macallister wasn't as quick with a new question. In his head, he ran through the topics that he had covered with Porter and Volkov. Petrikov didn't seem to mind the wait, and the prisoner remained quiet and motionless in his chair. Macallister asked, "Did you know that we located you in Caracas through your online chess games?"

Petrikov's eyebrows raised in authentic surprise as he answered, "No." After a brief pause, he grumbled, "I should have known. My addiction to those virtual matches became my downfall. I ceased playing in the real world." He shook his head in dismay before he added, "And, I suppose my daughter had something to do with that. You know, of course, that she is quite adept with computers."

Macallister bowed his head slightly. "I'd say that's an understatement." Petrikov's mouth curled in a slight, prideful smile as Macallister continued, "How did you get access to a device to play chess online? Seems to me like a security problem waiting to happen."

"Rodionov provided a smartphone."

"Really?" The surprise in Macallister's voice and face could have been genuine. The Deputy Assistant Director was pleased with his feigned response as he added, as innocently as he could, "And how did you come to select, um, Trampoline, to play chess?"

"It was the only application on the device that Rodionov gave me. I didn't have a choice."

Petrikov raised his gaze and eyed Macallister, who hadn't reacted visibly and blandly replied, "Thank you. Those are all my questions."

Retrieving the pages that Petrikov held, Macallister stuffed them in the satchel, and then added, "You've been forthright with a great deal of information, Mister Petrikov. That does not make amends, but it does deserve recognition. And, since I'm told that your health has failed, I'll part your company leaving you this."

Macallister pulled a compact, black, plastic tube from the satchel and unrolled it, revealing an even smaller, black, velvet pouch. He placed the unrolled plastic on Petrikov's lap; it was a checkerboard of black-and-white squares. Handing the pouch to the prisoner, Macallister stated, "Ben Porter asked that I give you this."

Petrikov choked as he coughed, "Ben Porter?"

"Yes."

Carefully unfastening the string closure at its mouth, Petrikov tipped the pouch onto the flimsy chessboard, and thirty-two figurines tumbled out, several bouncing to the floor. "These were mine, once before," Petrikov mumbled, recognizing the pieces. "Where did you find them?"

"Porter remembered that they were taken from Plattsburg. Collected as evidence. They were couriered to me last night from New York so that I could bring them to you."

"Why?"

"Porter told me that he parted ways with you in a manner that he regretted."

Nodding appreciatively, Petrikov muttered, "A worthy adversary. And one who can admit a misstep. I respect that. Please thank him for me."

"I will," Macallister agreed, as he banged on the metal door three times.

"May I impose with a question?" Petrikov moaned wistfully. "What of my daughter?"

"She has continued to work alongside Porter."

Macallister turned to look at the once-feared oligarch one last time; Petrikov's eyes were closed, and his head was nodding as his fingers absently toyed with two chessmen, a white king in his left hand, and a black pawn in his right. With a long sigh, Petrikov gently placed the king on the board and laid it on its side, still caressing the pawn with his right fingers.

✳ ✳ ✳

Ninety minutes later, inside the plush, smoothly flying Citation X in international airspace, Macallister lifted the secure telephone handset to his ear and, consulting a slip of paper, dialed a number. After a moment, Macallister said, "Hey. Porter. I delivered your package. He appreciated the gesture. But to my eye, he's not going to be around much longer to enjoy it."

"What do you mean?" On the satellite connection, transmitted into space and then thousands of miles away to a speakerphone, Ben Porter's voice was flat, digitized and devoid of inflection. Without the benefit of a video conference, Macallister couldn't see his covert agent, nor could he see the huddle of faces around the table aboard *Almaz*.

"He looks ill. Very pale, very thin. That's consistent with the medical evaluation reports that we've received. Petrikov ain't gonna be with us much longer."

It was Volkov's voice that replied, pointedly ignoring the Deputy Assistant Director's description of her father, "And what of Rodionov?"

There was a brief pause due to the satellite connection latency before Macallister confirmed, "Yeah. Petrikov identified both sketches without hesitation. Said both pictures were Vitaly Rodionov. Petrikov also said that he last saw him in December. In Caracas."

Volkov asked, "And what of the app?"

"You were correct," Macallister said, with a note of praise in his voice, probably lost by the time it reached the speakerphone due to the nature of the connection. "Petrikov said he was given a smartphone that had only one app on it. Trampoline."

"I'd say that's another piece of the puzzle," Volkov observed. "Rodionov controls the app. Through Trampoline, he could monitor my father, and see what he did. Who he conversed with. And so on."

"We gotta go to London," Porter barked, interrupting Volkov. "We gotta get face-to-face with Rodionov. Or Roddick. Or whatever he wants to be called."

Macallister concluded, "I agree, but it won't be that easy. I'll be back in the SIOC in two hours. We'll set up a conference. We'll need to coordinate with the Brits. Remember, these are international allies, and there's a global pandemic going on. If you're going to London, it's gotta be planned, surgically, to cover every contingency. We'll work on it through the weekend, at least. Probably into next week. We gotta do this slowly and carefully. Remember, we're talking about a Russian agent. And possibly taking down a Russian operation which has been ongoing, if you believe Melissa Zhao, for about eighteen months. They've presumably been building this Trampoline since they took over from Zhao. We cannot leave anything to chance."

Macallister terminated the call and placed the handset in its cradle. Twisting his forearm, he examined his watch. The dial indicated 12:35 p.m.

This is going to become a storm, he thought. *The Americans, the British, and the Russians. Mix them together, and we are going to have a tempest of epic proportions. With Ben Porter at the epicenter of it all.*

Macallister closed his eyes and reclined the leather-wrapped seat in the Citation X. He would have been far less nonchalant if he had known that the storm had already begun to form and swirl, deep inside the Lefdal Mine Datacenter.

CHAPTER
82

60° 52′ N, 003° 09′ E

AS MACALLISTER DISCONNECTED the in-flight call from the Bureau jet, I checked the time on the screens. 12:35 p.m. for Macallister and for the United States east coast. 6:35 p.m. local. And 5:35 p.m. in London—after hours on the last Friday in July. The offices in that pickle-shaped building would be emptied in anticipation of a summer weekend.

I looked at the screen that displayed our position but decided to get a proper answer from Lockwood. "How much farther to London?"

"Well, we're a few hours south of Måløy," he announced. "If you want to go visit the data center, now's the time. We're headed south at fifteen knots, about six hundred miles to go. We'll be at the mouth of the River Thames sometime during the morning on Sunday."

"Maybe we could greet Mister Karl Roddick as he arrives for work at the Gherkin on Monday morning," I suggested.

"I wanna be there," Volkov demanded. "I'd like to see his face when he recognizes me."

"That's actually a good framework," Havens offered. "We could set up Sunday afternoon and be in place for Monday morning. I like that. It's a conservative timeline. How do we proceed?"

"I think we will understand more in a few hours," I reported. "We've got a secure conference set up at four o'clock in the afternoon in D.C. You know, we gotta grab the bureaucrats before quitting time at five."

"It will just start getting dark here," Lockwood laughed. "Do we get overtime pay? It will be ten in the evening for us."

"Let's break for dinner," Hamid suggested. "I suspect we have a working weekend to look forward to."

* * *

At precisely 10:00 p.m., our screens lit with connections to the SIOC and to Boston. Appleton was alone on-screen; Melissa Zhao was not in the need-to-know circle as the FBI, CIA, and State Department planned to apprehend and interview Vitaly Rodionov, suspected to be an agent of the Russian GRU, Unit 29155, also known as Karl Roddick.

The dais in the SIOC was much more crowded than we'd seen it. Officials from State and Central Intelligence had all gathered. Grabbing the center seat, notably a power play, was the diminutive, white-haired Genevieve Sullivan, Under Secretary for Political Affairs. An operation by the United States on British soil was of grave concern to her, and she lectured, "This must be dealt with according to the protocols. I recognize the need for secrecy, but all the same, you must coordinate your efforts with MI5."

"I understand working with MI5 as the British government's domestic security agency," Director Ginachere of the CIA countered, "but what about MI6? Surely, the fact that your suspect is a foreign national will be of interest to them?"

"If we spread the net too wide, it will leak," Macallister cautioned.

"You don't understand," Ginachere said with conceit. "This is an overseas op. This is what we do. In fact, I've already sent the sketch of the target to my agents in London. They've made a discreet inquiry. Roddick is, indeed, working at that building. Do you have those types of resources? That foresight? Because if you do, I'm not seeing it."

"I think you're getting ahead of yourself," Macallister argued evenly, though I could tell that he was making an effort to control his temper.

"No, I'm acting in anticipation," Ginachere replied haughtily, condescension in her tone. "I like to know every possible detail. That is why, at the very least, the CIA should take command of planning, and we will place a tactful invitation for collaboration with *both* MI5 and MI6. We have a *substantial* presence in the United Kingdom."

I could hear Havens quietly moan, and I couldn't agree more. Words like "take command of planning" and "collaboration" were bureaucratese for "gimme the ball." The CIA was clearly angling to run the operation.

The debate among the honchos continued for thirty-five minutes, and I realized that it was a foregone conclusion, negotiated in private before the conference began, when I heard Director Toffer say, "Then it's settled. Central Intelligence will plan the operation and will coordinate with MI6. The Secretary of State's office will run diplomatic cover via the embassy in London, and the embassy attaché will liaise with MI5 as well as with the London police. You'll both have the full cooperation of the FBI. Whatever assistance we can provide, we are standing by."

I thought in dismay, *We're out. We're on the sidelines.*

The collective mood in the situation room was reflected by the darkening skies outside as *Almaz* continued to steam south, toward London, but now for no reason. One by one, wordlessly, the team trickled out. As I stood and departed, deciding that it was time for a beer, I looked back at Volkov. She was staring intently at her screen. I assumed she was dejected, glaring at nothing except perhaps her reflection, realizing that she would not have the opportunity to come face-to-face with Vitaly Rodionov.

I wouldn't have been so quick to crack open that beer if I had stopped for a moment and asked her what she'd been examining so carefully.

CHAPTER
83

ABOUT FOUR HOURS AND several beers between us later, Heather Rourke and I were sound asleep, twisted together in those luxurious sheets, when the phone in our stateroom rang. Annoyed, I lifted the handset.

It was Lockwood. "Porter. Situation room. On the double. Got it?" His voice was calm, but there was a distinct urgency in his tone. And he had used my last name—that was unusual.

"Yeah, got it," I confirmed, my senses at full alert. No sooner were the words out of my mouth, Lockwood disconnected. Rourke and I tugged on our clothes and ran.

Taking my usual seat, I examined the screens, first noting the time showing 1:30 a.m. – UTC-0. Lockwood had mentioned last night that we would cross out of the Norway time zone and into the London time zone; at sea, there's really no demarcation line since the Norway zone encompasses the nation even though, technically, the longitude line that marks the zone splits the nation. The mental gymnastics of figuring out the time came in handy; once the team was assembled, I had shaken off the sleep cobwebs.

Volkov wasted no time outlining the emergency. "It's on. It's happening. Trampoline's servers are running at full capacity. They are indexing records like mad."

"Yeah, but what does that mean?" I wondered aloud.

"The system looks like it is collating data by location. As we know, the platform has constant access to your location. It's organizing devices first by time zone, then by longitude, then by latitude."

Hamid sat up and asked, "When did it start doing this?"

Volkov examined the clock displays and said, "Maybe eight hours ago. I noticed something happening when Macallister called to tell us about his visit with my father, but at that time, it made no sense to me. And, I'd have to admit, I was kind of distracted by that call."

"I'm sorry about your father. It sounds like he is in very poor health," Lockwood murmured sincerely.

"I'm not," Volkov said with bitterness dripping from the tone of the short sentence. She paused, ran her hand through her hair, and continued in a normal tone. "I started to see a pattern of something happening while we were on the conference with D.C., when they pulled us from the case. I wasn't paying attention to the call—I was watching the server traffic, still trying to decipher the intent. I initially thought it was benign, simply a reindexing of their database, which would happen relatively frequently to maintain it. I finally figured it was sorting records in order to send out an application update, and I sounded the alarm."

I was getting impatient and demanded, "What do you mean? An application update? What's that?"

"It's the trigger." Volkov took a deep breath and began, "Working by time zone and then by location, every Trampoline user is being primed for an application update from the Trampoline servers. The update will be automatically installed on every device. That update initiates two actions. First, it sends instructions to transfer money out of any linked bank account, and then it locks out the user. Then there's a second wave. Remember that Trampoline has also collected every one of your contacts? Even the people you have not saved specifically as contact entries. If you receive or send an email to or from someone just once, Trampoline has that email address saved and indexed to you. They've got every phone number that has ever called your phone, or that you've called from your phone, saved and indexed to you—"

"What does that do for them?" Hamid asked, interrupting her.

"Trampoline sends a package, via either email or text, to everyone you have ever contacted or been contacted by. Within that package is a tiny program. A virus. If someone who receives the email or text, which has been sent from someone they know, and opens the message, the virus freezes their device while it sends that new device's contact list back to Trampoline. And the process repeats, over and over, as Trampoline finds new addresses or numbers to send the virus to."

"It's a Trojan horse, replicated millions of times," I suggested.

"Worse," Volkov responded. "*Billions* of times. According to Zhao, Trampoline has over a billion users. The first round steals their money, then locks them out of their own accounts. The second round attempts to freeze every device associated with those billions of users. There's a third round, which is automatic, as it runs replications of the second round until Trampoline runs out of addresses or phone numbers or manages to freeze every mobile device on the planet."

Hamid asked, "What's the point of freezing all those devices if they've already transferred the money?"

I realized in an instant and blurted, "It's to create time! Imagine the scenario. You get an email saying your account is being authenticated, and then your phone freezes. Then your friend's phone is all of a sudden bricked, too, and then your friend's phone freezes. You know something is happening. But through your phone, you can't access your usual news feeds, so you turn to television, which starts to report these strange occurrences. And all the while, money is being drained from accounts globally. But you don't know that yet, because how would you—you've been locked out of your accounts. And by the time everyone connected with Trampoline realizes that they are penniless, there's nothing anyone can do about it."

Hamid followed up on his question with a sharp insight. "If it started eight hours ago, that would have been 5:30, London time. After hours. Can you tell how many records are, um, processed?"

Volkov scrutinized her screen and guessed, "A lot? Hundreds of millions. Maybe eight hundred million."

I grabbed a piece of paper and did the math that Hamid was angling at. "Zhao told Appleton that Trampoline was at one point two billion users. If the system has indexed eight hundred million records in eight hours, they've got . . ." I scratched out the subtraction and gasped, "Four-point-two-hours left in processing time. That's like four hours and fifteen minutes!"

"Porter," Havens said deeply, "you're saying that Trampoline starts locking phones and draining bank accounts in just over four hours?"

"Yeah," I said, adding in a confused, almost whispering volume, "but why then?"

"Does it matter?"

I looked up at Havens. He was right. It didn't matter. And then it hit me. "Hamid said it earlier. 5:30 London time. After hours. And who's in London? The CIA said they confirmed this. Vitaly Rodionov. Or Karl Roddick. He's in London right now. We need to go there, right now!"

Rourke caught my eye and exclaimed, "I can fly a chopper way faster than Miles can drive this boat."

I barked, "How far to London, Miles?"

He consulted the display and said, "As the crow flies, about four hundred and twenty-five miles."

Rourke's face fell as she disclosed, "The maximum range of the chopper is four hundred and thirty-three miles. That's cutting it way too close. And we wouldn't be able to fly back."

"The hell with it. We need a one-way ride to London. By the time we prepare and load up, we'll be a little bit closer. Miles, full throttle!"

Lockwood bolted to the bridge, and as I continued thinking through my orders, I thought of him—always calm, cool, and collected. I kept my voice even as I ticked items off one-by-one, "Havens, you're on weapons and gear. What are we gonna need to get in that building? Volkov, watch the system. See if anything new emerges. And Hamid, get Macallister on the comms. If we don't call this in, we're gonna be shot down out of the sky by the British."

I looked at Rourke. Her green eyes were as focused as I'd ever seen them, and they got brighter and brighter as I instructed, "Rourke, prep the chopper, and make sure the fuel tanks are filled to the brim. Find a place to land as close to that pickle as possible. Shit, land on the top of it if you can. Wheels up in thirty minutes, tops. Fifteen minutes would be better. Let's go!"

CHAPTER
84

ALMAZ WAS VIBRATING AND shuddering, plowing and sloshing through the swell in anger, her engines straining as Lockwood called for maximum revolutions. The yacht was not designed for speed; it was intended for range and stability. I checked in with Lockwood on the bridge to find him on the intercom with Warren Parnell, our engineer. On the closed-circuit screen that showed the engine room, I could see a sweat-soaked Parnell, an unlit cigar clamped between his teeth, examining gauges.

Lockwood held a hand over the intercom mouthpiece and said with dismay, "We can't keep this speed up. Our designed max speed is twenty-one point five knots. We're exceeding that at twenty-three knots. Even if we could maintain these revolutions for another hour, it'll be inconsequential to the chopper range, but disastrous for our power plant."

"Fine," I said, "dial it back a hair. Rourke says we'll be ready to launch in minutes. She's going to warm up the engines with fuel lines connected, so we have max fuel."

"That sounds dangerous." Lockwood sounded dubious.

"Frankie Dunn is on the pad. He says he can manage it."

"Alright," Lockwood muttered. "What about you?"

I had already changed into my black night ops uniform but had not strapped on my weapons harness, and I glanced at the tactical watch on my wrist, numbers glowing green. "I got Macallister in one minute.

Rourke says she can manage the range, so keep us going as fast as you can, and as soon I talk to Macallister, we lift off."

"Copy that," Lockwood confirmed as I rushed to the situation room.

Hamid had also changed into the night ops tactical gear and was sitting in Lockwood's usual seat, to my left, while Volkov remained at her station, an empty coffee mug before her. The clock above the big center screen read 1:55 a.m., UTC-0, and that big screen was lit with an image of the SIOC. I looked at Hamid questioningly. He got the gist of my look and reported, "I called Macallister with your super-secret flip phone, and I said it was goin' down. Full court press. Told him to get his preppy ass in gear and get our peeps over to the SIOC."

"You really said it that way? Those exact words?"

Hamid punched me on the shoulder, "Fuckin'-a, man, I did. And it got his attention."

"Nicely done."

"Ah, there's more, bud. I called the duty officer at the Central spook headquarters and told them to get that Gina whatshername over on the double, and I called the Sec State's office and told them to track down the under elf."

Knowing that we were on-screen in the SIOC and praying that we were muted, I hissed, "You can't call her that."

He teased, "Just gettin' a rise from you, Benny boy. I kindly but sternly requested the presence of Under Secretary Sullivan, as soon as possible, as a matter of a national security emergency. That okay?"

The dais was filling with the familiar faces, but in my estimation, it was taking too long. When Macallister rushed in, the clock read 2:03 a.m., and I had Hamid unmute our microphone. I stood, mostly to get their attention and also to show that I was dressed in trendy head-to-toe black, the latest fashion in counterterrorism. I spoke directly and confidently. "Here is the situation. A Trampoline attack is imminent. By our estimation, in three-and-a-half or four hours. In less than fifteen minutes, my team and I will be airborne. We will land in London, we will infiltrate the Trampoline offices, and we will stop this. I have very little time for your questions, so make them succinct."

"I vehemently object to this," CIA Director Ginachere snapped. "The Russians have increased the pressure on my people in Moscow. They want answers. They want to know where their agent is. They—"

I cut her off, snarling, "Oh, so you answer to the Russians now, Director?"

Before Macallister or Toffer could intervene, Ginachere ranted, "And furthermore, you're now claiming the Russians are involved in this . . . this Trampoline thing? Based on a sketch? That's your evidence? What *actual* evidence do you have? This is outrageous."

"Volkov will brief you when my team is in the air."

"Absolutely not," Ginachere hissed venomously. "You're not going anywhere."

"I don't report to you. We're lifting off in minutes. Next question."

She wouldn't let it go, not willing to cede her authority, and turning to Toffer, Ginachere yelled, "This is unprecedented. Call off your team. Call off that loose cannon, whatshisname, Porter. We are planning a *proper* mission for next week. A fully-thought-out, carefully designed mission that is. We—"

"We don't have until next week," I said, cutting her off brusquely. "We have three or four hours. Will your team be ready by then, Director?"

"Easy, Porter," Macallister warned. "One step at a time. What's your flight duration?"

I took a deep breath and said, "Just over two hours. Max speed and max range. The chopper is not coming back."

"You have a chopper?" Ginachere's expression was blood-red-angry. I think she was jealous of my toys.

Macallister ignored her, asking, "Is Volkov going with you or staying on the boat?"

Volkov herself answered, "On the boat. I'll brief you, as Porter said. And I'll continue to monitor the Trampoline servers, and I can be a comms link to the team."

Director Toffer puffed out his chest and went with the flow in the room, saying deliberately, "Very well. What do you need from us?"

Ginachere sulked as I responded, "Urgent coordination with MI5 and local police. We'll notify you of our planned landing zone once we have it. We may have to wing it."

"Consider that done," squeaked the Under Secretary. "I can handle that. I'll get a priority message to our embassy, and I will reach out directly to my counterparts. And I'll connect with the British military. They will need to be informed. I'll caution you, however. It's early on Saturday morning there. I may not get them to move quickly."

I was watching the clock, and I announced, "That's enough. We need to get in the air. Volkov will explain what we've discovered."

Hamid and I ran to the helipad, leaving Volkov behind to watch our backs, both literally and figuratively, as she would continue to coordinate the mission with Washington. Havens met us on the pad and handed us weapons harnesses, saying, "Put 'em on in the air."

Ducking unnecessarily but instinctively under the spinning rotors, we climbed aboard the Eurocopter EC155B1, snapping the cabin door shut and donning headsets for internal communications. Out the window, I saw Dunn pulling the fuel hose away from the chopper, carrying a single set of wheel chocks in one hand. As soon as Dunn was clear, the whine of the engines increased, and with a wobble, the wheels separated from the teak planking of the helipad, and the helicopter took to the air.

Rourke lifted and banked the chopper only slightly clear of the towering antenna mast on *Almaz,* and she dipped the nose of the craft. As we began to gain speed, I watched the lights of *Almaz* below, imagining Lockwood pulling back the throttles with relief and then perhaps joining Volkov in the situation room, leaving Alverez on the bridge to con the yacht.

I inspected my wrist. The green numbers showed 2:21 a.m.

As the chopper bounced in a patch of turbulent air, my stomach flip-flopped. Was it nerves? Was it fear? Was it a premonition that we were already too late? I didn't know, but it seemed to me that the beat of the rotor blades had become synchronized with the seconds ticking off on my watch, and suddenly I realized that every passing second was critical.

CHAPTER
85

EIGHTY-SIX MINUTES INTO the flight, Rourke's voice, with an edge of stress, spoke via the headset system to Havens, Hamid, and me in the passenger cabin. "Two updates. One good, one bad."

"Bad news first, always," Havens responded quickly.

"Volkov says the index processing is running faster than she thought. She's pegged a time. Five in the morning."

"Five in the morning?" I wondered. "Why then?"

"I dunno," Rourke said. "Volkov suggested that it's midnight on the East Coast in the States. But whatever the reason, we are running out of time. We're exceeding the so-called *never exceed* speed of this thing by three knots. We're flying at one hundred and seventy-eight knots of airspeed. We're gonna be on fumes when we land. About forty-five minutes to touchdown."

I looked at Havens. His face was placid. The experienced CIRG agent had no doubt faced similar, high-pressure circumstances. I couldn't believe how calm he was in contrast to my racing pulse and sweaty palms. Havens asked casually, "Okay, so what's the good news?"

Rourke's voice, still edgy, replied, "Assuming the airframe holds together, and we don't run out of fuel, we have a landing zone near the target. Three minutes from LZ to the pickle building, at a jogging pace."

"Excellent," Havens confirmed with confidence. "Any word from Volkov on securing that LZ?"

"Not yet. My nav system says we will be landing at 4:35 a.m. Hopefully, that gives Volkov and the people in the SIOC enough time to get us some reinforcements on the ground."

"That should be plenty of time for the calvary to meet us at the pickle building," Havens commented, closing his eyes and crossing his hands across his chest in contentment.

I stared at him, thinking, *If he had a pair of cucumber slices covering his eyes, he'd be at a spa. Wait, aren't cucumbers and pickles related somehow?* I tried to follow suit, and I tried to distract myself. But all I could see in my mind's eye was that towering, glass-sheathed, gherkin-shaped building, and I wondered, *Were we even targeting the correct location?*

3:58 AM LONDON; UTC-0 / 10:58 PM US EAST COAST; UTC-5

"Ma'am. This is highly unusual." The British-accented voice dripped with a combination of superciliousness and disbelief.

"I know it's unusual. It's unusual for me to be calling you at four o'clock in the morning, your time, waking you, trying to get you to understand," squealed Genevieve Sullivan. "I'm the Under Secretary of Political Affairs, for heaven's sake. This is not some exercise." Sullivan turned to Director Toffer and added, with full knowledge that the listener on the speakerphone would hear the comment, "Are you making any progress with MI6?"

Toffer didn't respond, but the voice on the phone did, "Ma'am. I know who you are. I am the Assistant to the Minister of State for Security. And before I escalate this to the Minister and to MI5, and well before we escalate this to the Home Secretary, I will need evidence. All you have offered thus far are claims of some sort of manipulation of a social network."

Those last two words were spoken with scorn, and Sullivan responded in kind. "A manipulation is an understatement even for you, Assistant

Minister. I have neither the time nor the patience to present data. We have a team en route. They will land in London in a matter of minutes. They—"

"They shall do no such thing." The voice was clipped and deliberate.

To Toffer's surprise, Sullivan punched the button to disconnect the call as she announced, "He had one good idea. I'm going to escalate straight to the Home Secretary. I have her personal phone number."

As the white-haired woman swiped at a smartphone for the correct contact, Macállister whispered to Toffer, "Why the Home Secretary?"

Toffer replied, "She's a senior Minister of the Crown, a senior member of the Prime Minister's cabinet, and most importantly, has oversight of MI5. Sullivan has some serious connections. She'll get it done. Assuming the Home Secretary answers her phone at four o'clock in the morning."

4:29 AM LONDON; UTC-0 / 11:29 PM US EAST COAST; UTC-5

Rourke had called out, "Feet dry," as the view below the chopper, once the unbroken, black darkness of the sea below, became a patchwork of lights on the ground, getting denser and denser as we neared London, flashing over the city of Cambridge as Rourke picked up the M11 highway to follow as a visual reference. She pulled a weather report and gave us, in the back of the clattering machine, a quick briefing, "Skies are clearing and expected to be fair. The barometer is at 29.93 inches. Ground temperature will be in the mid-sixties Fahrenheit, with a light westerly breeze. Sunrise won't be until 5:25 a.m., but you'll have a little natural twilight as soon as we land."

"Lovely conditions," murmured Havens, finally opening his eyes. "ETA to LZ?"

"Six minutes. I am going to circle first. We're approaching from the northeast. Hold on."

The craft began to bank right and descend. My stomach floated into my throat. I looked at Hamid; he was grinning maniacally.

I blinked and tried to look outside, to find the horizon. The chopper leveled, and out the left side windows, I could just make out the twisting River Thames, a strip of blackness cutting through the lights of London.

I finally relaxed. We were almost there.

Buzzzz. Buzzzz. Buzzzz.

An urgent alarm tone sounded, and I heard Rourke mutter, "Shit," before she said loudly, "We've exceeded our fuel reserves. Out of fuel warning." Her voice was even but terse as she focused on the glass displays in the cockpit, the view through the curved-glass windows at the nose of the EC155B1, and the feel of the collective pitch control and the cyclic pitch control in her hands, along with the pressure of the antitorque pedals beneath her feet. She was conducting a physical symphony with her body; the movement and twist in her left hand adjusting the collective and the throttle, the angle of her right hand vectoring the flight direction, and the touch of her feet guiding the chopper's tail.

Muting the buzzing alarm, Rourke banked the machine to the right, and as the helicopter turned, the cylindric shape of the Gherkin became visible to the left of the chopper, just above the sill of the window glass. Rourke announced, "LZ below. Appears clear."

Havens was peering from the windows, too, and commented with just a note of concern in his voice, "I don't see any emergency lights. Either they are clearing the landing zone for us quietly and stealthily, or they haven't gotten the message."

4:32 AM LONDON; UTC-0 / 11:32 PM US EAST COAST; UTC-5

"To the best of our belief, it's happening at five your time. In just under a half-hour, Madam Home Secretary."

The tired, soft but precise female voice on the speaker responded, "I see. Thank you, Genevieve. Knowing you as I do, I don't doubt the seriousness of the situation. Kindly hold on this line. Let me make a call on a separate phone."

Sullivan's face showed triumph in contrast to the somber expressions gathered around the table. Above and beyond the group at the dais, one of the giant screens on the wall of the SIOC displayed a shaky, quickly moving aerial image of London, transmitted from the nosecone camera of the EC155B1 being piloted by Heather Rourke, relayed via the high-speed communications links aboard *Almaz*. Three other smaller screens were being fed by three helmet cams and showed only dark figures crouched in the cabin of a helicopter.

Macallister was grimly focused on a separate screen that mirrored one of Anastasia Volkov's monitors and showed a stream of data as well as a percentage indicator, currently at 96.11%. Every four to five seconds, the hundredths place would tick up to the next number. To no one specific at the dais, Macallister grumbled, "I hope the Home Secretary makes that call with a lot less politeness. We don't got time for that."

"It will reach 100% at midnight, east coast time," the disembodied voice of Volkov declared over the SIOC loudspeakers. "What happens after that is anyone's guess. It's not going to go global in an instant. It will take a little time. The Trampoline system is indexing from east to west by location, starting basically in North America. London actually gets hit last by the time the wave will go around the planet."

Before anyone could respond, the precise voice of the British Home Secretary announced, "MI5, the Metropolitan Police, and the City of London Police have all been notified. What time does your team intend to land?"

Macallister leaned to the speakerphone device and growled, "Now."

4:36 AM LONDON; UTC-0 / 11:36 PM US EAST COAST; UTC-5

I peeked forward into the cockpit. From what I could see, warning lights peppered the glass cockpit display, most of them fiercely red, some of them frantically blinking. Rourke had circled the landing zone for a second time at five hundred feet above the ground, but not a single emergency vehicle was in sight. I hoped that Havens' first guess—that they would meet us stealthily—was correct.

As a church spire flashed past the right window, the chopper banked hard right and nose up with a gut-wrenching motion, transitioning in almost an instant from forward flight to hover. My stomach lurched as the craft fell from the sky in a fast descent, the engines whining as the top of the church spire came level with the window.

I squeezed my eyes shut in terror.

With a scream of engine noise, the tail of the helicopter dropped slightly, then leveled abruptly as the wheels of the craft slammed into the earth. In a split second, the whine of the engines decreased in pitch as Rourke's voice said in my earphones, "Welcome to Saint Botolph Without Aldgate Church. This will be the end of your aerial tour of London. We're out of fuel. Go!"

Havens had already yanked off his headset, tossing it on the cabin floor. Hamid and I did the same as Havens kneeled at the left door and unlatched it, calling back to us, "Remember the briefing. Follow me."

During the final moments of the flight, we had put our three heads together to examine the map image that Volkov transmitted to Havens' tactical display, a small screen about the size of an iPhone strapped to his wrist. Both Hamid and I had identical devices. They'd be our guides, and Volkov would follow our progress through the cameras and location transmitters that were installed in our helmets. In addition, a tiny number showed in a red-outlined box at the corner of the small screen: 96.67%.

I mimicked Havens' leap from the chopper. My black, lace-up boots landed in grass, and after tucking a wheel chock that I carried under the nose wheel of the helicopter, I could survey the scene.

Rourke had nailed the landing, planting the rear wheels in the semi-circular patch of grass of Aldgate Square and touching the front wheel on paving stones. Volkov had warned us that the grassy area pitched down slightly toward the paved area, and I flashed Rourke, still in the cockpit, a thumbs-up sign once the chock was in place so that she could release the brakes. The engine noise died down, but the rotors still spun off their momentum.

Rourke herself appeared a moment later, having shut off the engines but leaving the electrical power on; we'd need the helicopter's telemetry relay to remain operational, linking us back to Volkov on *Almaz* and to the SIOC across the Atlantic.

The four-person squad took off at a jog, Havens and Hamid leading, Rourke and I as a pair in the second row, leaving the chopper behind and heading for Dukes Place. We could hear the squeal of car brakes as drivers in the early morning traffic realized that a helicopter, anti-collision lights still flashing but landing lights off, had perched itself in Aldgate Square.

"Aren't you worried that someone will board the chopper?" I gasped as we jogged.

She half-chuckled. "Nah. Where could they go? There's literally not enough fuel onboard to prime the engines."

"That close?"

"You have no idea."

4:39 AM LONDON; UTC-0 / 11:39 PM US EAST COAST; UTC-5

"They're on the ground," Under Secretary Sullivan reported as the bouncing images of now four helmet cam feeds showed an ominous, black-and-glass building to the left as the group traveled on foot northwest on Dukes Place, their movements also tracked on a moving map screen. "They're alone. Where's the local support?"

"Oh, dear," moaned the soft and precise voice of the Home Secretary. "They're on the ground already?"

Macallister stepped closer to the speakerphone, "Ma'am, the telemetric data from the aircraft showed a low fuel warning. I think they had to land. Regardless, the clock is ticking."

"Well done," Sullivan whispered. "You gave her a way to save face."

Macallister nodded as Sullivan updated the Home Secretary in a louder tone of voice, "Our team is ninety seconds out from the target."

4:41 AM LONDON; UTC-0 / 11:41 PM US EAST COAST; UTC-5

Dukes Place had become, for no apparent reason, Bevis Marks. We ran a few hundred feet further and turned left onto Saint Mary Axe, another oddly named street that was also the substance for the official name of the Gherkin, "30 St. Mary Axe." We'd already hustled some eight hundred feet, and we had to jog another two hundred and fifty feet. All in, less than a quarter of a mile, and I was panting.

Havens, Hamid, and Rourke seemed unaffected as we ducked left again, now running down the ramp to the underground garage.

With the target in sight, towering overhead, I mentally ran through the stats of the building that Volkov had compiled for our infiltration plan. Forty-one stories tall, it was round, with a decreasing circumference as it rose. The round core of the building, however, was a more consistent diameter, containing several mechanical chases, a series of eight elevator banks, some serving lower floors and halting partway up the core, and others skipping lower floors and accessing higher levels, plus two fire lifts, and two stair shafts.

Naturally, we'd take the stairs.

The security booth at the mouth of the ramp to the garage would not be manned until five in the morning, and we squeezed past the vehicle barrier. In the distance, I heard the wail of sirens, the noise getting louder and louder even as we descended into the bowels of the building.

We weren't going to wait for those sirens to arrive.

4:43 AM LONDON; UTC-0 / 11:43 PM US EAST COAST; UTC-5

"We're sending units to assist your team at the Gherkin, and sending police to secure your helicopter," the Home Secretary offered politely.

Staring at a tactical map displayed on one of the SIOC monitors, Macallister contained his frustration as the on-screen dots representing the team members moved closer to the center of the core of the target building. On another screen, the simulcast from the team's helmet cams showed a maze of columns within a small underground parking garage. Pushing a button on a tabletop-mounted console, Macallister said, "Volkov. The team is on its own."

"Copy that. I'll relay the message," Volkov responded calmly, from the *Almaz* situation room over three thousand nautical miles away from Washington.

On the data screen in the SIOC, the indicator ticked to 97.64%, now increasing by a hundredth every three or four seconds.

4:44 AM LONDON; UTC-0 / 11:44 PM US EAST COAST; UTC-5

Getting to the ground level of the Gherkin was easy; the emergency exit stairs from an underground garage were not secured. However, on the ground floor, in the vestibule where the garage stair shaft and one of the building stair shafts met, an exit-only door blocked access to the upper floors.

Havens extracted a small explosive device from his harness and rigged the door with a charge, commanding, "Stand back."

Hamid was pointing a neutralizing blue light at the eye of a security camera, but whether we were being watched by the building's twenty-four/seven security force was largely irrelevant. By the time a guard made it to our position, we'd be gone.

With a thud, the charge detonated, and Havens pulled the still-smoking door open with a gloved hand. "Let's climb," he said.

Ten floors. One tread at a time.

At least we don't have to climb to the top, forty-first floor, I thought with relief.

4:45 AM LONDON; UTC-0 / 11:45 PM US EAST COAST; UTC-5

"Intruders in Stairwell B."

"Pardon?" Vitaly Rodionov swiveled away from a glowing computer monitor and said, "What is that supposed to mean? Intruders?"

Fedor Ilin, seated at a nearby desk, replied, "I don't know. Someone just forced the door at the bottom of the stair open. The security camera recording shows a blank, blurry screen."

"Staff?"

"Not yet, I believe. The food and beverage staff for the top floor restaurant typically arrive after five. We're the only occupants of the building, as far as I can tell."

Rodionov rose from his seat and paced to the exterior, peering through the thick, double-glazed triangular glass skins that formed the exterior of 30 St. Mary Axe. At first at a walk, then at a trot, he circumnavigated the five-hundred-foot perimeter of the round office floor, at times diverting around the six triangles that encroached into the space and formed staggered, five-story high shafts at the exterior of the structure that promoted airflow and created energy efficiency.

Slightly out of breath, he returned to his terminal and reported, "There are emergency vehicles approaching this area from all directions, and perhaps several at the base of the building."

"For us? How is that possible?"

"Porter, I'm guessing," Rodionov snarled as he consulted his screen, stating, "The indexing routine is ahead of schedule. It will be complete in eight minutes. Set it up to transmit the update as soon as the index is complete."

Consulting his on-screen clock, Fedor objected, "But that will be substantially early. By seven minutes."

Rodionov grunted, "Who cares? Running it at midnight, East Coast time, was symbolic. It doesn't matter. By the time the Americans wake up for their first Saturday in August, it will be done. And not soon enough, if indeed Porter has found his way here."

Fedor had already begun to work at his terminal as Rodionov returned to the window, looking down toward the ground, eleven stories below.

He grabbed the shoulder of a third man seated opposite Fedor and ordered, "Gregoriy, come with me. Hand me that. We're covering the doors to Stairwell B."

A dark-haired man stood, lifting a black pistol from the surface of the desk. Handing the weapon to Rodionov, the man picked up a second gun.

4:48 AM LONDON; UTC-0 / 11:48 PM US EAST COAST; UTC-5

If I thought the run from the LZ to the target was tough, the stair climb was murder. Ten flights. I clutched my belly.

"Pull it together, Porter," Havens commanded without sympathy, completely unfazed by the climb as he set a second charge on the door marked with a giant, painted yellow *10*.

"I thought Volkov said the interior doors wouldn't be locked," I panted. "They're fire exits. You push them, and they open."

"No," Havens corrected me, "they're latched, not locked. You push from the inside, and they'll open. You pull from the outside, and they're latched. Otherwise, no floor is secure."

He pulled away from the door and quietly said, "Stand back."

4:49 AM LONDON; UTC-0 / 11:49 PM US EAST COAST; UTC-5

Rodionov was crouching close to the floor and facing a double exit door marked *Fire Exit—Stairwell B*. Hearing the sound of a soft *thump*, he first touched Gregoriy on the shoulder, and then, without a word, Rodionov tapped the muzzle of his gun on the grey carpeted floor. Gregoriy nodded his understanding.

4:49 AM LONDON; UTC-0 / 11:49 PM US EAST COAST; UTC-5

The charge made the sound of a soft *thump*, and Havens wasted no time striding to the door. He pointed to Hamid, then me, then Rourke, and finally held up three fingers. He folded one finger down, then a second finger, and then clenched his fist as he pulled the door ajar.

Hamid, wielding a H&K MP5 sub machine gun, slid through the opening silently and cut left past the door jamb, his boots soundless on a smooth, white, polished concrete floor.

Feeling Rourke's presence behind me and gripping a familiar FBI-standard issue Glock Model 22 pistol, I crept after Hamid, and I cut right.

The space was completely and totally empty.

4:50 AM LONDON; UTC-0 / 11:50 PM US EAST COAST; UTC-5

"Cover those stairs," Rodionov hissed, pointing to the head of a single, open, glass-railed staircase set into one of the triangle-shaped detents that encroached into the circular perimeter. Gregoriy trotted to the head of the stairs and squatted, peeking down to the lower floor in the two-level suite.

4:50 AM LONDON; UTC-0 / 11:50 PM US EAST COAST; UTC-5

"We're on the wrong floor. Fuck," I snarled softly. "The building directory indicated ten *and* eleven. We gotta go up one flight."

Havens followed Rourke into the cavernous space, the dawning light of a fair morning in London filtering through the entirely glass perimeter of the open, unfurnished, unoccupied space. Tapping me on the shoulder, Havens whispered, "Up," while pointing at the base of an open, glass-railed staircase set into a triangle-shaped detent that encroached into the circular perimeter.

"Wait," I hissed. Catching a glimpse of Hamid's SMG, I ordered, "Split it. Havens and Rourke, the glass stairs. Hamid, we're going up the fire stairs. You can blow the door open with the rifle."

"Got it," Havens confirmed as Hamid and Rourke nodded their understanding of the hastily adjusted plan.

"Give us thirty seconds."

Havens flashed a thumbs-up and glanced at the wrist display as Hamid and I hoofed it back into the stairwell.

4:51 AM LONDON; UTC-0 / 11:51 PM US EAST COAST; UTC-5

Gregoriy heard a soft footfall on the stair below, and risking exposure, he peeked through the glass rail to confirm his senses. Sure enough, a giant, ebony rock of a man was tiptoeing up the treads, clad from head to toe in black and wearing a tactical chest harness and a futuristic matte-black helmet. Raising the pistol, Gregoriy leaned his shoulder clear of the glass rail and fired three shots.

Across the space, Rodionov rushed toward the sound.

4:51 AM LONDON; UTC-0 / 11:51 PM US EAST COAST; UTC-5

Hamid and I both heard the *Pop! Pop! Pop!* of small arms fire as we reached the eleventh-floor landing, and without hesitation or command, Hamid blasted the fire door jamb with a burst from his MP5. I pushed him aside and yanked the door open.

Unlike the level below, this floor was brightly lit, a grey carpet topped with desk after desk, all bristling with computers and telephones and potted plants.

And, unlike the level below, this floor was occupied, and as I burst through the door opening, gripping my Glock, I caught a glimpse of a medium-height, dark-haired man facing in the direction of the stairs with a glass railing.

The man was facing the exterior of the building, and he turned back toward the fire door, no doubt turning toward the sound of Hamid's automatic.

I recognized him instantly. Vitaly Rodionov. Karl Roddick.

He raised his pistol as I raised mine, an almost synchronized reaction.

I felt strong. I felt the training at Quantico take over. I stood stock-still, my Glock aimed at his pistol.

Pop! Pop! Pop! Pop!

Rodionov was at a disadvantage as four shots were fired from the area of the glass stairs behind him. I could see his head twitch. He wanted to look. He dared not look away from me.

I, however, could see past him—and it was Rourke's helmeted head that poked up behind the glass of the rail, her hair tied back but still glinting red in the glare of the office lighting. She crawled over the still shape of a man who had collapsed at the top of the stairs.

"It's over," I announced. "Stop the computers. Stop the—"

With a staccato blast, Hamid fired his weapon to my left, and I watched Rodionov's eyes widen, but then, to my shock, he grinned, scrunching his nose so that the hairs above his upper lip splayed out, saying as his eyes darted once to his right, "Fedor already started the runtime routine. I spotted you, you know, at the data center. In Norway. With your friend Volkov. And because of your brashness and your arrogance, you're too late, Mister Porter. And you're dead."

Rodionov squeezed the trigger on his weapon, and a millisecond later, I squeezed my own trigger.

As a sledgehammer smacked into the left side of my abdomen, I began to fall, doubled over, trying to watch Rodionov dropping to the floor.

Gasping for breath, I hit the floor. My wind was knocked out of me like I'd caught a fastball in the stomach. I took a deep breath, then another, all the while staring at Rodionov, waiting for him to move, my Glock still pointed, mostly, in his direction. I saw Rourke spring from the stairwell and begin to run in the opposite direction, away from me, weapon outstretched, circling the perimeter and daring another target to appear.

Dragging myself to my feet, I felt my gut, where the thick, hi-tech body armor had done its job, deforming under the impact of Rodionov's bullet. I looked left. Hamid's shots had taken down another man.

I scanned the area, desperately seeking some sort of clue, wishing Volkov was at my side to take over, and I heard her voice, laughing at me in a New York hotel room, *"It's a computer. If you get stuck, sometimes it's more effective just to pull the plug."*

I spun toward the man to my left, who had been at Rodionov's right. He had been seated at a computer desk, and I raced to the machine. Not caring what was on the screen, knowing that it would be non-sensical to me, I started yanking cables from electrical outlets and from ethernet ports—one computer, then another, then another.

Hamid picked up on the task and then Rourke, and the three of us circled the eleventh floor of the Gherkin like lunatics, unplugging anything and everything in sight.

Sometimes, simply turning it all off is the solution.

CHAPTER
86

BREATHLESS, I COMPLETED THE circuit of the eleventh floor. "Where's Havens?" I wheezed.

Rourke bolted to the glass stairs, calling over her shoulder, "He's down! Hit!"

I heard the familiar *ding* of an elevator annunciator, and both Hamid and I spun to face the double glass doors that accessed the central core of the building. Two uniformed police officers burst from one of the elevator banks; both were armed with stubby black rifles with forward-curved magazines. Knowing enough, barely, about the British police forces, I recognized that these two men were from the limited ranks of AFOs, or Authorized Firearms Officers, and I motioned to Hamid to lower the muzzle of his weapon toward the carpet.

I could only imagine the image that the officer's eyes' processed: two black-clad, weapons-bearing, mercenary-looking figures, standing over two unmoving bodies splayed on the carpet, amidst overturned desks and scattered computer hardware. To their credit, and perhaps recognizing the gesture of lowering our guns, they proceeded cautiously and pulled the glass doors open.

I wasted no time with a greeting. "I'm Porter. United States Federal Bureau of Investigation. We have one of our team down. We have three targets down."

"How many of you?" was the quick reply.

"Four. Including the man down. He's on the level below."

"How many of them?"

"Only the three."

Another *ding* as a second elevator discharged more men, just as yet another group burst from the destroyed stairwell doors. I turned to Hamid, "I guess we're getting our reinforcements."

He agreed. "Yeah. You go deal with Havens. I'll take over here."

Hamid had the presence of mind to tear the Velcro-attached patch off his chest to reveal his Bureau badge, as I pointed to one of the first two officers and ordered, "Follow me."

I had lost track of time, once so critical to me, now meaningless, as Rourke and I watched the stretcher bearing the unmoving body of Leroy Havens being carried to the elevator banks.

Rourke did what she could to triage one bullet wound and two impacts; Havens' body armor, like mine, had done its job, but one projectile had connected with flesh and bone. He bled substantially, but he remained conscious, whispering to me as he was lifted, "Did we get 'em in time, Porter?"

I grinned, but, truly, I didn't know. Seeing Havens into capable medical hands was an opportunity to connect with Volkov, and for the first time during the mission, as Rourke and I climbed the glass-railed stairs to rejoin Hamid, I used my earpiece and spoke directly to *Almaz.* "Volkov? Do you copy?"

"Porter! Yes, copy." Volkov's voice was strident. "I've been monitoring the feeds. They're watching and listening in the SIOC, too, and they're demanding answers to their questions." She took a breath and added, in a much softer tone, "What's with Havens?"

"He's hit. Down but not out. Still conscious," I reported. "Did we get here in time?"

"Yeah," Volkov said.

Rourke and I reached the top of the stairs, and from the grin on his face, we could tell that Hamid heard that one word as well through his helmet link. He flashed a thumbs-up as Volkov continued, "The indexing routine was at 99.82% when it stopped. From what I could see, the application update was to disperse the instant the indexing work was complete."

I allowed myself a small smile before asking, "How much longer would the indexing have taken?"

Rourke, Hamid, and I stood shoulder to shoulder, waiting for Volkov's response. *One Mississippi. Two Mississippi's. Three Mississ*—when Volkov finally answered, curtly, "Thirty-nine seconds."

AUGUST

CHAPTER
87

SUNDAY, AUGUST 2, 2020 – LONDON, UNITED KINGDOM

TO EVEN THE MOST JADED Londoner, it had to have been a startling sight: a 235-foot expedition-style yacht rafted alongside the 613-foot Town-class light cruiser HMS *Belfast*. Even the stoic and calm Miles Lockwood was impressed when Her Majesty's government lifted the Tower Bridge, and the drawbridge beyond, to allow *Almaz* passage into the heart of London, on the River Thames.

The mooring location, however, was chosen not for its prominence, but for its security; the museum that typically operated on *Belfast* had been closed since March due to the pandemic, and Lockwood eased *Almaz* upriver on the Thames to tie alongside the warship, in order to discharge a package of the utmost secrecy.

Admiring the London skyline from the bow of *Almaz*, I reflected on the prior forty hours or so, since three body bags had been zipped closed and removed from Trampoline's eleventh-floor offices. Inside one of those bags was Vitaly Rodionov.

He was the first human being that I had killed. I recognized the weight, the remorse, and the burden that Volkov had described to me, months ago, as we drove in a rented Kia sedan toward New York City. Perhaps my actions were justified by the circumstances. It was him in that bag, but it easily could have been me.

It didn't matter. It remained a nagging, unpleasant feeling to know that I had taken another person's life.

Before I had the luxury of time to process all that, investigators from an alphabet soup of the United States and British government agencies began combing the Trampoline office space, documenting the gun battle with spent casings and trajectory calculations, packaging computer equipment for analysis elsewhere, and generally causing a shit-show of epic proportions as each agency vied to one-up each other.

Volkov had managed to coordinate a relay between Washington and the Metropolitan Police, who kindly spirited Hamid and me away in a Mercedes Sprinter van operated by the Territorial Support Group, the units within the Met Police responsible for terrorism response. It had been their two officers who were first on the scene. I told them that I owed them a pint, proudly recalling the local jargon for a beer, as they helped me into the van, the angry purple bruise caused by the backface deformation of the bullet impact into my armor now swelling and causing a bit of discomfort. Hamid poked me, telling me, "Walk it off."

Rourke was escorted back to the chopper, where she was able to top off the tanks in the helicopter with thanks to a fuel truck that had driven over from the London City Airport. By noon yesterday, on Saturday, she lifted off and flew to the helipad atop *Almaz*.

Havens was rushed to the Royal London Hospital, and the CIRG agent was expected to make a full recovery from his injuries.

In the meantime, Hamid and I were driven across the River Thames to the twelve-story "crystalline cube" of the United States Embassy, where I received a token compress for my bruise and a grilling, by secure video teleconference, by the suits across the Atlantic Ocean in Washington, D.C.

After we were questioned during a four-hour-long, play-by-play recap of the mission, completely unnecessary by my estimation, as they'd watched the whole thing unfold through our helmet-cam feeds that were relayed to the chopper, then to *Almaz*, and finally to their monitors in the SIOC, Hamid and I got a break, some food, and a place to rest. We reconvened on Saturday evening and again this morning. I'm quite certain that the bureaucrats were annoyed to be working on a Sunday in August.

However, there was planning to do. In a joint operation, the CIA and FBI would remove the server containers from Trampoline's data hall deep within the Lefdal mine. Volkov had identified the location of the backup servers: a second set in Langfang, China, and a third redundant backup outside of Las Vegas, Nevada. Teams of agents would be dispatched to those places, too, to take physical custody of the machines. The operation in three places around the world would have to be tightly coordinated to begin at the exact same moment as an upcoming announcement from Melissa Zhao, per her agreement with SAC Appleton, the timing of which had not been set.

And continuing throughout all that, Under Secretary for Political Affairs Genevieve Sullivan had been playing a chess match of international intrigue. After calls to and from London and Moscow, she was ready for me to execute the endgame on Sunday afternoon.

Hearing a chime on the yacht's public address system, I walked aft on *Almaz*, toward the wide stern area where the crew had placed a gangway across the narrow gap of water that separated our yacht from the much larger warship. Ducking into the main deck living area, I said, "It's time."

Perched protectively between Warren Parnell and Frankie Dunn, Nina Mishkin rose from her seat and, running a hand through her blonde hair, wordlessly joined me at the door to the aft deck. Two men appeared on *Belfast*, casually dressed, with their hands in their pants pockets. I nodded to them. They both nodded back at me. I nodded again. All the nodding made me feel a little foolish.

I turned to Mishkin and asked, "No hard feelings?"

The Russian agent gave me the tiniest of smiles and walked toward the gangway. Unable to contain myself, I called cheerily, "Thanks for sailing with us. See you around!"

The men atop the gangway remained unsmiling, and after watching the trio of Russians disappear on *Belfast*, surely under the watchful eye of both the CIA and MI6 who had jointly overseen the handoff, I returned to the situation room to rejoin a waiting Volkov, Rourke,

Hamid, and Lockwood, who had watched the exchange unfold via the closed-circuit camera system on *Almaz*.

"It's done," I announced.

Rourke shook her head. "Just like that? Do you trust them?"

"*Trust* is maybe a little subjective. But Sullivan assures me that the deal was done at the very top, with Vladimir Putin himself. He specifically agreed to dispense with a so-called bounty on Volkov and me, in exchange for Mishkin."

Hamid asked, "And no repercussions for taking out three of the members of Unit 29155?"

"No," I responded. "Sullivan said that Putin said that the Trampoline thing was an unsanctioned operation. He claimed he didn't know about it."

"Bullshit," snorted Hamid.

"That's exactly what Sullivan believes. But she says it doesn't matter. He's got plausible deniability, and if the United States government doesn't push for recriminations against the Russian takeover—for some very nefarious purposes, I might add—of a U.S.-based social network, Russia owes us one. Sullivan is playing a game that doesn't ever seem to end, and at this particular moment, she's holding some pretty good cards, thanks to that negotiation."

"But why wouldn't the United States government disclose it?"

"That's a good question, Miles. Imagine if it was disclosed. I mean, the United States would look just as bad, allowing it to grow to the point where it did with zero oversight. Our intelligence services, the British intelligence services, the Israeli Mossad, you name it—no one saw it coming. The politicians *and* the spies will sweep the whole thing under the rug."

Lockwood rolled his eyes a bit before asking, "And what about Petrikov? The guy who started this whole adventure?"

With a sigh, Volkov whispered, "He's dead."

Lockwood's eyes widened. "How?"

In a stronger voice, Petrikov's daughter reported, almost clinically, "He passed away in his sleep last night. They said they would list it as death by natural causes. That's ridiculous, you know. He merely gave up. Resigned. He had no more moves to make." Volkov smiled bitterly and added, "It was checkmate, and he lost."

Lockwood considered Volkov, then Rourke, then Hamid, and finally me, and he wondered aloud, "So that's it? It's over? Quadrant, and all this, is done?"

My team waited patiently for me to verify Lockwood's summary. Strangely enough, I was dejected.

I know, I should have been elated. Not only did we successfully accomplish our mandated mission by locating and apprehending Anatoly Petrikov, but we also took on the Russians and took down their audacious attempt to wreak havoc on the world through an addictive social media platform. On balance, a clear victory for the good guys.

The good guys—*my* Quadrant team. And now, we had accomplished our missions, and, well, I imagined that once we returned to the States, the team would disband. We'd go our separate ways. Lockwood was correct. It *was* over.

I looked them all in the eye, one by one, and I said sadly, "Yeah. We're done."

CHAPTER
88

MONDAY, AUGUST 3, 2020 – LIVE BROADCAST FROM NEW YORK CITY

SIX HUNDRED AND forty-two shows of *Welcome to a New Day, America* completed, and television director Vinay Panja expected this one to be no different than any of the ones before. Once more, he slipped his headset on, aligned the boom microphone to his lips, and cleared his throat.

Okay, folks. Let's do it again. Quiet on the set. Coming back from commercial in five. Four. Three. Two. One.

Cue theme music. Cue graphic: "Welcome to a New Day, America" title card. Fade to camera one. Slow trolly toward stage while panning to host. And . . . action.

"Good morning. I'm Cleveland Bauer, your host of *Welcome to a New Day, America.* We have breaking news this morning. I'm joined today by Melissa Zhao, the founder and Chief Executive Officer of Trampoline dot Live, the social network platform that we've come to love and enjoy during these difficult times. Welcome, Melissa."

Cut to camera two. Slow zoom to guest.

"Thank you, Cleveland. And thank you for letting me come on your show, especially on such short notice."

Cut to camera three. Full set.

"Well, Melissa, it's really our privilege to have you here, and with a big announcement, I'm told, about the future of Trampoline. I can hardly wait to hear it."

Cut to camera two.

What's happening? The guest isn't responding. Fast cut to camera one and pan to guest. Buy us some time.

"Melissa?"

Cut to camera two. Zoom in close. This is going to be good television, folks.

"Sorry. This is difficult for me. But it must be done . . .

"I regret to inform our one point two billion users that, effective immediately, Trampoline is shutting down. As of this instant, our servers are being turned off. The platform is closed. I'm sorry to everyone."

Cut to camera one.

"This—this is shocking news, Melissa. I—I don't know what to say. Except, maybe, why?"

Cut to camera two.

"Yeah, um, there's a lot of reasons. But mainly, we're too big, we're too sticky, and frankly, we're addictive. I've realized that we are running a service that went beyond our initial goal of connecting people happily. Now it's about ad revenue, and keeping user's eyeballs glued to the screen, and creating a vicious cycle that pretty much traps you and your friends into relying on us, and relying on the platform, for your connections. For your entertainment. To feed into your addiction. Honestly, it's just not healthy. It's toxic."

Close zoom to guest. Bring up stage right lighting. Catch that tear on her cheek.

"By the time I've spoken all these words, we'll have turned Trampoline off. And I encourage you to do the same. Unplug. Read a book. Write a book. Play some music. Take a walk. Make a phone call. Say hi to a stranger, like, in person. Face-to-face. Go have some actual, real-life, good, clean fun. That's it. That's all I have to say."

FRIDAY, AUGUST 7, 2020 – 51° 28' N, 037° 41' E

APPRECIATING THE LATE DAY and early sunset view though the forward-facing windows of the situation room, I had my chair swiveled with my back to the dark screens. I was sipping a late Friday beer, thinking that, out here on the Atlantic Ocean about a week since departing from London, it didn't matter that it was late Friday. It didn't matter where the boat was or how fast or in what direction it was going. Out here, surrounded by nothing and answering only to the waves and to the wind, it was always beer o'clock.

I heard a soft chime from the console behind me.

Rotating my chair, I saw a red light blinking, indicating an encrypted incoming voice call. I ignored it.

The console chimed for a second time, and my curiosity got the better of my hesitancy. I sipped my beer, slipped my headset onto my skull, and jabbed the appropriate button, hissing in my finest evil villain voice, drawing out the word, "Yesssss?"

"Who is this? I'm looking for Ben Porter."

I recognized that squeaky, creaky voice, and clearing my throat, I a-hemmed, "Ah, yes, um, this is Porter. Ben Porter."

"Oh, lovely. This is Genevieve Sullivan."

"Under Secretary Sullivan. Hello. What can I do for you?" I checked the clock displays. 8:22 p.m. local, somewhere in the middle of the

Atlantic Ocean, and 5:22 p.m. in Washington, D.C. After hours on a Friday.

"Are you alone?"

"Um, yeah."

"Good. I'm calling with a matter that requires the most careful discretion. If you share the topic of this conversation, the consequences could well be disastrous."

"I see. Okay, um, Under Secretary Sullivan. I understand."

"Please, call me Genevieve. That title is a mouthful."

"Um, okay, Genevieve." My throat dry, I slugged a gulp from my beer bottle, condensation dripping into my lap and onto the polished, black surface of the horseshoe-shaped table, creating glimmery little bubbles that caught the long, low rays of the setting sun.

"Thank you, Ben. First of all, congratulations. Your foresight stopped what could have been a disastrous cyber-attack."

"I appreciate that. But I doubt it will make a difference." I absently ran my finger through the little bubbles on the table, drawing a circle of moisture.

"Why is that?"

I gulped a slug of beer as I traced a wet horizontal line and then a vertical line, separating my circle into four quadrants. "Because people are cavalier about sharing everything and anything online. They tap and scroll mindlessly, craving the addictive feedback loop that social media creates. And those users don't seem to realize that they are merely pawns in a social network's game of subversive addiction."

"But now Trampoline is gone. Shut down," Sullivan objected.

I shook my head as I countered, "Nah. Not gonna matter. Trampoline's users will migrate to some other platform, and the cycle will begin anew. That's not even the worst part."

"Oh?"

"Yeah, because, I wonder what's going to happen to all the data collected by Facebook and all the pictures uploaded to Instagram and all the tweets on Twitter in twenty years? And furthermore, truly, how do we know that the remaining social media empires aren't doing something similar—or worse—to what Trampoline was doing?"

"That's a grim analysis, Ben." Her voice was indifferent.

"Yeah," I said. "It is grim."

There was silence on the connection, and I spun my chair to face away from the table and toward the solitude and the power of the Atlantic Ocean. Finally, Sullivan spoke again, quietly, contemplatively, "Be that as it may, Ben, we must move on. I've got an assignment for you *and* your team. I could use the resources of the blandly but cleverly named Quadrant Procurement Group—and Ben, I could especially use your unique and creative talents. As I've inferred, this is a matter of the utmost importance. It threatens the very security of the United States of America."

Suitably buttered up and very intrigued, I listened as Sullivan continued, sipping my beer slowly, thinking, *Quadrant is back in business.*

THE END

THANK YOU

I HOPE YOU ENJOYED this story!

Would you do me a favor?

Like all authors, I rely on online reviews to encourage future sales. Your opinion is invaluable. Would you take a few moments now to share your assessment of my book on Amazon or any other book review website you prefer? Your opinion will help the book marketplace become more transparent and useful to us all.

If you are new to Ben Porter's world, please check out the prequels to this story, *False Assurances* and *Threat Bias*, available on Amazon, Apple Books, or by order through your local bookstore.

Thanks for reading! I hope to see you back for Book Four in Ben's series. I teased it, a bit, in the last chapter that you read. But all is not what it seems . . .

ACKNOWLEDGEMENTS

WHAT A RIDE IT'S BEEN!

It's difficult to believe that less than a year has passed since I released *False Assurances* and *Threat Bias*. Since then, the books hit number one sales spots, picked up a film option, and garnered thousands of reader reviews. So, let's start with that last one: my deepest thanks to you, the readers, who have encouraged me to continue this journey. Your reviews, the good ones and even the not-so-good ones, inspire me. That you took the time to not only read my stories, but then to take more of your time to review them—it's humbling, to say the least. I can't name every one of you by name, of course, but all the same, please accept my gratitude.

That word "gratitude" barely cuts it when I think about James Patterson. He read my very first manuscript; the rest is history. I would not be writing this today without that early endorsement—and that critical early advice and guidance—from Jim. As I type this acknowledgement, it's early February 2021, and days ago, Jim had (once again) kindly provided a blurb for the back cover. I was, naturally, delighted to read the blurb, and I absolutely love Jim's GameStop reference. If, say, you're reading this later in 2021, or a decade later, the GME short-sale-squeeze episode will be just a blip in the history books—but it's relevant today. GameStop was news when Jim read this story, and what Jim has done has created a marker in time for his review of my story. It's so cool.

Also cool: places like the Lefdal Mine Datacenter and the Gherkin. Among other "real life" settings for this story, those in particular caught my imagination. I doubt I've done them justice in the text. *Almaz* is, of course, not real; I hope that actual naval architects accept the creative liberties I took to simplify the vessel. And those of you with expertise in information technology will recognize at once that, in the IP address that Anastasia Volkov pings, the last three numbers are out of range; I didn't want to use a valid IP address in the event that some resourceful and adventurous reader would want to actually ping it. However, the combination of numbers does have meaning—I wonder if anyone decoded the simple cipher while reading the story.

What's not so cool is the neuroscience of social media. Several years ago, I had the privilege of meeting Tricia McDonough Ryan, PhD. A specialist in pediatric clinical neuroscience, Dr. Ryan has taught me, and of course many others, about the risks to brain development that social media has created. This is not an isolated occurrence; it's something to be taken very seriously, and yet, few efforts have been made to address the addictions created by reliance on smartphones and social media. Dr. Ryan sent me a link to a Harvard University Graduate School article by Trevor Haynes which explains this in terms that even I could understand. It begins: *"I feel tremendous guilt,"* admitted Chamath Palihapitiya, former Vice President of User Growth at Facebook, to an audience of Stanford students. He was responding to a question about his involvement in exploiting consumer behavior. "The short-term, dopamine-driven feedback loops that we have created are destroying how society works."* My thanks to Dr. Ryan for her guidance and time; any errors in the depiction of addiction are mine as I tried to distill Dr. Ryan's depth of explanation into a few paragraphs.

Speaking of doctors, once again I am happy to recognize my dear friend and neurosurgeon Dr. Phillip Dickey (who has now appeared in all three of my acknowledgements) for his contributions on just how to go about knocking out a recalcitrant, Russian-born oligarch. Dr. Dickey first advised one medication, then changed his mind and recommended something else. Needless to say, don't try this at home.

---

* Haynes, Trevor. "Dopamine, Smartphones & You: A battle for your time." *http://sitn.hms.harvard.edu/flash/2018/dopamine-smartphones-battle-time/* Harvard University. May 1, 2018.

One of the best surprises about this journey has been meeting new friends. Many readers reached out to me after finding numerous typos in the first two books (and let me be the first to admit that proofreading is my least favorite part of the journey). Instead of criticizing, they offered help, and among them were two individuals in particular who I asked to pre-read this story. John House is an Air Force veteran with electronics and computer science expertise, along with a firm grasp of language. He has a knack for reading with a clever and nuanced eye to realism. Patricia "Tink" Harwerth has a wide range of experience, from game show host to founder of an academic school for children with autism and learning differences. She is also a perceptive reader, with a sense of humor to match. Her contributions within this story are matchless. I am very thankful for both John and Tink: for their time, for their thoughtfulness, and for their willingness to take on the story.

In the late summer of 2019, after I had received the last of my rejection letters from the big New York publishers, I had a chance meeting with a design/build client, who surprised me by sharing his independently produced private memoir and a second collection of essays. John Macleod was instrumental in encouraging me to follow the indie path, and then he himself wrote a novel. I encourage you to check out his story; it's a lyrically written, murder-mystery, legal thriller: *Justice Hill*.

Key to my independent publishing production is the team at 1106 Design. My thanks to them for their guidance as they've led the assembly of three books, showing me possibilities on everything from cover art to pixilation, all while guiding me through a myriad of decisions.

The toughest decisions, however, are left to my editor. I'm sorta amused that we've never met in person, and that the one time we've seen each other's face was during the live broadcast of "Night of 1,000 Authors" on November 3, 2020. And yet, I trust his judgement, his creativity, and his wise counsel implicitly, like I've known him forever. He pushes me without being pushy, and his insight has contributed immensely to these stories. Thank you, Ryan Steck. You are a champion of the craft and of the genre, and I am deeply fortunate to work with you.

If you're really paying attention, you'll remember the date above: election night, 2020, in the midst of an unsettled year. I've made it a point to keep politics out of my stories, and I ask that you set politics aside for a moment. My big publicity break came from an on-air review of *False Assurances* and *Threat Bias* by Rush Limbaugh, who said on his radio show, "I could not stop reading the book. It got to be about 1:30 in the morning and I had to put it down and I couldn't quit." For an independent, no-name author like me, that was a defining moment; it brought readers to a story that they'd otherwise be unlikely to see, and it was an opportunity for me to grab a toehold in the vast world of publishing.

And finally, I am grateful, as always, for family. A little plug for my brother, David, who has built, from scratch, a company to produce American-made medical-grade face masks (the Connecticut Mask Company), while also cheering on my journey as an author. My mom and dad have played an outsized role in this tale, always offering encouragement while also always advising me thoughtfully. My father has been the very first reader of each of these stories; for this third one, my eldest son Connor also read the first draft. Both dad and Connor pointed out paths to improvement, and I hope there will be a day soon when my son Keilan and my daughter Maggie also want to dive into the text before it's really finished.

Last but not least, my love to my wife of over two decades, Meghan. Wait—what? Wife alone is hardly an adequate descriptor. How about also: confidante, ally, cheerleader, teacher, mom, partner, and best friend. Here's to you, Meghan, to three books, done, and to many more books and years together!

—Christopher Rosow, February 7, 2021, Southport, Connecticut.

ABOUT THE AUTHOR

WHEN NOT WRITING, Christopher Rosow works in the design and construction space. And when not working or writing, or enjoying time with his amazing family, he's probably found out on the water somewhere, sailing. He lives in Connecticut with his family, his dogs, and way too many boats.

www.RosowBooks.com or www.ChristopherRosow.com
Facebook, Twitter, and Instagram: @RosowBooks

The Ben Porter Series by Christopher Rosow:
False Assurances – Book One (2020)
Threat Bias – Book Two (2020)
Subversive Addiction – Book Three (2021)

EBR

3 2400 0511 10710

CPSIA information can be obtained
at www.ICGtesting.com
Printed in the USA
LVHW090415240821
695915LV00004B/92